The World of Elven Alliance

SHIELD BAND

ANH T. LUU
632 LOCHSMERE LANE
ORLANDO, FL 32828

SHIELD BAND

ELVEN ALLIANCE BOOK SIX

TARA GRAYCE

SHIELD BAND

Taragrayce.com

Published by Sword & Cross Publishing

Grand Rapids, MI

Cover and Map by Savannah Jezowski of Dragonpen Designs

Dragonpenpress.com

To God, my King and Father. Soli Deo Gloria

LCCN: 2022906414

ISBN: 978-1-943442-30-0

CHAPTER ONE

Julien groaned and slouched in his chair at the small, sparse desk in his room in Winstead Palace, staring at the list of names Rharreth had provided before he returned to Kostaria. Here were twelve of the most esteemed female warriors of Kostaria, including Rharreth's shield sister Vriska. And Julien was going to have to try to woo one of them.

He rubbed his hand over the bristles of his beard and sighed. This felt like a scheme cooked up by one of the newspapers to sell the scandal sheets. He could just see the headlines. *Twelve eligible troll maidens. One Escarlish prince. Who will he choose?*

He had better hope the press didn't catch wind of this. It would be a nightmare. The Escarlish monarchy had only just survived the hit of Farrendel's illegitimate birth splashed across the newspapers. Another lurid story was the last thing they needed right now.

It was already turning into more of a nightmare than he'd expected.

He understood what Averett was trying to do by giving him time and options. Neither Averett nor Rharreth wanted to force anyone into marriage over a treaty. But right now, Julien almost wished someone would just tell him which troll woman he was going to marry, and then he'd do it. He'd make it work, just like Essie had when she married Farrendel.

His gaze landed on the name at the top of the first page. In truth, he, Rharreth, and Averett had already picked the ideal candidate.

Vriska of the family Ardon. Rharreth's one and only remaining shield sister.

She had been there, at the Dulraith months ago. But Julien couldn't remember her. He'd been too focused on the three trolls he was about to fight.

The Dulraith made Julien realize that Escarland would need a marriage of alliance with Kostaria, and that he would have to be the one to do it.

Julien rested his elbows on the desk, digging his fingers into his hair. The candle flickered, casting shadows onto the floor and flashes of orange against the blades of the historical Escarlish swords, daggers, axes, and other weapons hanging on his walls, his one decoration in the otherwise sparse room.

If he closed his eyes, he could dredge up the feel of his father's hand on his shoulder. *I never want my sons to harbor jealousy for each other. Your brother will be king. It is his duty. But you are his spare. That is a solemn duty in its own right.*

For years, he had been the loyal shadow at Averett's side. He had endured all the hazing that came with being a prince in an army barracks until he earned the respect of his fellow soldiers. All so that he could eventually protect his brother.

If something were to happen to Averett, he would quietly step into the role of regent until his nephew Bertie was old enough to take the throne, at which time he would just as quietly step into the background again.

Julien would marry an Escarlish noblewoman who was as quiet and content to be in the background as he was. They would dutifully serve Escarland and then humbly fade into the forgotten shadows of history when the time came.

Everyone would remember King Averett as the king who had brought peace and prosperity to Escarland. Legends would be told about Princess Elspeth, who married an elf prince and ushered in a new age. Even Edmund might get a few stories told about him, if the tales of his exploits were ever unclassified.

But no one would remember Julien, the spare Escarlish prince who had done nothing noteworthy as he quietly supported and protected his siblings.

At least, that was how he had always envisioned his future. And he had been content with it. Wanting more had never even occurred to him.

Now, his new future stared at him in the stark black-and-white list of names. Even though he had resigned himself to this new duty months ago—even before Averett had admitted it was necessary—it seemed he was not as content with it as he should be.

It wasn't that he was reluctant, exactly. Or that his planned future was such a closely held dream that he could not let it go. After all, he was twenty-six, and he'd yet to find that elusive Escarlish noblewoman from his expected future to marry.

No, it was simply unsettling to have a future that had been so starkly outlined for him from his youngest years upended so completely. What had once been a solid path was now crumbling sand that sent him reeling as he struggled to find his new footing.

Blowing out a long breath, he forced his shoulders to straighten. Just like when he had joined the army or when he'd gone into the Dulraith, there was no way forward but through.

Julien pulled out a fresh piece of paper and stared at the blank sheet. His elvish was still struggling, even though he had been working on it for months, ever since the Dulraith. Sure, he'd done it in secret and hadn't had a chance to practice without admitting to his siblings what he was doing and why he was doing it. Still, it didn't seem he had the same gift for languages that Edmund had. Even Essie had picked up elvish faster, though she had been helped along by her heart bond with Farrendel.

But according to Rharreth, Vriska didn't know Escarlish. Unlike the elves, few trolls were so academically inclined to learn a second language. Rharreth had, but he was a bit more far-sighted than most trolls. His shield brother Zavni had as well. But Vriska had not.

Gritting his teeth, Julien tried again to write a letter to Vriska that he could send to Rharreth to give to her when she was informed of this possible arrangement.

Perhaps he should keep the letter vague. He wouldn't address it to any one of the troll warrior women. Just in case Vriska didn't want to even consider this and Rharreth was forced to pass the letter off to the next troll woman on the list.

Vague wasn't a problem. His elvish writing was at the level of "See Spot run." Not a lot of depth could be conveyed with such simple words and lack of vocabulary.

"What has you looking so glum?"

Julien spun in his chair to find his brother Edmund leaning against the doorjamb, arms crossed. His brown hair was wet and tousled, his jaw freshly shaven. Except for the slight dark circles under his eyes, Edmund didn't look like he had just returned from a dangerous mission in Mongavaria. Julien couldn't see any pain in Edmund's stance, so the wound he'd received in Tarenhiel must be fully healed, nor must he have received any new wounds while in Mongavaria.

Julien jumped to his feet and gave Edmund a backslapping, brother hug. "When did you get back?"

It wasn't the first question Julien wanted to ask. But this wasn't the first time Edmund had mysteriously disappeared, then reappeared a few weeks or months later. It was best to just act casual and only ask the questions Edmund could answer.

Edmund grinned and stepped out of his hug. "Just a few minutes ago. I need to grab a few things and let the family know I'm safe. Then I'm off to Tarenhiel. I have an elven princess to ask if she will allow me to court her."

Julien forced a smile onto his face. He shouldn't feel jealous, seeing yet another of his siblings so totally in love while he was stuck in this cold political marriage.

This was his choice. He would make it work. And if he ended up miserable, then he'd hide it behind grins and banter so well that even Edmund wouldn't guess the truth.

Julien slapped Edmund on the shoulder. "I'm happy for you. I won't keep you. Unless…" He glanced back at his desk. "Would you have time to help me write a letter? You could take it to Rharreth for me."

Edmund shifted, glancing toward the door as if all he

wanted to do was run to Tarenhiel. But he shook his head and pushed past Julien. "Let's see what you have so far."

Julien winced, clenching his fists as Edmund picked up the letter he'd started. How bad was it?

Edmund chuckled and shook his head again. "Your elvish is...improving."

That bad. Julien sighed. "Did I at least use all the right words?"

"Yes." Edmund's grin faded a bit as he re-read the note. "And this probably isn't that bad. Trolls like things straight-forward rather than the more flowery elven style."

Julien sank onto the chair and gestured to the letter. "Just help, all right?"

Edmund nudged him aside to make room at the desk. He picked up a pen and tugged out a fresh piece of paper. "Dictate what you want to say, and I'll write it down. You can copy it out in your own handwriting."

Julien opened his mouth, then suppressed a growl as he tried to think of something he would want to tell the troll woman he intended to court that he also didn't mind his brother hearing.

This was ridiculous. Perhaps he would ask Farrendel or Essie for help with the next letter, whenever Farrendel and Essie returned to Escarland.

Though, Farrendel was likely to get more flustered and awkward about it than Edmund. And Essie would just sit there grinning at him. Normally Julien appreciated her cheeriness, but not about this.

Edmund raised an eyebrow. A very elven facial expression. "Well? If you don't want to do this, I have things to do, places to be, and an elf princess to woo."

What Julien wouldn't give for Edmund's glib tongue

right about now. He could banter just fine with his brothers. But actually sweet-talking a woman—especially a stranger via a stilted letter—was another thing altogether.

"No, I want to do this. Just give me a minute." Julien dragged his hand over his beard. The bristles were still stiff against his fingers, but far less scratchy since he'd started using elven shampoo and conditioner on his beard as well as his hair. The secret to a good beard was a lot of care, after all. "How about this..."

It took a good half hour of work—and even Edmund's good humor was fading to frustration—by the time Julien had a letter he was satisfied with.

"Here." Edmund scribbled a name on the edge of the paper with the list of possible marriage candidates. "That's the professor at Hanford University who teaches elvish. He will be able to help you with more focused studies. I'm not sure when I'll be back in Escarland, but I'll help you practice when I'm here. I'm sure Farrendel and Essie will help as well."

"Thanks." Julien grimaced down at the paper. He'd pushed through his schooling, even though he disliked it, knowing that a prince and an army officer needed a good foundation of history and military strategy. But he'd been rather glad that, as the spare, he was expected to join the military rather than attend Hanford University like the others.

Edmund gave him that eyebrow look again. "No, not *thanks*. I know you know the elvish for it. Farrendel uses it often enough."

How was Julien supposed to remember all the random elvish words that Farrendel used on occasion? He usually registered their meaning thanks to the context, then promptly forgot all about them. "Uh, lin-something?"

"Linshi." Edmund pushed away from the desk, already heading for the door. "But the trolls pronounce it with a guttural inflection and drop the *i* at the end so it sounds more like *linsh*."

"Thanks. Uh, linsh." Julien sighed and shook his head. Edmund had spent all of three months in Kostaria. How had he learned and retained all the nuances of the troll version of the language they shared with the elves in such a short time?

It really was frustrating sometimes, being the least smart of his siblings. Averett was politically wise. He was king. He had to be. Edmund was deviously brilliant with a quick, intelligent mind that remembered everything. And Essie was smart with people, picking up on their emotional cues even if she chose to ignore them at times. Even his brother-in-law Farrendel was proving that he had a gifted mind for mechanics along with his magical power.

Then there was Julien. He wasn't unintelligent, exactly. But he wasn't as quick as most of his siblings. It had been an asset, in some ways, when he had planned a life in the background.

It was less useful now.

Oh, well. He might not be quick, but he was determined. He might have to work harder at it than his siblings, but he would get there eventually.

While Edmund shifted from foot to foot, shooting glances toward the door, Julien labored to painstakingly copy the letter Edmund had written for him. When he flourished his signature on the bottom, the action felt strangely final in a way it hadn't even when he'd watched Averett and Rharreth sign the treaty that mandated this arranged marriage.

As soon as Julien folded and sealed it, Edmund snatched it from his hand. "If that's all you needed…" Edmund edged toward the door.

"Yes, go on." Julien waved Edmund away. "Say hello to Essie and Farrendel when you see them in Tarenhiel."

Julien wasn't about to mention the news that Essie was expecting. It would be good for his clever brother to be surprised for once in his life.

With a grin, Edmund all but ran for the door, disappearing into the corridor seconds later.

Would Julien ever get that smitten look when he thought about his soon-to-be bride? Or would his marriage be the one out of this alliance that didn't result in a happy ending?

CHAPTER TWO

Vriska ducked a sword swing, then lunged forward, ramming her shoulder into her opponent's gut. He lurched backward but didn't go down. The crowd of warriors gathered on the tiered stone benches of the fighting arena cheered, though the noise echoed only dimly past the focused beat of her heart.

Before he could grapple her, she came up, striking his jaw with her forehead. This time, he staggered. She got her sword up, swinging it at his neck.

He regained his balance and parried.

With a savage grin tugging her face and a snarl in her throat, Vriska swung her sword even harder, shoving forward. He parried three blows, but the fourth sent him stumbling. She caught his sword between her sword and the wall, ripping it from his grip.

She pressed her sword to his neck. "Do you yield?"

"Yield." The warrior saluted her as he eased away from her blade and stood. "Always a pleasure to be beaten by one of the king's shield band."

The cheering was now a deafening roar. Her people—the trolls of the far northern kingdom of Kostaria—loved a good fight. As did Vriska.

Her blood still running hot in the wake of battle, Vriska saluted the crowd with her sword before she strode to the edge of the sand-covered ring, vaulted up and over the low stone wall that separated it from the benches, and made her way toward the rest of her shield band.

Around her, the cheering started again as two more warriors took her place in the arena to show off their prowess.

Vriska's small shield band sat in a cluster around Rharreth, king of Kostaria, and his elven wife Queen Melantha. Amid all the gray skin and white hair of the trolls, Melantha's warmer complexion and black hair stood out, as did her willowy frame. Still, she sat with a straight-backed dignity beside Rharreth, as if she belonged there.

She *did* belong there. Vriska swallowed back the stirring in her chest. No longer a burning resentment. No, instead the bitter pang felt more like guilt. Vriska's resentment for Melantha had nearly cost Rharreth his life when Vriska hadn't warned him that Drurvas, his treacherous cousin, had been stirring up trouble.

And then there was the way Vriska had treated Melantha when she'd first married Rharreth. Melantha had forgiven her for that, but Vriska's actions had been dishonorable. It was a stain that Vriska had yet to cleanse from her honor, no matter how loyal she had been to her king and queen in the months since.

She and Queen Melantha were cordial now, and Rharreth once again trusted Vriska with guarding Melantha. But she and Melantha weren't close. Not like they might have been if

Vriska had embraced her new queen as a shield sister from the beginning.

Vriska took her seat on the bench in front of Rharreth and Melantha. Rharreth gave her a nod, a silent *well done*.

Zavni had the seat beside her, and he tossed her a towel. "You clobbered him good."

"I should hope so." Vriska wiped the rivulets of sweat that ran down her face. Then she scrubbed the damp sheen from her bare arms. There was nothing she could do about the sweat trickling beneath the layers of her thin, sleeveless shirt and leather vest.

She tried to ignore the way that Zavni was giving her sidelong glances, shooting looks past her to Rharreth. There was something going on. Zavni had seemed off since he, Brynjar, Rharreth, Melantha, and the rest of their squad of warriors had returned from Tarenhiel and Escarland a few days ago. Brynjar, too, had been casting her strange looks, before glancing at Rharreth. When she'd asked them about it, both of them had clammed up tight.

Vriska focused on the rest of the bouts. Zavni, Brynjar, and Eyvindur each fought a few rounds, and she tried to ignore the pang of missing Nirveeth and Darvek, the members of their shield band who had been killed in Drurvas's uprising.

Finally, amid the cheers of the final bout, Rharreth stood. His booming voice rang in the arena. "My warriors! You have shown your courage and your strength! Tonight, we feast to celebrate our new alliance!"

Amazingly, there were cheers, but Vriska wasn't sure whether they were for the new alliance or for the feasting.

She stood to protect her king and queen as the warriors

around them surged to their feet, charging to the doors to head for the feasting hall.

Instead of joining the crowd, Rharreth, Melantha, and their shield band waited, letting the stampede die down.

Rharreth rested a hand on Vriska's shoulder. "Vriska, come to my study tomorrow morning. We need to talk."

His deep voice was far too sober, as if something was wrong. Both Zavni and Brynjar were shifting again, looking anywhere but at her. Next to Rharreth, Melantha's smile had a twist that was almost…smug.

That, more than anything, tightened something inside Vriska's chest. What was going on?

But all she did was nod, then fall into place with the rest of her shield band around her king and queen as they made their way to the hall for the feast.

VRISKA DREW in a deep breath as she strode down the hall in Khagniorth Stronghold. She wasn't nervous. Of course she wasn't. She had worked too hard to earn her position as a warrior in the king's own shield band. She wasn't going to disgrace herself with a bit of nerves.

For that reason, she didn't hesitate in front of the door to Rharreth's study. No, she knocked forcefully and without any lingering pause outside the door.

"Come in," Rharreth called from inside.

Vriska stepped inside and shut the door behind her. Rharreth bent over his stone desk, its surface overflowing with paperwork. Abundant lighting kept the place from feeling cold while a fire crackled in the fireplace.

He glanced up at her, a hint of a weary frown playing

across his face. As if he wasn't looking forward to this conversation.

That made two of them.

Vriska clasped her hands behind her back. "You wished to speak with me, my king?"

"Yes." Rharreth pushed to standing, though he stayed behind his desk, staring down at it for a long moment before he met her gaze. There was something unreadable in his expression. "As you know, while Melantha and I were away, we signed a new treaty with Escarland and Tarenhiel that strengthens our alliance."

Vriska nodded, her stomach knotting tighter. She knew why such close alliances were necessary, and the trade with Escarland had gotten Kostaria through this past winter. For the first time in years, her family had not been hungry.

But she didn't like being so dependent on the elves or the humans. Her people were strong. They didn't need to stoop to begging from the other kingdoms like this.

Some of her thoughts must have shown on her face because Rharreth grimaced and shook his head. "I know many think I'm weak for making these alliances. But this is our chance to prove our strength to the other kingdoms in the alliance. In this case, they came to us because of the strength of our warriors. And we will stand strong as an equal partner, whatever it takes."

Vriska nodded again, though she wasn't entirely sure what he meant and why he was looking at her so intently when he spoke.

At least Rharreth hadn't gone groveling to Escarland and Tarenhiel for this new alliance. That was something.

Rharreth shoved from his desk and paced behind it. "As our alliance deepens, Escarland will realize just how much we have to offer. The bridge they want us to help build over the Hydalla River is just the beginning. Our people will find opportunities in Escarland that will take them away from our mountains."

Vriska wasn't sure she wanted to agree. Yet...her family had scraped by for years. Would they move to Escarland for an easier life if the opportunity arose? Her father was skilled at working with stone. Would he be one of those sent to Escarland to build that new bridge?

"Other human kingdoms will covet our resources once they learn of them. Without a strong alliance with Escarland, we will soon find ourselves beset from every side." Rharreth's pacing carried him the length of the small study and back again. "Times are changing. We can no longer stand alone, safe in our mountains, as we once did. We have seen a glimpse of that with Mongavaria's assassination attempt in Tarenhiel. Kostaria could easily be Mongavaria's next target, if they still wish to destroy this alliance."

Vriska hadn't witnessed the assassination attempt, but she had heard a detailed description of it from Zavni and Brynjar. Would Mongavaria try something like that in Kostaria? They would soon find that it was a foolish idea to attack the trolls.

She shrugged. "What does this have to do with me? I am loyal to you, King Rharreth. Your whole shield band is with you."

Did he still doubt Vriska's loyalty? She had done her best to prove herself, but had it been enough?

Rharreth's head shot up, and he met her gaze with his dark blue eyes. "I would never ask this of you if I didn't believe you were loyal."

What was he talking about? Vriska crossed her arms.

"Just spit it out. It isn't like you to dance around the topic like a flighty elf."

Rharreth's mouth pressed into a line, though it didn't seem to be with anger. "I know. But I need you to fully understand why I am asking this. Because this alliance is the only way forward for Kostaria."

Vriska was beginning to believe Rharreth was right, much as everything in her recoiled at the thought of Kostaria making such a close alliance with elves. And *humans*. "I understand, my king."

Rharreth sighed and paced away from her again. "For this alliance to work, it needs to be strong. We will need a troll in Escarland advocating for our people. Not just an ambassador, but someone with the power to see to it that our people are treated fairly. And the humans will need a voice here in Kostaria to do the same thing." He faced her. "That will take a marriage of alliance."

Vriska snorted, then coughed to cover her momentary disgust. A marriage of alliance with the elves was one thing. The elves, for all their delicate natures, were distant kin of a sort. The humans were so…human.

But she could not say those thoughts out loud. And the marriages holding the alliance together had worked so far. One more probably wasn't too much to ask. "I suppose it must be done. Who do you plan to send?"

Who would Rharreth marry off? It might take some doing, but there was probably a troll woman out there desperate enough to marry a human. Did Rharreth plan to send Vriska as her guard? Was that why he'd called Vriska into his study?

"Prince Julien of Escarland has volunteered to marry one of our warriors." Rharreth leaned against the wall behind him, still giving Vriska that unnerving, steady look. "The treaty doesn't specify his bride, only that she must be loyal to me. Ideally, she would have been related to me. I don't have any living relatives, but I do have my shield band. And you, Vriska, are my only shield sister."

No. Surely he could not mean for *her* to marry that human prince? Vriska's blood ran cold, then blazed hot in her chest. Rharreth would not have signed her life away without even asking her, would he? That wasn't the troll way.

Vriska crossed her arms and glared. "Surely you don't want *me* to marry him?"

She supported Rharreth's direction for the kingdom. She truly did.

But marrying a *human*?

No way was Vriska ever marrying a weak, pathetic human. He would never be a warrior who could stand at her side. He would never strengthen her in a true bond the way a troll would.

Nor could she endure the sneers that Rharreth had when he'd married Melantha. She had already dealt with enough of that when she became a warrior, after she'd fought long and hard to prove that a girl with from a non-warrior family was worthy to be in the younger prince's shield band. She had worked too hard to get where she was. She wasn't going to throw it away now.

Not even for her king? Her kingdom? Her duty? Was this what loyalty would demand of her?

Rharreth held her gaze unflinchingly. "It doesn't have to be you. There are others I can ask. But as your king, I would like it to be you. You are my shield sister, as close to me as a blood sister. There can be no stronger alliance than if you were to marry Prince Julien. Yet as your shield brother, I understand if you do not wish it. Neither King Averett nor I want to force anyone into this marriage."

Vriska swallowed, her hands clenched against her biceps as she flexed her crossed arms. "Who else have you asked?"

"No one besides you." Rharreth pushed away from the wall and strode a few steps closer. "If you agree, then I won't approach anyone else. But if you don't wish to consider it, then I will talk with the others who are eligible."

Vriska clenched her jaw. She was a warrior. Her stomach shouldn't be churning like this. "Zavni and Brynjar know, don't they?"

Of course they knew. This was the reason for their strange looks since returning.

"Yes. They were there when King Averett proposed this marriage alliance." Rharreth shook his head, his white hair trailing over his forehead. "But only our shield band and those necessary will know. King Averett and I are both working to keep this as quiet as possible so that all involved can be as free from pressure as possible."

It still felt like a lot of pressure, regardless.

She was loyal to her kingdom and her king. But was she willing to do something like this?

"I believe Prince Julien is a good man. He is the Escarlish prince who fought at my side during the Dulraith." Rharreth rested a hand on the elven dagger belted at his waist. "He is a warrior worthy to marry into my shield band."

Vriska squeezed her eyes shut, trying to remember the human prince who had fought in that Dulraith. To be honest, she hadn't paid much attention to him, besides to note with some surprise that he had survived more or less in one piece.

She'd been sure the human was going to get hacked to bits in the first few seconds.

All right, so he wasn't a pathetic, weakling prince as she had assumed.

But that Dulraith was hardly an accurate measure of his fighting prowess. Laesornysh had done most of the work while the human sheltered behind his shield. Perhaps he was not a weakling, but he still was not strong enough to stand against a troll warrior on his own.

"Vriska." Rharreth's tone changed to something softer, compassionate. The shield brother instead of the king. "I want you to be happy. And you aren't right now."

Vriska opened her mouth to protest, but no words came out.

Was she happy? She'd never stopped to think about it in so many words. Happiness had never been a goal. Becoming a warrior had been her purpose.

Then there had just been war. She hadn't thought much beyond the next fight, the next battle. So many of her shield band—her brothers and sisters—had been killed. It had seemed inevitable that she would die a bloody death in battle, and there hadn't been a point to think about a future that would never come for her.

And yet here she was, alive and well with no more wars to fight, no more battles to be won.

For the past months, she hadn't thought about what she was going to do. There was simply her duty to her king and queen. Standing guard in the corner and outside of doors for the rest of her life.

She hadn't become a warrior to do that. But she hadn't planned any other future for herself.

"Vriska?"

Rharreth's quiet voice dragged her out of her musing. Not that she liked being so stuck in her thoughts. It wasn't a warrior's way.

No, a warrior was straightforward. Bash. Hack. Fight. Win. Die. That was a warrior's life.

She sighed and sank onto one of the chairs in front of Rharreth's desk. "Does he know about my family?"

She wasn't from a warrior family, Kostaria's equivalent to nobility. No, her parents were common laborers in Osmana. Would an Escarlish prince see her family as nothing more than peasants to be scorned?

"I don't believe so." Returning to his seat, Rharreth pulled out an envelope, though he didn't give it to her. Instead, he turned it over in his hands. "He accepted an illegitimate elf prince as his brother-in-law. I think he has enough honor that he will treat your family well."

Right. Laesornysh was Prince Julien's brother-in-law. If Vriska went through with this ridiculous marriage, that would make Laesornysh her brother-in-law as well.

She wasn't sure she could do it. Rharreth had, but he didn't have to see his brother-in-law all that often.

"If I'm in Escarland…" Vriska had to pause, realizing what her words betrayed. She was considering this, crazy as it seemed. "Who will guard you and your queen? Our shield band is small."

"You and the others are stretched thin already. I understand that." Rharreth tapped the letter against the desk. "Many shield bands are shorthanded right now. I have already started the process of forming alliances between shield bands so that two or more shield bands work and train together. Adopted shield bands, as it were. Thanks to Drurvas, I know exactly who is loyal to me and who is not.

There are several shield bands who can help with the duties normally assigned to the king's shield band."

Well, Rharreth had an answer for everything, didn't he? He'd obviously put a lot of thought into this while traveling around Tarenhiel and Escarland.

"They will be honored to guard their king and queen." Vriska kept her tone neutral. What would she do with herself once the other shield bands took over some of the shifts guarding the king and queen? She didn't have a life outside of being a warrior.

"Yes." Rharreth leaned forward and rested his elbows on his desk. "Unlike the kings of Escarland and Tarenhiel, I don't have any siblings I can send on diplomatic missions. I will need my shield band to be more my brothers and sister than my guards. Even if you don't accept this marriage of alliance, you and the rest of my shield band will be asked to do more than the usual duties of a shield band. I will need ambassadors, diplomats, and leaders."

"So I could be sent to Escarland as an ambassador even if I don't marry their prince?" That didn't sound much more appealing than an arranged marriage with a human.

But it wasn't unexpected. Vriska and Eyvindur had been placed in charge of the kingdom while Rharreth and Melantha had been away. More of those kinds of tasks would fall on the shield band as Rharreth rebuilt Kostaria and made a place for it internationally.

"Yes, something like that." Rharreth's gaze swung away from her to the letter in his hands. "I saw the list of the stone workers who my chief engineer has recommended to be sent to Escarland to construct the bridge over the Hydalla River. Your father's name is on it."

Vriska stilled. Then it was as she had feared. Her father

would be gone for months on end, building that bridge in Escarland. What if he became one of the first to decide that the opportunities were better in Escarland? He was a skilled stoneworker. He would find a ready market in Escarland where troll stone magic was rare, instead of being one among many here in Kostaria.

This was what Rharreth had meant when he'd said they would need a troll in Escarland to speak on behalf of the trolls who decided to move there. And who better to give them a voice than a troll married to the Escarlish prince?

Did that troll have to be Vriska? Perhaps not. But Rharreth was, annoyingly, right. There were few others in Kostaria who had closer claims to Rharreth. The Escarlish king was offering his brother. It was only honorable that Rharreth give his shield sister.

Besides, Rharreth was granting her an honor by presenting this marriage of alliance to her, especially as his first choice. If Vriska married Prince Julien, she would become a princess. That was quite the step up for a troll girl born to a common, non-warrior family from a back street of Osmana.

Still, it would mean marrying a *human*. Perhaps everywhere else, she would gain the status of princess. But here in Kostaria, marrying a human, even a prince, would be a demotion, unless that human somehow had the guts and skill to prove himself to the troll warriors the way Melantha had.

Something Vriska highly doubted was possible. Melantha had her magic. Prince Julien was a magicless human who would always be physically weaker than any troll warrior, even if he was strong for a human.

Vriska dragged in a breath, straightened her shoulders, and faced Rharreth. "Do I have to decide right away?"

"No, but if you want to consider it, then you will need to start learning Escarlish." Rharreth shrugged, picking up the letter once again. "I've invited Ezrec, Zavni's father, to teach Escarlish to our whole shield band—and anyone else from the other shield bands who is willing to learn. I'm also working to secure teachers for those who will be sent to Escarland for building the bridge. They will need to be able to communicate with the Escarlish engineers and builders."

Vriska grimaced. "I think I'm considering it less now. Learning another language sounds like work."

"He's already learning our language." Rharreth's mouth quirked for a moment before he sobered. "The plan is for the two of you to spend the next three months learning each other's languages. At the end of that time, Prince Julien will come here to Kostaria under the guise of a diplomatic envoy. He will spend the next few months here. At that point, if you are still willing, the two of you will travel to Escarland and introduce you to the Escarlish people as Prince Julien's betrothed. As far as everyone else will be concerned, you met and fell in love while he was in Kostaria."

King Averett and Rharreth had this all planned out, didn't they? Neat and tidy as a strategically-sound battle plan.

Which meant, like a battle plan, it was likely going to fall apart on first contact with the enemy. Or in this case, her intended, Prince Julien.

Assuming she agreed to this. Why was she even considering it? Why hadn't she already said *no* and marched out the door? Marriage wasn't something she'd ever counted on as part of her future, much less marriage to a human.

But it wasn't like she had any better ideas. And going through with this might be the only way to prove her loyalty to Rharreth and Melantha once and for all and finally redeem her honor after the way she had treated Melantha and failed Rharreth.

"I understand." Vriska gave a sharp nod. At least Prince Julien wasn't going to show up on her doorstep tomorrow. She had three months to decide if this was a future she could live with.

Rharreth held out the letter, waving it in the air but not quite handing it over. "If you're truly considering it, then I can give you this."

"What is it?" Vriska didn't take the letter. Taking that letter felt like it would chain her to this scheme. This marriage.

"This is from Prince Julien. I'm to give it to the woman who agrees to consider the marriage alliance." Rharreth held it out to her.

This was really happening. Vriska hated herself for the hesitation. She was a warrior. She didn't hesitate. If she agreed to a marriage alliance, then that was that. She wasn't going to get all fussed over it.

She snatched the letter, then stood. "If that is all?"

"Yes. Take the day off. Read the letter and think this over. Talk to your parents if you wish." Rharreth speared her with a glance. "Though, I should not have to tell you that this can go no farther than that."

Vriska nodded and strode from the king's study, the letter clutched in her fingers.

CHAPTER THREE

Vriska found a quiet corner in the twisting passageways of Khagniorth Stronghold before she broke the seal—a royal seal of Escarland—and unfolded the letter.

A strong, bold script flowed across the page. For a moment, Vriska could just stare at the black words against the ivory page, not taking them in. Then, she drew in a deep breath and forced herself to read.

To whomever receives this letter:

What you have just been told is likely a shock. I have had months to prepare myself for the possibility that a marriage might be necessary for this alliance while you will have just been told your duty, if you choose to accept it.

Duty might seem like a cold reason to marry. Yet I have found there is love in it as well. The love for my family and for the kingdom that is their home is the heart of my duty.

I choose to believe that our duty to our kingdoms, our families, and each other will be enough. I can promise I will always treat you with honor, and I trust in the honor of your people that you will do the same with me.

I would be honored if you would write back. Please know that I am still learning and may need to consult with someone more skilled in your language to interpret your letter for me and help me write a reply.

Sincerely yours,

Prince Julien of Escarland

For a moment, Vriska could only stare at the letter in her hand. Something inside her chest twisted.

If she hadn't known better, she would have thought this was written by a troll, not a human. This Prince Julien understood a troll's heart for duty and honor.

If he'd written flowery words about falling in love and other mushy sentiments, then she would have marched back into Rharreth's study, tossed the letter on his desk to give to the next unlucky troll woman, and walked away then and there.

But honor and duty were the code by which she had lived her life, and any choice she made about this marriage would be based on them as well, not on something as weak and murky as love.

Vriska shook herself, growled, and haphazardly refolded the letter before stuffing it into a pocket. Enough of this staring and self-reflection.

Perhaps Rharreth had been right. It was time to visit her

family. Talking with them always gave her clarity to her purpose, and she was beyond due for a visit anyway.

She marched through the passageways and nodded to the guards at the gates as she stepped through. She crossed the small courtyard outside Khagniorth Stronghold before she exited the second set of gates onto the bustling streets of Osmana.

At this time of spring, slush still covered the streets from the last wet snowfall. Yet unlike last spring, when people had trudged about their business with slumped shoulders and haggard expressions, today people strolled in the sunshine. Laughter and boisterous voices echoed around the stone homes built into the mountainside. Shops along the main street actually carried food and goods, imported from Escarland.

Vriska turned down one of the side streets, winding between increasingly smaller and dingier homes. As she strode onto the street where her family lived, neighbors who had known her since she was small called out to her. She saluted them as she passed, though she didn't stop.

Her mother stood outside the door to her family's home in the mountain, scrubbing one of Da's shirts on a washboard. Next to her, Vriska's much younger sister Rikze cranked a skirt through the wringer to dry it.

Rikze glanced up to reach for the next dripping clothing item, only to promptly drop the shirt into the slush on the ground. "Vriska!"

Ma opened her mouth, probably to scold Rikze, before her head shot up at the shout. A smile creased her lined face, and she dropped the shirt into the gray, sudsy water. Wiping her hands on her grungy apron, she straightened. "Vriska, my warrior girl."

Vriska smiled at her mother, then opened her arms just in time for Rikze to slam into her. Vriska hugged her little sister, thankful that Rikze didn't feel as thin as she had last spring.

"It has been *so* long since you visited." Rikze squeezed even harder, as if she wanted to make sure Vriska wasn't going to disappear on her.

"I know." Vriska patted her sister's back. "It was busy while the king and queen were away."

She knew she didn't visit her family nearly enough. Through the wars, she'd told herself that it was her duty to her prince and kingdom that kept her away.

Now she didn't have that excuse. Was she ashamed of the poverty of where she'd come from? She didn't even live in that much luxury at Khagniorth Stronghold, not compared with how some of those from the lordly warrior families lived. But she still had much more than her family did, even with the money and provisions she gave them.

Vriska forced a lighter smile onto her face. "But the king and queen have returned, and I was given today off."

"I'm glad you could be spared." Ma's smile was warm, despite the lines in her face and chapped skin of her hands. "I made *iquitak*."

Vriska grinned as she followed her mother inside. *Iquitak* was a traditional desert made with animal fat and berries, like strawberries or blueberries or both. It was whipped until smooth, then frozen. At the king's stronghold, the cooks had taken to adding sugar or cream, but Vriska still preferred her mother's more traditional version.

"How have all of you been? And how's Da?" Vriska took a seat at the worn table. The bench underneath her wobbled a bit on the uneven floor. Or, perhaps, it was the legs that were uneven. Vriska had never been able to decide.

Had he been told that he was going to Escarland yet? Vriska would have to feign surprise when he made the announcement to the family. She wouldn't want to ruin her da's moment by giving away that the king himself had already told her.

"He was called away by the king's chief engineer this morning." Ma opened their cold cupboard, one lined with magical ice, and pulled out a bowl filled with the whipped dessert. She bustled over to the shelf and took down an empty bowl. "We are hoping this means he will be given more work. You know how he hates to be idle."

"Yes." Then he hadn't returned with the news yet. Perhaps if she lingered long enough, Vriska would still be here when he did.

She accepted the bowl and spoon that her ma handed her. The whipped desert filled the bowl. Far too much of it. Her family didn't have this much food to spare.

Yet Vriska knew better than to protest. Her parents were proud. They were proud of Vriska and what she had accomplished, yes. But they weren't going to accept her pity.

Instead, Vriska grinned at Rikze and pointed at her bowl. "I had a big breakfast. Want to help me eat this?"

Rikze grinned, snatched a second spoon from the drawer, then sat on the bench next to Vriska.

Vriska nudged the bowl so that it sat between them. She and Rikze clicked spoons, then they each dug in.

She had missed this. Her sister had been a surprise, born to her parents when Vriska was already nearly grown. She'd spent very little time with Rikze before her pursuit of her dream to be a warrior had taken her away.

Ma crossed the room and touched a tender spot on Vriska's face. "Are you all right? What happened?"

Vriska pulled away, though the bruise didn't hurt all that much. She could have had Melantha heal it, but she didn't mind wearing the proof of her victories on her face. "I got it in the fighting bouts to celebrate the king and queen's return."

"Did you win?" Rikze stared at her with wide eyes, spoon frozen partway to her mouth.

Vriska grinned, and she couldn't help the note of pride in her voice. "Of course I did. Only the very best can be a part of the king's shield band."

Ma's gaze remained on the bruise, and she frowned a little.

Rikze sighed. "I wish I could be more like you. You're so amazing and strong."

Vriska wasn't sure what to say to her sister. Their lives were just so different. Rikze spent her days here in Osmana, washing clothes and scraping by. Vriska lived in the stronghold, spending most of her days practicing her fighting skills and guarding the king.

Ma reached across the table to pat Rikze's cheek. "You are special, Rikze. You are our sunshine even during the sunless winters. And Vriska is our warrior, brave and strong." Now Ma was patting Vriska's cheek as well. "I love both my girls just how you are."

Still not sure what to say, Vriska simply nodded and turned back to her dessert before it melted.

She ate her *iquitak* in silence while her ma filled her in on the neighborhood gossip. Apparently one of the young women Vriska's age had just had her third child. Another was getting married in a week. An older woman who used to watch Vriska while both of her parents were working during those early, hard years was doing poorly. Rikze interrupted with updates about her own friends, all people Vriska didn't even know.

This was the life she would have had, if she had stayed here on the streets of Osmana instead of becoming a warrior. Would she have married by now? Perhaps had a child or two of her own?

She shuddered. Squalling babes and grubby children. Not a life she wanted.

And now she was faced with this. A marriage of alliance to a human prince who was neither the common stoneworker she might have married if she stayed here or the troll warrior she could marry, if she ever got serious about flirting rather than just bashing all the warriors' faces in.

She wasn't sure how to bring up the whole marriage thing, especially not in front of Rikze.

Heavy bootsteps stomped on the stoop outside a moment before the door creaked open. Da stood there, tall and burly with the stocky frame that Vriska had inherited from him. His muscles bulged beneath his worn shirt while patches covered the knees of his trousers. He ducked under the lintel and shut the door behind him, a few lingering clumps of slush falling from the soles of his scuffed boots.

As his gaze swept over the room, his grin widened, crinkling the leathery lines around his eyes and mouth. "Both of my girls are here!"

Rikze scraped her spoon around the bowl, claiming the last dregs of the dessert. "Vriska came for a visit. She said the king and queen gave her the day off."

Vriska willed herself to smile and nod in greeting.

Her da crossed the room and took the seat across from Rikze and beside their ma. "Good. Glad to see they are still treating you well, up there at the stronghold." His gaze flicked over her face, settled on the bruise for a moment, before he looked away.

Vriska had always appreciated that about her da. He took in the bruises, but he didn't pester her about them. He understood that they were a part of her job, the way his scraped knuckles and worn hands were a part of his.

Ma's gaze searched Da's face. "How did it go with the chief engineer? Does he have a job for you?"

Vriska forced her face to remain blank as she waited for her da's reply. Would her father be excited? Or would he turn down the opportunity? She wasn't sure which she hoped for.

Da took Ma's hand. "I've been asked to be one of the stoneworkers sent to Escarland to build a bridge for the humans."

Ma's face went blank, her eyes so focused on Da that Vriska could not hope to catch any glimmer of her true thoughts.

"Really?" Rikze froze with her spoon in the air, the surface licked so clean that it shone.

Da's gaze remained locked on Ma's, his voice giving away just how much he wanted to take this job even if his expression remained impassive. "It is a great honor to even be considered. King Rharreth wants only the best stoneworkers on this project. We have the honor and might of Kostaria to uphold in the eyes of the Escarlish humans."

"When would you leave?" Ma's voice was soft, its tone lacking any trace of her true thoughts on the matter.

"In a week. I would be gone for six to nine months. Maybe more, if the construction takes longer than the engineers have estimated." At this, Da's expression twisted for the first time. His gaze flicked briefly to Rikze before returning to Ma.

Vriska didn't let it sting that he didn't think of her when he worried about being gone. After all, she was a warrior and no longer a child like Rikze. Besides, she had been gone as long or longer while she had been fighting at Rharreth's side.

Rikze's face fell, and she slumped on the bench next to Vriska.

"The pay is good. Better than anything I've earned in years." Da wasn't even trying to hide his eagerness now. "And housing and food are included, so I would be able to send nearly all of it to you."

Vriska clenched her fists under the table and looked away. He didn't say it, but she could hear the undertone anyway. This was his chance to earn enough wages that they would no longer be dependent on Vriska's generosity.

Yes, her parents were proud of her and what she had accomplished, but they were also proud enough that they did not like accepting her wages, even if she was happy to give them whatever they needed. It wasn't like she needed it or had any aspirations to save it to turn herself into one of the warrior lords, ruling a stronghold.

Da reached out and traced a gentle hand over Ma's cheek. "This is the opportunity we have dreamed about all our lives, love."

Ma blinked, a sheen in her eyes, as she leaned into his hand. Her blank expression crumbled into a softer one that held a strange mix of love, hope, and resignation. "I know.

You must go. Of course you must go. We'll be fine here. Rikze and I can get on well enough on our own."

"And I'll look after them, Da." Vriska lifted her chin. If she was going to be stuck in Osmana for the time being—first learning Escarlish, then entertaining that Escarlish prince—she might as well put the time to good use.

Da met her gaze and gave her a single, understanding nod. Vriska was the family warrior. When Da was gone, she was strong enough to shoulder this duty.

"Of course you will. You always have." Ma smiled at Vriska before she turned back to Da. "The three of us will be fine. Now, let's see about getting you new work clothes. We can't send you to Escarland in those ratty things. We have the honor of our family to uphold."

Da hesitated, then nodded.

That hesitation was about the cost. They'd been saving that money to buy a new dress for Rikze for her birthday. And a whole new set of work clothes, including boots, would probably cost more than what they had set aside and they would have to dip into their emergency savings.

If only Vriska could convince them to accept more of her help. She had enough saved that she could buy Rikze's new dress, new clothes for her da, and a new dress for her ma while she was at it, and never miss the loss.

Even now, Da likely wouldn't take more of her coin than she already foisted on him. He probably thought dipping into their savings would be worth it, knowing they would be able to replenish the coin once he started work in Escarland.

Vriska resisted the urge to shake her head. If she married that Escarlish prince, she would have access to so much wealth that her family would never have to work another day in their lives, if they didn't want to. Yet her da would likely never accept a single coin, if he thought he could earn that same coin himself.

It was admirable. And frustrating, all at the same time.

While Ma and Rikze set out for the market with a large chunk of their savings in their pockets, Vriska set to work with the awl and leather to fix the hole in her father's travel bag.

Her father sat across from her and patched the sole of his boot. For several long minutes, they worked in silence, passing the tools and the spare bits of leather back and forth as needed.

She wasn't going to get a better chance to talk with her da about the marriage of alliance, if she ever was.

"Da..." Vriska trailed off, glancing at him before she focused on punching a new hole in the leather.

Da grunted, his signal that he was listening and waiting, without pausing in his work.

"King Rharreth has approached me with an opportunity in Escarland." Vriska moved the awl and worked to punch the next hole. She didn't like stepping around a subject. But, somehow, she couldn't bring herself to come right out and say that Rharreth wanted her to go through with an arranged marriage with an Escarlish prince.

"As an ambassador or something?" Da glanced up from his work, his fingers stilling only for a moment.

"Or something." It was close enough. And it might become true, if Vriska turned down the marriage. "The opportunity is a great honor. I was the first person Rharreth considered for it."

"But?"

Vriska sighed and set the awl aside, picking up a length of leather string. "But I don't know. All I ever wanted was to be a warrior. I never wanted to be an ambassador or—" Or a princess, but she wasn't going to say that. "—or anything else."

Her place was here. As a warrior of Kostaria. Not as a prissy princess of Escarland.

And yet, this might be her only chance to redeem her honor.

Da smeared animal fat sealant over his boot, then set it aside to let it dry. "You can do anything you set your mind to, Vriska. You showed that when you not only became a warrior but also got assigned to Prince Rharreth's shield band."

The pride in his voice made her chest ache. She didn't deserve it. Not after she had dishonored her family's sacrifices by harassing Melantha and listening to Drurvas's drivel.

But her family only saw the honored warrior. They didn't know the life she lived.

"I know." Vriska shoved the leather string through the hole.

"Kostaria is changing." Da picked up his other boot and started rubbing it with the animal fat. "We will do what we have to in order to survive the change. If that means I go to Escarland for a job, then that's what I have to do. And I trust that you will do what you have to do, Vriska. Your ma and I will be proud of you no matter what you decide and where you go."

"Linsh, Da." Vriska nodded before she turned back to finishing the patch.

She didn't have more clarity than she'd had before. But she at least felt a bit more settled. No matter what she chose, she would have her family.

CHAPTER FOUR

THREE MONTHS LATER...

Julien strained to push himself up, his body held out in a rigid line balanced on his toes and hands. Sweat poured down his face, stinging his eyes. His training for the army had been tough, but perhaps he'd gone soft since then. He groaned as he shoved himself the last few inches upright.

"Only five more." Farrendel's voice was far too chipper, considering he was currently sitting cross-legged on Julien's shoulders and back, adding weight and difficulty to the exercise.

Julien could only grunt as he slowly lowered himself to the ground. He was seriously regretting asking for Farrendel's help in training. Farrendel didn't yell in his face the way the drill sergeants had, but somehow Farrendel's nonchalant orders were just as bad. It was rather annoying to struggle through something that Farrendel found easy.

Though Julien would like to sit on Farrendel's back and

see how easy he found exercise then. Considering Julien probably weighed nearly double what Farrendel did, even his elf brother-in-law might struggle.

The early summer day was already building to a humid heat, even at this time of morning. The trees of the palace parkland provided shade for their sheltered clearing, a refuge away from the prying eyes of guards or family members.

After pushing himself up once again, Julien glanced over his shoulder.

Farrendel was swiping a cloth over one of his blades, as if entirely unconcerned about how much Julien was struggling through these pushups.

"You could at least show some sympathy," Julien gasped between breaths as he lowered himself again.

"You will thank me when you are locked in a fighting bout with a troll warrior." Farrendel sheathed his sword, then drew the other one.

Julien grunted and strained to push himself up again. He had seen the muscled arms of the troll warriors. He wasn't sure he had any hope to compete, even after exercising rigorously these past few months. Gritting his teeth, he forced himself through the last few pushups before he collapsed onto his face in the dirt, gasping.

Farrendel uncurled his legs and rose to his feet, sheathing his sword. "Take a moment to rest, then we will spar."

Julien groaned and didn't bother to move. How was he going to spar with Farrendel when he couldn't even lift his arms? "I'm beginning to wish you went with Essie this morning."

Farrendel gave an exaggerated shudder. "She is with Paige. Doubtless they are discussing pregnancy again. I like babies. I am excited to be a father. But there are some details I do not need to know."

Julien chuckled into the ground, then pushed himself upright with shaking arms. He eased into a sitting position, resting his trembling arms on his knees. "Knowing Essie, she hasn't been shy about chatting about all the details."

Farrendel's smile quirked in a tilt that was somehow both wry and lovingly indulgent.

The expression made something ache inside Julien's chest. Would he ever feel that way about his bride? Farrendel and Essie had an arranged marriage, and they'd had far less time to get to know each other than Julien did Vriska…or whoever he ended up marrying if he and Vriska didn't actually like each other when they met in person.

Perhaps Julien should look at Farrendel's expression with hope rather than pain. If Farrendel and Essie could fall in love, then surely Julien could fall in love with Vriska.

Julien forced himself to his feet and started to stretch out his muscles before they stiffened up. "I suppose we should get to it. I can still stand."

Farrendel drew his swords, his stance instantly going from relaxed to dangerous.

Julien picked up his sword and shield from where he had leaned them against a tree. This sword was a longer, heavier one than he had used before, better suited for hand-to-hand combat with the trolls than his original, lighter cavalry sword.

These past months, he had re-learned the old ways of sword and shield, things that had been all but set aside in Escarland in the age of guns and bayonets.

No sooner had Julien faced Farrendel, raising his sword,

than Farrendel leapt into the air and stabbed downward with one of his short swords.

Julien raised his shield to block one of Farrendel's swords, then barely got his sword up to parry Farrendel's other sword.

His brother-in-law was *fast.* It was all Julien could do to move to parry him.

He'd thought he'd learned how to fight when sparring with Captain Merrick, Iyrinder, and Farrendel, back when he'd started those practices as a way to help Farrendel. But he'd since learned just how much Farrendel had been holding back.

Julien got in a couple of strikes, though he was pretty sure that he only managed it because Farrendel let him.

Farrendel whipped another strike at Julien's head. Julien blocked, only to find that Farrendel's other sword trapped his. Before Julien could pull free, Farrendel ripped his sword out of his hand.

Julien groaned and leaned his hands on his knees, letting his shield drop to the ground. "Agh. That doesn't get any easier. Tell me the truth, am I improving? Or am I going to totally embarrass myself the first time I'm challenged to a bout with a troll?"

"You are improving." Farrendel sheathed his swords and swiped a sleeve over his forehead.

Julien was gratified to see that Farrendel was sweaty too. Not breathing hard, and not quite as drenched in sweat as Julien was. But the bout hadn't been too terribly easy.

"Fighting a troll will be different than fighting me." Farrendel gestured at Julien's shield. "Your style will probably be better for it. Your shield will be of more use against their larger weapons, though they will hit like a battering ram."

"I remember." Julien grimaced and rubbed his arm. He'd taken a few hits in that Dulraith, and they had knocked Julien to his knees. "At least the trolls keep their feet on the ground."

"Not you too." Farrendel grinned and elbowed Julien. "If you say I fight like a grasshopper, I am going to pull out my swords and show you just how deadly I can be."

Julien held up his hands in surrender. "Please don't. I've had enough."

Farrendel eyed him, getting that mischievous tilt to his smile that warned he was up to something. "You can still walk. That means you can still fight."

Julien picked up his sword and shield, exaggerating a limp. "Nope. Can't walk. See?"

"Hmm." Farrendel raised an eyebrow, but he didn't suggest they go back to sparring. After a moment, his expression sobered. "Julien, shashon. I know the treaty is signed, and…"

Not this again. Julien was rather tired of his family trying to talk him out of this. They'd gotten even worse as the day for his departure to Kostaria neared.

But his mind was made up. The treaty was signed. There was nothing Julien could do but make a good life out of this choice.

Julien clasped Farrendel's shoulder, waiting until his brother-in-law's silver-blue eyes swung up to meet his gaze. "I'm going to be fine. This is what I want. And I appreciate all you've done in helping me better my fighting skills and my elvish."

Farrendel gave a slight nod. "I will do whatever I can to help."

"I know." Julien released Farrendel's shoulder and set out for Buckmore Cottage once again.

As they strolled into the back gardens of Buckmore Cottage, Farrendel and Essie's home here in Escarland, they found Julien's sister Essie and sister-in-law Paige seated at an outdoor table with cups of tea and a plate of desserts between them. Bertie and Finn, Julien's nephews, alternated between playing with toy elf warriors and waggling a string for Mustache, Essie and Farrendel's half-grown kitten.

Paige and Essie glanced up, and a wide smile broke across Essie's face. She jumped to her feet and crossed the small patio to Farrendel's side.

Julien glanced away as his sister kissed Farrendel on the cheek. It was good to see them happy, but it was still mildly uncomfortable to see his little sister go all smoochy with someone. Especially now as she was beginning to show a little bit of a bump from the baby. It was still hard enough for him to think of her as old enough to be kissing a husband and having a baby.

"Did you have fun beating Julien up again today?" Essie's voice was light with suppressed laughter.

Julien gave a groan and rubbed at a bruise forming on his arm. "Yes, he did."

Farrendel wrapped an arm around Essie's shoulders, still holding her close. "Your brother is becoming a good warrior."

Coming from Farrendel, that was a huge compliment.

But would it be enough? Would Julien have the skills to prove his worth to the troll warriors—especially his warrior bride?

Paige set aside her teacup. "Julien, Avie said to tell you that he wants to see you, Edmund, and Jalissa in his study once you're done with your practice."

Julien nodded. "I'll tell Edmund and Jalissa that I'm done."

Bertie and Finn had raced up to Essie and Farrendel, and now gripped Farrendel's hands, begging him to play with them.

Since none of them were paying any attention to Julien anyway, he stepped into Buckmore Cottage and followed the sound of voices to the parlor.

There, Jalissa sat at a small desk while Edmund paced back and forth. As Julien stepped inside, Jalissa was saying, "I should have known you would have a second, scheming reason for encouraging me to become the patron of the Kingsley Gardens."

"Don't deny that you're already plotting a few schemes of your own." Edmund grinned down at her, leaning forward as if about to kiss her.

Julien knocked on the open door and cleared his throat. A part of him was immensely thankful that he was finally leaving for Kostaria. It was starting to get suffocating, being surrounded by so many disgustingly happy couples.

Not that Julien minded that all his siblings were so happy. It just ached a bit, wondering if he would find that himself.

Worse, he knew himself. He would fall in love with his troll bride. He would give her his heart for the simple reason that she was his wife, he would choose to love her, and his heart thus belonged to her.

Yet would she feel the same? Or would he be stuck in a marriage where he loved, yet his feelings were never returned? That sounded even worse than an entirely loveless marriage.

At least once he was in Kostaria, he would finally know one way or the other, instead of being stuck in this endless wondering. Once he was there, he could handle whatever he would find.

Jalissa started and nonchalantly slid the top sheet of paper under the blank ones below, hiding it from view.

Julien wasn't even going to ask what Edmund and Jalissa were plotting now. He knew that they had been searching out any remaining Mongavarian spies or Escarlish traitors that remained in the kingdom, but the less he knew, the better.

Edmund straightened slowly, as if not at all concerned that he had nearly been caught kissing Jalissa.

Julien forced a grin onto his face as jabbed a thumb at Edmund. "Jalissa, are you sure you want to marry this schemer?"

Jalissa smirked and glanced at Edmund. "I am sure. Besides, I know his greatest secret. I can blackmail him whenever I wish."

Surprisingly, Edmund shifted, looking a bit…guilty. Julien wasn't sure he could remember his brother ever looking that uncomfortable.

Then Edmund's smile softened as he rested his hands on Jalissa's shoulders. "You have me well and truly wrapped around your finger."

She held up her hand, wiggling her fingers to make her ring sparkle in the light. "I have the ring to prove it."

Edmund again looked about ready to kiss her, even though Julien was standing right there.

Julien shifted. Would Edmund and Jalissa even notice if

he quietly slipped away? He cleared his throat again. "Anyway, I'm done with my morning practice. Give me a few minutes to wash up, then I'll meet you at Avie's study. Paige already told you he wanted to talk to us, right?"

Edmund nodded, straightening a bit even though he continued to rest his hands on Jalissa's shoulders. As if he was impatiently waiting for Julien to leave before he and Jalissa went back to whatever scheming they had been doing before Julien walked in.

Pasting an easy smile on his face, Julien ducked out of the parlor. He had to cut through the back garden of Buckmore Cottage, and he tried to be as unobtrusive as possible as he passed Paige and Essie, who had gone back to talking. Farrendel now sat cross-legged on the patio bricks as he built a fort out of stray sticks with one hand while petting his purring cat with the other. Bertie and Finn made noises as they raced around, a wooden elf warrior clutched in each fist.

Julien strolled down the gravel trail that led from Buckmore Cottage to the back garden of Winstead Palace. He ducked into the palace, then headed for the wing that held the royal apartments. Once in his room, he washed and changed into clothes that weren't stained with dirt from being pummeled by his elven brother-in-law.

As he headed back out, he paused by his desk. His latest letter from Vriska lay on top where he could easily re-read it yet again, if he wished.

It was just as short and stilted as all of her letters. And all of his, truth be told.

Writing letters had been a good idea to try to get to know each other over the past few months. But he hadn't taken into account how hard it would be, working with a limited vocabulary as he learned a new language or putting up with awkwardly dictating a letter.

Not to mention, Julien was not a verbose person. He just wasn't the type to pour his heart out in person, much less in a letter.

He liked to think that Vriska was the same way and that was the reason for her short letters rather than a reluctance to communicate with him.

Once they met in person, things would be different. They would bond over sword practice and duty to their kingdoms. He wasn't going to let himself worry that it wasn't going to work out just because both he and Vriska failed to bond through letters.

Giving himself a shake, Julien strode from his room.

When he arrived at Averett's study, the door was partially open, the sign that Averett was expecting them and didn't mind being disturbed. Julien nodded at the guard stationed outside the door, then knocked on the doorjamb, sticking his head inside. "Avie?"

Averett glanced up from the paper he was reading. He gestured to the three chairs stationed on the other side of his large sturdy desk. "Since you're here first, you get your pick of seats."

Julien was tempted to sit in the middle one, forcing Edmund and Jalissa to take the seats on either side of him, just to needle his younger brother. But that would probably backfire as he found himself awkwardly sandwiched between Edmund and Jalissa as they bantered and shot each other romantic looks.

Instead, Julien took the chair on the far right. It put his back to the wall, which would be a more subtle dig at

Edmund, who also preferred to sit with his back protected. "Edmund and Jalissa should be here shortly."

"No need to wait. We're here." Edmund strolled into the room, tugging Jalissa gently after him with his grip on her hand.

Julien held back a groan. Essie and Farrendel's snuggliness had been bad enough—something that had gotten even worse now that Essie was expecting and Farrendel was hovering atrociously. Now Edmund and Jalissa rarely went anywhere without holding hands. As if Edmund's pining all winter hadn't been enough to deal with.

Still, it was good to see his siblings happy. Even if that happiness came with an excessive amount of public affection.

Edmund paused next to the chairs, shooting Julien an exaggerated, annoyed look. Julien held his brother's gaze and didn't budge from the seat he'd claimed.

With a small shake of his head, Edmund held out the middle chair for Jalissa, then sank into the farthest chair to the left. This put his back to the closed door, something that probably itched at him even if he knew the door was well guarded.

"Good, you're all here." Averett's smile dropped from his face, replaced with a grave frown and weary lines around his eyes.

Edmund leaned forward. "Is something wrong? Have there been delays on the new bridge?"

Julien shifted, waiting for Averett's answer as well. While he wasn't as invested in the construction of the new bridge as Jalissa and Edmund—they were planning to get married on the newly completed bridge and wouldn't want any wedding delays—he still felt a responsibility for the construction. Once he married Vriska, he would be the official link between Kostaria and Escarland.

"No, the bridge is right on schedule. A little ahead of schedule, even." Averett stared down at his desk, his gaze latching on an opened, ivory envelope.

Julien studied the envelope, but he couldn't make out any details that would tell him its origins. Edmund's eyes widened, though, so he must have seen something that Julien didn't.

Averett drew in a deep breath and tapped the envelope. "I have received a missive from Mongavaria. They have requested an exchange of emissaries to resolve the current tension between us."

"Tension." Jalissa gave a soft snort.

"It is a rather polite way to phrase their assassination attempts." Edmund's light tone didn't match the hard look in his eyes. While all of them had taken the near assassination of Essie, Farrendel, their unborn child, and all of the elven royal family rather personally, Edmund had the extra anger at the execution of the brave Escarlish spies who had been captured in Mongavaria.

Tension didn't begin to cover it.

"I know. I'm suspicious of their motives. But if they are willing to negotiate, I would like to pursue the opportunity." Averett grimaced down at the letter. "They are sending their princess. They insinuated that they would like to consider a marriage of alliance between her and Julien as a way to resolve the issues between our kingdoms."

Julien froze, trying to process what this meant. Mongavaria didn't know about the marriage of alliance between Julien and Vriska—or whoever agreed to it on the Kostarian end. Besides keeping the whole process quiet for privacy's sake, especially if Julien found himself with a sudden change of bride if Vriska decided she didn't want to marry him, they had also wanted to keep the news out of Mongavaria's ears as long as possible. It was gratifying to know that they had succeeded in that, at least.

"Surely you aren't considering it?" Edmund gestured from Julien to the envelope. "Even setting aside the damage it would do to our relations with Kostaria if we backed out of the marriage alliance now, you know what happened to the Nevarian royal family. They married into what was then Mongalia and started mysteriously dying off until Mongalia inherited the entire kingdom by default. The Intelligence Office hasn't been able to confirm exactly what role Mongalia's royal family played, but we have our suspicions."

Last Julien had heard those suspicions involved poison, too-convenient "accidents," and a ruthless king plotting the annexation of Nevaria for over two decades before making it a reality.

Edmund's frown deepened, his green-blue eyes darkening. "It is my belief that Mongavaria wants to do the same thing to Escarland. They failed to marry their crown prince to Essie, so now they're trying to hitch their princess to Julien. He's actually a better option for them, if you think about it. He's higher up the line of succession. That leaves fewer people to kill off before Julien would inherit the throne."

"I know exactly what Mongavaria is doing and, no, I'm not about to marry off Julien to their princess." Averett blew out a breath through his teeth, shaking his head. "We are all in agreement that a marriage of alliance with Kostaria is far more beneficial, even regardless of the fact that Julien and I gave our word and we aim to keep it. Parliament might argue, but they don't have access to some of the information about Mongavaria that we do."

"So what do you plan to do about Mongavaria's offer?" Julien gripped the arms of his chair. Playing politics was more Averett's and Edmund's thing than his. Why had he even been included in this meeting if Averett wasn't going to take Mongavaria up on this marriage of alliance? Julien was leaving for Kostaria in a few days. He would marry Vriska—or another troll bride—and that would be that.

"I can't outright tell them no, especially since we aren't ready to reveal your marriage of alliance with Kostaria just yet." Averett glanced from Julien to focus on Edmund and Jalissa. "But I do want to agree to an exchange of emissaries. If we can work out some kind of peaceful resolution, then I want to try. Their princess is their only heir, so our emissaries should be safe enough, knowing we could retaliate. But..."

"But we need to send an emissary with nearly an equivalent rank. We can't just send any random ambassador." Edmund shared a look with Jalissa, resignation filling his gaze. "You want to send me."

It would make sense. Edmund's skills as a spy would be useful in this situation. Especially since he had been in Mongavaria before, if rather unofficially and not for long.

Still, why was Julien here? This seemed like something for Edmund and Averett to work out between them. Of course Jalissa should be here, since this would affect their wedding plans, depending on when the exchange happened.

But it wouldn't affect Julien, would it? Surely Averett wouldn't delay Julien's trip to Kostaria over this. The alliance with Kostaria was too important as a deterrent to Mongavaria if a peaceful solution couldn't be reached.

"Actually, Weylind and I want to send both of you." Averett's mouth twisted into what could only be described as a wry frown. "Well, we'd rather send neither of you. But we need representatives of both Tarenhiel and Escarland. And the two of you are the only ones qualified to take this on. It will be dangerous, and I'd rather send in a spy than simply an ambassador."

Julien didn't like the thought of sending both his brother and his soon-to-be sister-in-law into Mongavaria. If this was some kind of trap, Mongavaria could do whatever they liked, and Escarland wasn't in a position to contest it.

What other option did they have? If Averett refused this overture outright, Mongavaria could use it as an excuse for more attacks. Even outright war. And they would paint themselves as the innocent party who had reached out, only to be rebuffed.

Edmund turned to Jalissa, squeezing her hand again as he spoke in elvish. "This will be dangerous."

Julien shifted, looking away. He would celebrate the fact that he understood the elvish, except that he was now overhearing what was a quiet moment between Edmund and Jalissa.

"I know." Jalissa shifted to face him, her shoulders straightening. "But I knew something like this was a possibility when I agreed to marry you. This is for the good of my kingdom as well as yours. We have to do this."

Edmund nodded and turned to Averett again. "We'll do it."

Averett's gaze flicked between them. "We'll send you with guards, of course. And you *should* be safe. As I said, we'll have their princess here. They wouldn't dare harm you, knowing we could harm their princess or hold her hostage in return. And, politically speaking, she is more valuable than the two of you. We'll have more leverage than they will."

True, if they were looking at the cold surface facts. Neither Jalissa nor Edmund was the heir to a kingdom.

But Mongavaria likely knew that Escarland was far more merciful and would hesitate to harm their princess. While that kingdom had already proved with its treatment of the captured Escarlish spies that it was prepared to be ruthless. Not a situation that Julien liked. At all.

But there wasn't anything he could do about it.

Edmund sighed and met Averett's gaze. "I guess the only question remaining is when do we leave?"

"I tried to push it back as far as I could, but Mongavaria is impatient." Averett's gaze dropped back to his desk. "If you both agree to this, then you'll leave the week after your wedding."

Edmund's posture eased, as if he was relieved by the news. He had likely been worried that they would have to leave as soon as possible, which might mean postponing the wedding.

With his easy grin, Edmund glanced at Jalissa. "Honeymoon in Mongavaria?"

"Official ambassador mission. Possible spying. Definite danger." Jalissa shrugged, a twist to her lips. "Sounds romantic. What else should I have expected, marrying you?"

"We can take a more romantic honeymoon later, if you'd like. Explore the forests of Tarenhiel, perhaps. Or maybe wander through Kostaria." Edmund's smirk widened. "It is very beautiful up there."

Julien shook his head. He was pretty sure Edmund was still banned from Kostaria.

"Would the visit be authorized or unauthorized?" Jalissa raised her eyebrows.

"Probably unauthorized. Unless my brother's romance turns out extremely well and he can convince Rharreth to allow me back into the kingdom." Edmund's grin remained in place, but he flicked a glance in Julien's direction.

Julien held back his grimace. He could only hope his arranged marriage turned out that well. He wanted to have what his siblings had found. Love.

Not just the mushy, fleeting kind. But the kind that would walk into an enemy nation to stay together, like Edmund and Jalissa were doing. Like Essie had done to fight her way across Kostaria to get Farrendel back.

With a hint of a smirk still playing around his mouth, Edmund nodded to Averett. "Thanks for delaying the mission until after our wedding. I wouldn't want to postpone, and we'll be safer in Mongavaria once we're married and can stay together. I don't intend to let Jalissa out of my sight while we're there."

"And I will not let you out of my sight." Jalissa's fingers tightened on Edmund's hand, her chin lifting. "You will need my magic."

Edmund nodded, the smirk softening as he held her gaze. "I have a feeling your magic is going to be crucial in getting us in and out of Mongavaria safely."

"Hopefully it won't come to that," Averett stated, though Julien could tell he was trying to reassure himself as much as Edmund and Jalissa. "I know you'll be busy with wedding plans over the next three months, but you have until then to prepare. I've already submitted the signed paperwork to allow General Bloam to share information about our spying operation in Mongavaria with both of you. He won't tell you everything, of course, but you will be asked to memorize anything he deems useful."

"Good." Edmund gave a brisk nod. "It will be easier if both of us know the information."

In case something happened to one of them. He didn't say it out loud, but the implication was there all the same.

Julien shifted in his chair. Why was he here again? If he could, he would take Edmund and Jalissa's place in Mongavaria.

But he didn't have Edmund's training. Besides, his place was here, securing the alliance with Kostaria.

Though if the diplomat exchange wasn't happening until after Edmund and Jalissa's wedding, what did that mean for Julien? The plan had been for him to return to Escarland by then with his betrothed on his arm.

Averett's mouth twisted into a grim line as he turned to Julien. "When I sent my agreement to the exchange to Mongavaria, I won't make any promises while leaving the impression that a marriage of alliance is still a possibility. By the time the Mongavarian princess arrives, you will have just returned from Kostaria. We'll use the same story we planned to give to the people all along, that you went to Kostaria and happened to fall in love while you were at it. Since I made no promises, Mongavaria can't really argue."

Julien nodded, seeing the logic in it. "By that point, the diplomat exchange will have already occurred and Mongavaria can't back out."

"Exactly." Averett's smile didn't hold any mirth. "When you return, you will also have your troll betrothed with you. With Tarenhiel represented in these negotiations by Jalissa in

Mongavaria, Kostaria will be represented by her here in Escarland."

Julien frowned. That would plunge his betrothed into the diplomatic deep end on her first visit to Escarland. And the two of them wouldn't even be married yet. Or know each other all that well.

Would whatever fledgling relationship they had formed by then survive the pressure?

He would have to hope so. Both for the sake of his future marital happiness and for his kingdom's safety. With Mongavaria still making noise, it was more important than ever that the new alliance with Kostaria remained secure and strong.

Too bad it all rested on Julien, the least smart and charming of all his siblings. And Vriska, the troll king's prickly shield sister.

CHAPTER FIVE

Julien hugged his sister Essie, keeping his bear hug gentler than he usually did. Behind her, an elven ship waited at the dock to carry her, Farrendel, Edmund, and Jalissa across the Hydalla River to Tarenhiel.

Essie pulled back, resting her hand on his arm as if she wasn't ready to let him go. "I wish you were traveling with us as far as Estyra."

Julien didn't. He had been the one to suggest that he stay the night at the encampment for the troll workers before catching the weekly supply train across Tarenhiel the next day. He was looking forward to the undisturbed time to think before he reached Kostaria.

Besides, the farewells were bad enough. He'd said goodbye to Averett, Paige, his nephews, and his mother that morning. Now he was saying goodbye to the others. They were making a much larger fuss than was warranted, and he was glad this was happening now in Escarland rather than in Estyra with Weylind and the rest of the elven royal family looking on.

"I'll be fine, Essie." Julien released her. "Enjoy your trip to Lethorel."

"I will. I love Lethorel." She glanced over her shoulder to Farrendel. "Though I'm really hoping this trip isn't cut short with an ambush, assassination attempt, or other kind of danger. A holiday that stays simply a relaxing holiday sounds wonderful."

Behind her, Farrendel nodded, a hint of a grimace twisting his mouth. The last two times he and Essie had gone to Lethorel, they had been attacked. Julien hoped for both their sakes that this holiday was entirely uneventful.

Uneventful, except for Edmund doing his level best to see just how far he could push Weylind before he snapped.

Essie started to step back, then hesitated before giving Julien another, tighter hug. "I just want you to be happy, Julien. You've always been there for the rest of us, stepping in as a big brother since we didn't have Father looking out for us. But I have Farrendel now. Edmund has Jalissa. Averett has Paige and a whole palace full of staff and guards looking after him. We'll be all right if you take a step back so you can pursue your own happiness."

Julien stared off over Essie's head rather than down at her. He wasn't sure what to say, even as he tried to swallow past the uncomfortable choking sensation at the back of his throat.

His little sister was all grown up and dispensing wise advice. He'd gotten a taste of his own, protective medicine this spring as his siblings pitched in to help him prepare for this trip to Kostaria. He still wasn't sure how to handle being protected instead of doing the protecting.

Finally, he cleared his throat and gave her another hug. "I'll try."

Essie stepped out of his hug and grinned. "Enjoy your trip to Kostaria, fall head-over-heels in love, and come back with a new soon-to-be sister-in-law for me. I can't wait to meet her."

Great. No pressure there. As if finding love in this situation wasn't hard enough, he had to worry about disappointing Essie if this troll sister-in-law didn't fit as well with the family as Paige and Jalissa did.

Shaking the thought away, Julien turned to Farrendel. When Farrendel didn't back away, flinch, or otherwise indicate that he wasn't up for a hug at the moment, Julien gave him a back-slapping hug. "Thanks for all your help."

"Of course, shashon." Farrendel even gave him a tentative back-slap in return. He opened his mouth, as if he intended to say something else, but he closed it again and shook his head. Perhaps it had been another attempt to talk Julien out of this. When Farrendel spoke, all he said instead was, "Do not forget that you are a warrior."

Julien nodded. That was Farrendel's way of saying, *Stay safe. Don't die. Don't let the trolls pummel you too badly.*

Farrendel stepped back and picked up the wooden cat carrier formed of delicate branches that was clearly of elven design. Inside, the plump and fluffy orange cat sat with its tail curled around its paws, a disgruntled look on its smushed face. Farrendel rested a hand on Essie's lower back and steered her toward the ship.

Essie gave one last wave over her shoulder at Julien before she fell into step with Farrendel.

Julien faced Edmund and Jalissa, not quite sure what to say. He just wanted to get this over with. He wasn't into drawn-out farewells, and there had already been far too much talking and emotions for his liking.

Jalissa reached out, hesitated, then grasped Julien's shoulders in an elven-style hug. "I hope you find happiness, shashon, with…everything."

Everything. That was a diplomatic way to put it. Julien would probably call it *the mess that passed for his romantic life.*

"Linshi, isciena. That is the right word, isn't it?" Julien grinned at her and squeezed her shoulders in return. Even though it wouldn't be official for another three months, it was good to hear Jalissa call him *brother* and claim her as *sister* in return.

"Yes, it is." Jalissa's smile flickered, then died once again. She glanced down, her hands clasped in front of her. "Could you give my best wishes to my sister for me?"

"Of course. Do you have any letters or anything else that you wish to pass along?" Julien had gathered that Jalissa's relationship with her sister Melantha had been improving over the past three months.

Jalissa gestured toward the train that had delivered them to the border. "I already packed my items for Melantha in the trunk of stuff Essie and Farrendel are also sending. The trunk should be with your things?"

"It is." Edmund's mouth twitched.

Julien nodded, not questioning how Edmund would know that. When they'd boarded the train that morning, Essie had pointed out a trunk the servants were loading, informing Julien that it was filled with hot chocolate, Escarlish candy, and other items for Rharreth and Melantha.

"Linshi." With another smile, Jalissa stepped away and strode toward the ship, following Essie and Farrendel.

That left Julien alone with Edmund.

Edmund stepped in to give Julien yet another back-slapping brother hug. "Don't let the trolls beat you up."

Somehow, Julien didn't think he could avoid getting beat up once or twice while in Kostaria. "I'll try not to, but I think it's rather inevitable."

"In that case, give as good as you get." Edmund glanced around, then lowered his voice. "Are you sure about going alone? Perhaps you could take a handful of guards with you? I have a few people I could recommend."

People who would likely be spies doubling as guards.

Julien shook his head. "The trolls will respect me more if I come alone. Besides, Essie went to Tarenhiel all by herself. I can do no less now."

"Well, she wasn't exactly alone. She just didn't know she wasn't alone." Edmund shifted, glancing over his shoulder at the ship before turning back to Julien. Edmund gripped Julien's shoulder. "You don't have to be alone either. I can—"

Julien shook his head, harder this time. "No. First of all, if King Rharreth were to catch you spying in Kostaria again, it would undo everything I'm trying to accomplish with my marriage. Second, you're needed here. You're taking a family trip to Lethorel with your future in-laws. You have a wedding to plan and a mission to Mongavaria to prepare for. I'll be fine."

Edmund shifted, as if he wanted to glance over his shoulder at Jalissa again but didn't dare give away that she was what kept him from rushing off to Kostaria. "I know. But I'm willing to drop everything for you. Just know that, all right?"

"I know." Julien wasn't sure how to convey how much his brother's willingness to go back to spying for him meant. "You have Jalissa now. You can't take off like you did before. Besides, you don't want to disappoint Jalissa. I've gathered that this trip is rather important to their family. This is your first visit to Lethorel, isn't it?"

Edmund's smile had a wry quirk. "Actually, yes, it is. The elven summer palace was never considered a prime source for my type of *visiting*, even when the king was in residence since all important information still flowed through Estyra. But let's just say its general location in Tarenhiel isn't a surprise."

And thus the reason those Mongavarian spies could find the information for their assassination attempt several months ago.

"I'm surprised Weylind is even letting you go, knowing what he does about your past activities in Tarenhiel." Julien kept his grin in place. It was strange, realizing that Weylind knew more about what his brother had been doing the past few years than he did. But Edmund's past as a spy was need-to-know, and Julien didn't need to know. He probably shouldn't even know Edmund had been a spy.

Though, *had been* probably wasn't quite right. Once a spy, always a spy. Edmund was just doing it more officially under the guise of an ambassador these days. There was no use pretending that he wasn't going to be taking notes when he and Jalissa went to Mongavaria.

Edmund shrugged, still grinning. "I think there was some debate on whether I counted as family since Jalissa and I aren't married yet. But Weylind is starting to get a little resigned to the whole thing, and he probably figures I'll be there next year, even if I was banned this year, so there's no point in doing anything but conceding to the inevitable."

"Well, I hope the time with them goes well. Try not to annoy Weylind too much." Julien lightly punched Edmund's shoulder, then gestured toward the ship. "Now go on. They'll leave without you if you don't hurry up."

Edmund shrugged even as he started toward the boat. "Not a problem if they do. I have other ways into Tarenhiel."

Julien laughed and lifted a hand in one last wave as Edmund strode onto the ship. The gangplank was pulled up, and the ship glided away from the dock.

For long moments, Julien remained standing there, watching the ship as it slipped across the water. Other boats, both elven and human, plied the waters, ferrying workers, materials, and trade goods across the broad, muddy brown expanse of the Hydalla River, making a final run before nightfall.

Before him, the partially constructed bridge soared into the orange, sunset sky. The sloping causeway jutted out from each bank of the river, ending abruptly in space. Coffer dams held back the river around each of the footings for the massive pylons that would support the span. In the center of the river, Linder Island had been cleared of all guard shacks and communications outposts and instead was piled high with rock quarried from Kostaria and hauled down the coast and up the river.

The army outpost remained perched on the hill overlooking the river on the Escarlish side, but construction had started on new, stone fortifications near the river, which would hold gun emplacements to protect the bridge and the train depot from attack.

"Your Highness?"

Julien turned and found a tall, thin man standing there. The man wore a white shirt underneath suspenders with black trousers and coat. A black bowler hat completed the look. Something about his bearing simply screamed *clerk*. "Yes?"

"I'm Sam Kent. I'm the administrator assisting the engineers for the construction projects." The man bobbed a bow.

Yep, a clerk. Which meant he was likely the single most important and under-appreciated person here at the construction site. People who pushed around the paperwork kept the world running, after all.

Now that Julien had turned, he was facing the second, sprawling construction site, this one for the large train depot that would provide the transfer point for goods traveling between Escarland and the kingdoms to the north. A large swath of ground had been cleared of vegetation until it was down to bare dirt. The outlines of foundations for buildings stood in rows while piles of gravel waited to be spread for the rail bed.

Beside the train depot's site, what looked like a town lay in neat rows of stone buildings that hadn't been there the last time Julien had gone north.

Sam Kent gestured in that direction. "If you would come with me, Your Highness?"

Julien glanced toward the train. It appeared his luggage had already been unloaded, and a troll was currently carrying the last of it down the hill toward the settlement. With a nod, Julien followed Sam down the graveled road.

As they neared the town, the noise and bustle drifted to Julien on the light, river-scented breeze. The main street below was filled with both trolls and humans. What looked like a tavern spilled light and raucous noise into the street. Stores lined each side, looking for all the world like any other small town in Escarland, except for the fact that every single building was made from stone.

Sam waved in that direction. "As you can see, we have a fully functional town."

A town that wasn't going anywhere, even after the bridge was finished. Julien could see that now. These buildings and homes were too permanent. Besides, the train depot would need workers. The bridge would turn the focus of trade to this section of the border, taking it away from other port towns like Ayre. In a few years or decades, this little start of a town would bloom into a full-blown city. And these troll-built homes would be at its heart.

"How has it been going, integrating the troll and human workers?" Julien eyed the bustling street as they entered the far side of the town. He didn't see anything that would indicate problems.

"It wasn't without issues, especially right at first." Sam shrugged and nodded toward where a mixed group of trolls and humans were gathered around two trolls who were having a wrestling contest in the middle of the street. "But it has gone better than many expected. The leaders have enforced the rules as kings Averett and Rharreth outlined, and any troublemakers have been immediately sent home. The dishonor of being sent home is enough to keep the trolls in line, and the humans don't want to lose the work opportunity. There are still some on both sides that harbor prejudices, but they keep to themselves. The majority have learned to get along."

"Good." It wasn't easy to integrate when both sides harbored discrimination toward the other. While it was impossible to stamp it out completely, they could do their best to place the expectation of decency on their people and be an example for them.

Within a few years, there were likely to be more and

more elves and trolls walking the streets of many towns and cities in Escarland. Already, an elven healer worked in each hospital in Aldon while another healer was now permanently stationed at Winstead Palace to assist the royal physician. And the elven and troll cities were likely to see more humans in their midst, from tourists to those looking for new opportunities in those kingdoms.

"Some of the troll workers have joined the crews building the railway depot. Their head engineer has expressed interest in having our help in constructing new railways in Kostaria." Sam paused in front of a building.

"Have they contacted King Rharreth and King Averett about this idea yet? I believe that is something the kings would be interested in approving." Julien resisted the urge to shudder at the thought of the train ride across the Kostarian mountains. Right now, Kostaria only had the single rail line running from the border to their capital city, and that line was less than what Julien would call comfortable. Or safe.

"We have a message for you to carry to King Rharreth. The trolls' head engineer thought it best if King Rharreth approach King Averett from there." Sam's gaze strayed down the street, then he gestured in that direction.

Julien turned to find a troll and a human approaching them. The human was slim, though his arms were muscled. He still looked tiny next to the brawny troll next to him.

Sam Kent gestured between them, introducing them as the head engineers for the bridge project.

Julien shook their hands, greeting each of them. All four of them stepped inside the building, which turned out to be the main administrative office. A table had been placed in the center of the room, and it was set for four.

Over dinner, Julien listened as the engineers described the progress of the bridge. From what he could gather, Edmund and Jalissa had nothing to worry about. The bridge would be finished in time for their wedding.

After dinner, the engineers gave Julien a full tour of the town. Julien made a point to stop and talk to many of the trolls and humans wandering the street.

Vriska's father was somewhere in this town. She had mentioned that he was one of the stone workers building the new bridge, something that he considered a great honor.

What would Julien even say to him, if he met him? *Hello, I'm Prince Julien. I'm on my way to Kostaria to court your daughter. Maybe. If she still wants to once she meets me. Otherwise, I'll court someone else. So, do I have your blessing?*

It sounded lame even in his head. Did Vriska's father even know about the arranged marriage? Had Vriska or Rharreth told him? Julien certainly didn't want to be the one to tell him if he didn't know.

It didn't matter. Julien didn't meet him and didn't have to decide what to say. As the darkness of night descended and the stars winked overhead, Julien was shown to a room where he could sleep.

He lay on the bed, staring at the ceiling, for long minutes. Tomorrow morning, he would cross the Hydalla and board a train headed north for Kostaria.

Three months. It was the longest he had ever been gone from Escarland—from his brother's side. Even though Averett's safety was no longer his duty as it had once been, he struggled to let it go. If something happened to Averett, Paige, or his nephews while he was gone…

Nothing was going to happen. The palace security was well trained. The Mongavarian spy ring had been arrested and fully shut down. Edmund and Jalissa had made sure no more traitors lingered among the Escarlish nobility, though Edmund suspected a few were dabbling in illicit smuggling.

It was time for Julien to let this duty go and face his new future, whatever it might hold.

CHAPTER SIX

Vriska waited on the new train platform, forcing herself to remain steady rather than shift. Prince Julien, her possible intended, would arrive any minute now.

That spring, the train tracks had been extended from the old platform near the ruins of what had been Gror Grar to a new station next to the capital city of Osmana. This new station had a sprawling complex to handle the new trade with Escarland.

After so many years with few changes to their kingdom due to the focus on war, it was strange to see how things were shifting, growing, even in the short time since Rharreth and Melantha had become king and queen.

Would Vriska have a place in this new Kostaria? She didn't know anything else besides war and weapons. She wasn't equipped for peace.

She likely wasn't the only warrior wondering that. What would the warriors do, now that they weren't in a state of war with Tarenhiel?

Next to her, Rharreth stood firm, wearing his large sword at his hip, as he clasped Melantha's hand. She wore a wool dress fringed in fur, but it was far lighter than the heavy coats and furs she'd donned through the winter.

Around them, Zavni, Brynjar, and Eyvindur gathered, guarding their king and queen. Several members of other shield bands stood with them, starting their new jobs of assisting the king's shield band.

Catching Vriska glancing her way, Melantha spread her free hand and smiled. "I am loving all this sun."

"I told you that summer in Kostaria is pleasant." Rharreth smiled down at his wife. "Perhaps we should travel even farther north. There are places where the sun never sets at this time of year."

"That does sound lovely." Melantha glanced at Vriska again, as if realizing that it would not happen this year. She and Rharreth were needed for Prince Julien's visit. "Until then, I'll enjoy the long summer days we have here in Osmana."

Vriska turned away, staring off into the countryside instead.

Only the peaks of the tallest mountains remained touched by snow. All the valleys were filled with green while even the evergreen trees seemed brighter and livelier now than they did in the dark months of winter. Summer flowers bloomed in the high meadows, turning them into vibrant swaths of yellow and purple, while distant herds of caribou could be seen grazing.

Movement in the far distance caught her gaze. She shaded her eyes, spotting the plume of steam and smoke chugging from the train.

Vriska's stomach churned. Only a few more minutes,

then Prince Julien would be here. She could no longer pretend this arranged marriage didn't exist.

Sure, she could still back out. Only Rharreth, Melantha, their shield band, and Prince Julien himself knew about the plan. As far as everyone else was concerned, Prince Julien was here on a diplomatic visit. If he happened to fall in love with Vriska, then all the better for Kostaria. No one would know it had been arranged.

Vriska wanted to punch something. She was a troll warrior. She didn't suffer from angst like this. No, she didn't think. She just followed orders, fought for her kingdom, and died with honor.

Except that she hadn't died in the wars. Instead of dying with honor, she had failed to even live with honor.

The train rumbled around the far mountain peaks, then swooped into the valley in which Osmana lay. It screeched to a halt alongside the platform in a billow of steam. Within moments, the troll engineers bustled around the train, lowering the gangway to the platform.

The door to the passenger car opened, and a figure stood there, still mostly hidden in the shadows of the train car. Then, he stepped forward into the sunlight, giving Vriska her first glimpse of the human she might end up marrying.

Well, she had seen him before, briefly, during the Dulraith. But she hadn't paid any attention to the human who had fought at Rharreth's side.

Prince Julien was tall, perhaps as tall as she was, if not a little taller. His shoulders were broad and muscled, showing that he was a human warrior, not the weakling prince as she had feared. His hair was brown with a few reddish highlights in the sunlight while a thick beard covered his cheeks and chin. His eyes were brown and held a steady earnestness, though his gaze remained carefully focused on Rharreth and Melantha, as if to avoid looking at Vriska before he was ready.

Should she feel some kind of instant connection? An attraction? She wasn't sure if she felt anything.

But she'd never tried to have a relationship before. She didn't know what it felt like. For years, she hadn't given so much as a passing thought to ever marrying since she had been too focused on being a warrior to dwell on anything else.

It was hard to wrap her mind around it, especially since she wasn't sure this future was one she wanted. She was willing to try, for duty's sake. But that was the only reason she was here. She had no dreams of romance and love.

Rharreth stepped forward with Melantha at his side. "Welcome to Kostaria, Prince Julien."

Vriska spared herself only a moment of pleasure at the fact that she understood the Escarlish that Rharreth spoke. Her dogged determination to learn Escarlish had paid off.

Prince Julien stepped forward and gave a half-bow to Rharreth and Melantha. "Thank you for welcoming me into your kingdom."

Vriska understood that bit of Escarlish as well. Perhaps she and this Escarlish prince would be able to fumble their way into talking to each other. That was a step in the right direction.

Assuming that was the direction she wanted.

Prince Julien cleared his throat, a hint of a grimace twitching his mouth for a moment. When he spoke, it was in the shared language of the elves and trolls, though his Escarlish accent was thick. "Queen Melantha, I have greetings from your family. And letters. Did I say that right?"

Melantha smiled her serene, court smile and nodded. "Yes, and thank you. I trust all of them are well? Essie and the baby?"

"Yes, they are well." Prince Julien nodded, a smile on his face. "You will wish to read your sister Jalissa's letter right away."

Melantha's smile widened into something genuine. "Did your rogue brother finally ask her to marry him?"

"I'm not going to give away her news." Prince Julien's smile held something of a smirk.

It was an expression Vriska liked. She wouldn't want a stuffy, too proper prince.

"The letters and gifts from your family are in one of my trunks." Speaking in Escarlish again, he gestured toward the trunks and bags that several troll servants were unloading from the train. "I don't pack that much for myself."

Rharreth suppressed a grin, as if he had been wondering at the amount of baggage the human prince had taken along. "Prince Julien, let me introduce you to my shield band. You've met Zavni and Brynjar."

Zavni and Brynjar nodded, then sent glances at Vriska. They knew what was going on, after all. They had been there when Rharreth agreed to this marriage of alliance.

"This is Eyvindur." Rharreth waved to him. Then, everyone turned to Vriska. Her skin prickled as Rharreth gestured to her. "And this is Vriska, my shield sister."

Vriska kept her expression blank, her arms crossed. Yet, as Prince Julien finally turned his gaze toward her, her breath caught. Not in a romantic way. But in that tight, awkward way of meeting a stranger for the first time.

Prince Julien's gaze was as neutral as hers, though his brown eyes remained soft. Once again, he spoke in her language rather than his. "It is a pleasure to meet you, Vriska."

How long had he practiced those words to get them right? He was dedicated, she would give him that.

Prince Julien was still watching her—everyone was watching her—waiting for her response.

Vriska forced her mouth to move, her dry tongue to form a word. "Likewise."

As she turned away, she could see the flash of disappointment on Rharreth's face.

Apparently she wasn't trying hard enough.

The thing was…she wasn't sure she wanted to try. A part of her—a large part—wanted to turn prickly and make this Prince Julien go away.

Rharreth and Melantha turned toward Osmana, and Prince Julien fell into step with them.

Vriska hung back, letting Eyvindur, Brynjar, and the rest of the guard detail follow first.

As the others strode ahead, Zavni halted next to Vriska and elbowed her. "So that's your human prince."

Vriska scowled, staring at the back of Prince Julien's head rather than at Zavni. "He isn't my prince."

Zavni waggled his eyebrows. "Uh-huh."

Vriska punched his arm. She didn't want to talk about this. Especially not with Zavni while he was smirking at her like that.

Brothers. She was so glad she'd never grown up with any.

JULIEN STROLLED next to Rharreth and Melantha, surrounded by their shield band. Trolls lined the streets of Osmana, gaping at him. Had any of them even seen a human before? Few had ventured out of the safety of Osmana's walls when the Escarlish army had been camped outside the ruins of Gror Grar.

The citizens of Osmana remained mostly silent, though a few smiled and some of the children waved. They didn't know about the arranged marriage part of the treaty. As far as they were concerned, he was simply a prince of Escarland on a state visit.

Feelings for Escarland were probably mixed. On the one hand, the trade with Escarland was causing a boom for the Kostarian economy. Not to mention the extra jobs for all the workers and engineers who had been sent to Escarland for building the bridge over the Hydalla River.

But on the other hand, Escarland had sided with Tarenhiel and, together, the two kingdoms had soundly defeated Kostaria. And defeat was something the proud trolls didn't handle well.

The main street of Osmana lay in a straight line from the gates to Khagniorth Stronghold at the far end of the walled city. The other side streets wound off into the sloping mountainsides before ending at the walls formed out of the surrounding mountains. Unlike the multi-story tenement housing and tall, stately homes in Aldon, the homes here only formed small, rounded structures while most of their rooms were deep inside the mountains.

Khagniorth Stronghold loomed over the city, built into a small mountain with the peaks turned into spires. It might not have the stately grandeur of Winstead Palace, but there was a brutal beauty to the stronghold.

Julien glanced over his shoulder at Vriska as they stepped inside the fortress. She had remained their silent, stalking shadow throughout the walk. He'd thought she was warming to him in their letters, but now that he was here, he couldn't tell. She seemed...angry.

He had not expected her to welcome him with open arms, but he had thought she wouldn't be this cold.

Though if Vriska had changed her mind, there were the eleven others on that list. It would mean going back to the beginning. Back to trying to pick a wife at random from a list.

Julien worked to keep his expression neutral. This might have been easier if his brother and King Rharreth had simply picked for him. Julien would have dutifully loved whoever he married, and that would have been that. None of *this.*

He tried to appear attentive and listening as Rharreth and Melantha gave him a tour. He managed to keep up the appearance until he was finally shown to his room and given a moment to wash up before supper.

Julien braced himself against the wall and took in the stone room. The bed was piled with blankets and furs. The furniture was formed mostly of stone with only a few wood and leather touches to soften them. A grotto provided a bathing area. So very different from his home in Winstead Palace.

His luggage was stacked in the corner. Not that he had much. The larger of the two trunks he'd taken along was filled with gifts for Melantha and Rharreth.

The other, much smaller trunk was stuffed with random courting gifts. It had been difficult, trying to pick out gifts that would appeal to Vriska and yet be impersonal enough that they could be gifted to another troll woman if Vriska refused him. Somehow, he didn't think the standard flowers and jewelry that he would have given an Escarlish woman he courted would work for a troll woman here in Kostaria. In the end, it had ended up a very small, nearly empty trunk.

His personal belongings fit in the single, army-issue rucksack tossed on top of the two trunks. Some habits died hard, and he still packed the way the army had taught him during basic training.

How had Essie managed this? Getting tossed into a new kingdom and a new culture?

Julien huffed and pushed away from the wall. He knew exactly how Essie had handled it. She had waltzed into Tarenhiel, gaped at everything with wonder, charmed everyone she met, and had Farrendel head-over-heels in love so fast the elf hadn't even known what hit him.

But Julien wasn't Essie. All the charm in the family had gone to Essie and Edmund. Whatever had been left went to Averett.

That left Julien as the quiet, non-charming one in the family. He could banter just fine with his family, but anyone else…not so much.

No use standing here ruminating.

He changed into fresh clothes and located the trunk with all the letters and gifts. At least for tonight, he didn't have to think about Vriska and the marriage alliance. Tonight, he was going to enjoy a quiet evening with his sister's sister- and brother-in-law and try to acclimate to this new place where he found himself.

Picking up the trunk, he nodded at the trolls guarding his door. They weren't members of Rharreth's shield band, though Julien assumed the troll warriors were trusted. Then he strolled the short distance down the passageway and halted in front of the door Rharreth and Melantha had shown him earlier.

Zavni and Vriska stood there, guarding their king and queen. Zavni smirked and knocked on the door behind him, announcing to Rharreth and Melantha that Julien was there.

But Vriska didn't give him so much as a glance. She scanned the passageways with an alacrity that would be commendable in a guard yet showed just how determined she was not to even look at him.

Julien sent one last glance in her direction before he stepped inside.

Rharreth and Melantha lounged on a long bench softened with layers of furs and blankets. They both glanced up and nodded as he entered, though they didn't get up.

Good. Julien didn't want to stand on formality the entire time he was in Kostaria.

Julien set the trunk on the table before he took a seat on a fur-lined chair across from them. "Here are the letters. And gifts. I think Essie might have gone a little overboard in sending hot chocolate and candy."

Melantha leaned forward, opened the lid, and laughed. "You are correct. But her generosity is appreciated."

She gently removed the stack of letters from the top, her slim hands fingering each one. Her dark eyes took on a sheen while her smile twisted into something wistful.

It must be hard for Melantha, being so far from her family now that she was working to restore good relationships with them. Especially right now, since she had to know the rest of her family was at Lethorel for their annual holiday.

While Melantha sorted through the trunk, Julien held out the letter from the engineers to Rharreth. "I stopped at the worksite for the new bridge on my way here. The bridge is coming along well, and the engineers are pleased with the way the human and troll workers have come together. They have been so pleased, in fact, that the engineers have discussed the possibility of Escarlish engineers helping with more train tracks here in Kostaria."

Rharreth took the letter, nodding as he opened it. "You humans do have more experience with laying track. I could see how working together would be beneficial to modernizing travel in my kingdom."

Melantha paused in sorting the contents of the trunk to give an exaggerated shudder. "Any help would be appreciated. If your human engineers could make train travel here in Kostaria feel less precarious, I would be doubly grateful."

"I'm sure they will do what they can. Kostaria's mountains pose challenges that Escarland's flat farm fields don't." Julien shifted in his seat. Things like this were the reason why he was marrying a troll to secure this alliance.

Still, this was more Averett's thing than his. Even Edmund and Essie took more joy in politics than he did.

"I will send a message to King Averett to start discussing the details." Rharreth stated, then leaned his elbows on his knees. "Now about the reason you're here..."

Julien grimaced and shot a glance toward the door. "She didn't seem eager to meet me."

"Vriska is still considering her future." Rharreth sighed and shook his head. "She is my shield sister. I want what is best for her. I'm not going to pressure her to accept you."

"I don't want you to pressure her or anyone." Julien realized he was clenching his fingers, and he forced himself to relax. "I want whomever I marry to volunteer for this marriage of alliance as willingly as I am."

Rharreth nodded, his gaze dropping to his hands.

Melantha's mouth pressed into a line. "With the prejudices against humans, it will be a challenge to convince Vriska or any of the others to accept a marriage to you without some reluctance. The hatred is not as great as it was between elves and trolls, but the stereotype of humans being weak and inferior is no less real."

"I know I'm going to have to prove myself as a warrior." Julien forced a grin and flexed his arms. "I've been working to build my strength and endurance for the past several months, and I practiced with Farrendel for some of that time."

Hopefully all that work would be enough. It would be embarrassing if, after months of work, he was still soundly trounced when he came up against a troll one-on-one. Sure, he'd fought trolls before in the war and in the Dulraith. But never by himself. He'd always had either his brothers, an army, or Farrendel watching his back.

Melantha's hard expression broke with the hint of a smile. "Then I am sure you are well-prepared."

Rharreth's mouth also twitched in a smile before the smile faded. "It will still be a struggle. If you lose, you will be dismissed as a weakling. If you win, there are some who will resent that a human defeated a troll, seeing it as a dishonor."

Julien nodded, his jaw hard. He was not afraid of a little hard work and pain.

"You will be tempted to try to ignore them and simply take their slights." Melantha's back straightened, her eyes flashing. "I know from experience that they will not stop."

Rharreth reached out and clasped her hand. "We are trying to change the cultural emphasis on strength that leads to bullying those that are perceived to be weak. But it has been deeply ingrained for generations, and there is no way to change the heart even if we manage to change everything else."

"What do you suggest I do instead?" Julien glanced between Rharreth and Melantha. Like many among royal families, he had been raised to keep a stiff upper lip and ignore such attacks and slights. In most cases, ignoring the bullies was the best policy.

But not here in Kostaria, apparently.

Rharreth sighed and shook his head. "Don't start a fist fight over every slight. That would be just as bad. But stare them down, letting them know that you aren't scared off by their attacks."

All right. Julien could do that.

Melantha shared a look with Rharreth before turning to Julien. "You are not alone here in Kostaria."

"My shield band and I will have your back." Rharreth held Julien's gaze, his deep voice low and unwavering. "Here in Kostaria, we might emphasize individual strength. But we also have a sense of the strength of the shield band. You will gain more respect if they see that you have a shield band standing by you than you will if you attempt to handle it on your own."

"Good to know." Julien rested his elbows on his knees and stared down at his hands.

Sadly, gaining the respect of the trolls as a whole would likely be the easiest part of his mission in Kostaria.

Convincing Vriska to give him the time of day—much less give him her heart—would be far more difficult.

CHAPTER SEVEN

Vriska hefted her sword as she gathered with her shield band in the training arena the next morning. As the king's shield band, they had first choice of times to practice, and that usually meant first thing so that Rharreth could finish before the work of the day started.

Zavni swung his ax in an easy grip at his side. "Guess we'll get to see what your prince is made of."

Vriska punched him in the arm. If only her shield brothers would quit hassling her over this.

Brynjar drew his sword. "Better to figure out now than at the fighting and feasting tomorrow."

"Well, he can't be too shabby. He did all right in the Dulraith." Eyvindur hopped over the low wall of the training arena instead of using one of the openings.

"Still doesn't mean he can hold his own against troll warriors when he doesn't have Laesornysh at his back." Brynjar shrugged, flexing his brawny arms as if prepared to pound Prince Julien to pulp.

Vriska fought back the heat rising in her chest. "Don't go

beating him up. Just because he can't stand up to us doesn't mean he isn't a decent warrior. We're the king's shield band. We're better than the average troll warrior."

Brynjar took a step back. Eyvindur raised his bushy white eyebrows.

Zavni smirked and rested the handle of his ax on his shoulder. "Look at you. Standing up for him already. Maybe you like him more than you think."

"Just shut it before I shut your mouth with my fist." Vriska flexed her fingers on the hilt of her sword. She was thoroughly tired of this ribbing.

Any reply was cut off as the door opened, and Rharreth entered, followed by Melantha and Prince Julien. Before the door shut behind them, Vriska caught a glimpse of several members of the other shield bands guarding the door. Taking over additional guard duties for their king, as Rharreth had said they would.

Rharreth wore a fitted leather tunic that left his arms bare. He had both a sword and a dagger belted at his waist. At his side, Melantha wore a thin red shirt beneath her leather tunic. She carried her hardwood staff.

Behind them, Prince Julien also wore a leather tunic, though his was of a lighter, human design than the one worn by Rharreth. Prince Julien had donned a blue shirt beneath while a long, straight sword hung at his hip.

Hopefully he could prove he was worthy to carry it. It would be even more embarrassing for Vriska if she stood up for him, only to find out he hadn't been worth the effort and the teasing.

As if realizing he was the subject of their scrutiny, Prince Julien strolled forward and drew his sword. His glance swept around each of the members of the shield band, lingering only a moment longer on Vriska than the others. "I see you are all waiting to get a piece of me. Who would like to go first?"

"I would." Zavni sauntered forward, swinging his ax down from his shoulder.

Vriska shot Zavni a glare, but he ignored her. Then Brynjar was before her, ready for sparring.

She fought horribly, since she was trying to keep Prince Julien and Zavni in sight even as she fought Brynjar.

Prince Julien moved well with a quick, fluid grace. His muscles, less bulky than that of Vriska's shield brothers, played beneath his light shirt with each swing of his sword. He sidestepped a swing of Zavni's ax, then quickly slithered in a thrust at Zavni's unprotected side.

A sword whistled so close to her head it must have lopped off a lock of her hair.

"Heads up, Vriska." Brynjar eyed her. "Your mind isn't on our fight."

She growled and put even more power behind her upper cut, aimed at his neck.

Brynjar triangle-stepped as he parried, placing himself off line and forcing her to match his move. Thanks to her distraction—and only that—he got a good thrust in and had his blade at her neck.

Strangely, when she glanced toward Prince Julien and Zavni, it was Zavni with his hands raised and the human prince's sword at his chest.

That was unexpected. This human was no slouch when it came to his weapons.

Vriska nodded to Brynjar, then hurried to face Prince Julien before any of the others had a chance.

Prince Julien swiped at a drop of blood trickling from a

small slice across his cheekbone. He smiled, his brown eyes warm. "Your turn to test my mettle?"

She crouched, taking in his easy stance and the comfortable way he gripped his sword. "You did well enough against Zavni, I suppose. Though he was likely so taken aback by such skill found in a human that he went too easy on you. I won't make that mistake."

Prince Julien's smile tightened as he prepared for battle.

Vriska lunged forward and threw the power of her arms and back into a swing. He was quick, his footwork light, as he stepped and parried her blade, using her momentum to turn her sword away.

Even as he parried, he turned his sword and thrust at her, and she was forced to pull back and dodge.

He was fast, far faster than she had been expecting. He didn't fight exactly like an elf. There was no flipping or maneuvers like that. But something about the way he moved spoke of elven training.

She probably should have expected he would train with his brother-in-law, the infamous Laesornysh. Yet that would mean that he spent the months since this marriage was arranged not only learning her language, but also honing his muscles and skills so that he could fight well enough to take on a troll warrior.

His sword came at her again, and she shook herself. Now was not time to think. It was time to react with the instincts of honed muscles and long practice.

She turned his sword and swung back with a cut of her own. He stepped and swung in defense, seeking a weakness in her guard.

She found herself grinning, a thrill deep in her bones and savage on her face.

Here, in battle, there was no future. There was no marriage alliance. No politics and treaties. Just the surge of muscle and the weight of her sword in her hands. The thrill of danger and the jitters of adrenaline coursing through her veins. Here her world was as simple as blood and steel, strike and parry, life and death.

She caught Prince Julien's blade with her own and twisted it, sending him off balance. Before he could recover, she had her blade pressed to his neck. "Do you yield?"

"Yield." Prince Julien lowered his sword, still wearing a hint of a smile that tugged at his red-brown beard. Blood trickled from a cut across his forehead and a slice along his shoulder that she had given him. Yet instead of appearing resentful for losing to her, his smile tugged wider. "You fight well."

There was no irony or mocking in his words. Just a sincere observation. A compliment, even.

Perhaps that was why she found herself replying, "You do too."

He grinned, as if she'd given him a grand compliment, before he turned away to face Rharreth in a bout.

Vriska stood for a moment, watching him. While female warriors were common in Kostaria, some among the male warriors still displayed resentment and ruffled pride when beaten in a bout by a female warrior. Not among Vriska's shield band, but it still happened.

Yet this human prince, despite females not fighting among Escarland's army, had taken his defeat at her hands well. Another thing to his credit.

Giving herself a good shake, Vriska turned as well, this time to face Zavni. At least this human prince wasn't an embarrassing weakling. Even if she didn't agree to marry him, he would at least give a good accounting of himself here in Kostaria. That would earn his kingdom favor, even beyond the treaty.

She might have been against such close ties with other kingdoms at the beginning, but she was starting to see the benefit. Even if she couldn't, Rharreth did, and she trusted Rharreth. Wherever he led, he would lead Kostaria to a far better future than the one his father and brother had envisioned.

As Rharreth and Zavni finished their final bout, Julien leaned against the short wall surrounding the arena, trying to make the move appear casual. He struggled to keep his breathing even so that the others couldn't hear how hard he was panting.

Julien's arms, shoulders, and back ached from the "warm-up" bouts that had been as difficult as any bout he'd ever fought. Farrendel had been correct. The trolls hit like battering rams, and they were far faster than any human Julien had ever sparred with.

Yet they didn't quite have Farrendel's or Iyrinder's speed and agility. All his practice fighting those elves this spring gave Julien some advantage. He had honed his own speed and agility to the peak of what his human body and mind could achieve to keep up with Farrendel. That made him fast enough to match, or even best, a few of the trolls, at least.

He touched a spot of wetness on his face, and his fingers came away bloody, both fresh and dried.

"Here, allow me." Melantha stepped closer and brushed green-wrapped fingers across his temple.

A soothing warmth spread over his face, then spread into the slices on his arms and legs.

"Linshi, Your Majesty." He realized after he spoke that he'd used elvish and Escarlish, and it was a good thing Melantha spoke both to understand what he meant.

A hint of a smile crossed the hard lines of her face. "You did well this morning."

She nodded with the shared understanding of someone who had also faced the hard task of earning a place here in Kostaria. Then she stepped past him to join Rharreth.

Julien glanced around, then hurried to Vriska's side before she could follow the rest of her shield brothers from the arena. Perhaps she had been actively avoiding him, but they weren't going to get anywhere if they didn't talk.

He fell into step with her and tried not to take it personally when the knot at the corner of her jaw flexed and her stance tensed.

He didn't want to force his presence where it wasn't wanted. But he'd thought she had agreed to this as willingly as he had. Hadn't she exchanged letters with him for that purpose?

If she would allow, then they would talk. Clear the air. If she truly no longer wished to spend time with him now that she'd met him, then he would rather know sooner rather than later.

She turned away, making a show of sheathing her sword at her side.

"Can we talk?" He winced when he realized he'd said that in Escarlish. He fumbled to repeat the question in elvish.

"I heard you the first time." Vriska whirled back toward him, her fists clenching like she wanted to punch him.

Julien forced himself not to take a step back. He wasn't

used to attempting to court a woman who was more likely to break his nose than flutter her eyelashes.

Not that he had ever done much courting. He'd talked to a few young ladies of the court. Flirted with a few. But none of that had ever led anywhere. The ladies always seemed to be after his title more than him as a person.

Besides, his duty to his brother had always come before his personal life. He'd rarely had time to pursue anything, even if he had found himself drawn to anyone.

Vriska glanced past him to where the rest of the shield band gathered around their king and queen, as if seeking an excuse to get away from him. "I should…"

Rharreth turned to them, and he motioned at Vriska. "You are excused from your duties."

"But…" Vriska glanced between Julien and Rharreth, as if desperate for any excuse.

Julien shifted, heart sinking. If she really didn't want to spend time with him, then he wouldn't press the issue. Why had he even asked? This had been a mistake.

"Take whatever time you need." Rharreth glanced at the others in the shield band, then motioned to Eyvindur. "Go with them, though stay back and be discreet. Julien, I hate to saddle you with an escort, but in case Vriska stomps off, I can't leave you unprotected. While I wish I could, I cannot trust everyone among my people in these halls."

Great. Even King Rharreth believed that this conversation would go badly. Not to mention it seemed likely Julien would get mugged if he wandered the halls alone.

Vriska crossed her arms, jaw working. But she didn't protest again as Rharreth, Melantha, Zavni, and Brynjar left. Eyvindur took a spot by the door, out of earshot unless this conversation involved shouting.

Which it might, based on the way Vriska was scowling.

Julien dragged a hand over his beard. What could he say that would convey what he was thinking?

What *was* he thinking? He didn't know Vriska. He didn't even know her well enough to be attracted to her. Not yet.

She was lovely. Tall and muscled. A square jaw that was jutting even now. Her smooth face and high cheekbones held the resemblance to the elves that showed their peoples had once been one, a long time ago, yet her features were stockier than the slim, angular look of the elves. Part of her white hair was done in braids with bone and leather decoration tied into the strands while the rest was loose and flowing over her shoulders and down her back.

There was nothing of what Escarlish culture would deem traditionally feminine about her. Yet he would never mistake her for a man either.

Julien drew in a deep breath and faced her. She was no delicate Escarlish miss who would expect him to dance around the topic. She was a troll. Being blunt was probably the best course of action. "I made my choice when I agreed to a marriage of alliance with one of your people. I no longer have a choice. But you still do. If you find me repulsive, then just say so and don't prolong this."

She whirled back to him and blinked, as if that was not at all what she was expecting him to say. "I don't…" She growled and paced away from him, her hand clenching on the sword at her side. "I don't know, all right? I just don't know, and I hate feeling forced into this."

His stomach twisted. He had never wanted whatever troll woman who agreed to this to feel forced into it. "Then walk away. I don't want you to feel forced. I don't want that for anyone. Yes, our kingdoms need this alliance. I understand that, and I'm taking that duty on willingly. But I don't want…"

He scrubbed at his beard again, unable to look at her. What a mess this had become.

"My duty has always been to guard my king." Vriska's voice rang cold, yet it held a hint of bitterness. "I don't know how to embrace a new duty that will take me away from that."

Julien searched the hard angles of her face. "I understand that. My duty, too, has always been to guard my king. My brother."

For a long moment, the silence stretched between them, each of them searching the other's face.

Was that a softening Julien could read in her dark blue eyes? Perhaps an understanding that they both shared the same struggle in this arranged marriage?

Or was he reading too much into her expression, seeing what he wanted to find instead of what was actually there?

Vriska's sigh came out on a growl. "So where does that leave us?"

"Is there an us?" How he hated all this uncertainty. He preferred his life to be straightforward. "If this isn't what you want, then you are free to back out. You owe me nothing. You will not be betraying your duty to your king or kingdom."

"Yet if I don't, someone else will have to." Vriska spun on her heels again, pacing away, then back again. Her eyes burned. "Where is the honor in placing a burden on someone else that I'm not willing to carry?"

Julien forced the smile to remain on his face. "Glad you're being honest about what you think of me. Don't hold back."

"You know what I meant." Vriska gestured at him with another growling huff.

"Yes." He let his smile slip as he glanced away from her. "You meant the burden of the treaty. The burden of uniting our kingdoms. You didn't mean the specific people who have to carry that burden on both sides of this."

When he glanced up again and met her gaze, he was almost certain he wasn't imagining the frisson of understanding this time.

He softened his tone. "Is duty enough, do you think?"

She crossed her arms again, more a wall to protect herself than a barrier to keep him away. "I don't know. Perhaps it is."

He'd had his conversation, but now he sensed it was time for him to retreat and give her space. He nodded to her and took a step away. "You don't have to decide today. As I said, I don't wish to pressure you. But if you do decide to proceed with this arrangement, then I want you to know that I hold my honor and duty as close to my heart as any troll does. You will never have to fear that I will be less than honorable and faithful to you."

Unable to watch her reaction to words that felt too honest, Julien turned and strode toward the door.

He had meant what he said. No matter who he married —even if it was for a treaty and not for love—he would be faithful and honorable to her. She would be his wife. He would choose to show her love every day, even if it wasn't the love of ballads and legends. He might never become as disgustingly in love as his sister and brother were with their elf prince and princess, but Julien would love regardless. What was love, anyway, but duty lived out in actions?

CHAPTER EIGHT

Julien's sword felt heavy at his side as he marched with Rharreth and his shield band into the crowded training arena. Unlike the morning practice the day before, the benches were packed with trolls. Shouting and stamping and loud voices rang inside the room until his ears ached and he began to think he should have asked Farrendel for some of that charmed moss to dampen the noise.

The noise became even worse as the troll warriors around them saw their king and sent up a growling, stamping cheer.

Rharreth held up his hand, his antler crown on his head as he acknowledged his people. Beside him, Melantha wore a red dress trimmed in fur, the troll queen diadem tied around her forehead while her short black hair spiked in a fierce manner. Julien had only glimpsed her from a distance before she had become queen of the trolls, but she seemed like she belonged here. There was an edge to her that would have been out of place in the peaceful branches of Ellonahshinel.

Julien took his seat on the bench behind Rharreth and Melantha. Strangely, Vriska took the seat beside him without the prickly glare she had given him yesterday. Still, she didn't sit particularly close, and she didn't look at him.

It was progress, at least, even if she hadn't given him an answer as to her willingness to continue to pursue this or not.

As the last of the troll warriors squeezed into the remaining seats in the benches, Rharreth stood and held up his hands. It took several moments before the trolls packed into the arena noticed their king and fell silent.

Or as silent as a horde of trolls ever managed to be. The room was still filled with a clanking of weapons against stone and a hushed bloodlust for the coming fights.

"Today, we celebrate the visit by Julien, prince of our worthy Escarlish allies." Rharreth gestured around the benches and gathered warriors. "Now let us show to our visitor just how worthy an ally we trolls are to Escarland."

Another rousing cheer shook the stone of the training arena until Julien risked a glance at the ceiling, hoping it wouldn't fall down on their heads.

Yet when he glanced back at the gathering, he could see what he hadn't noticed before. Not everyone was cheering. There were groups clustered together who were glaring at him rather than cheering. Even some of those cheering wore scowls, as if they were willing to cheer to make their king happy but they also allowed their true feelings free rein on their faces.

He drew in deep breaths, trying to keep the tension in his

chest from tightening his muscles. He would need to remain loose and limber for what lay ahead. Unlike Rharreth's shield band, there were those here who would not hesitate to take off an arm. Or a leg. Or even his head, if they thought they could get away with it as an "accident."

Rharreth swept one last glance over the gathering. "Let the challenges begin!"

As he took his seat, a troll immediately jumped to his feet and challenged another warrior to a bout.

For the first few bouts, it seemed that Julien's fears were unfounded. No one challenged him. Several of Rharreth's shield band accepted and gave challenges, including Vriska.

Julien let himself admire her in a way he hadn't been able to do while busy fighting the practice bouts the morning before. She moved with a lethal grace as she hammered her sword into her opponent's. Her dark blue eyes flashed, her square jaw hard as the granite of the mountain around them.

It sent an uncomfortable feeling into the pit of his stomach. If he went through with this marriage, his wife would likely be stronger than he was. A better warrior. She wouldn't need his protection or his strength. He had always been the strong warrior among his own people. A good soldier. It tweaked his manly pride to think that he would likely be the weaker one in his marriage.

Yet that was what this ugly feeling was. Pride. And pride was never a good thing. Never something to be lauded and nurtured in his heart, even under the guise of "manliness."

It was not Vriska's problem if she was an excellent, strong warrior. It was his problem if he let it bother him.

And, truthfully, it bothered him that it had bothered him, even for a moment.

With a long exhale, he released the momentary pride and instead joined the cheering when Vriska trounced her opponent, her blade at his throat forcing him to yield.

If Julien was going to be second to her, then so be it. He was used to being second, after all. He had been second to his brother all his life, and his brother was far too important to him to ever let himself resent it even for a moment. In the Dulraith, he had been second to Farrendel, there merely to provide a shield while his brother-in-law did the bulk of the fighting. And Julien would never resent Farrendel for being the warrior he was.

It would be the same with Vriska. He would quietly stand in the background and celebrate her accomplishments. It was what he was good at. Being second.

Among the cheers and the calls of another challenge, Vriska made her way back to the benches and took the seat next to Julien once again.

Sweat covered her bare arms and stuck strands of her hair to her forehead. Trickles of blood dribbled from a few stray cuts. She even reeked a bit, like one of his soldiers after a training session, reminding him again that in this moment, she was all warrior.

Julien picked up one of the ragged towels the shield band had taken with them and handed it to her. "You fought well. That was impressive."

As she took the towel, her gaze searched his face, as if looking for any resentment in his words.

It made him glad he'd banished his moment of giving in to pride so that he could say those words with sincerity now.

After a moment, she looked away and wiped the towel over the sweat on her face, then down her arms. "Linsh."

The word sounded like it cost her. And it made him smile a bit. He didn't think she had gotten the same lectures against pride from her parents the way he had from his. She was a troll. Pride and honor were a way of life.

The current bout in the arena ended. Amid the cheering, a new troll stood. He was one of the warriors who had been scowling instead of cheering during Rharreth's short speech.

Julien's body tensed as the troll turned to stare at him, a sneer curling his mouth. "Rharreth, my king, is your *guest* accepting challenges? Or is the human too weak to stand before a troll warrior?"

In answer, Julien stood and began to peel his shirt over his head. He had known it would come to this.

Rharreth must know it too, since he didn't try to assure Julien that he didn't have to accept. "Fight bravely. Even if you lose, you will gain the respect of many."

"Just make sure you do not get your head lopped off." Melantha's mouth was tight as she glared at the troll who had challenged him. "Even a limb I might be able to reattach, if it is a clean slice and I get there fast enough."

So reassuring that she felt the need to provide him with that attempt at comfort right now.

Rharreth stood as well and faced Julien's challenger. "Yes, he is well able to accept challenges. But remember, Brathac, this is a challenge. You are bound by the rules of the arena. Let this fight be one of honor as befitting warriors."

If Brathac acknowledged the warning in Rharreth's words, Julien didn't bother to look. He tossed his shirt on the bench, the heated air of the arena brushing his skin. He had to agree with Farrendel. The trolls' obsession with fighting half-clothed was rather annoying. Especially since Julien felt particularly pasty compared to the sea of gray-skinned trolls surrounding him.

His challenger strutted down the stairs and stepped into the arena. A hush, even more complete than the one when Rharreth spoke, fell over the gathered trolls.

Hefting his shield in one hand, his sword in the other, Julien ignored the crawling feeling of so many eyes focused on him as he strode down the few steps and landed on the soft sand of the center arena.

Dropping into his stance, he faced Brathac. All he had to do was lose valiantly enough that he gained the respect of the trolls from whom respect could be gained.

But in this moment, he didn't want to simply lose bravely. He wanted to win. Just this one bout, even if he lost the others.

Not to soothe his pride, though it was itching uncomfortably again at Brathac's sneering.

But so that Vriska would be impressed. He might be second to her in skill and strength, but it would be nice if she saw him as a worthy second.

VRISKA GRIPPED the edge of the bench, attempting to keep her face placid. Why would watching Prince Julien march down into the training arena make her heart beat harder in her throat?

It wasn't because of any of this marriage nonsense. It had to be because it would look bad for Rharreth and for the treaty he had signed if the human prince failed to fight well.

And it would go even worse for the alliance if Brathac killed Prince Julien and claimed it was an accident.

With a roar, Brathac charged and swung his huge, two-handed sword. Prince Julien side-stepped to take it as a glancing blow to his shield. His own sword whipped forward, slicing Brathac's upper arm.

Enraged, Brathac charged in, forcing Prince Julien back by force of his superior height and bulkier muscles.

Yet even when retreating, Prince Julien did so with light, easy steps. He moved with a grace that few among the trolls could master. But he didn't have the flightiness about him that characterized the elves. He still retained the steadiness of a well-grounded fighter.

He hadn't taken off his shirt during the practice bouts with the shield band. She'd thought the thin fabric of the shirt he'd worn then had displayed his broad shoulders and muscled arms well enough.

But now that he fought as shirtless as his opponent, his muscles were well defined beneath his pale, human skin. Broad shoulders, a strong chest, a trim waist.

Not a weakling human by any means.

Though, he was far hairier than any troll, from the thick beard on his face to the hair on his chest. While trolls were not as hairless as elves and a rare troll would occasionally be able to grow a thin beard or sport a few curls of chest hair, none of them were like Prince Julien.

Yet it wasn't a bad look. Vriska found the beard strangely manly. Kind of rugged, actually.

A fist lightly punched her shoulder from behind. She whirled and glared up at Zavni's smirking face.

He didn't have to say anything. And her punch in return was all the answer he was going to get.

Annoying shield brothers.

A clang filled the hall as Prince Julien took another blow on his shield. He staggered beneath the blow.

Even as Brathac grinned, Prince Julien spun on a heel, his shield still braced beneath Brathac's sword, and slammed the hilt of his sword into Brathac's jaw.

As Brathac stumbled, Prince Julien hammered his sword into Brathac's, pinning it between sword and shield. With a yank, Brathac was disarmed. In another blink, Prince Julien's sword pressed to Brathac's throat. "Do you yield?"

Somehow, the prince even had the presence of mind to say it in their language instead of his own.

Brathac snarled, his face twisted.

Prince Julien's sword pressed harder against his neck, drawing a bead of blood.

Brathac spat, a glob of spittle landing on Prince Julien's face. "Yield."

Prince Julien held Brathac's gaze, not backing down, before he stepped back. Julien gave a nod, an acknowledgment of a well fought battle, before he strode away, leaving the arena without any gloating.

For a moment, only a stunned silence reigned over the arena. Brathac whirled and stalked back to his seat.

Then Zavni shot to his feet, hooting and stamping. Brynjar joined him, followed by Eyvindur. Rharreth and Melantha joined in as well, though in a dignified, royal kind of way.

Vriska sat frozen. She should cheer. Against all odds, Prince Julien had actually won that bout.

But she couldn't force herself to move. Not even as the others returned to their seats and the cheering died down. Two more warriors entered the arena, facing each other for a bout.

Prince Julien slid into his seat beside her. If he'd noticed her lack of cheering, he didn't show it. Instead, he set down his sword and shield, picked up a rag, and swiped the sweat and troll spit from his face with a hint of a grimace. That grimace deepened as he gave a soft groan and gripped his shield arm. "That hurt."

Melantha half-turned in her seat, her eyes sweeping over him for a moment before meeting his gaze. "I am sorry, but unless the wound is dire, I cannot heal you until the bouts are over. It is considered tampering."

"I wouldn't ask for it." Prince Julien shook out his arm, flexing his fingers as if testing his remaining strength.

It was honor worthy of a troll that he was willing to bear the sore muscles of battle. Yet this prince displayed a humility rarely seen in a troll warrior. Vriska wasn't sure how to wrap her mind around it, to be honest. A humble warrior seemed a bit of an oxymoron, yet he wore it well.

Vriska shook herself free of her paralysis and held out his shirt. "Here."

When Prince Julien smiled, it tugged at his beard, causing a hint of deep grooves around his mouth beneath the facial hair. "Thanks."

With the rag in his other hand, he dabbed at the blood dribbling from a cut on his arm, and Vriska tried not to watch the play of his muscles as he sat this close to her.

The bouts continued, and Prince Julien was challenged to several more. He didn't win all of them, but he gave a good account of himself. Vriska fought several more bouts as well, and she lost only two of them.

Prince Julien congratulated—or commiserated with—her after every bout. Her shield brothers did too, of course. But

Prince Julien's smile and quiet words were different than her brothers' arm punches and ribbing.

Whether it was a good different or a bad different, Vriska wasn't sure yet.

Not sure yet. That was a good way to describe everything she felt about Prince Julien.

CHAPTER NINE

Julien strode into the feasting hall at Rharreth and Melantha's side. He tried not to gape, but he still probably looked as awed as he felt. The black obsidian of the feasting hall's ceiling glittered high above the rows upon rows of tables filling the space. Trolls packed the benches, gripping tankards filled with some kind of alcohol, while roast meat—probably caribou or moose—heaped on platters.

Rharreth and Melantha paused to talk to some of the trolls as they strode through the maze of tables toward the dais. Julien smiled, nodded, and tried to contribute to the conversation where he could once he was introduced.

It only took until about the third time they stopped before Julien realized that Rharreth and Melantha were subtly introducing him to all the others on his list of possible brides, along with their families.

Julien appreciated the gesture. He supposed he should find out if he had an instant attraction with any of the others.

But it still seemed odd, even thinking about an attraction

with someone else when he had this thing with Vriska. It wasn't like they had an understanding or anything. Both of them were free to walk away.

Not that it mattered. None of the others drew him the way Vriska did. Perhaps that was because he knew Vriska better, at least somewhat, due to their letters.

But in his heart, he already knew. He'd decided on Vriska, and he would pursue a relationship with her for as long as she wanted one.

Finally, Rharreth and Melantha took their seats on the dais. Julien had the seat next to Rharreth with Vriska on his other side.

Vriska remained quiet as platters of meat and roast vegetables were placed in front of them.

Julien tried to think of something to ask to start the conversation. What would Vriska find interesting to talk about? It seemed that neither of them was any more verbose in person than they were in letters.

What he wouldn't give for a measure of Edmund's wit. Or Essie's ability to effortlessly start a conversation.

Instead, he was just himself. The least charming prince of Escarland.

After scooping some of the meat and vegetables onto his plate, Julien gestured toward the trolls gathered on the benches below. "Is your mother here? You said your father was in Escarland helping with the new bridge."

Vriska stiffened as she transferred a large chunk of meat onto her plate. "No, she isn't here."

Julien waited, but she didn't elaborate. Now that he thought about it, the work on the new bridge wasn't something a troll warrior was likely to take on. Was her father, perhaps, not a warrior? Or not from one of the rich, near-noble warrior families?

"You said you have a sister?" Julien speared a forkful of the meat.

"Yes." Vriska stuffed a large bite in her mouth, as if to make sure she couldn't answer any more questions.

This was going well. Julien stuck his own bite in his mouth. Perhaps eating in silence was the better option.

As Julien ate, he caught the looks that some of the trolls were sending him. Across the room, Brathac sat at a table with a cluster of other warriors. All of them were shooting glares in Julien's direction.

But many of the other trolls gave him a nod of respect when he caught their gaze. He had made some progress, at least, even if it wasn't with Vriska.

Rharreth turned to Julien, opening his mouth as if he planned to strike up a conversation.

The doors to the hall slammed open. A young adult male troll stood there, though he only paused at the doorway a moment before he hurried between the tables, headed for the dais. Around him, the gathered troll warriors halted in their feasting, watching as the troll passed by their tables.

The troll bounded up the three stairs, then thrust a folded piece of paper at Rharreth. "A message for you, my king."

Rharreth took the paper, glanced up, then motioned to the hall at large. "Please. Continue feasting."

After another moment, most of the trolls turned back to their food, and the hall filled with the buzz of conversation once again.

Once the attention of the hall was no longer on him, Rharreth opened the note and read it quickly. His jaw tightened, something in his eyes hardening. He mumbled something to Melantha before he stood and ushered the messenger from the feasting hall.

Julien went back to his food as well, eating in silence since Vriska still didn't seem inclined to talk.

Rharreth returned after about half an hour, and all he did was give a grim nod when Melantha sent him a questioning look.

Something was going on, but Julien resisted the urge to ask. He was a foreigner here, despite the upcoming marriage. Rharreth would only tell him if he thought it necessary. Until then, this was Kostaria's problem and Julien would be kept out of it.

Still, when he walked past Rharreth and Melantha's door that night, he could hear raised voices inside. Voices that the guards stationed outside their door—and the guards escorting Julien—were pretending they didn't hear.

VRISKA STALKED along Osmana's main street, Prince Julien walking briskly at her side. He glanced around, taking in the buildings and bustles of the city.

For nearly two weeks, Vriska had avoided Prince Julien as much as possible. It wasn't as hard as it might have been. Since he was ostensibly in Kostaria as a diplomat, he needed to attend several meetings with Rharreth, discussing various points of trade between Escarland and Kostaria.

Each day, new members from the warrior families arrived at Khagniorth Stronghold, and that kept Prince Julien even more busy in meetings.

Vriska considered it a win-win. A win for Kostarian-Escarlish relations, which she had to grudgingly acknowledge was important for Kostaria's future. And a win because she got to avoid the prince.

But all good things came to an end. And Rharreth giving her the next few days off and all but ordering her to give Prince Julien a tour of Osmana had decidedly ended her reprieve.

She probably should point out places of interest and act the part of tour guide. But she couldn't think of what to say. He could see well enough for himself that they were passing various businesses. If he wanted to know more, he would have to ask.

Would it be odd if she avoided the area of the city where her family lived? Would her family's feelings be hurt, if she had been in Osmana and hadn't stopped to visit?

No, better to introduce Prince Julien to them now before whatever this was between them progressed any further.

As she led Julien off the main street and through the maze of the back pathways, Vriska's chest tightened to the point of pain. Prince Julien didn't seem to be the type to behave badly when introduced to her family, but she didn't know how this would go. He was still a prince, after all. He might not intentionally scorn them, but that didn't mean he would respect them once he saw their tiny home and humble furnishings.

Oh, well. If he was going to scorn her family for being common, it would give her an excuse to back out of this arrangement once and for all. She just didn't want her family hurt in the process.

The homes around them grew tinier the farther they walked into the city. Laundry flapped in the summer breeze, strung between homes. People eyed them as they walked by, gaping at the human in their midst.

Prince Julien's eyes darted back and forth, scanning their surroundings. Yet he didn't reach for the sword buckled at his hip, nor did his confident stride falter.

Finally, they reached the nondescript gray stone wall with its arched, stone door that formed her parents' home. Only a short, curved entrance jutted from the mountainside, while the rest was buried into the rock.

Prince Julien's gaze settled on her as they halted. Instead of asking why they were stopping, he simply faced her, waiting.

She drew in a deep breath, then gestured at the house before them. "This is where I grew up. My parents and sister still live here, though my da is in Escarland right now."

But of course, he already knew where her father was. She'd told him that in one of her letters, and they talked about it during the feast.

Prince Julien's mouth tipped into a smile, framed by his beard. "Taking me home to meet your mother? Already? I didn't realize we were that serious."

"We aren't." Vriska clenched her fists and glared. She wasn't about to explain that this was a test. Or that she was hoping he'd fail it so she could walk away without guilt for failing her duty to her kingdom.

"Ah." Prince Julien's smile didn't slip, but something in his gaze sharpened. Perhaps he'd read more into her expression than she'd intended to tell him.

Tamping down a growl, Vriska turned to the door and pounded on it.

The door creaked open, and her mother stood there. A moment later, both her eyes and the door widened. "Vriska! And..." Somehow, her eyes widened even more, and she jerked into a bow. "Your Highness."

"It's just Julien." Julien smiled and bowed to her. "It is a pleasure to meet you, ma'am."

Something in Vriska's chest eased. This was going well.

No, wait. She didn't want it to go well. Why was she relaxing as if relieved?

Her mother stepped out of the doorway, gesturing to them. "Please come in."

Julien gestured for Vriska to enter first. She brushed past him and stepped inside the cozy, stone walls where she'd grown up. A part of her didn't know what to do or where to stand as Julien followed her inside and closed the door behind them. The room felt so much smaller, poorer, with him taking up space in it.

She glanced around at the tiny main room with its table filling most of the space, the kitchen cupboards, and the fireplace molded into the other wall. A passageway disappeared into the mountain, the doorways to the individual rooms covered by curtains rather than actual doors.

It was a far cry from Khagniorth Stronghold, much less the opulence she had heard was displayed in the human palaces.

Julien's smile gave nothing of his thoughts away. He nodded to Vriska's mother. "You have a lovely home."

"Thank you." Her mother's smile widened. "Please, have a seat. I still have some *iquitak* left. Rikze is currently out, but she should be back soon. I know she'll want to meet you."

Vriska stiffened at the undertone, and she avoided her mother's gaze as she took a seat at the table. Her mother must be dying to ask about Julien, especially now that they had shown up together like this.

She resisted the urge to slouch lower. Rharreth had kept the news about the arranged marriage quiet, but Vriska's and Julien's stroll through Osmana would send the rumors of a romance flying. It would be noised about all of Osmana by nightfall. If she wasn't careful, she'd find herself so stuck that she'd never get herself free, if that was what she wanted.

It was, wasn't it?

Julien took the seat on the bench next to her. Not too close, but close enough that she was still all too aware of him. Sitting next to him felt different than sitting beside her sister at a family meal. Different even than sitting in the feasting hall with her shield brothers. She had never been aware of her shield brothers the way she was of Julien.

Ma bustled to the cold cupboard and pulled out the remaining *iquitak*. She divided it into two bowls and placed them in front of Vriska and Julien.

Julien dug into the *iquitak*, taking a bite without hesitation. "This is good."

"It is *iquitak*. A traditional dessert." Ma hesitated, as if she didn't dare say anything else.

"It is made with berries and animal fat." Vriska eyed Julien, waiting for his reaction. If he was going to react poorly, now would be the time.

He paused with his spoon partway to his mouth. He swallowed, then popped the bite in his mouth. "Never would have guessed. It tastes good."

"It packs a lot of fat for staying warm during the long winters." Vriska dipped her spoon into her own *iquitak*.

Ma lingered next to the table and glanced between the two of them, as if she didn't dare speak in the presence of royalty.

Prince Julien gestured to the bench across from them.

"There is no reason to stand on ceremony on my account. Right now, I'm here as Vriska's friend, not as a prince."

Vriska resisted the urge to elbow him. Did he *want* her mother to all but have them engaged by nightfall? Bringing a single, male *friend* home to meet her mother was an entirely different thing to showing up with a bunch of the guys from the shield band just to hang out.

Ma slid onto the bench across from Vriska. With her tension, the wrinkles around her eyes and mouth were more prominent.

Prince Julien smiled, took another bite of his *iquitak,* and glanced at Ma. "I had the opportunity to tour the construction site for the bridge over the Hydalla River before I came here. They have made incredible progress, and the accommodations for the workers appeared comfortable."

"My husband has had nothing but praise in his letters." Ma held herself stiffly, her tone a hint too smooth. She likely wouldn't have told the Escarlish prince something negative to his face, even if Da had mentioned anything.

But in this case, Ma was being entirely truthful. Da had been effusively enthusiastic about the work he was doing in Escarland.

For a long moment, they sat in strained silence, broken only by the faint clinking of Vriska's spoon against her bowl as she halfheartedly stirred her *iquitak* instead of eating it.

What was there to talk about? Every topic that crossed Vriska's mind seemed far too personal. Or not personal enough.

He had asked after her family, and she probably should ask about his.

But she knew his family. At least, she knew of them, even if she didn't know more about them than that. The elf scourge Laesornysh was Prince Julien's brother-in-law, and Vriska wasn't sure she would ever be up for discussing him without bitterness crossing her face.

Before the silence lingered longer, the door flung open, and Rikze burst inside like a morning breeze gusting down from the mountain peaks. "Vriska! You're..." She trailed off, her gaze focused on Julien, as she skidded to a halt.

Vriska attempted a smile. "Rikze, this is Prince Julien."

Julien stood and bowed to Rikze. "It is a pleasure to meet you."

Rikze grinned and plopped onto the bench next to Ma. "Are you going to court Vriska? Everyone in the street is talking about it, after you were seen strolling together."

"Rikze!" Ma hissed, sending her a quelling glare. "It isn't polite to ask such things, especially of a prince."

Vriska choked, not daring to glance at Julien. This whole courting thing was still so *new*. She couldn't wrap her mind around being in a pair instead of just herself as she had always been. Not that she was even sure she and Prince Julien were courting. Not officially, anyway.

Yet that annoying, good-natured smile never dropped from the prince's face. "Your sister is very special. Whoever courts her is a very lucky man."

Vriska's breath caught, but Prince Julien kept his gaze firmly locked on Rikze across the table from him. He had neatly dodged the question, and yet his answer held far too much meaning.

Did he consider himself a lucky man, forced into this arrangement like this? Or was he just saying what he thought she would want to hear?

"Our da is in Escarland right now. He's helping to build

that new bridge for your king." Rikze reached across the table and took Vriska's bowl.

Vriska let her. She was too tense to do more than stir it, and Rikze would appreciate the dessert far more.

"I was just telling your mother and sister that I toured the town that was set up for the workers. Your father should be well provided for while he is in my kingdom." Still, Prince Julien didn't look at Vriska, and that not-looking made Vriska all too aware of him next to her.

"I would love to visit Escarland." Rikze scraped the last of the dessert out of Vriska's bowl.

Julien pushed what remained of his *iquitak* toward her. "You're welcome to visit. I'd be happy to give you a tour."

"Really?" Rikze grinned and claimed his bowl. "I have never been farther than a dog sled trip outside of Osmana."

Vriska refused to wince. She had traveled all over Kostaria as part of Rharreth's shield band. Her status as a warrior had taken her life in a vastly different direction than the rest of her family.

Julien leaned his elbows on the table, focusing on Rikze as if sharing a great secret. "Well, I've never traveled by dog sled. So there's something you've done that I haven't."

Rikze brightened and turned to Vriska. "We should take him out on the sled!"

Julien raised his eyebrows at Vriska. "The sled? But it's summer. There isn't any snow right now."

"There's a summer sled with wheels on it." Rikze jumped in before Vriska could answer.

Vriska scowled. She would have to ask to borrow Rharreth and Melantha's dog team, since her family was too poor to own one.

But it likely wasn't too much of a hindrance. Rharreth

and Melantha hadn't had a chance to run their team often, and considering how invested Rharreth was in making this marriage of alliance work, Vriska could probably ask for just about anything and he would make sure it happened.

Ma spoke quietly to Rikze, probably reminding her to rein in her exuberance.

Julien lowered his voice and leaned closer to Vriska. "We don't have to, if you don't want to."

Vriska shrugged. "It sounds like fun. Besides, I wouldn't want to disappoint Rikze."

Until she decided one way or another about this arrangement, then she would have to spend time with Prince Julien. Perhaps a jaunt into the mountains without all the prying eyes of Khagniorth Stronghold was just what she needed to finally make up her mind.

CHAPTER TEN

Julien trailed behind Vriska as they, together with her sister Rikze, left one of the side gates of Osmana in the early dawn hours. A chill still nipped in the air while a hint of fog lay in the valleys and ravines. He drew in a deep breath of the fresh, clear breeze whispering down from the mountain peaks.

A small pack rested on his shoulder, containing a few emergency items that he would never travel without and some of the Escarlish chocolate he'd brought with him as a courting gift. This dog sled trip into the mountains with Vriska and her sister seemed like the best opportunity for courting he'd had so far.

Next to him, Rikze chattered about the various parts of Osmana as they strode by, and her non-stop talking reminded him of Essie. Rikze carried the picnic basket, even though he had offered several times to carry it for her.

Rharreth had been more than happy to lend the use of his dog team. Melantha had even had the stronghold cook prepare the well-stuffed picnic basket. Somehow, they had managed to wedge in the added provisions that Vriska's ma had also sent along.

As much as Julien was looking forward to spending the day with Vriska, a niggle of unease worked its way into his chest, both because of Vriska's aloofness and because of the weary set to Rharreth's face that said something more was going on. Something he had yet to tell anyone besides Melantha, if Julien were to guess.

Vriska stalked ahead of Julien and Rikze, also carrying a pack. She didn't glance over her shoulder to check if Julien and Rikze were keeping up. Instead, she marched onward with a brisk stride as if she hoped to outdistance her own thoughts.

After they exited Osmana, Vriska led the way up a rocky ravine until they reached a flat, grassy meadow bordered by spruces and pines just out of sight of Osmana. A constant barking echoed off the surrounding trees of the glade and the cluster of buildings at the far end. Rows and rows of doghouses lined the meadow with dogs in varying shades of black, brown, gray, and white jumping and lunging on their leads.

A few trolls bustled about, caring for the dog teams. One of them paused and nodded as he saw their approach. "We have your team hooked up for you as the king requested."

Julien tried not to shift at the way the trolls were sending sidelong glances in his direction. As long as the glances remained curious, then he likely wasn't in any danger.

"Thanks." Vriska strode through the kennels of dogs, headed for the far side of the meadow.

Rikze hurried after her, occasionally pausing to give one of the sled dogs a pet or a scratch behind the ears.

Julien trailed behind her, but he kept his hands at his

sides. A few of the dogs growled at him, and he wasn't sure which ones were safe and which weren't. Besides, wasn't there some rule against petting working dogs? He didn't want to cause trouble.

At the far side of the meadow, a dirt road was worn into the grass. A ten-dog team waited there, hooked to what must be the summer sled. It looked a bit like a tiny wagon, with four small wheels, a platform, and an arched, upright back at the rear. A place for someone to stand jutted from the back. The platform was covered with layers of furs and blankets. For padding and protection against the chill wind, Julien guessed.

He'd heard of the Kostarian dog sleds, but it was still strange to see all those dogs, and yet no reins or string for guiding them as one would a horse. No, the dogs would be guided solely by voice.

Vriska dropped her pack on the sled and started to lash it in place. "Well, climb on."

Rikze grinned and hopped onto the front, cradling the picnic basket in her lap. Julien glanced at Vriska before he folded himself onto the sled behind Rikze. There was nothing for him to hold on to but a low railing along the side with Vriska's pack wedged beside his hip. He squirmed out of his own pack and tied it in place on the other side.

While Vriska climbed onto the back, standing upright behind the arched frame that Julien leaned against, the dogs remained sitting, ears alert and eyes shining. She gave a command in her language, and the dogs sprang to their feet, quivering and barking with anticipation.

Then, she called another command, and they lunged into motion.

He tightened his grip on the rail as the sled jerked, then

rolled forward at an increasingly fast clip. It jounced over the ruts and bumps in the dirt road, but the furs beneath him helped cushion his tailbone somewhat.

Rikze craned her neck and yelled over her shoulder, "It's a lot smoother in the winter when there's a good hard pack of snow!"

He nodded to let her know he'd heard, but he didn't try to reply. The cold breeze stung his face, and he blinked rapidly as his eyes watered. In front of him, Rikze didn't seem as affected, but she was a troll. She was better suited to the chill of a Kostarian summer morning than he was.

Vriska directed the dogs with shouted commands, following the meandering valley trail between the mountains. She kept them heading roughly northwards. Stands of spruce trees grew along the lower slopes of the jagged mountains on either side of them. Their trail ran along a rocky creek, its water clear as it flowed over dark river stones.

Julien had never felt the wildness of the land itself so keenly as he did when he took in the deep green trees, brown riverbed, whitewater splashing over dark gray rocks, and the brightest blue sky arching above. It called to something deep inside him, resonating with a part of himself that he hadn't known existed.

He drew in a deep breath of the river-scented air, though he grimaced as he caught a whiff of the stench of dog urine. Apparently dog teams were louder and smellier than they sounded in the stories told down in Escarland.

No matter what happened with Vriska or whoever he ended up marrying as a part of this marriage of alliance, he would at least love the land.

The trail turned away from the river and wound up the

gentle slope of a rise. As they reached the top, they broke out of the trees onto a grassy meadow that ended in a cliff overlooking a broad valley ringed by mountains.

Vriska called the dogs to a halt, and they sat or lay on the ground where they had halted, panting and tongues lolling. She climbed off the sled. "Rikze, Julien, could you set up the picnic? I'll give the dogs some water."

Rikze hopped to her feet, snatched the picnic basket and an armload of the furs from the sled, and raced toward a flat, grassy spot near the edge of the promontory. She set the basket down, then started spreading out the furs.

Julien uncurled from the sled more slowly, his knees a little stiff after being crammed in the tight space. After a glance at Rikze, he grinned at Vriska. "I don't think she needs my help."

"In that case, can you grab the water jug?" Vriska unhooked the dogs and started staking them in a line out of reach of each other so they wouldn't start fighting.

Julien sorted through the small pack of gear lashed to the sled and located a stone jug filled with water, along with a stack of thin stoneware bowls. He carried them to Vriska, and she set a bowl in front of each dog while he poured the water. Last, she produced a bundle of meat-covered moose bones and distributed them. The dogs set on the bones with gusto, their barking quieting to an aggressive cracking and gnawing.

Once they were finished, Julien and Vriska strolled to where Rikze had set up the furs and picnic basket. She hadn't unpacked much of the food, only a few snacks that they could nibble on until it was time for lunch.

Julien sank onto the furs and took in the view from the promontory. To one side of where they sat, the river they had followed cascaded over a cliff in a roaring, frothing waterfall. From there, the river broadened into a winding stream with cattails and brush along its banks. The green of the valley spread for miles before ending at the gray, craggy mountains that loomed in the distance on all sides.

"Look at all this food." Rikze rifled through the contents of the basket. "We could feed the family for a week on all this."

Julien turned just in time to catch Vriska's wince. What must it be like for her, constantly stuck in the middle between the life she lived as a warrior in the king's shield band and the life her family lived as commoners?

And now he was asking her to become a princess. No wonder she was hesitant. It was one thing for Farrendel and Essie to agree to a marriage of alliance. They had both grown up with the weight of kingdoms, courts, and politics on their shoulders.

But Vriska hadn't.

No matter who he married among the trolls, the Escarlish court was going to do their best to eat her alive. Every little faux pas and hint of awkwardness would be mocked. The court could get ruthless when they sank their teeth into someone.

Could Vriska handle it? Could any troll woman? The troll court had its intrigues, but mockery was done face-to-face. Retribution was handled openly with the violence of a quick bout in the arena, and that was that.

As much as he'd love to see Vriska punch the lights out of the snooty court matrons, such actions would only make any scandal worse, not solve the problem like it would here in Kostaria.

Worries for another time and place. Right now, he didn't

know if he could convince Vriska or any of the others on the list to willingly agree to this marriage of alliance.

Vriska plucked a handful of nuts from a small jar. "Yes, the cook at Khagniorth was generous."

Julien leaned over and also dug out a handful of nuts, letting his fingers brush hers as he did. She shot him a look, and he just grinned as innocently as he could back at her. "The food looks good. And this view is amazing."

He kept his gaze on Vriska, rather than on the mountains around them. Let her take that sentence as benignly or as flirtatiously as she wanted.

Vriska's eyes narrowed at him, as if she didn't know what to think about his sudden attempts at flirting.

Perhaps the standard human gestures weren't going to work on a troll warrior. But he'd already tried impressing her with his muscled physique and his fighting skills in the arena. If that hadn't worked, then he didn't know what else to try.

"This is one of our favorite spots." Rikze gestured toward the valley, as if oblivious to Julien's and Vriska's silent exchange. "We would hike here as a family. It has been easier since Vriska started borrowing dog teams to get us here faster. I think I saw the field glasses around here somewhere."

A moment later, Rikze pulled out three sets of field glasses from the picnic basket. She handed one each to Vriska and Julien before she sprawled on her stomach and inched toward the cliff's edge.

Vriska motioned toward the edge. "We're a little late in the morning to see wolves, most likely. But a lot of other wildlife should still be out there, if you want to take a look."

Julien nodded, then motioned for her to go first. He'd

like to say it was out of chivalry, but really it gave him an opportunity to sprawl next to her, close enough that their shoulders brushed whenever either of them shifted. As Vriska had Rikze on her other side, she couldn't put more space between them without moving entirely.

She shot him another look. Not really a glare. More an *I know what you're doing* look. But she settled in and lifted her field glasses without making any move to push him away.

He shifted a stone from where it had been poking into his stomach.

Rikze scanned the valley with her field glasses before she pointed. "Look. There's a herd of caribou on that far mountain."

Julien tore his gaze away from Vriska, lifted his glasses, and scanned the indicated mountain until he spotted the dense herd of caribou grazing along the brushy slope.

"There are some moose down by the river." Vriska pointed, bumping his shoulder as she did so.

He swiveled his field glasses and searched the riverbanks until he found two large brown animals—moose—half-hidden in the stands of thick brush next to the river. Even at this distance, he could tell the animals were huge, and one had a set of thick, spreading antlers that looked downright dangerous.

"And there's a grizzly." Rikze pointed out the shaggy, lumbering brown bear that appeared to be noshing berries on a far slope.

He made a mental note not to wander off. Even the animals here in Kostaria were deadlier than anything they had back in Escarland.

But this kingdom suited Vriska. The breeze tossed her white hair around her face, her gray skin smooth and unlined. She was as tough and beautifully rugged as the mountains around her.

How could he justify taking her away from this place? He couldn't imagine her in the urban environment and the stuffy court of Escarland. Kostaria was her home. Could he ask her to leave, even for the good of both of their kingdoms?

But now that he'd started to know her, he couldn't imagine marrying anyone else for this treaty. She was brave, tough, and had a strong beauty that reminded him of Kostaria itself. More than that, she loved her family with a fierceness that called to him.

Yet marrying someone else was still a distinct possibility, if Vriska decided she wanted to back out.

After all, why should she settle for him? He was no troll warrior. No, he was a human prince who came with all the burdens of politics and court life. Compared to the troll warriors she saw every day, of course he was a weak second.

Second, yet again. If Vriska agreed to this marriage alliance, would she always see Julien as a second choice to a troll warrior?

Julien would do his best to make sure the troll woman he married never felt like *his* second choice.

They watched the wildlife for the rest of the morning. At noon, they feasted on the roasted and shredded moose meat sandwiches, fresh berries, and vegetables the cook had provided.

As they finished, Julien fetched his pack from the sled. When he returned to his seat on the furs, he resisted the urge to swipe his suddenly sweaty palms on his trousers. He shouldn't be this nervous. He was just giving her a box of chocolate.

But he'd never had much practice at courting before. And with Vriska, he never knew how she would react. All he knew was that it wouldn't be with the soft smile and effusive thanks that an Escarlish noblewoman would have given him.

"I brought something for dessert." He dug into his pack, pulled out one of the tins of chocolate, and held it out for Vriska. "For you. It is Escarlish chocolate. It is a variety of flavors from dark chocolate to milk chocolate to chocolates filled with caramel."

Vriska eyed first him, then the tin with wariness, as if he was holding out a snake instead of chocolate. After a moment, she took the tin and pried the lid off.

Rikze leaned forward, peering into the tin as well as if she'd never seen chocolate before in her life. Perhaps she hadn't. Due to the tensions, neither Kostaria nor Tarenhiel had done much trading with the surrounding kingdoms until recently. Neither kingdom had even gotten their hands on hot chocolate until Essie introduced it.

Vriska pinched a chocolate between her fingers and bit into it as if she half-expected it was poisoned or would taste foul. As she chewed, her eyes widened, and she froze, her gaze shooting up to meet his. "This is good. I've never tasted anything like it."

"Can I have one?" Rikze was already reaching for one of the chocolates in the tin.

"Actually…" Julien pulled a second tin from the pack and held it out to her. "I have one for you as well."

It seemed his guess was correct. Even though a troll woman's heart wasn't likely to be won with flowers or poetry, chocolate was universal.

Rikze grinned and tore the lid off the tin so fast that it

flew a few feet before landing in the grass behind her. She popped a chocolate into her mouth, then made a noise between a gasp and a moan. "This is beyond amazing."

"I have a tin for your mother as well. We can give it to her when we return." Julien set his pack to the side, the last tin of chocolates clinking faintly against his large survival knife, flint and tinder box, and small medical kit that he'd stashed in his pack in case of emergencies.

When Julien turned back to Vriska, her gaze was still focused on him, emotion roiling through her deep blue eyes. "Thank you for the chocolate. And for thinking of my family."

Since she'd written to him about her family, he'd made sure he had enough of some of the simple gifts, like the chocolates, to give to her sister and mother as well. He figured that, if Vriska had refused him, it would not hurt to have extras of things like tins of chocolates.

And now that he better understood the commoner background that Vriska had come from, he was especially glad he'd brought enough to share. While Vriska's family wasn't living in the squalor he'd seen in some of the poorest districts of Escarland's capital of Aldon, they were clearly considered among the poor here in Kostaria. Even with the increased trade between the kingdoms, they wouldn't be able to afford luxury items like expensive chocolates. No wonder Vriska's father had taken the job in Escarland.

Rikze crammed another piece of chocolate into her mouth. "Now I really want to go to Escarland. Do you eat chocolate like this every day?"

Julien chuckled and patted his stomach. "Of course not. My waistline would be a lot pudgier if I did."

Rikze grinned and punched Vriska's arm. "Well, Vriska is glad you aren't some pudgy, chocolate-stuffed prince."

Vriska glared at her sister with a look that clearly said, *Don't you dare say another word.*

"What?" Rikze gave her a look right back. "He's giving you chocolate and clearly trying to flirt with you. And you haven't punched him in the face yet."

Julien stilled, keeping a pleasant and neutral smile on his face with some effort. Rikze had seen through his not-so-subtle attempts at flirting. But was she right about Vriska's reaction? Was Vriska more attracted to him than he'd thought, given her glares and aloofness?

Vriska's glare deepened, and she opened her mouth. Her eyes flicked toward Julien, then she seemed to change what she had been about to say. "Don't eat all your chocolate right now."

Rikze gave Vriska another impish smile before she stared down at her tin of chocolate, heaving a mournful sigh. "I suppose I shouldn't eat all of it. Who knows when we'll get more?"

"If your da doesn't send you some, I'll make sure you get more." If Rikze had been Essie, Julien would have tweaked her nose. Instead, he stood and retrieved the lid of her tin for her. "Besides, chocolate is very sweet. You'll give yourself a stomachache if you eat too much all at once. Trust me. I ate a whole tin once, and I was miserable for the rest of the day."

Rikze nodded and placed the lid on the tin firmly, as if to shut away the temptation.

Before Julien could return to his seat, Vriska stood, gripped his arm, and hauled him a few yards away. When he faced her, whatever soft look she'd had a moment ago had been washed away, replaced with a hard, bright anger.

What had he done to get her angry now? He thought it had been going well a moment ago.

"What do you think you're doing?" she hissed as she poked his chest with her finger.

Julien blinked at her, bracing himself against the force of her jabbing finger. Why was she so riled? He hadn't done anything. "What are you talking about?"

"Stop making promises to Rikze that you can't keep." Vriska jabbed his chest again with enough force he winced. "This arranged marriage is bad enough, but I won't see her disappointed."

"What do you mean? Of course I'll keep my promises to Rikze." Julien refused to take a step back, and he kept his voice low enough that Rikze wouldn't be able to hear what they were saying.

"And if I back out of the marriage and you're forced to move on to the next female on Rharreth's list? What happens then, huh?" Vriska's blue eyes snapped with a fire that drew him even as an angry heat built inside his own chest.

Did Vriska really know him so little? Sure, they'd only been together here in Kostaria for two weeks, and she'd spent most of that time avoiding him. But they'd been writing to each other for three months. Shoot, he was here to keep a promise that his brother had made in a treaty. If that wasn't enough to prove that he kept his word, then he wasn't sure what would.

He drew in a deep breath and forced himself to let it out slowly, expelling the heat before it built into true anger.

Vriska didn't know him well. That was why he was here in Kostaria, after all. She had no reason to think that he would care for her and her family beyond what they could do to help him fulfill his duty to the treaty.

"Even if you don't agree to marry me, I will still see to it that your sister gets to visit Escarland and that she will receive more chocolate. I am a prince of Escarland. I have the power to see that it is done regardless of whether you marry me." Julien held Vriska's gaze, hoping she could read in his eyes how earnest he was. "I know you don't know me well yet, but I do not make promises lightly. Whether that promise is to you or your sister or your king, I will see that it is done."

VRISKA STARED into Julien's deep, brown eyes, and her anger deflated, replaced with something else she couldn't name.

Humans were notoriously untrustworthy when it came to their word and honor. She shouldn't trust the sincerity she saw in his eyes.

Yet it was hard not to believe him when he was looking at her with such naked honesty. She couldn't read any shifting to his gaze or his stance that would denote a lie.

And she was familiar with liars and schemers. After all, her guilt over Drurvas was not that she had been deceived but that she hadn't been deceived and yet hadn't said anything of her suspicions.

Besides, Rharreth seemed to think the human king and his brother were trustworthy. He wouldn't have signed such a close treaty with them if he had thought otherwise.

If she believed Julien was sincere, then that meant the depth to his words was real. If he promised her sister a trip to Escarland, then he would make it happen.

If he promised to love and cherish Vriska in marriage

vows, then he would do it. Even to his own hurt, if that was what it took.

And she wasn't sure how she felt, contemplating a relationship with a man like that. If anything, he was too humble. Too good.

"Oh." It was all she could think to say.

She glanced away, needing to look anywhere but at his earnest eyes set in his rugged, bearded face. A few yards away, Rikze had gone back to scanning the valley below with her field glasses, thoroughly distracted or doing a rather good job of pretending to be so.

"Vriska." His voice was low. Gentle in a way that begged her to meet his gaze again. "If this isn't what you want, then don't hesitate to say so. I won't think any less of you. King Rharreth won't either."

Perhaps Vriska could believe that about Julien, but Rharreth? He might not wish to, but he would be disappointed if Vriska wasn't the one to marry Prince Julien. Once again, Vriska would fail her king. Fail her duty. Fail to regain the honor she'd lost by her treatment of Melantha and her silence about Drurvas.

Was duty enough? He'd asked her that question once before. She hadn't been sure then, and she wasn't any more sure now.

Yet if she truly found an arranged marriage with Prince Julien repulsive, then why hadn't she walked away yet? Why hadn't she taken the way out that both Prince Julien and King Rharreth had offered her?

If it wasn't duty holding her here, then what was? She wasn't attracted to him. At least, she didn't think she was. She had never dreamed of marriage or anything like that.

Yet here she was, unable to let him go either.

"I don't know what I want." She clenched her fists at her sides, struggling to keep her voice low so that it wouldn't carry to Rikze. "I just…"

All she wanted was to be a warrior. Yet she didn't want a return to the war and bloodshed either.

Perhaps she simply didn't want to be the one to walk away. If she did that, then the shame of her dishonor would remain. But if he walked away, then she would be free since she had done her best.

Vriska met Julien's gaze with a glare, shoving away any vulnerability she'd felt a moment ago. "Why don't *you* walk away? After all, I'm not the only troll woman under consideration. Why keep pursuing me? I'm a warrior. I'm never going to be a pretty, perfect princess to stand at your side. I'm not even sure I want to marry, much less have children. You'd be better off looking elsewhere."

Julien started as if her words slapped him, his expression shuttering. "You don't want children?"

"No." At least, she'd never given it much thought. It ranked up there with marriage as things she'd never dreamed about since she had been too focused on becoming a warrior.

He drew in a deep breath, then let it out slowly as if to absorb the shock of her words. After a long moment, he stepped back, and the easy-going smile returned to his face. He gestured toward the dog sled. "Would you like to show me how to drive this thing? Or steer? Or whatever you call controlling a dog team?"

Good. A distraction. She could handle that. He hadn't said what he planned to do, but he would likely walk away and start pursuing someone else once they returned to Khagniorth Stronghold.

But until then, they might as well enjoy the rest of the day.

"Of course. Here." She led the way to where the dog sled waited for their return trip.

Instead of hooking up the dogs, she showed Julien where to stand and talked him through the various commands. It took several minutes for him to memorize the commands and the correct troll pronunciation so that the dogs would be able to recognize the words through his thick Escarlish accent.

As she adjusted his grip on the back of the sled, her fingers brushed his, and he met her gaze with his brown eyes.

And, for the first time, her heart started thumping just a bit harder. Which was terribly inconvenient, since she had just shoved him away.

CHAPTER ELEVEN

Julien strode through the passageways of Khagniorth Stronghold after a practice bout with Vriska and Zavni. The three of them were silent. Perhaps Zavni had picked up on the tension that remained between Julien and Vriska in the past few days.

Julien still wasn't sure what to think, after her revelation that she didn't want children.

He did. And he knew better than to hang his hopes on her changing his mind. This was her decision, and if he wanted to be with Vriska, he'd have to respect that.

So either he would have to give up that dream to pursue Vriska, or he would have to give up Vriska. Easier said than done, now that he'd started to let himself fall for her.

Needless to say, the morning practice sessions had become rather awkward. Especially since only Vriska and Zavni had been able to make it that morning.

He wasn't sure where Brynjar and Eyvindur were. He'd gotten the impression that Rharreth had sent them on a mission of some kind, but no one had informed Julien of just what that mission might be. Whatever was going on had kept Rharreth and Melantha so busy that they had been unable to join Vriska, Zavni, and Julien for a morning bout in the arena.

A group of troll warriors headed in their direction down the corridor, likely for their turn in the training arena. Julien vaguely recognized the leader as one of the trolls he'd fought—and defeated—in the bouts that first week. What was his name again?

Zavni and Vriska closed in tighter around him, their hands going to their weapons. Julien tensed, though he resisted the urge to reach for his sword.

The lead troll halted, a sneer curling his lip. After holding Julien's gaze for a long, deliberate minute, the troll leaned forward and spat onto the floor at Julien's feet. "Filthy human. Bringing your diseases and weakness here. Go back to where you belong."

"Back off, Brathac." Vriska's hand tightened on her sword's hilt, her face stony.

Julien eased to the side, putting himself in a better position to draw his sword if necessary. Hopefully it wouldn't be.

"The king will not be pleased if you harm his guest." Zavni's normally cheerful expression had dropped into a cold, deadly look as he reached over his shoulder to rest a hand on his ax.

"I'm sure he won't. We've all seen how our king caters to the humans. If he wasn't so busy groveling to them, perhaps he would have done something about this disease that has been plaguing our people." Brathac shot another glare at Julien. "But he's too weak. First an elf for a wife, now a human welcomed into his halls."

Now wasn't the time to ask what Brathac was talking about when he mentioned a disease.

Instead, Julien forced his posture to relax into nonchalance, and he gestured at the sword sheathed at Brathac's side. "Is that a new sword? I assume it must be since my brother-in-law Laesornysh melted your last weapon."

Julien didn't know for sure that Brathac had been among the army supporting Drurvas that day along the southern border of Kostaria, when Farrendel had disarmed all of them and incinerated their weapons with his magic. But it seemed a safe gamble, based on the disdain in Brathac's words.

Brathac's jaw tightened, his brown eyes flashing. Yep, Julien's words had found their mark. Perhaps taunting the troll wasn't the wisest move, but Julien wanted to remind Brathac and his cronies about one of the biggest reasons why Rharreth was so determined to maintain the peace.

And that reason was, largely, Farrendel and his magic.

While the trolls might dismiss elves and humans in general, even they couldn't dismiss Farrendel's strength, even if they hated him for it.

With a growl, Brathac spat on the floor again, then stalked down the passageway once again, his three minions following in his footsteps.

As soon as they disappeared around a corner, Zavni heaved a breath and lowered his hand from his ax. "He's heading for trouble one of these days. Did you have to taunt him?"

Julien shrugged and relaxed his grip on his sword's hilt. "If he was going to attack, he would do it whether I taunted or groveled. I figured it was best to remind him that I have a powerful family."

Vriska shook her head, not looking at him. "Still, I

wouldn't recommend being alone in a corridor with him. He might not hesitate to take a swing at you, especially now that he's backed down once."

Julien nodded as they set off down the passageway once again. After a moment, he glanced between Vriska and Zavni. "What did he mean, about a disease?"

The muscle at the corner of Vriska's jaw knotted. He might have guessed the emotion was anger, except for the glimpse he got of her eyes before she turned away. "King Rharreth will explain. He asked to speak with you after our practice bout."

Some of Julien's disquiet eased. Hopefully that meant Rharreth had intended to tell Julien, his ally, what was going on even before this confrontation with Brathac would have compelled him to do so.

They finished the walk to Rharreth's study in silence. As they neared, the sound of raised voices reached them, too indistinct to pick out the words, though Julien could hear Melantha's and Rharreth's tones in the sound.

Zavni knocked on the door, then he and Vriska took positions on either side of it, joining the two guards already stationed there.

The argument within halted. Then Rharreth called out, "If that is Prince Julien, send him in."

He glanced at Vriska, but she was focused on scanning the corridor for threats. Right now, she was on duty as a guard and he was on duty as a prince. Besides, they weren't courting or betrothed or anything official yet that would allow her to remain at his side for meetings.

Julien pushed the door open and strode into Rharreth's study. There, a number of magic-powered lamps provided light. Rharreth slumped behind a stone desk, a pile of papers spread in front of him. Melantha stood next to him, leaning over as if in mid-argument. As Julien entered, she straightened and instead sank into a chair next to Rharreth behind the desk.

"I heard something about a disease?" Julien sank into the chair facing the desk and crossed his arms. "What haven't you been telling me, Rharreth? I am here as your ally. There was no need to keep me in the dark."

Rharreth sighed and dragged a hand over his face. The light of the lamps highlighted the depth of the circles and the weary lines carved around his eyes. "I kept it quiet from everyone, not wishing to worry the kingdom needlessly. But the situation is out of my hands now."

Melantha made a noise in the back of her throat, her mouth pressed into a tight line. "It seems I was right."

"Yes. But I still maintain there was nothing we could have done at the time, even if we had acted." Rharreth sighed, glancing at Melantha, before he turned back to Julien. "Shortly after you arrived, I received word of a mysterious illness that struck two of the small, coastal towns. Many men, women, and children sickened and died within two or three days. I ordered those two towns placed under quarantine, as is standard practice for a town afflicted with an illness. For nearly a month, the quarantine seemed to have worked. Then, this past week, I have been flooded with reports of an illness spreading rapidly, striking villages faster than those villages can send in reports."

"Brathac insinuated that humans were to blame for the disease." Julien searched their faces, trying to read their thoughts on the matter.

"That is the rumor that has been going around." Rharreth's jaw tightened, and he glanced down at the papers on his desk rather than meet Julien's gaze. "Many seem to think that since this disease is following the trade routes, the trade with Escarland is what brought it to Kostaria in the first place."

"It is a possibility." Melantha spoke quietly but, unlike Rharreth, she met Julien's questioning glance with a steady, almost belligerent gaze. "It is not unreasonable to think that there is a disease that is rampant among your people which had not reached Kostaria before now and thus the trolls would have no immunity to it. The same could also be said of a Kostarian disease that could be transmitted to Escarland with devastating effect."

Julien opened his mouth, wanting to deny that his kingdom could be the cause of harming Kostaria, even unintentionally. But he wasn't a physician. Melantha would know far more about how diseases spread than he did. If she thought it a likely possibility, then he couldn't argue with her logic.

Instead, he turned back to Rharreth. "If this is an Escarlish disease, then we will provide all the help we can. We would also consider it a courtesy if we were kept informed of the situation. If this disease is following the trade routes, it could strike both Tarenhiel and Escarland."

Assuming it hadn't come from Escarland in the first place.

Rharreth's jaw worked, as if he didn't want to admit such weakness even to allies. "That is why I am informing you now."

"I have been telling my rather stubborn husband that perhaps this is the time to call the treaty into effect." Melantha gave Rharreth another, sharp look. "Weylind will help."

Rharreth sighed and for just a moment, his mouth quirked with the hint of a smile. "I should know by now to listen to you. But it seems I still cling to too much pride. It isn't an easy thing to admit that I need to ask the elf king for aid."

"I know." Melantha's expression and voice softened. "I am not sure how thrilled the healers will be to be sent to Kostaria, but they will go if he gives the order."

Julien shifted in his seat. This seemed like a discussion the two of them should have hashed out before he'd arrived.

"I will send a message to both Weylind and Averett as soon as we are done. But I wished to discuss it with you first." Rharreth raised his head, facing Julien squarely once again. "Based on the reports I've received, this disease strikes seemingly with no warning symptoms. The afflicted suffer vomiting, which often turns bloody. They have great internal pain, and over three quarters of the sick die within two or three days. It strikes all ages indiscriminately, and whole sections of towns fall sick within the same night. Do you have such a disease in Escarland? Do you know a cure or something we can do until the elf healers arrive?"

A seventy-five percent death rate? He had never known a disease to kill so effectively.

Julien shook his head. "There is the flu, which causes vomiting and fevers. And cholera has plagued the cities of Escarland for years. But even cholera isn't nearly that deadly, and it often kills within hours, not days. Besides, we have recently discovered that cholera is spread through contaminated water. From what I've seen, your cities don't have issues with sewage contaminating the fresh water supply."

Aldon was in desperate need of sewage tunnels. Dumping sewage in the streets and trying to clean it up afterwards wasn't a great way to deal with waste, as the outbreaks of cholera and typhoid proved. Another thing the trolls could help build, if this disease didn't send them back into isolation.

"But I'm not a physician. I'm no expert." Julien shrugged, sagging against the back of his chair. He had some training in recognizing cholera, typhoid, and other diseases that often struck large army encampments. But his knowledge ended at the basics.

"I understand. I knew it was a long shot that you would have some insight into what we're dealing with." Rharreth scrubbed a hand over his face again.

"We need to visit one of the afflicted towns." Melantha rested a hand on Rharreth's arm. Her voice was soft, gentle, even as her posture remained steely. "I am a healer, Rharreth. I need to be out there, helping our people. Right now, I am the only one in Kostaria who can figure out how to fight this disease."

"Melantha..."

"I know you don't have an heir yet, and it would be very bad for Kostaria if the two of us died. But I can protect us." Melantha held Rharreth's gaze with a steel that said she wouldn't be budged. "Your one objection was that the coastal towns were so far away that we could not get there quickly enough to be of any help. But the disease has come close enough that we can journey to the nearest town and still save some of the sick."

"Melantha." This time, Rharreth drew her closer, meeting her gaze. "I was going to say that yes, you're right. We need to visit one of the towns. I need to see what has been afflicting my people, and your magic will be invaluable."

Julien squirmed in his chair once again. Would Rharreth and Melantha even notice if he quietly left?

Melantha's smile broke across her face, warming the hard lines. "It might take a week for Weylind to gather healers willing to travel to Kostaria. That should give us enough time to visit a village and see what needs to be done."

If they left, they would likely take Zavni and Vriska with them. Besides, Julien didn't want to sit here at Khagniorth Stronghold while a threat like this disease was ravaging an ally's kingdom.

"I would like to go with you, King Rharreth." Julien kept his back straight as Rharreth swung his gaze on him.

"I cannot guarantee your safety. It wouldn't look good if you were to die of a disease here in Kostaria." Rharreth's mouth flattened into a hard line. "It might even be best if you cut your trip short. It is only a matter of time before the disease reaches Osmana, at the rate it is spreading."

"I understand, as will my brother. I will send him word of my intentions, along with your message informing him of the situation. He will not place the blame on you if I should take ill." Julien worked to keep his voice and expression neutral.

Going into battle was one thing. There he at least had a chance to defend himself. But a disease with a seventy-five percent mortality rate was something altogether different. He had no defense, no way to even know if he had been afflicted until it was too late.

But he could not turn coward now. If he intended to marry into Kostaria, then he needed to stand with that kingdom during this.

"If this disease is as virulent as it seems, then it is only a matter of time before it spreads beyond Kostaria's borders."

Julien held Rharreth's gaze. "My brother will want my first-hand account so he can prepare. Something like this would devastate Escarland."

For the first time, Melantha's hard expression gave way to something more like fear. "I truly hope the reports are exaggerated or there is something simple that can be done. Because if it is as claimed, then even Tarenhiel might not be impervious. We elves have such an abundance of healers that my people never face illness, and thus they have no immunity to anything. If this disease should reach Tarenhiel's shores and if it should overwhelm our healers..." Melantha shivered, her gaze dropping to her hands.

"All the more reason for Weylind to send however many healers he thinks he can spare to stop it here in Kostaria before it can spread elsewhere." Rharreth reached out and took Melantha's hand.

Julien didn't want to contemplate it. The cholera outbreak a few years ago had been bad enough. But something like this? The bodies would pile up faster than they could be buried. And if Tarenhiel was also struggling with the same thing, then there would be no help from that direction.

Hopefully it wouldn't come to that. Perhaps this was simply a virulent flu that a few elf healers could cure easily enough.

Julien jogged alongside the pack mule on the trail to the tiny village of Carth, which was their destination for the evening. Ahead of him, Vriska jogged beside the mule where

Melantha perched, looking uncomfortable since she was the only one who didn't take a turn on foot.

While sled dogs were the preferred travel for the long winters, mules still provided better transport in the summer. Still, the trolls only had a limited number of mules, since they had to be cared for all winter. That meant the troll warriors all took turns running and riding.

Rharreth had offered that Julien could ride the whole way if he wished. But there was no way Julien would remain on a mule while Vriska and the others took turns jogging. He would look weak before the troll warriors if he did, not to mention that it went against the way he'd been raised to ride while a lady walked. Even if that lady was a tough, troll warrior who likely had better endurance than he did.

As he ran, he gazed at the looming, gray mountains. Their slopes were covered with green before giving way to gray stone, then white snow at the peaks. The lower slopes were covered with scrub brush and spruce trees. It was hard to believe that a deadly disease was lurking in this pristine wilderness, killing the trolls who were hardy enough to make their home here.

The setting sun warmed his back while the pink, blazing sky stretched overhead. Sweat trickled between his shoulder blades, and he struggled to keep his breathing even as he leaned into the slope. The trail wound upward, following the edge of a mountain's side. But he wouldn't beg for a rest. He could keep going just as long as the trolls could.

Hopefully. If he admitted to weakness, he would never live it down.

Finally, the first structures of the village of Carth appeared on the next mountainside, bathed orange in the sunset. Rounded stone buildings lined each side of the road, forming the main street, while the entrances to homes dotted the mountainsides on either side.

As Rharreth called a halt before the largest building in the small town, Julien took in the sight of the quaint troll village. After the war, it was too easy to imagine all the trolls were large, muscled warriors.

But many trolls were like the people peeking from their homes and shops at their king. Normal people living their lives in their tiny villages away from war and politics. Despite their different culture and manner of dress, there was something homey and familiar about the place, as if it could just as easily be a human town in Escarland or an elf village in Tarenhiel.

The door to the large building in front of them opened, and three trolls strode down the steps.

The first two were Eyvindur and Brynjar, and the two of them bowed to Rharreth. The third troll stepped forward and also bowed. "Your Majesty. It is good you've come."

Rharreth glanced from the troll to his shield brothers.

Brynjar grimaced and gestured toward the rest of the town. "We stopped on our way to meet you to report and learned that a family here fell ill just a few hours ago."

Julien gripped the lead rope of the pack mule tighter. They had planned to spend the night in Carth, then move on to the next village.

But it seemed that the disease had come to them.

Melantha joined Rharreth and gave a sharp nod. "Then let us set up here. While I want to help as many of our people as possible, I believe there may be more benefit if we are here to observe the beginning of the disease's encroachment on a village. I might be able to learn more about how it spreads."

"Very well." Rharreth turned to face their traveling party which, apart from Julien, Vriska, and Zavni, was also formed of a small army of other warriors. Rharreth shouted orders, and the warriors jumped to set up the large tent that would serve as a hospital ward if the disease spread that much here in this town. They set up their own camp just outside of the town.

While they worked, Melantha and Rharreth followed the town's leader to the home where the afflicted family was quarantined.

Julien worked alongside the troll warriors. He ate a simple meal and fell onto his bedroll. Sleep claimed him within minutes.

CHAPTER TWELVE

Vriska woke to shouting and blazing torchlight. As she pushed onto an elbow, shoving aside her bedroll and tarpaulin, she blinked blearily into the night.

Rharreth stood at the door of the hospital tent that they had set up that evening, barking orders. Townsfolk and members from the other shield bands who had traveled with them carried stretcher after stretcher past him. From within, Melantha's voice rang sharp and strident as she gave further orders.

Vriska shoved to her feet. She already wore her light tunic and trousers, and it was the work of a moment to throw on her vest and boots.

How had so many people sickened so quickly? Just one family had been sick when she'd turned in for the night, and that family had been properly quarantined.

It didn't matter how or why. That was for Melantha to figure out, since she was the healer.

Vriska strode to Rharreth and bowed to him. "Where do

you need me, my king?"

He pointed over his shoulder at the tent. "Assist as you can inside."

Vriska nodded and braced herself before stepping into the tent. She was a warrior. She wasn't naturally nurturing or soft or anything conducive to nursing the sick.

But this was a crisis, and hands were needed no matter a person's preferences. Based on the long line of those already carrying stretchers, they already had enough volunteers for that job. That left tending the sick, and Vriska wouldn't shirk her duty no matter how it went against her nature.

She pushed into the tent and had to stagger to the side as the smell hit her. Already, the cots they had set up were full of the sick, and more were laid on pallets on the floor. It seemed every bucket in town had been commandeered either for puking or hauling clean water. The whole tent reeked of vomit and excrement while the sick curled on their sides, clutching their stomachs and crying at the pain.

A young girl, no more than ten, stood next to the door. She held out a scrap of fabric to Vriska. "You must put on a mask while by the sick. The queen's orders."

Vriska took the scrap of cloth and tied it over her nose and mouth. It smelled faintly floral, providing a modicum of relief from the stench of illness.

Also wearing a mask, Melantha raced from cot to cot, her fingers laced green as she healed patient after patient. Those she'd healed rested easier, but they didn't spring from the cots and leave as Vriska might have expected.

Some of the female townsfolk went from bed to bed, cleaning up the patients and tending those in the throes of distress. Zavni and Brynjar were there too, fetching buckets of fresh water and leaving to dump out and clean puke buckets.

But the person who caught Vriska's eye was Julien. He knelt next to a cot, the cloth mask over his face puffing out oddly due to his beard. He held a bucket for an older male troll as the troll alternated between puking and spouting insults at Julien. It seemed the troll was not happy to have a human helping him in his time of weakness, even though he was too weak to resist the offered aid.

Julien didn't flinch at the invectives or at the vomit that seemed to purposely miss the bucket. His voice was calm and even kind as he handed the elderly male troll a wet rag to wipe his face.

Here she was, reluctant to get her hands dirty with this kind of nursing even though these were her own people, while Julien was already there in the thick of it, covered in the mess and grime without complaint, for a people not his own.

With a deep breath that she instantly regretted, Vriska grabbed a bucket and waded into the fray of the tent.

For hours, she held buckets while patients vomited. She cleaned up messes and bedding. She fetched clean water and washed out the soiled buckets. At first, she just about gagged each time she tended a patient. But, eventually, her senses grew numb to her surroundings.

It was hard to remain numb, though, when the stretcher bearers kept bringing in patients as more of the town fell ill. The illness seemed to strike everyone. The elderly, the adults in the prime of their life, the young children. Whole families fell sick all at once.

It was even harder to remain numb when the stretcher bearers were called in to carry out the first dead body. Then the second. Then a third, a child still clutching his toy sword.

As the faint light of dawn brightened the tent's canvas weave, Vriska held a bucket for a young mother as she vomited, the vomit stained with a bright red that told of internal bleeding. The woman's face whitened further at the sight before she turned pained eyes toward the toddler on the next cot over. The child curled around her stomach, whimpering at the pain.

A few cots over, Julien bowed his head and solemnly closed the eyes of the elderly troll who had so railed at him at the beginning of the night.

Vriska's fingers tightened on the bucket she held as she pushed to her feet. What was this disease that it could kill so quickly? There were winter plagues that occasionally laid many low, but nothing like this.

As she headed for the exit, she passed where Melantha had her hand pressed to a child's forehead. Before Vriska could pass her, Melantha's face whitened to an even paler shade than her already silvery elven tone, and she swayed.

Vriska dropped her bucket and lunged forward, catching Melantha as her knees buckled. Vriska glanced around, then shouted, "Rharreth!"

Rharreth shoved aside the tent flap, then his gaze fell on Vriska where she clutched Melantha's limp form. Eyes widening, he raced across the tent, all but jumping over a few of the cots in his haste. He scooped Melantha into his arms, sinking into a crouch as he cradled Melantha's face. "Melantha, love, are you all right? Is it the illness?"

Melantha weakly shook her head against Rharreth's arm, though she didn't open her eyes. "No. I am just exhausted."

Rharreth's jaw clenched, his dark blue eyes flashing with

pain. "You promised you would not exhaust yourself. You were supposed to keep enough magic to heal yourself if needed."

"And I still can. I have not expended every last drop of magic." Melantha blinked, gripped the front of Rharreth's shirt, and pulled herself more upright.

Vriska relaxed her clenched fists, her shoulders slumping. For a moment there, she'd thought Queen Melantha had succumbed to the illness. If that happened, there would be no one standing between all these people and death until the elven healers arrived.

Assuming King Weylind of the elves would still send them if his sister died.

"It is this disease. I have never seen anything like it." Melantha's eyes fell closed again as she pressed her face against Rharreth's shirt. "It attacks so many organs at once. I need so much magic to heal even one person and yet, when I check on that person hours later, the illness is back and attacking them again. I cannot...I cannot heal everyone, Rharreth. I cannot save them."

"I know." He pressed a kiss into her hair.

It was such a tender gesture that Vriska turned away. She would have left, but she was boxed in between the wall of the tent, two cots, and Rharreth and Melantha in the aisle between. And there was the bucket and splattered vomit at her feet that she would need to clean.

"I do not think ten healers will be enough." Melantha's face twisted, and a tear slid down her cheek. "If this disease spreads, I do not know if all the healers in Tarenhiel will be enough."

Vriska froze where she stood, a weight settling deep in the pit of her stomach. They had been placing so much hope in the elven healers. But if even they couldn't stem the tide of this thing?

It was too horrible to contemplate. And there was nothing Vriska could do to fight it but clean up puke buckets and fetch glasses of water for the sick.

Rharreth stood, holding Melantha in his arms. "Rest for a while. You will do no one any good if you collapse."

Vriska didn't hear whatever Melantha might have mumbled in reply as Rharreth carried her from the tent. As they left, a deeper darkness settled over the tent despite the morning rays of sun beaming through the tent flaps.

It was the lack of hope. The realization that their one and only healer had been carried out of the tent in exhaustion.

Vriska picked up the bucket she had dropped. Most of the vomit had soaked into the ground, leaving a wet, gloppy spot. She kicked at some of the surrounding dirt to further soak up the rest of the disgusting mess.

"Here." Julien appeared next to her, then he poured a bucketful of sand over the spot.

"Linsh." Vriska nodded and followed him from the tent to the nearby stream where they rinsed their buckets.

"Are you doing all right?" Julien's deep brown eyes searched her face. He reached out a hand, as if to touch her, before he halted and grimaced at his fingers.

She stared down at her own hands. Her calloused fingers were chapped and dry from all the handwashing she'd done.

As to his question, she didn't know how she was doing. She was mostly trying not to think about it too much.

She had seen plenty of death during the war. It had been brutal and bloody and gory.

And yet this was a different kind of horror. The war, at least, struck down warriors who went into battle knowing what it could cost. But this disease took the young. The elderly. Mothers and fathers. Sisters and brothers. Whole families.

If this disease kept spreading like this, it would reach Osmana soon. In Osmana, the death toll would be devastating.

"I don't know." Vriska sighed and pushed to her feet. It was better not to dwell on it. Not right now. "We should get back."

When they returned, however, Rharreth ordered them to wash up and get some rest as well. He was setting up a rotation of helping in the tent, digging graves, collecting the sick from their homes, and resting.

Vriska washed off the grime and changed into clean clothes. She added her dirty clothes and mask to the pile of laundry waiting to be washed by the remaining, healthy townsfolk. Then, she collapsed onto her bedroll, pulled the tarpaulin over her head, and tried to relax enough to rest.

When she woke, bleary-eyed and groggy, to the sound of hoofbeats, she poked her head out of her blankets and blinked into the early morning sunlight.

A troll reined in a snorting, lathered mule to a halt as Rharreth strode to meet him. The troll swung down, gasping out something that Vriska was too far away to overhear.

But by the way Rharreth's shoulders slumped, lines digging deeper into his face, she didn't have to. She knew.

The illness had struck Osmana.

CHAPTER THIRTEEN

Julien stood next to Rharreth at the doors to Khagniorth Stronghold. Before them, sick trolls on cots, blankets, litters, or furs lay in packed rows, filling the courtyard from one end to the other. More trolls filled the street outside as they sought help from their queen and only healer.

His chest ached with a strange, painful numbness as he took in all the sick and dying. The trolls weren't his people, not like they were for Vriska and Rharreth, yet that didn't negate the compassion he felt. The hurt at seeing so many suffering people.

Beside him, Rharreth wore a weary frown. Lines dug deeply into his face around his eyes and mouth.

It was an expression Julien had seen on Averett over the years. The weariness of carrying the crown while the kingdom was in crisis.

Yet in this crisis, there was very little Rharreth could do besides organize care for his people...and coordinate the burial efforts for all the dead.

And very little Julien could do. Rharreth wasn't his king or his brother the way Averett was. He wasn't sure what to say or do besides stand there and be the visual proof of Escarland's support.

Shouting erupted outside of the stronghold gates, growing louder and louder. Rharreth straightened the slump of his shoulders, going from such a defeated posture to a more regal air.

Troll warriors swung the gates open, revealing a detachment of fifty troll warriors, led by Vriska and Zavni, as they shoved their way through the crowds of desperate trolls. They had their shields outward, pushing the people back as some of them scrabbled at the warriors, begging and pleading.

At the center of the detachment of troll warriors, twenty elven warriors, distinguishable by their swords, shields, and bows, surrounded the ten elven healers, protecting them from the desperate trolls.

Trolls. Begging for help from elves. It would have been a moment to appreciate, if the situation hadn't been so dire.

The troll guards closed the gates after the warriors, but that didn't dim the shouting.

Most of the troll warriors guarding the elves dispersed, leaving a small escort to pick their way through the sick trolls waiting for care. Once Zavni and Vriska in the lead reached Rharreth, they halted and bowed.

The two of them stepped aside, and one of the elven warriors strode forward. Julien thought he recognized the elf as one of Weylind's commanders during the war.

The elf gave a half-bow. Respectful, but not the depth it would have had to his own king. "King Rharreth, I wish to convey my king's deepest condolences to your kingdom as well as my king's promise of aid. I have with me ten healers who have volunteered to come to Kostaria to aid your people. More healers will be coming once my king ensures that Tarenhiel will not be left short-handed if this disease should spread."

Amazingly, the elf didn't sneer with the usual elven superiority complex. Weylind had chosen well, in both the healers he'd sent and the warriors chosen as their escort.

"I thank you, and I thank your king and kingdom for your aid in Kostaria's time of need." Rharreth nodded back to the warrior. "If you would follow my warriors Zavni and Vriska, they will show you to the healing clinic where my queen will assign your tasks."

It was subtle, but even Julien could hear the warning in Rharreth's tone. Melantha was in charge of the healers, no matter what the elves might think of her past betrayal of Tarenhiel or her marriage to a troll.

A few of the elven healers shifted, but none of them sneered. They had volunteered, after all. If they were among those who clung to prejudices against the trolls, then they wouldn't have come.

The elf warrior in charge gave a few quiet orders, and the elven warriors fell into place around the healers as Zavni and Vriska led the way inside. The elf leader, however, didn't follow. Instead, he reached inside his tunic and pulled out a folded and sealed letter that somehow hadn't gotten so much as a crease in it. "I also carry a message from King Averett of Escarland."

Rharreth took it. With a glance at Julien, he broke the seal and quickly read. He glanced up, meeting Julien's gaze. "Your brother has also promised Escarland's help. He is gathering volunteers among the Escarlish nurses and doctors to provide extra hands. He is also sending blankets, cots, and other medicinal supplies."

"My king hopes to send such aid as well, once he has organized more healers," the elf warrior added, as if to make sure Rharreth knew that Tarenhiel was not about to be outdone in generosity by Escarland.

"All help is appreciated." Rharreth refolded the letter, glancing between the elf warrior and Julien. "King Averett also reports that he has brought in a group of doctors and scientists in Escarland to theorize on what this disease might be. They have been reviewing the reports I've sent and consulting with the head elven healers. It is likely that several of them will travel to Kostaria with the supplies and additional aid."

Julien's shoulders relaxed. He hadn't doubted that Averett would send help but it still eased something inside him to know his assurances to Rharreth were being carried out. "Of course. We are allies."

Rharreth nodded, though the lines in his face remained deep and weary. "I knew having allies would be important to Kostaria's future. But I never expected to need our allies in this way."

"No king does." Julien swept another glance over the courtyard. Two trolls carrying an empty stretcher exited a side door of the stronghold. They lifted one of the sick trolls onto their stretcher, then returned inside, bringing another troll in for healing.

Would this soon be Escarland's fate as well? Would the hospitals of Aldon overflow with the sick and dying? Would there be enough elven healers to cover all three kingdoms?

If the way this had spread through Kostaria was any indication, it would hit the poor sections of Aldon the hardest. So far, very few of the upper class warrior trolls had become sick. Even after being exposed many times, none of Rharreth's shield band had gotten sick. Nor had Julien, thankfully.

It was strange. If this was an outbreak of a disease like cholera that was from polluted water, then it would have struck one town or one section of Osmana. Not spread across the kingdom like it had. Nor were the water sources in Kostaria polluted with waste the way the cities in Escarland were.

But if it was passed from person to person, then why hadn't any of those tending the sick gotten sick themselves? Why such a class division among the sick?

The elf warrior gestured toward the door. "If I may, King Rharreth, I would like a tour of the healing clinic so that I can send a report to my king as soon as possible."

"Of course." Rharreth took a step toward the door, then turned back to Julien. "Prince Julien..."

Julien nodded toward the trolls in the courtyard. "I will stay here and help those waiting for a healer."

Rharreth nodded and led the way into the stronghold, the elf warrior following at his heels.

Julien turned back to the courtyard with Brynjar and Eyvindur sticking with him as his guards.

The three of them claimed buckets of clean water and went from sick troll to sick troll, giving them something to drink. Dehydration was a danger with the amount of vomiting and diarrhea that the sick experienced with this disease.

As he reached the far side of the courtyard near the gate, the guards opened the gates for another long line of volunteers carrying stretchers with the worst of the sick found in the town. Rharreth had organized squads of volunteers to go door-to-door in Osmana, seeking the sick—and finding the dead when whole families had succumbed together before anyone had realized something was amiss.

"Julien."

His name was a hoarse whisper ending in a whimper. He snapped his head up, searching for the one calling out to him.

On the stretcher carried past him, a young troll girl curled around her stomach, her white hair lank and straggling around her face.

Yet her dark blue eyes—so like her sister Vriska's—focused on him.

"Rikze." Julien scrambled to his feet and hurried to her side as the stretcher bearer started to set her down in a clear patch on the courtyard's stone. He squeezed her limp, clammy hand, then glanced up at those carrying her stretcher. "Bring her straight to the healing clinic."

The troll's jaw worked. He wouldn't like taking orders from Julien. "She has just arrived..."

"She is sister to Vriska, member of King Rharreth's shield band." Julien kept his voice steely. He just had to bluff that he had the authority to give these orders.

After a long moment's hesitation, the stretcher bearer nodded. Then he and the other troll lifted Rikze again, turning toward the stronghold's doors.

Rikze let go of Julien's hand and weakly gestured. "Ma..."

"I'll find her." Julien forced himself to smile before he turned away, frantically searching the nearby stretchers.

There, a few stretchers away, Vriska and Rikze's mother lay still and pale.

Julien gestured to those stretcher bearers as well. "This patient, too, needs to be brought right inside."

These trolls didn't argue but followed after the others. A few of the surrounding trolls lying on the ground protested, and perhaps Julien shouldn't give cuts to anyone, no matter who they were.

But this was Vriska's family, and he couldn't imagine leaving them here, untreated in the courtyard.

Brynjar joined him and gave him a nod. The troll's way of telling him he'd handled that well. "I'll tell Vriska, if you wish."

Julien shook his head. "No, I will."

Perhaps Vriska would take the news that her family had fallen ill better if it came from her shield brother instead of Julien.

But Julien was attempting to court her. He needed to show her that he would be there for her even in something as awful as this.

VRISKA SAT on a cot and held her little sister in her arms. Around them, elven healers bustled from cot to cot, healing just enough to keep the patients alive and comfortable. Trolls—both warriors and commoners—tended the sick.

Rikze curled into Vriska, tears running down her face. "It hurts, Vriska."

"I know." Vriska tightened her hug around her sister. If only she could take the pain onto herself. She was the warrior. She could handle pain.

But this was her sweet little sister. She shouldn't be suffering so much pain that she was crying from it.

At the next cot over, Julien dabbed a damp cloth over Ma's fevered brow. Vriska's mother still hadn't woken since she'd been brought to the clinic, despite the amount of magic Melantha had poured into her. The grim set to Melantha's mouth hadn't eased Vriska's worries any.

Would she lose both her sister and her mother to this disease? How would her father handle that, since he wouldn't even know they had been sick until after they were dead?

Rharreth had ordered that the trolls working on the bridge in Escarland remain where they were. It was hard, knowing that her father couldn't come to be here with Ma and Rikze. But Vriska understood why Rharreth wouldn't want trolls to travel back and forth, potentially spreading the disease to Tarenhiel and Escarland.

This disease was awful. And there was nothing Vriska could do about it. No enemy she could fight. No weapon she could wield to defend her family.

Instead all she could do was hold her sister, stroking her sweaty hair from her face. "Just take slow, steady breaths. One of the healers will be back to tend you."

Rikze gave a weak nod, another tear tracing down her cheek. After a moment, her body shuddered, and she scrabbled for the bucket.

Vriska kept one arm wrapped around her sister while she held the bucket for her in the other.

Her sister heaved and vomited. The clear liquid in the bucket was tinged with red, and it stabbed something inside Vriska to see it. Her little sister was internally bleeding. As far as the elven healers could tell, this disease attacked the internal organs, causing them to fall apart and shut down. And that was happening to Rikze.

Melantha halted next to Vriska and rested a hand on Rikze's cheek. Melantha's serviceable gray dress bore darker spatters while her short black hair lay limp rather than spiked. Dark circles smudged underneath her eyes, and her elven features appeared gaunt rather than simply angular.

Despite her exhaustion, green magic glowed around her fingers. Rikze's vomiting eased, and her body shuddered, then relaxed in Vriska's arms.

"That feels nice," Rikze mumbled against Vriska's shoulder as her eyes fluttered closed.

Vriska set the bucket aside and wrapped both arms around her sister as Rikze went fully limp.

Melantha drew her hand back, the green glow disappearing. "She should sleep peacefully for a few hours. The rest will do her body good."

Vriska nodded, but she didn't let go of Rikze. A part of her worried that if she let go, Rikze would slip away from her.

Melantha moved to Vriska's mother and rested her fingers on her forehead. Once again, the green glow surrounded Melantha's fingers and seeped into Vriska's mother. Yet this time, Melantha frowned, giving her face even more weary lines.

Vriska held her breath, waiting for Melantha's verdict.

Melantha withdrew her fingers and glanced at Vriska. The smile that creased her mouth didn't ease the somber depths of her eyes. "I am doing all I can."

No false promises. No assurances Ma would be fine when she clearly wasn't.

Yet Vriska appreciated the honesty. And the fact that here Melantha was exhausting herself for her people.

Yes, *her* people. Vriska had acknowledged Melantha as

her queen long before this. But now she truly felt that reality. Melantha was the queen of Kostaria, and she was showing her care for her people in a very real way right now.

"Linsh, my queen." Vriska held Melantha's gaze, hoping she would see how much Vriska appreciated everything Melantha was doing.

Melantha nodded, then swept a glance over the healing clinic. The entire space was packed with cots, as were many of the surrounding rooms which had been commandeered for more sick rooms. The space stank of vomit and sickness, yet Vriska barely smelled the stench anymore.

"I only wish I could do more." Melantha sighed and glanced at Rikze before she strode toward the next cot.

Vriska pressed one last kiss to her sister's forehead before she gently lowered Rikze to the cot. Rikze gave a small moan, and she curled in on herself on the cot. Vriska tucked the blanket over Rikze's shoulders.

Her ma and sister couldn't die. They just couldn't. Vriska had long ago accepted her own death. She was a warrior, after all. But her ma and sister were supposed to be safe here in Osmana, far removed from the blood and death that Vriska had witnessed. It was not supposed to be like this.

"Are you all right?" Julien's voice was too compassionate. Too gentle.

It broke something inside her. She couldn't bring herself to meet his gaze. She might just fall apart if she did.

She was a warrior. She had faced plenty of death with a heart of stone. She didn't cry. She didn't break.

But she couldn't do this anymore. She had tended the sick, dredged up a caring she didn't even know she possessed, and gave of herself in a way she never had before.

This wasn't her. She was a woman of war. Her hands were rough, made to hold a weapon rather than gently nurture.

Vriska pushed away from the cot and brushed past Julien, ignoring Julien's gentle queries that blurred against her ears. She stumbled around the cots and into the main entry hall of Khagniorth.

Zavni was there, directing stretcher bearers to the different rooms. Rharreth was there, talking to the sick with the elven leader at his side. Brynjar and Eyvindur were there, guarding the door to the healing clinic.

Too many people. Vriska couldn't break in front of them anymore than she could break in front of Julien.

She ignored Zavni's call and strode down one of the side passageways, winding her way through the warren of corridors until she could no longer hear the bustle from the entry.

This deep into Khagniorth, the magic lights were not lit, and Vriska didn't bother saying the word to light them. The darkness of the passageway suited her mood.

Drawing on her magic, she coated her fists in a fizzling, gray light. With a shout, she punched the wall as hard as she could. Her magic protected her hands so that the stone bent around her fists instead of breaking her fingers.

Again and again Vriska shouted and pummeled the wall. All her feelings of helplessness and fear and anger bled through her chest into her fists as she pounded the wall over and over, leaving divots.

She wasn't sure when her shouting turned to tears. She slammed her fists into the wall one last time, then leaned her forehead against the stone as her sobs came harder, faster.

"Vriska." Julien spoke her name with that same gentle tone that had broken her in the healing clinic.

When he touched her shoulder, she didn't resist as he turned her to him. She'd never been the type to cry on someone's shoulder, and yet when Julien wrapped his arms around her, Vriska found herself sagging against him. She was too tall to rest her head on his shoulder, but she pressed her face into the crook where his neck met his shoulder.

The strength of his arms, the warmth of his body, steadied her in a way the stone wall hadn't. Even as she sobbed, the tide of tears ebbed, leaving exhausted numbness in its wake.

How she hated crying in front of anyone. It was embarrassing—not to mention uncomfortable—to let anyone see her that vulnerable. Especially because she normally wasn't weepy. She was a warrior. She could take care of herself and her own emotions.

Walling away her tears, she drew in a deep breath. As she did, she became aware that her face was still pressed against Julien's neck. Like her, he reeked of sickness and the cleaning alcohol the elves insisted they use on everything. And yet, beneath those odors was the whiff of a different scent. The spice of his soap and a smell that was uniquely him. It made her want to hold him closer and draw him in.

"Vriska?" Julien's voice was still soft, but it had a different note to it than it had before.

What was this feeling tightening her chest and catching in her throat? Was this what attraction felt like?

Vriska pushed away from Julien, her back bumping into the wall behind her as she put a step of space between them.

Julien cleared his throat and also took a step back, looking away from her as he rubbed a hand over his beard. "I…uh…"

Vriska scrubbed a hand over her face, swiping away the

signs of her tears. She had to say something to break the tension. "I hate crying. Especially in front of people."

Warriors didn't cry. At least, they didn't cry where someone else would see. And Vriska was tough enough that she didn't succumb to tears often.

Julien's mouth tipped into a hint of a smile. "I don't like crying either. But there's no shame in shedding a few tears. Even if it's embarrassing."

Vriska studied his face for a long moment. Only the rare troll warrior would admit to shedding tears, and that was probably the same for a human warrior. Yet here Julien was, not only admitting to tears of his own, but not judging her for the ones she had cried. Finally, she gave him a nod. "Thank you for coming after me. For being here."

"Of course." Julien shrugged, as if it wasn't a big deal.

Yet it was. He cared. He'd stayed to help fight this disease when he could have returned to Escarland and safety. He'd tended her family while they were sick. He'd come after her just now and stayed while she worked through all these emotions.

She wasn't sure how she felt about that. A part of her wanted to run, to go back to trying to push him away. Yet another part of her was starting to get used to having him around.

"I...should get back to my family." Vriska edged around him, dropping her gaze to the floor. Her skin prickled, and all she wanted was a moment to collect herself. Why was it more awkward around him now that he'd seen her cry than when she'd met him the first time?

"Go ahead. I'll follow in a few minutes."

She released a breath and hurried down the passageway,

thankful he understood that she needed a moment of space. Perhaps he needed a moment alone as well.

As Vriska neared the entry hall, she quickened her pace until she was almost jogging. An irrational gnawing settled into her chest, a fear that her mother or sister might have taken a turn for the worse simply because Vriska wasn't there to watch over them.

Pushing her way into the healing clinic and between the cots, she returned to their side. Rikze slept peacefully, some of the lines of pain on her face easing with the healing sleep. Her mother rested as well, though her sickly pallor hadn't gone away.

They were still alive. That was all that mattered at the moment.

CHAPTER FOURTEEN

For a long moment, Julien leaned against the wall, drawing in the quietness of this dark corner of Khagniorth Stronghold. He had been so rarely alone since he'd arrived in Kostaria, except for nights in his room. Even then he had guards stationed outside of his door.

He had been craving a few minutes of quiet to settle his thoughts. So much had happened from meeting Vriska to this disease ravaging Kostaria. That had allowed very little time for him to process where he stood with Vriska, with Kostaria, with the treaty.

Not that the quiet time was helping. That moment when Vriska had held him tighter and buried her face against his neck had sparked something in his chest.

Attraction to her wasn't a problem. But she didn't want children. Could he set aside his dreams of children for her? Or would it be better if he pursued another troll woman instead? Yet, at this point, he had been in Kostaria for over a month of his three-month stay. Was it too late to even attempt a courtship with someone else?

Besides, it felt wrong to even worry about something that felt trivial when so many lives currently hung in the balance. Trolls—men, women, and children—were dying. Julien's love life was hardly the most important thing right now.

With a sigh, Julien pushed away from the wall. Which way did he need to go? He had followed the echoing sounds of her shouting last time when he'd decided to go after her to offer comfort.

Perhaps he should have returned with Vriska rather than risk getting lost.

His footsteps echoed hollowly in the cavernous passageways, so strangely empty with everyone focused on the healing clinics set up around the entry hall and in the courtyard.

Which way was the entry hall? He still hadn't heard its bustle. He must have taken a wrong turn since this corridor didn't look familiar. Then again, they were all just blank stone so it was hard to tell one corridor from another.

A sound broke the stillness behind him. He whirled, then brought up his fists.

Four male troll warriors stood at the entrance of the passageway, led by Brathac, the troll who had given Julien trouble when he'd first arrived. It was no great leap of logic to see that they were up to no good.

"What do you want?" Julien shot a glance around. He was still all alone.

Brathac's sneer curled his face into an ugly expression. "You are a human. Do you think you are worthy to stand in these halls as a warrior?"

"I do not have to claim it." Julien assessed the warriors

before him, trying to pinpoint their weaknesses. "I defeated you in the arena in the time-honored tradition of your kingdom."

Brathac growled, his fists clenched. "It doesn't mean anything. You are just a weakling human. That defeat meant nothing."

The fact that Brathac was so bent on revenge for a single defeat even weeks later said that it meant a great deal.

Could Julien take four troll warriors all by himself?

Brathac stepped forward, a gray glow already surrounding his fingers.

Nope, he couldn't. Not when those trolls had magic, and he didn't.

Julien planted himself in the center of the passageway and braced for the attack. He couldn't defeat them. He would have to give as good as he got and hope he could hold them off long enough for help to arrive.

Or that he would at least get in enough hits to mark them so that Rharreth could avenge him.

"Worse than your dishonorable actions in the arena is this disease that you and your fellow humans brought to our mountains," Brathac growled, his magic swirling brighter around his fists. "Our king never should have consorted with humans. You weaken us."

"Who did you lose?" Julien kept his tone compassionate rather than antagonistic. Few warrior families had been affected, but perhaps Brathac, like Vriska, had come from commoners. Or his was the rare warrior family who had fallen ill. This disease was one Julien would wish on no one, not even on Brathac.

Brathac's jaw worked, and his eyes flashed. Behind him the other three trolls glanced at each other, as if knowing

Julien had struck a nerve. Brathac pointed a finger at Julien. "You brought this on us. You came here, and only weeks later our people are falling ill. Rharreth is too spineless to stand up to you humans and take Kostaria back for the trolls."

Julien didn't bother to point out the flaws in Brathac's logic. Yes, many blamed humans for this disease. And perhaps there was some truth to it. Only more research on the part of the elven healers and the Escarlish scientists, when they arrived, would provide an answer there.

But Julien personally couldn't be responsible. The first cases of this disease had shown up on the far coast in towns where Julien had never stepped foot in his life.

"But the worst of your transgressions is the way you've been looking at Vriska, the king's shield sister." Brathac stalked a few more steps forward. "Do you really think you are worthy to woo a troll warrior?"

Apparently his attempts at flirting with her had not been that subtle. He had not realized they would be noticed and so scorned by the other trolls. Had Brathac followed him and Vriska and seen their embrace a few minutes ago?

What would Brathac think if he knew Rharreth had been the one to agree to a marriage of alliance between a troll and a human?

"It is Vriska's choice whether she accepts my attentions or not. It's not your place to make her decision for her." Julien braced himself. "Nor is it your place to protect her. She can protect herself, and she has her shield band protecting her back already."

The time for talking was over. Brathac just wanted to rant, and Julien wasn't going to give him the continued satisfaction of reveling in his supposed grievances.

Instead, Julien charged the trolls. If he couldn't win, his best chance was to take the offensive.

They stumbled back, surprised that he would dare charge them.

He slammed a punch into Brathac's face, breaking his nose with a gush of blood. Spinning, he rocketed a punch at the face of another of the attacking trolls.

That was all the time his surprise earned him.

A fist slammed into his gut, and Julien doubled over, gasping for breath. He forced himself to throw another punch, grazing another troll's cheek. He had to hit them in their faces where the bruises would be visible.

More fists pounded him, and this time it was all he could do to curl in on himself and try to protect his head with his arms.

He was slammed against the wall. Stone wrapped around him, and he cried out as something snapped deep inside him.

For a moment, the four trolls halted. Brathac smirked, chuckling and saying something in a low tone to the troll next to him as if this was all just entertainment for them.

Julien strained against the stone holding his arms and chest, but his efforts were useless against the inexorable grip of the rock. Something hot and panicked rose in his throat, and he had to swallow it down as he glared at the laughing trolls.

Was this how Farrendel had felt both of the times he'd been captured by stone? This utter helplessness? The rising panic and the clawing resignation? And Farrendel had been pinned to the floor, suffering like this for days rather than mere minutes.

Julien braced his feet, hoping the trolls wouldn't think to

secure his feet the way they had his arms. He would have one last chance to get in a blow or two before he'd be entirely helpless.

After a few more chuckles among themselves, the trolls advanced, raising their fists to resume the beating.

Julien lashed out with his foot, catching the last troll he hadn't marked in the ear. Blood dribbled down the side of the troll's face.

The troll growled, then the four of them were on him. Fists and pain and stone cutting into his chest, his wrists, his ankles.

This was helplessness. There was nothing he could do besides tensing his muscles to lessen the blows as best he could. Nothing left for him but to take it and hope he survived.

Another fist crunched into his face, and the blackness consumed him.

A CRACKING SOUND rang in his head. He groaned as pain burst inside his skull.

"Do not try to talk. Your jaw is still healing." A soothing voice spoke nearby. It took him another long minute to get his sluggish mind to register that it was Melantha's voice.

Julien drew in as deep a breath as he could manage and lay there, eyes still closed. What had happened? Why was he lying here in such pain?

"Do you know who attacked you?" Rharreth's voice this time, harder and colder than Melantha's.

"Give him space. Let him rest." Melantha. Chiding.

The attack. Julien groaned again as images flashed

through his aching head. Brathac and his three troll cronies. The way they'd pinned him to the wall and beat him until he blacked out.

"Do not try to talk yet. Rest." Gentle fingers rested on his forehead, and more healing magic flowed into him, banishing the pain.

He drew in another deep breath, then two. His ribs ached, but the magic dulled the pain.

So much magic. Magic that should have been used on the sick and dying trolls rather than him.

Julien groaned and struggled to shake his head. "No. No."

"Easy." Melantha's magic didn't stop flowing into him.

Julien managed to peel his eyes open. Images blurred, and he blinked several times until the dark gray ceiling above him came into focus. Melantha, her short black hair lank against her forehead, stood next to him where he lay on a table.

Sucking in a deep breath, Julien forced his aching jaw to move. "No, save your magic. I will heal."

Melantha's jaw worked, the dark circles under her eyes even deeper than they had been before. "I am the healer, not you. I will decide how much magic I can spare to heal you."

Julien sighed and tried to relax back onto the table. He knew better than to argue with that tone of voice, especially coming from a queen. Even if she technically wasn't *his* queen.

He glanced around the room. It seemed to be one of the private examination rooms in the back of the healing clinic, with a wall of cupboards and shelves filled with jars and supplies on one side and the table where he lay in the center.

On the other side, Rharreth paced outside of the open

doorway, his fists clenched at his sides. He glanced into the room, his gaze flicking from Julien to Melantha. "Is he healed enough to answer questions?"

"Yes." Melantha waved Rharreth inside. "But keep it brief. He needs rest."

Rharreth nodded, strode into the room, and planted his hands on the table next to Julien. "Who did this to you?"

"Brathac and three others. I don't know their names." Julien's jaw hurt as he spoke, his voice coming out rasping, but at least he was alive. He could speak. "I hit them. All of them should have cuts or bruises on their faces and heads."

Rharreth rested a large hand on Julien's shoulder for a moment. "Well done. Rest. We will hunt down Brathac and his conspirators."

Julien wanted to join him, but he could feel that his body was in no shape for hunting troll warriors.

Rharreth strode from the healing ward, the door slamming behind him.

"I am sorry you were attacked." Lines dug into Melantha's smooth face, as if her duty as the troll queen was a heavy burden. "I had hoped that the changes Rharreth and I have made would be enough. This kind of bullying has become ingrained in troll culture after hundreds of years under kings who modeled this behavior, and it seems the tensions caused by this disease have brought out the worst."

Her jaw flexed, and Julien could only guess at what kind of bullying she had endured when she married Rharreth.

"Rharreth and I won't tolerate this dishonor." Melantha sighed and leaned against the table. "But changes don't happen overnight. Nor is it possible to change hearts."

"I understand. I don't blame you or Rharreth for this." Julien gave a harsh chuckle that hurt deep in his chest. "I was expecting to get beat up at least once on this trip, though I thought it would likely be Vriska's father or perhaps Vriska herself."

Melantha sighed and shook her head. "It is a sad commentary on Kostaria that you would come here expecting a beating."

Gathering his strength, Julien pushed to a sitting position, letting his legs dangle over the edge of the table. He groaned and hunched, breathing hard. His head spun, and he wasn't sure if he was going to vomit or pass out.

"Take it slow." Melantha pressed a hand to his bare arm, and only then did he realize he was missing his shirt. Her gaze remained firm. "You will need to rest for a few days. You are human. I cannot heal you as quickly as I could a troll or an elf. Nor do I have the magic to spare for a full healing."

He nodded, trying not to let the reminder of his human shortcomings gnaw at him. He had been too human—too frail, too magicless, too weak—to protect himself against the troll warriors.

Perhaps they had been right. No matter how good a warrior he was, he would always be human. He would never be truly worthy of a troll warrior like Vriska.

CHAPTER FIFTEEN

Vriska paced between the cots in the healing clinic, waiting for the back door to open and Rharreth to give them word on Julien. Zavni paced with her, and the elf healers and troll volunteer nurses dodged around them as they cared for the patients. Brynjar and Eyvindur remained outside the door of the healing clinic, guarding those within.

What kind of dishonorable troll did something like this?

She stopped short, her chest tightening. She had done exactly that, except to the king's wife instead of his guest. Sure, she had never beaten Melantha within an inch of her life, but Vriska had spit on her. Hurt her. Looked the other way when others hurt her. Those actions had besmirched her honor just as much, even if the results had not been as drastic or as life-threatening.

She had apologized to Melantha, sort of. How could her guilt over her actions months ago keep growing?

Vriska halted next to her mother's cot, checking on her

yet again. Ma and Rikze still slept peacefully. One thing to be thankful for, at least.

She never should have left Julien behind in that passageway. Rharreth had been so careful about ensuring that Julien was always guarded while here in Kostaria. Vriska had known that something like this was a possibility, yet she had been selfish enough to want a few more minutes away from Julien to process what had happened that she hadn't thought through the risks of leaving him alone.

Yes, it had been his choice, too, to stay behind rather than return with her. But that didn't ease the tightness in her chest. He had been there for her as she vented her feelings over her mother's and sister's illnesses. Yet when he had needed her to fight at his side, she hadn't been there.

The door to the exam room opened, and Rharreth stepped through, shutting the door behind him so quickly that Vriska didn't get more than a glimpse of Julien laid out on the table, blood still crusted over his face and in his beard.

Vriska hurried to Rharreth's side, Zavni at her heels. When they reached their king, Rharreth directed them into a corner where they were out of the way of the healers and nurses.

Rharreth faced them, grooves lined around his eyes and tightening his hard jaw. This latest situation only added to the weight sagging his shoulders and the exhaustion pooling beneath his eyes. "Prince Julien has awakened."

Vriska released a breath. At least he had woken. When a servant had found him, he had been a bloody, unconscious mess dangling from the restraints that had pinned him to the wall. By the way Melantha had set to work, her brow pinched, her magic flooding from her hands, he had been near dead after that beating.

Those fools! What had they thought would happen if they killed the Escarlish prince with their fists? Did they really think another war with Escarland was the best thing for Kostaria? Especially right now?

Even if Escarland didn't start another war, they likely would end both the defense treaty and the trade that provided much-needed goods and food. Even more trolls would die if they didn't have the grain and medical supplies Escarland had and would send.

Not to mention that healing Julien had taken magic that Melantha could have used to heal the sick instead. Would someone die—would Vriska's ma or sister die—because Melantha had been forced to use her magic to heal Julien?

Apparently Julien's attackers didn't care about the common Kostarians who would suffer. Their prejudice against humans was so strong that they didn't even think about the consequences.

Rharreth swept a glance over them. "He said his attackers were Brathac and three others. He got in a few hits, so they should have visible bruises or cuts on their faces or heads."

"Good for him." Zavni slapped his fist into a palm.

Vriska glanced toward the closed door, something warm filling her chest. Even when outmatched by four trolls, Julien had fought until the bitter end. That was courage, to face such odds without backing down.

She had seen so much of Julien's gentle, humble side lately that she had nearly forgotten the courage she'd seen in him that first week he'd been here, when he'd walked into the practice arena and taken on troll warriors in fighting bouts.

"We're going to track Brathac down." Rharreth led the way toward the door. As they stepped outside, the five members of one of the other shield bands bowed to him. Rharreth nodded. "Three of you, guard Queen Melantha and Prince Julien. Don't let anyone besides the members of my shield band enter the examination room."

"Yes, Your Majesty." The other shield band members bowed again and stepped inside the clinic to station themselves outside of the inner door.

Vriska eyed the other shield band as they left. It was strange, seeing another shield band taking on the duties that would normally be reserved for Rharreth's shield band alone.

But they were down to only four members besides Rharreth, and all four would be needed to hunt down these attackers. If not for the war, their shield band would have been fourteen strong. More than enough to guard a door and protect their king.

Rharreth turned to face the entry hall, taking in the bustle. Several of the trolls hurrying about their tasks glanced their way. Many had seen Julien getting hauled into the healing clinic, limp and bloodied. Raising his voice, Rharreth shouted to gain the attention of those in the hall. "Prince Julien of Escarland was attacked in the halls of Khagniorth. He named Brathac and three others as his attackers. They should all have bruises and cuts. Everyone who can be spared, I want you to search the halls. Shut the gates of Osmana. I want them found and arrested."

Several of the gathered warriors bowed and hurried off to carry out his orders.

Rharreth glanced back to the three of them. "Zavni, Brynjar, Eyvindur, I want you to lead the efforts to search the stronghold. Vriska, remain here with me."

Vriska clenched her fists, though she didn't argue. She should be out there, too, hunting down the despicable lowlifes who had attacked Julien.

But once they were caught, they would be brought here to face Rharreth's justice. Besides, she wouldn't want to be off in the passages of Khagniorth if Julien, her mother, or her sister took a turn for the worse.

With a salute, Brynjar, Eyvindur, and Zavni split off, going down different hallways and gathering more warriors around them as they went.

While she waited for news, Vriska stalked back and forth beside the door to the healing clinic, her blood boiling with every step she took. When she got her hands on Brathac, she was going to make him wish he'd never laid a finger on Prince Julien.

"Your Majesty!" A group of trolls headed their way, a struggling figure in their midst. "We caught Brathac, as you ordered."

Vriska's gaze latched onto Brathac. Dried blood crusted under his nose, over his mouth, and onto his chin. A lump was forming over his nose while a bruise was spreading from his nose to surround both of his eyes.

She smirked at him and crossed her arms. Julien had gotten in quite the punch. She'd have to compliment him on it, once she had a chance to talk with him.

Brathac stopped struggling and simply glared, first at Rharreth, then at Vriska.

Rharreth halted in front of Brathac and stared down at him with a cold, deadly gaze. "Brathac of the warrior family

Cherdor, you have attacked the king's guest. Not only have you dishonored these halls, but you also caused Queen Melantha to expend magic healing Prince Julien that should have been used to heal those suffering this disease. Some of our people might die because she lacks the magic to heal them. What do you have to say in your defense?"

Brathac spat onto the floor, the glob landing a foot shy of Rharreth's boots. "I was only doing what you are too cowardly to do. We all know that the humans brought this cursed disease, and it is your fault for allying with the weak, disease-ridden humans in the first place."

"I see. Your problem is with me, not the human."

"My king!" Another group of warriors led by Brynjar dragged one more troll out of another passage. This warrior, too, bore forming bruises and bleeding cuts.

"Look who we found!" This time it was Zavni strolling into the entry hall, pinning the arm of a third captive behind the troll's back. Eyvindur held the other arm while several other warriors surrounded them.

The two trolls were forced to kneel next to Brathac. That left one of Brathac's minions still at large somewhere in Khagniorth Stronghold or in Osmana, if he'd decided to flee.

Rharreth glared down the line of them as even more servants and warriors gathered at the edges of the hall, drawn there by news of what had happened. "The three of you have dishonored yourselves and Kostaria by attacking my guest here in the halls of Khagniorth. Do any of you wish to deny these charges?"

Vriska struggled to keep her expression blank as she remained in her place a step behind and beside her king.

Brathac spat again, then glared at Rharreth. "You're the one dishonoring Kostaria. You weaken us by your treaties with the elves and the humans. And now this human is sniffing around your shield sister, and you seem to be encouraging him. I won't stand by and allow a warrior of Kostaria to tie herself to a human."

Vriska clenched her fists and resisted the urge to punch Brathac. Who was he to make such a decision for her? If she wanted to tie herself to a human, it was no business of his.

Then again, he was intent on making decisions for Rharreth as well. Just like Drurvas had been.

Rharreth crossed his arms, his back straight and posture regal. "Is this about honor or about revenge? We all saw Prince Julien defeat you in a bout, the time-honored tradition of testing strength and fighting ability. He proved his abilities according to our traditions. Unless you are saying you no longer believe in the traditions of our people?"

Brathac opened his mouth, as if he planned to protest.

But Rharreth waved a hand. "I have no wish to hear any more of your excuses. Your dishonor is clear, while the effects of the alliances have been proven. I won the Dulraith against my traitorous cousin with an elf and this human at my side. When the humans needed their borders protected, they asked for my help. When the humans and the elves needed a new bridge, they turned to us, the trolls, to build it. And now, when we are suffering from this new, deadly disease, the elves and humans are providing us with much needed aid. This is a new era for Kostaria, one where we work with humans and elves. One where honor is found in humility rather than arrogance. I am humble enough to recognize when our nation could benefit from an alliance with others."

And that was why Escarland was willing to make this

alliance with Kostaria. They had recognized that this king and his Kostaria would make worthy allies.

Vriska shifted, the memory of Julien's arms around her shivering down her back. Would Julien make a worthy ally for her? Not just as a fellow warrior to guard her back, but as an ally in life?

Brathac's lips curled. "Hear your king, people of Khagniorth. Hear how your king will weaken Kostaria."

Many of those gathered in the hall shifted, a low murmuring breaking the tense silence that had blanketed the onlookers. But no one spoke up in solidarity with Brathac. Hopefully that meant they saw him for the bitter, dishonorable troll that he was.

"You and your men will be sent to the mines of the far north to serve a sentence of hard labor, and your status of warrior is hereby stripped from you." Rharreth met Brathac's gaze. "However, this dishonor will not rest upon your family. There will be no more charging to your deaths to regain honor for your family. This dishonor rests upon your shoulders and your shoulders alone."

Even Vriska could acknowledge that this was far better than the old troll custom, where they would send packs of dishonored trolls to attack Laesornysh in the hope of regaining their honor for their family's future. Perhaps it was because of her upbringing, but an innocent family should not be dishonored for a family member's failings.

One of the trolls who had joined Brathac in the beating sagged. Perhaps he, at least, had some honor left. Even if he was still a miserable excuse for a warrior for participating in beating a man pinned to the wall with stone.

Brathac glared, meeting Rharreth's gaze. "Then I challenge you, Rharreth, to a Dulraith. I would rather die in honor than live in servitude."

Vriska had to suppress a rush of bloody satisfaction rising in her chest. Rharreth had not wanted to sentence Brathac to death when Julien hadn't actually died. But Brathac had chosen death anyway. And right now, Vriska was more than happy to oblige him.

Rharreth's jaw tightened, his dark blue eyes flashing. "Perhaps a lesson in the strength of this alliance would not be amiss. Do any of the rest of you wish to join Brathac in this Dulraith?"

The one who had sagged in relief edged back, shaking his head.

Brathac glared over his shoulder at him. "Coward!"

The troll hung his head. "If the dishonor will only rest on me, then I would rather live and perhaps see my children again someday than die in a useless attempt to regain honor for myself. I was wrong to follow you into this in the first place."

Brathac lunged against the grip of the warriors pinning him in a kneeling position. "Then live with your disgrace. You are not worthy to be a troll warrior."

The other troll straightened his shoulders as much as he could while held in place. "I will fight at your side."

"Very well." Rharreth gave a sharp nod, then glanced up to the warriors holding the accused trolls. "Take this one to his room where he can gather his things and say farewell to his family before he leaves for the north. As for these two"—Rharreth gestured almost dismissively to Brathac and the troll who had volunteered to fight with him—"take them to cells where they can be held until the Dulraith. It would be dishonorable to hold the Dulraith while our people are still suffering from this disease. Only after this disease is conquered can we attend to other matters."

Vriska couldn't help but smirk. Rharreth had agreed to Brathac's challenge of a Dulraith, but he had just asserted his authority by announcing the Dulraith would be held in Rharreth's timing, not Brathac's.

Brathac lunged again, baring his teeth and snarling as if he was a rabid wolf instead of a troll warrior. More warriors rushed to hold Brathac down as he fought, ranting unintelligibly about Rharreth and humans and how Kostaria was being dishonored.

Vriska started to turn away. She had seen enough, and it was time to check on Ma, Rikze, and Julien.

Her movement must have caught Brathac's eye. He halted, his gaze swinging to her, a sneer breaking through the dried blood coating his face. "You should be thanking me, Vriska. The way that animal was looking at you…he was getting ideas about…"

Vriska barely heard his next, crude words. She had resisted punching him before, but now he had gone too far. She could take the insults to herself. But Julien was a good, honorable man. He didn't deserve to be so slandered.

She shoved past Rharreth, past the warriors holding Brathac, and slammed a punch as hard as she could into his already broken nose, savoring the grinding of bone beneath her fist.

Brathac howled, his head snapping back.

"What makes you think I don't welcome his attentions? That human prince has more honor in a drop of his blood than you have in your whole body." Vriska cocked her fist back to throw another punch.

Someone grabbed her, yanking her arm around before

she could land the second punch. She fought, trying to free herself from the constricting, muscled arms that held her fast. How dare anyone stop her? Hadn't they heard what Brathac had said? He deserved to get a taste of his own medicine.

"Vriska. Enough." Rharreth's voice, close to her ear.

"Vriska. Steady." Zavni's voice, at her other side.

Vriska blinked, shuddered, then sagged. Both Zavni and Rharreth gripped her, holding her back.

Brathac remained slumped against the grip of those who held him, and Vriska took some satisfaction in the fact that he was still reeling from her strike. Hopefully Melantha wasn't too quick to heal whatever had been broken. It was one thing to spare magic for Julien. But it was another to heal Brathac when others needed the magic more.

Rharreth released Vriska, then spoke in a low tone so that only she and Zavni could hear. "You'll get your chance in the Dulraith. Now return to the healing ward and check on your family."

She could hear what he wasn't saying. He didn't voice the reprimand, even though she deserved it. She had lost her head. And had she really said that she didn't mind Julien's attentions in front of everyone in the hall? The servants might keep their mouths shut, but the warriors were the worst gossips.

She bowed to Rharreth, not meeting anyone's gaze. Then, she turned and strode across the entry hall toward the healing clinic. At the door, the members of the shield band nodded to her and let her past.

After the commotion in the entry hall, the packed healing clinic almost seemed like a peaceful reprieve. Serene elven healers moved between the cots, keeping the patients stable.

Three of the elven warriors remained on guard around the edges of the room while several elven warriors had joined the efforts in nursing the sick. The rest of the elf healers and warriors must be in one of the other rooms-turned-healing-clinics or perhaps they had gone to the courtyard to start healing the sick there.

Vriska wound her way through the cots to where her ma and Rikze lay. She halted and rested her hand on Ma's forehead. Ma's eyelids fluttered, and she mumbled something Vriska couldn't make out.

"I'm here, Ma. Just rest." Vriska squeezed Ma's shoulder before she turned to Rikze. Her sister remained deeply asleep, but some of the normal gray had returned to her skin instead of the pallor. "I'll be back."

With one last glance to assure herself that both of her family members were resting well, Vriska headed for the far side of the room where Melantha knelt next to a small boy.

Melantha glanced up at her before returning her focus back to her patient. She didn't ask, but the question hung in the air between them.

"We found Brathac and his cronies." Vriska gestured at the door behind her, then realized that her knuckles were bloody and bruised from hitting Brathac.

"I see." Melantha's gaze flicked to Vriska's knuckles, a frown wrinkling her brow. She didn't offer to heal Vriska, as she normally would have. Healing magic was too precious to waste on something so superficial as bruised knuckles.

Vriska rubbed at her knuckles. "Where is Julien? How is he recovering?"

She would let Rharreth explain about the Dulraith and why Vriska had punched Brathac. Right now, Vriska was too wrung out to explain anything else.

Melantha waved toward the examination room. "I had a cot brought in where he could rest more comfortably until he can be moved to his room. He was awake when I checked a moment ago."

Vriska might not be great at picking up subtext, but even she could tell that Melantha was telling her to head on back there.

Strangely, Vriska wanted to see him, though she didn't want to examine her reasons for wanting to do so too closely.

"I guess I'll go guard him." Vriska shifted, then marched the short distance to the closed door of the exam room. With a deep breath, she knocked on the door. "Prince Julien?"

"Come in." His voice sounded strong, at least.

Vriska pushed the door open and shoved into the room, leaving the door cracked open behind her.

Julien lay on the cot crammed into the room, the exam table shoved to the side to make room. Blankets were pulled over his bare chest. His bare shoulders were well muscled, though bruises showed along his collarbone and around each of his wrists. Both of his eyes were blackened with dark bruises that spread down onto his cheeks. A few cuts lacerated his face and dried blood still flecked his beard, though it appeared that Melantha had attempted to clean him up as best she could.

As badly as he had been beaten, he still gave Vriska a lopsided smile. "Have you come to tend me, my lady?"

Vriska snorted and perched on the exam table, the only place to sit in the room besides Julien's cot. "If you wanted someone to tenderly mother you, then you'd better turn right around and hook up with one of those kindly human women. I'm not the gentle, tending type."

"You could have fooled me in the last few days." Julien's smile remained strong, though it held a somber tilt.

They had all spent a great deal of time tending to the sick in the past days. Or was it weeks at this point? The time was blurring together.

Vriska didn't want to talk about the disease. Or her mothering skills.

"We caught Brathac." Vriska rubbed her aching knuckles again, her fingers coming away bloody from split skin. "I punched him. I think I shattered whatever was left of his nose."

"Good." Julien weakly reached up and touched his own nose. "I doubt his face will ever look the same again."

He probably meant for her to laugh, but Vriska leaned her elbows on her knees, staring at her hands. Julien was a good man. An honorable man. And she couldn't let him keep thinking that she had the same honor.

"I'm just like Brathac, you know." Vriska stared at her hands rather than look at him.

"Vriska?" Julien reached out and clasped one of her hands. As if he thought he had to give her comfort right now.

Well, he'd pull away soon enough.

She thought about tugging her hand free. But, somehow, she couldn't find the strength right then. Besides, she'd already cried all over him. Holding his hand was nothing at this point. "I never beat anyone up like Brathac did. But I harassed Queen Melantha when she first married Rharreth. I listened to Drurvas's prejudicial talk—agreed with it, even. I've been trying to regain my honor ever since, but I'm not sure I ever can."

"Is that why you agreed to think about this marriage of

alliance? To regain your honor?" His voice was soft, and he squeezed her fingers.

"Yes. No. At first." Vriska stared down at their clasped hands. Why hadn't he pulled back yet? She had confessed her failings to him. He now knew how she had dishonored herself. "You deserve someone with honor."

Vriska finally got the courage to yank her fingers free of his grip. It was too hard pretending she was worthy of him while confessing how dishonorable she truly was.

He drew his hand back and rested it on the blanket. For the first time, his gaze swung away from her, as if she had done more than just pull her fingers free. As if he had been reaching out to her, and she'd pulled away.

Julien stared up at the stone ceiling arching above them. "You have recognized your dishonor and changed. You have grown from where you were."

Had she? Or was she still the same person who had hurt Queen Melantha and agreed with Drurvas even briefly? She shook her head. "I'm not so sure."

"I am." Julien's smile returned, though he didn't reach for her hand again. "You punched Brathac in the face over what he did to a human. You have tirelessly tended the sick even though nursing isn't something that's in your nature. And even though many have entertained the rumor that this disease came from humans, you haven't listened to them or treated me any differently. Those are not the thoughts and actions of someone who still harbors the prejudices she once did."

Vriska glanced away, flexing her fingers. She didn't like all this self-examination. Punching people in the face was much easier, and far more satisfying.

But speaking of Brathac, that reminded her…

"Brathac implied that we were…that we are…and I didn't exactly deny it, and…" Vriska growled and fisted her hands against her thighs. "It will be all over Osmana by nightfall that we're courting."

Julien flicked a glance at her before he once again focused on the ceiling. "And how do you feel about that? The rumors were already there, when we were seen in Osmana together when we visited your family. The disease took attention away from us for a while, but this isn't the first time we've been the topic of the gossips."

Vriska stared at her fists. More disgusting soul-searching. She was tired of all this angst over Julien. It was time she just made a decision one way or the other.

Yet hadn't she already made her decision? She hadn't denied it when Brathac accused her of courting a human. If anything, she had all but confirmed it.

And if she hadn't wanted to court Julien, then there would be no angst about it. She would have just ended things, no matter her duty to her kingdom. Rharreth wasn't forcing her into this. There were other options.

But she didn't want him to choose another option. It made her go all hot and punchy just thinking about it.

How did she go about telling him?

She huffed out a breath. "It isn't as bad as I thought it would be. I'm getting used to you." She punched his shoulder.

He groaned and gripped his shoulder.

Oops. She probably should have held his hand or something romantic like that. Not punch him like she would one of her shield brothers. Apparently she had a lot to learn about this romance stuff. She grimaced. "Sorry."

He chuckled and released his grip on his shoulder. "I'll be fine. As you can see, I can take a punch."

Vriska was saved from having to answer by a knock on the open door. When she looked up, she spotted Zavni leaning inside.

He smirked. "Sorry to interrupt your little romantic chat, but I thought you'd want to know that we caught the last one. He was trying to flee but found out that his views on humans and the alliance aren't shared by the majority of Kostaria's citizens. Especially not the commoners who survived this last winter on Escarland's grain and produce."

Julien nodded, then yawned, his eyelids drooping. "The way to a person's heart is through their stomach. That is just as true for a troll as it is for a human."

Vriska hopped to her feet. "Yes. Now I should let you rest. You haven't finished healing."

Julien's mouth tipped in a smile, though he let his eyes fall all the way closed. "You're just looking for an excuse to leave."

Well, yes. But it was uncomfortable that he could read her so well even after such a short amount of time.

She spun on her heels, stomping toward the door. "Just rest."

If only she could go back to just not thinking as she punched her kingdom's enemies. Life was much simpler when she believed she was going to die in the war.

CHAPTER SIXTEEN

Julien suppressed a groan as he pushed himself first to a sitting position, then swung his feet off the bed. For a moment, he leaned his elbows on his knees, waiting for his head to stop swirling.

He'd given himself three days to rest after his injuries. Well, that and Melantha had banned him from helping and gave strict orders that he was to rest.

But three days were all he would allow. There was far too much to do.

The second group of healers would arrive on the train shortly. Averett had also sent some of the scientists who wished to study the disease since there was only so much they could do while theorizing from afar. They needed to conduct tests in person to send information back to both Tarenhiel and Escarland.

Julien had to be there in the courtyard to welcome them. Not that Rharreth had required it. But Julien refused to hide in his room any longer. His cracked ribs had healed, thanks to Melantha's magic, as had the other broken bones in his face and arms.

The bruises remained, splashed deep purple and green across his face and chest. At least he was here in Kostaria where he likely wouldn't be sneered at for appearing in public with such bruises on his face.

With a steadying breath, Julien pushed to his feet. He had to grit his teeth through changing into his clean clothes and buckling on his sword. Everything ached from the bruises, and every muscle strained tight. Hopefully getting up and walking would loosen the stiffness.

Julien opened his door and stepped into the passageway.

Zavni stood next to the door, and he swept a glance over Julien. Thankfully, he didn't ask why Julien was up and about. Zavni was a troll warrior. He understood why Julien would need to be back on his feet as soon as possible.

Instead, Zavni shook his head and fell into step with Julien as he headed down the passage. "You are a sight. You're going to give those new elf healers a fright."

"It's the human scientists who will worry the most. I'm their prince, after all." Julien shrugged, the movement twinging pain through his shoulders and down his back. "Is Vriska with her family?"

Zavni nodded, then veered down a side passageway. "Yes. They've been moved to a room down this way where they can rest away from the bustle of the main healing clinic."

Julien nodded and followed Zavni's lead down the side corridor. Zavni had correctly guessed that he would want to check on Vriska's mother and sister before heading for the courtyard.

They reached another, larger passage, and this one

bustled with quiet activity. An elf guard followed one of the healers while trolls walked between the rooms, likely checking on patients who were recovering. From what they had observed, the main disease only lasted two or three days. If the afflicted person survived past that, they usually recovered, though they were often weak for a while.

Zavni halted and knocked on one of the doors. At the call from within, he opened the door and stepped aside for Julien.

Julien stepped inside, closing the door behind him.

Two beds filled the small room while a few fur-covered chairs filled the remaining space.

Vriska glanced at him from her seat beside the far bed. On the bed, Vriska's mother lay propped on pillows. But she was awake and alert, and that was a vast improvement from where she had been several days ago when Julien had last seen her.

Rikze rolled off the closer bed, slamming a book closed and tossing it onto the bed behind her. "Prince Julien! You look awful."

"And you look much better than the last time I saw you." He forced himself to give her a gallant bow, as if greeting a lady.

Rikze's smile broke across her face, creasing her still too-hollow cheeks. Yet her skin held a warmer tone than it had, and her eyes were bright instead of dulled with pain. "Queen Melantha and the other elf healers fixed me and Ma all up."

Vriska's mother gave a weak smile, her hand lifting before dropping back to the blanket.

"I'm glad you're feeling better." Julien smiled at Rikze,

then gestured at his own face. "Queen Melantha fixed me up too."

Vriska pushed to her feet. She awkwardly patted her mother's shoulder. "I'll be back later to check on you. More elf healers are arriving today."

"Good. I'll be resting here." Her mother smiled, her eyelids drooping as she settled deeper into the pillows.

"I'll be here too." Rikze flopped back onto the bed and reached for the book. "I'm already bored with resting."

"I'll come back and keep you company this afternoon." Julien would probably need a rest by then anyway, so he might as well sit here.

"I'd like that. I'll be finished with this book by then." Rikze squirmed deeper into the blankets and furs on her bed.

Perhaps Julien and Vriska would have to track down another book for her by the afternoon. If there was another book. Julien hadn't seen a library or an excess of reading material lying about. The trolls didn't seem to revere learning and reading the way humans and elves did.

Vriska led the way from the room, and Julien followed her, shutting the door behind them. As he, Vriska, and Zavni started for the exit to the courtyard, he asked, "How are they doing?"

"Rikze is healing quickly, and Melantha doesn't think she'll have any long-term effects. But my ma…" Vriska shook her head, clenching her fists. "Her body has been permanently weakened. She should recover, but she will always be weaker than she was. The winters are going to be especially hard for her."

"I'm sorry." He wasn't sure what else to say. He sneaked a glance at Vriska next to him. "Your family will always be welcome in Escarland. We still have cold winters, but nothing like you do in Kostaria. I know moving isn't likely to be something that your family would consider, but I thought I'd make the offer anyway."

He snapped his mouth shut. Perhaps he shouldn't have said anything at all. This probably wasn't the time for solutions, just for comfort.

But Vriska heaved a sigh, her shoulders rising and falling. "I know. My da has written about the opportunities that have already been offered to him and the other workers after they finish building the bridge. I don't know if he and Ma will consider moving, but if it is the best thing for Ma..." Another sigh. Another shrug. "I don't know what they will do."

He could hear what she wasn't saying. She didn't know what she would decide either. He had hoped they had turned a corner in that charged moment when he'd comforted her, and then again when she held his hand after his beating.

The three of them exited a side door into the courtyard. Even with the ten elf healers, the courtyard remained packed with trolls waiting for healing. Julien shuddered to think of how many were still dying.

Hopefully the additional elf healers would help. If the Escarlish scientists and elf healers could figure out what this disease was and how to treat it, then even more trolls could be saved.

Julien, Vriska, and Zavni joined Rharreth and Melantha in front of the main doors. Even though it had been only a few days since Julien had last stood there with them, they appeared even more worn. Rharreth appeared years older, with deep lines etched into his face, while Melantha was downright gaunt, her skin translucently pale and her hair straggling.

Something needed to change, otherwise both Rharreth and Melantha would collapse from the strain and exhaustion.

Once again, the shouting of the crowd announced the approach of the group before the gates opened to admit them into Khagniorth Stronghold. The troll warriors clustered around the elf healers and human scientists so thickly that the elves and humans were barely visible. Elf warriors with their bows and swords and human soldiers carrying muskets marched among the troll warriors, protecting their charges.

Rharreth went about the same rigmarole as before, welcoming the elf healers and letting them know they would be under Melantha's command.

Julien only partially paid attention. He was too tired and sore to do more than stand there and play the role of the quiet, background prince that he usually was.

As the elves dispersed, the group of humans stepped forward. The middle-aged man with dark hair bowed first to Julien, then to Rharreth. "Your Highness, King Rharreth, my team and I look forward to working with your people and the elf healers to find a cure for this disease plaguing your kingdom. Is there a room where we can set up our equipment?"

"Yes, we have set aside a room for your use next to the healing clinic for the convenience of you and the healers involved." Rharreth gestured from the human scientists to Zavni. "My shield brother Zavni will show you to the room. Do you require any assistance in setting up?"

"Thank you, but we prefer to set up our equipment

ourselves. But your people's help in toting the crates has been much appreciated." A smile creased the scientist's face as he glanced over his shoulder at the eight especially burly trolls who carried four large wooden crates between them. The scientist's smile faded as his gaze swept around the courtyard and took in the rows of groaning, miserably sick trolls. "We would like to get started as soon as possible."

"Right this way." Zavni motioned to the scientists, turned, and strode toward the doors.

Julien stepped out of the way, making more room for the pack of scientists and the crate-carrying trolls to get by him. As the soldiers followed and passed by him, each of them paused long enough to give him a salute.

Julien saluted them in return, a pang shooting through him that wasn't only caused by the pain of his sore muscles and bruises. These men were a part of the castle guard, Julien's previous command. He had given that up to come here, and he likely would never return to that old position once he married Vriska and took up a more political role.

Once the last of the soldiers disappeared inside Khagniorth, Julien faced the courtyard again, only to find that four people still remained in the center of the troll warriors. Two human men stood with the bearing of soldiers, yet with an extra wariness and sharpness that reminded Julien of the way Edmund always calculated every detail of his surroundings. They didn't carry weapons but seemed no less dangerous.

The two remaining figures wore cloaks, obscuring their identities and race. One was smaller and something about the figure seemed feminine. As for the other...Julien crossed his arms with a sigh. If his guess was correct, things were about to get interesting.

Rharreth glared at the two cloaked figures, his tone turning frosty. "And who are you? Reveal yourselves."

Edmund, Julien's brother, tossed back his hood and stepped forward, that easy grin on his face disguising any unease he might feel at this situation. "I apologize for the disrespect of concealing my identity, King Rharreth, but I wasn't sure you'd allow me entry otherwise."

Julien resisted the urge to snort. Mostly because it would hurt his nose rather than any compunction against scoffing openly at his brother's words. Sure, Rharreth's lack of welcome was part of the reason. But the other part was that Edmund rather liked his dramatic entrances and big reveals. For a former spy, he liked showmanship a little too much sometimes.

Rharreth crossed his arms, his face hardening further. "You are correct. I know what you are, and I thought I made it clear that you are not welcome in Kostaria."

"I understand that, but I'm not here in my former role. I have turned over a new leaf, as it were." Edmund's grin grew as he held out a hand to the second figure.

Jalissa, as she revealed once she delicately lifted her hood, rolled her eyes and took Edmund's hand.

Melantha swayed forward, as if all she wanted to do was run to her sister to give her a hug but couldn't while Rharreth and Edmund were in a diplomatically tense standoff.

Edmund held Rharreth's gaze, something in his grin slipping a bit to show the hard calculation beneath. "Right now, I'm here as an official ambassador from Escarland, nothing more. You have my word on that, and my brother Averett's as well."

Rharreth jabbed a finger in Julien's direction. "Escarland doesn't need a second ambassador. I already have him."

Julien shifted, wishing he'd paid more attention to his classes on diplomacy. Was he supposed to take Rharreth's side to keep him happy? Or take Edmund's side as his brother and fellow countryman?

"Well, yes. But Averett wishes to convey the level of his support by sending both of us." Edmund gave a nonchalant shrug and held up his and Jalissa's clasped hands. "Weylind also wanted to send an ambassador to show his full support, and Jalissa and I are a package deal."

Rharreth's scowl deepened, as if he wanted to argue but couldn't. Edmund might have been caught spying on Kostaria a while back, but he was still an Escarlish prince. Rharreth couldn't afford to cause an incident by kicking him out of the kingdom.

Jalissa gave a soft huff that conveyed another eyeroll as she glanced from Edmund to Rharreth. "Look, we are here to help. Edmund has a theory about this disease that he wishes to investigate, and I am here to help him with that investigation. These two men"—she gestured to the two men standing behind her and Edmund—"are former colleagues of Edmund's and they are also here to assist him."

"And what is this theory?" Rharreth's tone dropped two more icy degrees as he took in the fact that there were actually three Escarlish spies standing before him.

"I'd prefer not to say just yet." Edmund glanced around at the courtyard packed with people, including the squads of troll warriors still standing there listening impassively to this entire conversation. The grin entirely dropped from Edmund's face, leaving behind a deadly cold expression in its place. "Especially not in public. But trust me when I say I desperately hope I'm wrong."

"Trust you? That's the problem. I don't trust you." Rharreth's jaw worked. "Do you really expect me to allow the four of you to wander about my stronghold conducting a mysterious investigation?"

Julien struggled to remain standing where he was. This was something Rharreth and Edmund needed to have out between them, and it was better they got this tension out of the way as quickly as possible, no matter the awkwardness for the rest of them listening.

Melantha and Jalissa shared a glance, and Julien caught the twitch of a smile that crossed Melantha's careworn features before she stuffed it away again. If he were to guess, the sisters had shared some silent communication about the ridiculousness of male posturing, or something like that.

When Julien glanced at Vriska on his other side, she caught his gaze and gave a tiny shrug. As if she, too, wasn't sure what her role was besides to be the silent bystander at her king's back. At least Julien wasn't the only one feeling out of place in this duel of words.

"Of course not." Edmund's smile didn't return as he gestured from Rharreth to Julien and Vriska. "I will be happy to report my theory to you in the privacy of your study, and I welcome you, my brother Julien, and any of your shield band to tag along as I investigate."

"Very well." Rharreth gave a sharp nod. "Come along, then. I'd like to hear this theory of yours. Julien, Vriska, I would like you to come as well."

Rharreth turned and marched back into the stronghold. Melantha waited for a moment, glancing over her shoulder at Jalissa.

Jalissa hurried to catch up, and the sisters exchanged a brief, elven hug before they entered the stronghold together, talking in low tones. But Jalissa was smiling, and

Melantha gestured about her as if excited to show her sister her new home for the first time, despite the dire circumstances.

Edmund joined Julien and swept a glance over him, a hint of his grin returning. "I thought I told you not to let the trolls beat you up."

Julien shrugged, winced, and strode through the stronghold's doors. "It was unavoidable. I didn't exactly give as good as I got, but they fought dirty. I at least got in enough hits to mark them so Rharreth and his shield band could round them up for punishment."

"I see." Edmund nodded, the grin fading into a frown as he took in Julien's appearance again.

Julien turned away, keeping his focus on Jalissa and Melantha ahead of him rather than his brother. Edmund probably saw all the things Julien didn't want to tell him. Like the fact that Julien had been too hurt to join Rharreth and the shield band in rounding up his attackers.

"How have things been, otherwise?" Edmund's gaze was sharp enough that Julien could feel it even though he didn't glance at his brother.

Instead, he glanced over his shoulder. Vriska trailed behind them, looking everywhere but at their backs as she pretended she wasn't listening to their conversation. She had fallen back into guard mode, silently following with a hand on her sword's hilt.

Behind her, the two Escarlish spy-soldiers walked in silence with Brynjar and Eyvindur keeping watch over them in the rear.

"I've been well." Julien halted and half-turned to Vriska. If only he could reach a hand to her, but he didn't think she'd take it, especially not with Edmund there. "Vriska, I don't know if you've officially met my brother. Edmund, this is Vriska."

Vriska shot him a glare before she strode to his side. She held her chin high, her back straight, a proud warrior.

Edmund grinned and held out a hand to her. "Nice to meet you. Julien has told me a lot about you in his letters."

Julien grimaced. He didn't think he'd said that much. He wasn't much for letter writing, after all. But Edmund was the type to successfully read between the lines.

Vriska eyed Edmund's hand for a moment before she clasped his forearm in a warrior's clasp rather than the handshake Edmund had likely been expecting. Vriska's hand was large enough to nearly circle Edmund's forearm while Edmund's fingers looked almost small against Vriska's muscled arm. Vriska gave a nod before she released Edmund. "Prince Edmund."

Edmund shot a grin in Julien's direction. Julien just grinned back. Oh, yes. His girlfriend could totally beat up his brothers, except, maybe, Farrendel.

Girlfriend. Was Vriska that? Julien didn't let himself think of Vriska that way often, not yet.

But he wanted it to be true. The more time he spent with her, the more he couldn't picture anyone else at his side.

She wasn't anything like the quiet Escarlish woman he'd envisioned marrying. And he likely would have been happy if he'd married someone like that, if his life had turned out differently.

But Vriska was a fellow warrior. She understood how awkward he found politics and how armies and weapons were comfortable. Of course she understood, since she was the same way. Neither of them knew what their changing futures held, yet Julien hoped they could find out together.

Both Vriska and Edmund were looking at him, as if waiting for him to make the next move.

Julien cleared his throat and waved toward the hall ahead of him. "Looks like we've fallen behind."

"I'm the man of the hour. They aren't going to start without me." Edmund's grin remained in place as he set out through the entry hall with the confidence of someone who knew exactly where he was headed.

Perhaps he did. Julien didn't know exactly where Edmund had lurked during the three months he'd spied on Kostaria.

Just as an experiment, Julien dropped back half a step, letting Edmund take the lead instead of him. At the far end of the entry hall, Edmund paused before the correct corridor. He glanced over his shoulder, a knowing glint to his gaze, as he waited until Julien waved in that direction.

Not that Edmund needed the confirmation. He was just putting on a show to make it look like he didn't know his way around as well as he did. He'd done the same thing in Ellonahshinel, going so far as to pretend to be nervous crossing the smaller branches, when he and Julien had gone there to plan the war with Kostaria to rescue Farrendel. Essie hadn't seemed to notice. Understandable, considering how worried she'd been over Farrendel. But Julien had, though he'd known better than to do more than share a look with Edmund.

As he did now before they set off once again. Apparently Edmund *had* explored Khagniorth Stronghold at one point or another.

No wonder Rharreth wasn't thrilled with having Edmund back in his kingdom.

After climbing a set of stairs and going down another

short stretch of corridor, they reached Rharreth's study. The door stood open, and the others were just settling into seats.

Brynjar, Eyvindur, and the two Escarlish men remained outside while Edmund, Julien, and Vriska filed inside.

Edmund took the seat next to Jalissa across the desk from where Rharreth and Melantha sat. Edmund and Jalissa were a sharp, well-rested and healthy-looking contrast to the worn and exhausted Rharreth and Melantha.

Vriska shut the door and stood with her back to it, providing another layer of security.

As there were no more chairs available, Julien took a position along the wall next to her, content to observe Edmund's reveal rather than participate.

After a glance at the door, as if to ensure they were now alone and guarded, Rharreth focused on Edmund, the lamp casting shadows in the deep, weary grooves in Rharreth's face. "Well?"

Edmund drew in a deep breath, all traces of the light-hearted grin and easy manner disappearing in a blink. "I've read the reports of the disease plaguing Kostaria, and I think it might not be a disease at all, but a poison."

CHAPTER SEVENTEEN

Julien stared at the back of his brother's head. A poison? How could anyone poison this many people across a kingdom? It didn't make sense.

"Poison." Rharreth stared at Edmund, as if it was a struggle to turn his mind in that direction after so long of assuming this was a disease.

"Oh." Melantha sucked in a breath, slumping against the back of her chair. "That would explain so much."

Rharreth glanced at her. "It would?"

"Yes." Melantha nodded, her eyes brightening for the first time in days. "I have been unable to find a bacteria or a virus causing the disease, but if it is caused by a plant-based toxin, then my healing magic would struggle to detect it. I have only been able to detect and heal the results of the toxin. It would also explain why patients do not stay healed, since the healers and I have only been healing the effects while leaving the toxin to continue its work as it moves through the body."

"Could you find the toxin, now that you know that it

might be the cause?" Rharreth's shoulders straightened, an urgency in his tone as if he was starting to believe Edmund's theory.

Julien's stomach sank, and he clenched his fists at his side

"Maybe. There is a fine, complicated line between healing magic and plant magic when it comes to how toxins and nutrients from food interact with the body. Only the most advanced healers among us can use their magic on such a microscopic level." Melantha glanced at Jalissa across the desk. "Perhaps if Jalissa and I used our powers together?"

Jalissa gave a tiny tilt of her shoulders. "Maybe, though I do not have the strength of magic to do more than detect the toxin. I am not sure I could aid you in removing the toxin from the entire body, if that is what you are asking."

"Detecting the toxin would be a good start. If this is a poison." Rharreth turned back to Edmund. "What poison do you think it is?"

"There are several that exhibit similar symptoms, but my guess is ricin. It is found naturally in castor beans." Edmund clenched his fists against the arms of his chair. "We don't grow castor beans in Escarland. At least, not legally. I can't speak for those who might be illegally growing a plant or two. My grandfather banned castor beans when they were first brought from across the ocean. But the bean became popular in what was then Nevaria and the southern part of Mongalia."

"Mongavaria." Julien hadn't meant to growl the new name of the expanded kingdom out loud.

Next to him, Vriska flexed her fists, as if she wanted to march over to Mongavaria and personally punch its king.

"Exactly." Edmund didn't look at Julien, but he nodded

as if Julien's outburst had been planned. "Escarland's Intelligence Office suspects that the current Mongavarian king used poison—likely ricin—to kill off the Nevarian royal family and give himself an excuse to annex the kingdom, though we can't prove it."

Rharreth frowned, his gaze distant as he stared at the wall. "Nor can you prove Mongavaria is behind this, though I'll admit they would have motive to weaken Kostaria and thus weaken the entire alliance. But how could they possibly poison so many of my people all at once?"

"I suspect the food." Edmund grimaced. "In the past year, you've imported more food than ever from foreign sources. I don't know if they are smuggling the tainted food in the Escarlish shipments or if they are being dropped off at the coast, but that would be the easiest way to widely distribute the poison."

Rharreth pinched the bridge of his nose, squeezing his eyes shut. "The disease seemed to originate at the coast."

"But how do we know this theory is correct?" Vriska stepped forward, her fists still clenched, her eyes flashing.

Of course this news would hurt. It was bad enough, coming to terms with the fact that both her mother and sister had fallen ill with a deadly disease that was sweeping the kingdom. But it was another thing altogether to think that they had been deliberately poisoned.

Julien wished he could reach for her to comfort her again, but she wouldn't want that at the moment. Right now, she needed to punch the wall to vent her anger.

Poison. Julien saw again the mass graves in the town of Carth. The young children who had succumbed despite the healers' efforts. Vriska holding Rikze as her little sister cried in pain.

If Mongavaria had done this, then it was beyond a mere act of war. It was...Julien couldn't even think of what to call something of this disgusting level of dishonor and horror.

"How do you know he's telling the truth?" Vriska took another step forward, her eyes blazing, her fists clenched white-knuckle tight. "This whole thing is too convoluted to be true!"

Julien sighed and resisted the urge to go to her. Of course Vriska wouldn't want to believe it. It was too terrible.

Edmund half-turned in his chair to face Vriska, unflinching beneath the blaze of her anger. "You wouldn't recognize it as a poison, since elves and trolls rarely use poison, as it is considered dishonorable to kill in such a manner. But poison isn't uncommon among humans, especially in what was once Mongalia. I've been trained to recognize the signs of a number of poisons, and the two men who came with us are experts in various poisons. Not that Escarland has employed such methods since before my grandfather's reign, but it pays to have the knowledge to fight those who do."

Vriska crossed her arms, still glaring.

"Vriska." Rharreth's sharp tone snapped through the room. "I need to consider all options, including this one."

After a moment, Vriska deflated, and she bowed her head to Rharreth. "Yes, my king."

When she stepped back to her former place in front of the door, Julien reached out and put a hand on her shoulder. She stiffened, but she didn't shake his hand off. After a moment, she relaxed and gave him a nod.

"We feel the same way. I am going to investigate the possibility that this is poison, but the Escarlish scientists are going to research it as if it is a disease." Edmund straightened in his seat to face Rharreth once again. "While one of the scientists is an expert in infectious diseases, the rest are more flexible in their specialties. If this turns out to be a poison, they will switch to researching the poison."

"Does ricin have an antidote?" Melantha leaned forward, some of the weariness dropping away.

"No." Edmund didn't sugarcoat it, even though Melantha's shoulders fell at the word, the hope in her eyes dying. "At least, not one that we humans have discovered. But we've never had access to elven magic before. Perhaps there is an antidote that can be created with a combination of healing and plant magic, if the poison and its specific mechanism can be pinpointed."

"Better yet, we can stop the poison at its source so that my people aren't getting poisoned in the first place." Rharreth pounded a fist into a palm, as if prepared to deal a swift death to whoever had been killing so many of his people. "If it is a poison."

"We should know soon enough." Edmund gestured to Jalissa at his side. She had remained serenely silent throughout the discussion, the picture of a graceful elven princess.

Jalissa nodded, a hint of something secretive playing around the corners of her mouth. "I was already training to recognize various poisons with my magic in preparation for the diplomatic trip to Mongavaria. I can examine your food and tell you in moments if it is tainted or not."

She said it so matter-of-factly, as if it was totally normal to practice finding poisons with her plant magic. The fact that she took such things in stride just proved how perfect she was for Edmund.

"Then let us go examine the food stores." Melantha pushed to her feet, her movements brisk.

Rharreth was only a second behind her, as if he, too, was desperate to know if this was the answer to why so many of his people had died, even if it wasn't a good answer.

Julien waited by the door as the rest of them filed past him. Edmund paused to let Jalissa go first, but before Edmund could follow, Julien gripped his arm, lowering his voice so the others couldn't hear. "Are you still planning on going to Mongavaria? Even if we discover that they've been purposely poisoning the trolls?"

"Yes." Edmund sighed, serious lines replacing his normal, easy grin. "We have to go now more than ever. We need to know if this was sanctioned by the Mongavarian king or if rogue elements within Mongavaria took it upon themselves to perpetrate this. And we need to know if he plans to send poison to Tarenhiel or Escarland next."

"He would have a harder time poisoning us." Julien stepped through the door, trailing behind Jalissa as the group trekked toward the store rooms. "Neither we nor the elves import food from outside our borders the way Kostaria does."

"No, but that doesn't mean Mongavaria couldn't find a way." Edmund frowned, his expression going pained. "Believe me, I don't like it any more than you do. Jalissa and I have had some rousing fights over her going along, but she's stubborn."

Jalissa glanced over her shoulder, her mouth twitching with a hint of a smile that said she'd heard that last comment. She dropped back and took Edmund's hand. "I am also right. You need my magic to get both of us in and out of Mongavaria safely."

"Yes, I do." Edmund's smile returned, though this one was softer, more genuine, than the grin he normally wore. His gaze warmed to something adoring and mushy. "We make a good team. How did I get along without you on my missions before?"

"I do not know." Jalissa's gaze was a touch coy in return as she and Edmund shared a look that held far more meaning than Julien understood—or wanted to understand.

Another sibling going all mushy. Julien had rather enjoyed escaping all that for a while.

He quickened his pace to leave the two lovebirds behind, catching up with Vriska instead.

Vriska glanced at him before she continued stalking down the corridor with her eyes focused ahead, her hands clenched at her sides.

"Are you all right?" Julien wasn't sure what else to do or say.

"No, I'm not." Vriska ground the words between clenched teeth. "If Mongavaria poisoned my ma and my sister, I...I don't know what I'll do."

His stomach sank even further. Would Rharreth declare war over this? He would be in his rights to do so, if it could be proved that Mongavaria was knowingly behind this. It was an attack on Kostaria.

But if Kostaria went to war with Mongavaria, Tarenhiel and Escarland would be dragged into it as well because of the alliance. Even more people would die. For what? Vengeance? Could it be called justice, if that justice killed more innocent lives?

If Rharreth didn't go to war, he would look weak in the eyes of his people. And Mongavaria would be free to continue to plot such strikes against all three kingdoms of the alliance.

Perhaps Edmund was right. The diplomatic swap needed to go through. It was their last hope to negotiate and avoid war.

VRISKA LEANED against the wall in the cavernous space deep inside Khagniorth Stronghold that served as its food storehouse. Barrels upon barrels of grain, dried produce, and salted meat filled the space. More dried vegetables and smoked meat hung from rafters. Layers of magic embedded in the stone protected the room from pests that would otherwise have infested the room.

Julien had joined her, offering the same silent support that he had on the walk here. A part of her wanted to reach for him, as she had after finding out her mother and sister were sick. But the rest of her was too proud to admit she needed support, especially with so many others around.

The elf princess Jalissa—Melantha's sister—went from barrel to barrel, opening each and touching the contents with green-laced fingers. The green was a deeper color than the green of Melantha's magic.

Would this elf discover poison? Heat flooded through Vriska's chest and boiled inside her head. If Julien's brother was correct, then an enemy had been attacking their kingdom for weeks, and they hadn't even known it. Worse, the enemy had been striking at the non-warriors. The innocent men, women, and children who should have been protected from the horrors of war.

As much as Vriska didn't like the elf warrior Laesornysh,

he at least had the decency to only use his magic on the troll warriors. He'd never attacked an innocent village across the border—something even those among her own people had done when they raided into Tarenhiel. Laesornysh had honor, elf though he was. These Mongavarians did not.

The tension stretched as Jalissa continued to make her way around the large room. Even though she wore brown trousers, a green shirt, and sturdy boots, she moved with an elegance that Vriska would never be able to match.

Was elegance and grace something that Julien would expect in his bride? Sure, Jalissa had an extra measure, being an elf. But how would Vriska compare with the human women who would no doubt be waiting for Julien to return to his kingdom so they could dig their claws into him?

And why did the thought of other women add to the boil in her head? Surely Vriska wasn't jealous or entertaining thoughts of punching those imagined Escarlish women.

Finally, Jalissa inspected the final barrel. After a moment, she withdrew her hand and shook her head. "I do not sense any poison here."

Melantha sighed, sagging against Rharreth in a renewed weariness. "It was a theory, I suppose. Even if I want an answer, poison would be a terrible one."

Edmund shared a look with Jalissa before he faced Rharreth and Melantha. "Just because there's no poison here doesn't mean that this disease hasn't been caused by poison. It only means that the official trade coming from Escarland remains untainted."

"A good thing for diplomatic relations between our kingdoms," Julien muttered under his breath, glancing at Vriska. "It shows how far our kingdoms have come that Rharreth hasn't made the accusation that Escarland was behind this."

It hadn't occurred to her either to blame Escarland. What did that say about her that she had so subconsciously dismissed that possibility? Had she become so used to having Julien around that she associated his honor with the rest of his kingdom?

Rharreth and Melantha shared a look. Rharreth's mouth took on a grim line. "It is odd that few of my warriors have come down with the disease, and almost no one here at Khagniorth Stronghold has become ill, despite our close contact with so many of the afflicted. The disease seems to strike the poor harder than the warrior families."

Prince Edmund nodded, as if Rharreth's words proved his poison theory. "Something that is common in Escarlish cities, where our waste removal leaves a great deal of room for improvement, but it is strange for Kostaria. But if the tainted food is being smuggled in at lower prices than the official trade from Escarland..."

"The poor are the ones who will take advantage of the cheaper food, never knowing it is poisoned." Rharreth swiped a hand over his face.

Vriska sagged against the wall, her blood roaring in her ears. Of course. Her mother would buy cheaper food, if there were some available. And she would congratulate herself on getting a good deal.

She only partially heard Rharreth, Melantha, and Edmund as they discussed the Escarlish-Kostarian trade and how the smuggled food might be dispersed once it reached Kostaria.

It didn't matter how it happened. At least not right then. Vriska squeezed her eyes shut, resisting the urge to pound the wall behind her. With all the magic lacing it, she probably would break her fingers despite her magic.

"Do you know where I could examine food that we know was eaten by someone who is sick?" Princess Jalissa's voice broke through the clamor in Vriska's head.

"I do." Vriska snapped her eyes open and pushed away from the wall. Everyone in the room turned to look at her, and she straightened her shoulders to face them. "My mother and sister became sick only a few days ago. Their home should still be untouched."

"Are they all right?" Princess Jalissa's deep brown eyes held a compassion that only made Vriska wanted to punch something.

"They survived." Vriska couldn't help the short, clipped tone to her voice. Only time would tell if her family would be all right. "Now do you want to take a look at their food or not?"

Rharreth gestured to her. "Lead the way, Vriska."

Julien reached for her as she spun on her heel, but she shook off his hand. She didn't want his attempt to comfort her right now.

Blindly, she stalked through the passages of Khagniorth, letting her feet carry her by memory rather than thought. The walk through the streets of Osmana passed in a blur until she blinked and found herself facing the door of her childhood home.

With a deep breath, she pushed the door open and stepped inside.

The kitchen remained as neat and clean as her mother always kept it. All the dishes from her ma and sister's last meal here were washed and put away. Everything looked like her mother would bustle into the room at any moment, pulling out food and telling Vriska to sit and eat.

Except that Ma lay in a bed at Khagniorth Stronghold, still too weak to stay awake for long stretches at a time.

Everyone else strode into the room, pressing against the walls to fit inside the tiny room.

Vriska stood to the side, crossing her arms and staring numbly as Jalissa went through the cupboards until she found the one storing food.

Jalissa sent her green magic through the dried fruit, smoked meat, and a bag of grain. At the bag of grain, she paused and sent another burst of her magic through it, her delicate mouth curving into a frown. She glanced over her shoulder at Prince Edmund. "As you suspected, the grain is poisoned with ricin."

Prince Edmund nodded, then swept a glance around all of them. "No one touch anything until Jalissa has swept the whole place, looking for ricin."

One of the two Escarlish men stepped forward, putting on a mask and pulling on gloves as he did so. While Edmund and Jalissa stood back, the man carefully closed the bag of grain and tied the top. The man gingerly picked up the bag. "We will run some tests to determine the strength and potency of the ricin."

It was apparently plenty potent, given the number of dead. Vriska clenched her fists at her side.

Rharreth straightened his shoulders and glanced at Melantha. "How many of the elf warriors have plant magic? Will they be willing to help?"

"I have not asked, but plant magic is the most common magic among the warriors." Melantha, too, stood straighter, as if an answer strengthened her, even if it was such a terrible one. "They will help."

"We need to search the entire city and confiscate the

poisoned grain." Rharreth glanced at Edmund. "Is there a method we should use to destroy it?"

"Don't burn it. You don't want the ricin to become airborne, even if it should be quickly diluted on the breeze." Edmund frowned. "You could probably bury it, though I would suggest you do it carefully. You don't want the poison to seep into the water supply or poison crops. Perhaps surrounding it with your stone magic would work."

"We'll order the poisoned grain taken to the ruins of Gror Grar, and we'll worry about destroying it later." Rharreth reached for Melantha's hand. "First, we need to keep more people from getting sick."

Vriska nodded along with everyone else standing in her family's tiny home. The sooner they could stop this poison, the better.

CHAPTER EIGHTEEN

Julien sat to Rharreth's left in the tiers of stone benches around the practice arena.

Though this morning, it wouldn't host a benign practice. No, today the sand would be stained red with the blood of a Dulraith.

Next to Julien, Edmund's face remained unreadable. Yet on his other side, Jalissa's serene composure showed strain, and she gripped Edmund's hand so tightly Julien wondered if Edmund's blank expression was hiding his pain rather than tension.

Julien leaned closer to them and whispered, "You don't have to stay, Jalissa. I know a Dulraith isn't pleasant to witness up close."

She had seen one before, when Rharreth, Farrendel, and Julien had fought the Dulraith against Drurvas and his cronies. For that Dulraith, Jalissa had remained across the Gulmorth Gorge so while she had been close enough to see who survived, she hadn't been able to clearly see the blood and sweat of the battle.

Her face a little white, Jalissa shook her head. "Edmund will stay, and I do not want to remain in a room alone, waiting to be told the outcome."

Edmund rested his free hand over their clasped fingers, his eyes searching Jalissa's face in a way that said he read far more into her words and her expression than Julien did. Edmund leaned closer and whispered to Jalissa too quietly for Julien to catch the words. Not that Julien wanted to overhear whatever sweet assurances Edmund was giving her, likely in elvish since he seemed to lapse into elvish whenever he wanted to say something meaningful to Jalissa.

Julien sneaked a glance over his shoulder at Vriska before he straightened and sat forward again. Would he and Vriska ever develop such habits between the two of them? Would their language be hers or his or the mix of both that they tended to use, since neither of them was as eloquent in either language as Edmund was in both elvish and Escarlish?

A roar filled the arena as troll warriors led Brathac and the two of his cronies who had chosen to join him in this Dulraith into the arena.

As ordered, Rharreth had waited to hold this Dulraith until after the disease—as they'd assumed at the time—was defeated. In the month since Edmund and Jalissa had arrived and figured out that it was a poison instead of a disease, the numbers of new cases had dropped dramatically.

Rharreth had sent messages to the entire kingdom, warning each and every town about the poison and that only the authorized trade with Escarland was safe. To make sure of that, Weylind had elves with plant magic inspect all the food that passed from Escarland through Tarenhiel before it was hauled into Kostaria.

To find the poisoned grain already in Kostaria, Rharreth stationed teams of troll and elf warriors in the courtyard of Khagniorth so that the citizens of Osmana could bring their grain to have it checked for safety. Other teams had been sent out to the larger villages where villagers and those from the surrounding, smaller villages could also have their food checked for poison.

The tainted grain from all over Kostaria was hauled to Osmana and currently formed a massive pile inside of a stone and ice shield that Rharreth had built on the ruins of Gror Grar, since he was the only troll strong enough to work with the stone that was infused with Farrendel's magic.

Additional warriors had been sent to the coast. So far, word had come that two ships attempting to smuggle goods into Kostaria had been turned away. One had been able to flee before capture, but the other had been apprehended. The crew had been reluctant to talk, but when they had, they had claimed to be from Escarland, though the goods they carried had been picked up at a port in Mongavaria. They had claimed to have no knowledge of the poison, though they had known that smuggling goods into Kostaria—and thus bypassing the taxes in the various kingdoms involved—was illegal.

Julien clenched his fists as he stared down at a smirking Brathac. As galling as it was, Brathac had been partially right. Humans had caused all this death in Kostaria. And while Mongavaria seemed to be behind the poisoning, humans from Escarland had done the smuggling.

Edmund suspected someone among the nobility of Escarland was behind the smuggling operation, but he was being close-lipped about whom he thought it might be. He would probably return to investigating once he returned to Escarland tomorrow. At least, when he found the time between the last-minute wedding plans and preparations for his trip to Mongavaria.

In the arena below, Brathac and the two trolls with him claimed their weapons while their guards exited. Brathac thumped his sword against his shield and faced Rharreth. "Your time of reckoning has come, Rharreth. Face me with the honor due a troll warrior and pay for the weakness you have brought to Kostaria."

Rharreth's deep blue eyes flashed, but his expression remained stony as he stood. He didn't waste time trying to refute Brathac. Instead, he turned to Julien next to him. "Prince Julien, you will fight at my side. You, too, Vriska."

Julien nodded. Rharreth hadn't asked him about it ahead of time, but he hadn't needed to do so. It was expected in the troll culture that Julien would fight in this Dulraith, and there had been no reason for Rharreth to assume anything less with Julien.

Zavni grimaced and reached as if to draw his ax from its place strapped to his back. "Are you sure, Your Majesty?"

Julien refused to wince. Yes, he was a human. Yes, he was weaker than any of the other warriors here. But he could hold his own. He was quick. He had trained with Farrendel for this purpose.

"Prince Julien has more reason than any of us to fight in this Dulraith. It is his honor, his status as a warrior, that is in question." Rharreth shrugged, then started shrugging out of his leather vest. He handed the garment to Melantha.

Melantha sighed as she accepted his vest, then his shirt. "Can you trolls go so much as a year without a fight to the death?"

"Apparently not." Rharreth rested his hands on her

shoulders, but Julien turned away before he witnessed the king and queen kissing.

Instead, he stood and pulled his own shirt over his head, the coolness of the underground room brushing against his skin. He handed his shirt to Edmund.

Edmund took the shirt and met Julien's gaze. "Don't die, got it? You need to be there for my wedding in a month."

"Yes, that's your only concern. That my death doesn't unbalance your numbers for your wedding." Julien forced a grin and lightly punched Edmund's shoulder.

Behind Edmund, Jalissa gave a tiny huff that broke through some of her tension.

"Yes, that's it." Edmund grinned back, but the expression didn't reach his eyes any more than Julien's had. He lowered his tone. "You don't have Farrendel watching your back this time."

"No, but I have Vriska." Julien glanced at her where she stood one tier up from him.

Vriska's tight, leather vest left her arms bare, showing off her toned muscles. As he met her gaze, a hint of a savage smile cracked the hardness of her jaw.

Melantha glanced between the three of them. "Remember. Do not get your head chopped off."

"I have no intention of dying." Rharreth leaned closer and kissed Melantha's forehead. When he lowered his tone, his words seemed to hold an extra meaning. "Especially not now."

"Dying usually is not intentional," Melantha muttered, though something in her eyes remained soft as she met Rharreth's gaze.

Julien turned away, peeking another glance at Vriska. By the way she stared down at Brathac below, the light of blood and battle in her eyes, he didn't think there would be any sweet, romantic moments before battle for him and Vriska.

Rharreth led the way down the stairs and into the arena, Julien and Vriska following. At the edge of the arena, Julien found his shield waiting for him, and he drew his sword, testing its comfortable weight in his hand.

After a month, his bruises had faded to faint, brown smudges. His sore muscles were gone, and he'd resumed practicing with Rharreth's shield band. He was as ready as he could be for his second Dulraith.

This time, there was no ceremonial cheering or rune painting. Perhaps there was no time. Or maybe Rharreth wasn't going to dignify Brathac's Dulraith with such things. Unlike the Dulraith against Drurvas, the fate of the kingdom didn't rest on this battle. Unless, of course, Brathac managed to kill Rharreth. That would turn this throwaway fight into something bigger.

Also stripped to the waist, the three troll warriors faced them. All three wielded swords, thankfully. An ax would be much harder to fend off, much less a mace like the one Julien had faced in the last Dulraith he'd fought.

Who would have guessed that he would end up having to fight multiple Dulraiths?

If he married Vriska, this might not be the last one he fought, considering the prejudices still lingering in Kostaria.

Brathac faced Rharreth, still sneering. "So let it begin."

"So let it end." Rharreth raised his sword, ice to Brathac's molten hatred.

With a growl, Brathac swung his sword at Rharreth's head. Rharreth parried easily.

The other two trolls both rushed Julien. He parried one sword, then Vriska parried the other. Almost as one, he and

Vriska sidestepped together, keeping each other protected as they attacked. They pushed back the two trolls, forcing them to give ground step by step.

One troll lashed out, catching Julien across the top of his shoulder. He stumbled back, and the two trolls took advantage. They both swung at Vriska, and she struggled to block the blows.

Julien regained his balance and launched back into the fight. He swung hard enough to send a troll off balance.

Vriska lunged and stabbed the troll through the chest.

Before she could withdraw her sword, the other troll was already swinging for her neck.

Julien lunged and blocked the sword inches from Vriska's skin. The troll's eyes widened, and Julien kicked him in the stomach, sending him stumbling back. It gained them a few feet and enough time for Vriska to yank her sword free of the dead troll.

She spun and blocked the troll's next strike. She shot Julien a glance, and she didn't have to say the words out loud for him to understand. *Finish him.*

While she swept the troll's blade high, he thrust his sword into the troll's chest. He suppressed any pang he might have felt at the death at his hands. This was the trolls' Dulraith. This was their law. These trolls had known what it might cost the moment they chose to fight.

Even as Julien withdrew his sword, he caught sight of Rharreth straightening, Brathac dead at his feet.

At least this time, the only wound any of them had suffered was the small gash on Julien's arm.

Vriska turned to him and, despite the blood and the dead bodies before them, she was grinning. "We fight well together."

Yes, they did. They had moved in that fight as if they had been fighting together all their lives. Never getting in each other's way. Communicating what they planned with just a glance. Perhaps their morning practices could explain it. She fought like that with her shield brothers, after all. But could they really have developed that rhythm after less than two months' worth of mornings?

Or was it something deeper?

"Yes, we do." Julien drew a rag from a pocket of his trousers and wiped the blood from his sword before it had a chance to dry.

He'd fought well, and he'd survived. Brathac was gone, and now it was time to turn his attention to the real threat posed by Mongavaria and whichever Escarlish noble had been foolish enough to take up smuggling.

Though, that fight was likely more Averett's and Edmund's than Julien's. Even less so, now. Before, Julien might have led the raid as the Intelligence Office and the castle guards cooperated to make an arrest. Now, even that was taken from him and given to his replacement.

His duty was to woo Vriska. Something that would hopefully become easier now that Brathac was dead and the threat of the poison was diminishing.

Amid the cheers, Julien returned to his seat and only half-listened to the short speech Rharreth gave about the strength of Kostaria and the trolls' resilience even in the face of this poison.

Edmund leaned over and whispered, "I've had my doubts this past month, but just now, I saw something between you and Vriska. I look forward to your wedding."

Julien elbowed his brother in the ribs. Even if he couldn't help but hope Edmund was as astute about this as he seemed to be about everything else. With only a month remaining in his stay in Kostaria, it was far too late to try to fall in love with someone else. Julien was going to marry Vriska, or he'd have to return to Escarland unbetrothed and have to start over.

Except starting over might not be that simple. Because he suspected his heart might be a little broken if Vriska rejected him.

CHAPTER NINETEEN

Vriska stood in the center of what was once her childhood home as her family's meager belongings were packed up and loaded in the wagon out front. Her ma sat on a bench in front, saying farewell to the neighbors stopping by to give her their best wishes. Rikze flitted between staying by Ma, helping with the move, and talking about Escarland to anyone who would listen.

Didn't Rikze feel the same twinge at the thought that this place would no longer be home? Sure, it had been years—decades, even—since Vriska had lived here. Yet it was still home. This was still the place where Vriska had gone when she needed solace after a battle. Here at this table, she'd eaten Ma's *iquitak,* dreamed about becoming a warrior, and soaked in a slice of peace away from war.

But Ma and Da had made their decision via letters sent back and forth. Da enjoyed the work in Escarland, and he was eager to explore the additional work that life in Escarland promised. And they both hoped that the warmer climate in Escarland would be better for Ma.

Yet that meant they were uprooting their family for an unknown future in a kingdom only Da had seen so far, and he'd only seen a tiny piece of it.

Zavni returned and gripped the other end of the worn, stone table. "Do you have the other side?"

Vriska shook herself. "Yes. Of course."

She gripped the other end of the table top and sent her magic into it to detach the top from the two stone supports, which would be carried to the wagon separately.

Both she and Zavni sent their magic into the tabletop, using their power to help carry the stone slab. Together, they maneuvered it through the doorway and hefted it into the second wagon. Brynjar and Eyvindur followed a moment later, each of them carrying one of the benches.

As they settled the benches into the wagon, Julien tottered from the doorway, lugging one of the stone pedestals. His face screwed up with the strain, his cheeks turning a shade red, as he panted in his struggle.

Vriska hurried to his side and took the stone from him, propping it against her shoulder. "Someone else could've gotten it."

"I know. And I'm probably going to regret attempting it in the morning when my back hurts." Julien straightened and stretched his back with a grimace. "But I couldn't let all you trolls show me up."

She wasn't going to point out that all of them were far stronger than Julien. Instead, she shrugged as she carried the pedestal to the wagon. "We have our magic to help."

Julien's mouth quirked with a hint of a wry smile that said he knew exactly what she was doing in preserving some of his manly pride.

Zavni re-entered the house, then exited a moment later, hefting the second stone pedestal. He set it in the wagon, then patted the wagon's side. "I think that's the last of it."

Vriska swallowed back the lump in her throat. No way was she going to be caught crying by her shield brothers and the neighbors gathered around. "Go on ahead with the first wagon. Ma, Rikze, and I will follow in the second in a few minutes."

Zavni nodded. After exchanging looks, he, Brynjar, and Eyvindur climbed into the first wagon, its bed piled with canvas sacks filled with her family's things. Julien climbed onto the bench of the second wagon, indicating that he planned to wait for Vriska and her family. With one last glance in Vriska's direction, Zavni took the reins, and the mule team brayed as they set out down the street.

Vriska turned and held out a hand to Ma. "Would you like to step inside one last time?"

Ma nodded and took Vriska's hand. She didn't lean on Vriska as she had only a few weeks earlier, but she still walked slower than she used to as she led the way into the house.

Rikze trotted into the house after her, and Vriska trailed after them. The three of them halted in the center of the front room, bare except for the built-in stone cabinets along one wall.

The emptiness stabbed into Vriska's chest, swelling that annoying lump in the back of her throat.

For the first time that morning, the smile dropped from Rikze's face. "It seems strange, that this won't be home anymore. I…" Her words wobbled, a tear spilling down her cheek.

Ma wrapped one arm around Rikze's shoulders. "We had a lot of good times in this home, didn't we? But we are what made it a home, not the place. We still have each other, and that won't change once we reach Escarland. We'll make a new home and new memories there."

Rikze nodded, leaning her head against Ma's shoulder as a few more tears streaked down her face.

Vriska swallowed again. She refused to cry. She had to be the strong one. If she was going to give in to the weakness of a few tears, then she'd do it when she was alone in her room at Khagniorth Stronghold.

Except that she wouldn't be alone. Ma and Rikze were staying there for the next few days before the three of them boarded the train that would eventually take them to Escarland.

Ma's eyes glittered with a wet sheen, but she smiled as she reached up and put her other arm around Vriska, pulling her into the hug. "And with Vriska marrying her Escarlish prince, we will all be together there."

That helped clear the clogging tears from her throat, though the replacing apprehension wasn't much better. Vriska wrapped an arm around her ma in return. "You don't know that for sure."

"He's smitten. I can tell." Ma's smile held that knowing, motherly look to it. All she saw was the supposed romance. Not the arrangement due to the treaty.

Did Vriska want to marry Julien? Become a princess of Escarland? She'd always thought her heart was in Kostaria. Her duty as a warrior was here, serving in the king's shield band.

Yet her family would be in Escarland. Where did that leave her heart, torn between her family and her duty?

Or…did her heart no longer fully belong to either her family or her duty? When she was with Julien, she caught glimpses of a different future. And it no longer scared her the way it once had. Instead, something in her relaxed when she was with him. For so many years, she'd had to keep her guard up around everyone, even her family and her shield band. For them, she had to be the tough troll warrior. And that was all right.

But with Julien, she didn't always have to be tough. He'd seen her cry and hadn't embarrassed her for it. He hadn't seen her as less tough, less a warrior, because she'd given in to tears when her family had been so sick. Perhaps, if she found herself alone with him, she'd give in to tears again over the loss of her childhood home.

"Rikze, why don't you go out and make sure no one is bothering Julien?" Ma released Rikze and gave her a nudge in the direction of the door.

With one last glance around the room, Rikze nodded and strode from the door with a deliberate stride, as if she'd said her goodbye and wasn't going to look back.

The sight ached inside Vriska's chest. The past few months had forced her little sister to grow up. She'd suffered from the poison, nearly lost Ma, and now said farewell to the only home she'd ever known. Hopefully she wouldn't lose her starry-eyed enthusiasm and would take to life in Escarland the way Ma seemed to think she would.

Once Rikze shut the door behind her, Ma turned to Vriska, her gaze soft. "You've always been my tough girl, Vriska. You're capable of standing on your own, and you've been happy with your life as it is. Don't be in a hurry to change that if you don't want to. If Julien is the right one, he will love you for the fierce woman you are, not the woman he thinks you should be."

Vriska nodded, glancing toward the door even though she couldn't see where Julien waited with Rikze and the wagon. In the last three months, Julien had shown over and over again that he saw her exactly that way. He never resented her greater strength or skill with weapons. He never made snide comments about her gender, as some of the male warriors of other shield bands sometimes did. And he'd given her time to think about their marriage, flirting and spending time with her yet never pressing.

Was it enough? Even if he was the perfect man, that wouldn't be enough if Vriska didn't think life with him would be better than the life she had by herself.

Or perhaps not better. But a different kind of good.

"And from what I've seen, he does that." Ma gave Vriska one last side-hug before she stepped away. "I rather like him."

"I do too." The words came out almost by accident. Vriska forced herself to smile to hide the momentary lapse into vulnerability. "Speaking of Julien, he and Rikze are probably wondering what's taking so long."

With one final glance around the house, Ma headed for the door. Vriska followed, then Ma shut the door one last time, her hand lingering on it for a moment before she pushed away, headed for the wagon.

Ma climbed into the back of the wagon, sitting next to Rikze. That left the seat on the driver's bench next to Julien for Vriska.

Vriska climbed onto the wagon and settled next to Julien. He sent her a searching glance before he faced forward again, flicked the reins, and sent the wagon lurching forward on the stone road.

Even as the wagon shuddered and rumbled down the back street, Vriska didn't glance back. Her future—and her family's future—lay ahead, not behind.

JULIEN SAT NEXT to Vriska on a ledge tucked into the side of Khagniorth Stronghold. They each had a bear fur over their lap, more furs beneath them, as a chill breeze washed down the mountains, already holding the hint of the coming winter as autumn weather descended on Kostaria. Above them, stars glittered in the dark sky far above while faint shimmers of green and pink streaked across the sky.

They would leave in the morning for Escarland to arrive before Edmund and Jalissa's wedding.

After long moments of silence, Vriska sighed. "I'm sorry. The lights aren't the best tonight."

"They are still beautiful. I've never seen anything like them back in Escarland." Julien glanced from the sky to her, then back to the sky when she didn't turn to meet his gaze.

In the months he'd been here in Kostaria, he'd fallen in love with the kingdom. The inky blackness of the sky and the vibrant stars that shone with a clarity he'd never seen in Escarland. The shimmering northern lights casting a green glow over the jagged peaks of the mountains. The crisp taste to the air even in the warmth of summer, a reminder that winter was never that far away here in the upper north.

When he'd left Escarland, he hadn't been sure he could leave his duty and his kingdom behind. Now, if Vriska asked it of him, he thought he could give up Escarland if he got to live in the wildness of Kostaria instead.

Would she ask it of him? Would she ask anything of him? His fingers strayed to his pocket, feeling the lump of the item he'd tucked inside. After three months with her, he had peace with what he was willing to give up for her. Because she was worth it.

But did she feel the same way? While he could adapt to Kostaria, he wasn't sure Vriska could adapt to Escarland, even if her family would be there. Nor did he want her to. He wanted her to be herself, not the person the court would pressure her to be.

Still, he needed to talk with her about this before they left. He still wasn't sure where they stood. They were courting, kind of. But it was still tentative and didn't feel as real as he thought it would by this point.

Yet she was the woman he wanted at his side. Even in Escarland.

Slowly, he reached for her hand. She didn't pull away, her hand strong and as large as his. Though her fingers were just a little bit slimmer. Not delicate by any means, yet still different against his hands.

"Are you all right with going to Escarland? With this?" Julien held up their clasped hands.

Vriska shrugged. "Besides a few raids into Tarenhiel, I've never left Kostaria."

"Escarland will be very different from anything you've ever seen." Julien couldn't see her face well in the dark. "But you'll be with me and my family. We'll keep you sheltered from the snobbery of the court."

He could see her well enough to make out her scowl. "I don't need protecting."

"I know." Julien shrugged. "But Escarland is different than Kostaria. You can't go around punching anyone who makes a snide comment. Disappointing, I know. A few of them could use a good sock in the nose. But that's the way it is."

"Sounds like a terrible place." Vriska's voice held a note of a laugh along with apprehension.

"It's not as bad as I'm making it sound." Julien shrugged, rubbing his thumb over the back of her hand, the pad of his thumb catching on dry skin and scabs on her knuckles. "And your family will be there."

Vriska nodded, all but her frown hidden in the darkness. "I hope Ma is up for the trip. She still gets tired so easily."

"The Tarenhieli train is very restful, even if it will be a long day of travel." Julien tried to keep his voice reassuring. He didn't want her to think that he was dismissing her concerns for her mother's health. "And Melantha will be there, so she'll have a healer on hand."

"I'm glad for that, though Melantha could use the rest herself." Vriska frowned, the twist of her mouth barely visible in the darkness of the night. "It has been two months, and she still seems tired and worn."

Julien had noticed that, though Melantha had improved a great deal once the tide of poisonings was stemmed and the demand for healings lessened. By the way Rharreth was hovering, much like Averett had hovered with Paige and Farrendel was currently with Essie, Julien had his own guess as to what might be causing Melantha's weariness.

But he wasn't going to tell that news until Rharreth and Melantha decided to share it.

He let the silence stretch for several long moments. As he

waited, his heart beat harder and faster in his throat, throbbing at his temples.

Was this the right time? While he would have preferred to do this properly and spoken with Vriska's father first, he wanted to speak with Vriska before they left.

Besides, he couldn't imagine a better setting with the lights blazing across the sky and the mountains spread out before them.

He tried to surreptitiously wipe the palm of his free hand on his trousers, visions of fumbling the ring and sending it bouncing across their ledge, down the craggy side of Khagniorth Stronghold, and into the blackness of night running through his head.

Julien cleared his throat, shifting to better face her as he still clasped her hand in his. "I wanted to talk with you. Before we left. The plan was for us to return to Escarland and announce our betrothal."

Now did that sound unromantic or what. He snapped his mouth shut, hating how cold the words sounded.

Vriska gazed out at the city spreading below them, the mountains dark against the sky far beyond. "I know." Her shoulders lifted, then slumped. "Before King Rharreth approached me with this, I never thought I'd get married. I thought I'd fight and die in the war. But now that the war is over, I don't know what to do. Yet you've given me the first glimpse I've had of what life could look like."

It wasn't a stirring declaration, but it was a baring of her heart that was unusual from Vriska. That spoke of the trust he'd earned with her, even if she hadn't gone so far as to say that she was attracted to him or falling in love with him.

"I hope, together, we can find our purpose." Julien

settled more comfortably against the rock wall behind him. The night grew colder around them, a slight breeze shivering against the back of his neck. "We're entering a new era of peace for all our kingdoms, I think. We warriors will need to find a new place."

Oh, yes. Discuss politics in the middle of trying to declare his love. Well, not his love, even if he was about to propose. Good thing the setting was romantic because he was utterly failing.

"Yes." She sighed, still staring off into the distance rather than looking at him. "I don't know yet what place I want. All I've wanted to be is a warrior. It is simple. I always knew my duty. But this…"

"Is a lot more complicated." He gently squeezed her hand. "I want to figure it out together. I respect you. You respect me. There's something between us, I think." Like Vriska, he wasn't ready to use the word *love* yet. Besides, it would just scare her away.

Still it seemed strange to reach into his pocket, pull out the diamond ring, and hold it out to her without telling her that he loved her.

Vriska blinked at the ring, her forehead scrunched. "What is that?"

"It's a ring. In Escarland, it's a sign of our betrothal." Julien turned the ring, letting the simple embedded diamonds catch the light of the sky above. As Vriska opened her mouth, probably to protest that she wasn't about to wear a ring on fingers she needed unencumbered to wield her weapons, he added, "I know you won't wear it on your finger. I was thinking you could tie it into your hair."

"Ah. That would be acceptable." Vriska still didn't make

a move to take the ring. Nor did she look at him as she stared first at it, then out into the night. "You want children."

Right. This had been one of the hardest things for him to come to grips with.

But she was being asked to give up her place as a warrior, something so integral to her identity, to figure out a new life at his side. For her, he could give up a few of his old dreams to form new ones. Because she was worth it.

"If you don't want children, then we won't have children. I'll be the best uncle I can be to my nephews, and any future nieces or nephews we might have." Julien kept his voice steady, his gaze focused on her even if she wasn't looking at him. "I'll never pressure you. Not in this. And not to marry me, if this isn't what you want."

She continued staring off into the night, her jaw working a bit at the corners. Even if he had been able to see her expression, he likely wouldn't have been able to read it.

"You don't have to accept. I understand." Julien lowered the ring and rested his hand on their clasped ones. "But I'd like it if you did. Will you marry me, Vriska?"

Her gaze dropped from his eyes to the ring he still held out between them. But her expression remained neutral, her posture stiff.

His heart pounded out the seconds, though the time stretched out into agonizing hours.

Finally, Vriska gave a sharp nod and plucked the ring from his fingers. "Yes."

As she tied the ring into one of the leather strands woven into her hair, she didn't look at him, her posture just as stiff as it had been before her agreement.

Julien released a breath and slumped against the stone behind him. She'd said yes out of duty. Then again, had he asked for anything other than duty? He was attracted to her, yes, but if not for duty, he would not be asking now. Not this soon.

They had respect. Perhaps the beginning of a spark.

But in the end, it all came back to cold, hard duty.

CHAPTER TWENTY

Vriska resisted the urge to gape, first at the massive trees of Tarenhiel, then at the flat, rolling hills of Escarland spreading out to the horizon from the Hydalla River. The bridge itself was awe-inspiring, even knowing what her people were capable of. It soared across the Hydalla River in a series of graceful arches supported by massive stone pillars, a beauty of magic and engineering highlighted by the setting sun.

Rikze had done enough gaping and talking for the two of them, and even Ma hadn't been able to hide her wonder at the sights flashing past the windows.

They'd ridden in the royal car of the Kostarian train to the border, then walked across the bridge over the Gulmorth Gorge. The Tarenhieli train had been so eerily quiet and plush beyond belief as it glided through the serene forest.

At the Escarlish border, it took a while to ferry all of them across the river. Between the warriors and families of the workers, a small army of trolls would be there to witness the completion of the new bridge. Well, that and the wedding between Prince Edmund and Princess Jalissa, though the trolls were less excited about that than they were about the bridge that their people had built.

Would Julien expect this much hoopla for their wedding? Vriska fingered the ring tied in her hair, her skin getting all tight and itchy just thinking about enduring an event this large.

And the Tarenhieli and Escarlish parts of the wedding and guests hadn't even arrived yet.

The Escarlish side of the river bustled with both trolls and humans. Rharreth waded into the fray of disembarking warriors and troll families reuniting with loved ones.

Rikze gripped Ma's arm and all but tugged her from the ferry dock toward the horde of people. Ma glanced over her shoulder at Vriska, sharing a smile, before she let Rikze yank her forward.

Vriska picked up the sack of her mother's personal items that she hadn't wanted to trust to others for shipping. As she reached for her sister's, Julien appeared at her side.

"Here, let me help." Julien reached for the second sack.

Vriska swiveled them out of his reach, scowling at him. She might wear his ring tied in her hair, but that didn't make her too weak to carry two small sacks. "I can handle it."

He managed to snag one of the sacks, halting her, as he met her gaze with those soul-deep brown eyes of his. "I know. I'm not saying that you can't. I'm simply offering to help. Just because you can do something by yourself doesn't mean that you have to if someone is willing to come alongside you."

Why was she being so huffy with him? Of course he didn't think her weak. Nor was she weak for accepting his help. That was the point of a relationship, after all. He had her back, and she was supposed to have his.

The betrothal just kind of itched at her. She'd said yes, and it wasn't that she was regretting her choice, exactly. But her answer didn't sit right with her either, and she wasn't sure what was wrong.

Shaking herself, she shrugged and forced herself to let go of the sack. "Fine. Take this one."

Since Julien had one of the sacks, she had a free hand to grab her own rucksack. Julien, too, grabbed his army-issued rucksack, slung it over his shoulder, then picked up his shield, its surface a bit more worn and dented after all the fighting bouts.

Some of that prickly feeling faded just a bit. There was something so comfortable about a man who packed in a rucksack. He was organized with that edge of discipline that she appreciated as a fellow warrior.

"Let's get your family settled." Julien gripped her sister's sack of belongs at his side and led the way off the dock, headed for the milling crowd.

Within a few minutes, they located Ma and Rikze near the edge of the mob. Rikze stood on her tiptoes, craning her neck as she tried to peer over the heads of the surrounding people, all of whom were taller than her.

Vriska peered around as well, though she didn't stand on her tiptoes. Even if she stood much taller than Rikze, many of the male troll warriors were even taller.

How were they going to find her father in this horde of people? The streets of the simple town were packed with troll workers hurrying toward the dock, the families of those workers running toward them, and the troll warriors unloading their gear and setting up a temporary camp at the edge of the town. Even a few humans milled among the crowd, as if undaunted by the horde of trolls descending on Escarland's border.

Yet Julien pushed his way into the crowd, greeting a few of the humans, troll workers, and troll warriors as he went.

The farther they went, the more the bustle died off until they were only surrounded by the quieter common workers who had settled here for the months it had taken to build the bridge.

"Thera? Rikze?"

Vriska whirled toward the sound of her da's voice.

"Vriska?" His eyes widened, then a broad grin broke across his face. He stepped toward them, but he only made it two strides before Rikze raced toward him and flung herself into a hug.

"Da!" Rikze clung tightly before she spun and waved toward the rest of them. "We rode in the royal car! And Vriska is going to marry Prince Julien!"

Vriska stifled her groan. She'd wanted to break that particular news in a better way than that. Or at least enjoy the reunion with her da before she brought up the uncomfortable topic.

Da started. His gaze flicked from Vriska to Julien, then back to Vriska.

Julien shifted, then held out his hand. "It is my pleasure to finally make your acquaintance. I have heard a lot about you from your two wonderful daughters."

From anyone else, that might have come across as blatant, smarmy flattery. But Julien's straight face and truthful tone showed he was sincere.

After a moment, Da shook Julien's hand. He had likely become familiar with the human custom during his months working in Escarland. "I hope we will have a chance to get to know each other better."

An edge of a threat laced through Da's voice, and he must have tightened his grip on Julien's hand. Julien's face twisted with the hint of a wince before he schooled his features.

"That is my hope as well." Julien didn't shake out his hand when Da released it, though he must have wanted to. Instead, he held out the sack he had carried. "I must make sure King Rharreth has all he needs for his warriors. I'll leave you to settle in."

After sharing a last glance with Vriska, Julien turned and strode away through the crowd once again.

When Vriska turned back to her family, her da's gaze focused on her. She kept her expression blank, and she lowered her voice. "We'll talk later."

Her da nodded as he set the sack on the ground. He pulled Ma in and hugged her, resting his face against her hair for a long moment, mumbling something too low for Vriska to hear.

Vriska blinked and turned away at the emotion on her parents' faces and the rare public display of affection. Ma had nearly died, and this was Da's first chance to hold her close. It must have been agony for him to be here, not allowed to leave to take care of his family.

Even Rikze didn't make any disgusted noises at the affection, though she joined Vriska in looking everywhere but at their parents.

After a moment, Da and Ma stepped apart, and he hefted the sack to his back. He held out his hand to Ma, smiling. "Come. Let's get you settled in, and I'll show you around the settlement. We've been calling it Bridgetown, though I don't think the name is official."

Ma took his hand with a return smile while Rikze crowded in close. Vriska fell into step behind them, trying to absorb the changes in her family.

Her da was happy here in Escarland. Despite his worry for Ma, his step had an extra confidence to it, his back a little straighter, his head held higher. The lines were not etched so deeply into his face. While they had made the decision to move to Escarland for Ma's health, perhaps that hadn't been the only reason. Had Da already been thinking about making Escarland their new home even before Ma was poisoned?

He led them to a small, stone house. It had two rooms, a front sitting room and kitchen with a bedroom in the back. Sleeping pallets currently rested off to the side along the wall, waiting for nightfall when Vriska and Rikze would sleep here in the kitchen.

"This is where I've been staying." Da pointed back the way they'd come. "There's the main street of shops back that way."

"Can we see them?" Rikze stepped back toward the door, as if she planned to leave right now.

Da's smile widened as he set the sack on the table, then headed for the door again. "Yes, but we should hurry. Many of them will start closing for the evening."

The four of them hurried back into the street, then turned onto the main street. There, they discovered that they weren't the only ones who decided to explore rather than settle in for the evening. Most of the shops remained open while reunited troll families strolled the boardwalk from shop to shop. At the far end of the street, musicians had set up drums and pipes and troll couples stomped and whirled and hooted in traditional troll dances.

Vriska couldn't help but be drawn into the lightness that seemed to fill her parents and sister. For a few moments, she was a young girl again and they were a family as they'd rarely had a chance to be.

Da stopped them at a human-run café and bought them all beef sandwiches for supper, plunking down the coin for the purchase with an ease Vriska had rarely seen, as if the coin wasn't as dear as it used to be.

Once they all polished off the sandwiches, he purchased something the Escarlish called ice cream for dessert.

Rikze took the bowl of chocolate ice cream, dug in her spoon, and popped it into her mouth without hesitating. Her eyes widened, and she moaned as she swallowed. "This is the best thing I've ever tasted."

Vriska tentatively scooped a spoonful of her own chocolate ice cream and ate it, closing her eyes as the rich, creamy substance washed over her tongue. It was cold and rich and tasted as sweet as the chocolates Julien had given her—chocolates she'd savored far more than she wanted to admit.

Yet something inside her twinged, as if she would be disloyal to Kostaria and her ma's *iquitak* if she admitted that she liked this ice cream. Would Escarland replace everything, including her ma's traditional dessert? By moving to Escarland, would her family lose everything that had made them Kostarian? They would have to adapt to their new kingdom. Adopt its culture and language.

What about Vriska? What would she give up about herself and her kingdom and culture if she married Prince Julien?

When she married Prince Julien. She had his ring woven

in her hair. Tomorrow, all three kingdoms would know they were betrothed. Sure, she could still back out. But it would be a major international incident if she did.

The four of them finished their ice cream and returned the bowls and spoons to the café. As the night deepened around them, Da pulled Ma into a dance, the two of them smiling and laughing as they hadn't in years.

Some of the warriors had joined as well, clapping and stomping around the edges of the dance since there were more men than women. Rharreth and Melantha were whirling through the dance, Melantha grinning and laughing as loudly as any troll.

"Do you wish to dance?"

It took all her control not to jump at the sound of Julien's voice next to her. She turned to him and shrugged. "You probably don't know how to dance like a troll."

"No, but you can teach me." Julien's grin flashed as he glanced from her to Rikze. "If you won't, I'm sure Rikze will."

Rikze grinned and nodded. "Of course I will. But I think Vriska wants to dance with you more."

Vriska didn't. Not really. Even if she felt all too aware of Julien's strong, steady presence next to her, filling the space at her side so completely that it felt empty when he wasn't there.

With a sigh, Vriska took Julien's hand and dragged him into the pack of dancing trolls.

To his credit, Julien picked up the rhythm quickly, stomping and clapping as they circled each other as if in a swordfight. He grinned, a wild light filling his eyes as the rhythm increased.

She grinned back, laughing as that same wildness welled

up inside her. They might be standing on Escarlish soil having eaten Escarlish food, but this dance was a slice of Kostaria.

The night deepened, the time blurring, as she danced first with Julien, then with each of her shield brothers except for Rharreth, then back to Julien. Zavni and Julien each made sure Rikze had a chance to dance, looking out for her little sister.

By the time Vriska and her family returned to the little stone house and collapsed into bed or on their pallets in the main room, there wasn't time to speak with her da about Julien. Not that Vriska was too disappointed to put off that conversation for another day.

Especially since she fell asleep smiling at the memory of Julien's grin and how like a troll he'd looked while caught up in the dance.

VRISKA WOKE to the sizzle of cooking sausage and the rich smell of breakfast filling the room. She pushed upright, swiping her hair out of her face. Julien's ring thumped against her hand.

Next to her, Rikze still slept on her pallet, her mouth hanging slightly open, her body relaxed in sleep. Ma bustled around the kitchen, scrambling eggs in one pan, roasting sausages in another.

Vriska rolled out of her bedroll and smoothed the wrinkles out of the trousers and shirt she'd worn to bed. "You could have woken me."

"You were exhausted. You danced late into the night." Ma's eyes held a bit of a twinkle as she dished out some of the eggs and a sausage on a plate. "Eat up. It will be a busy day today."

It would. The elf king and human king would be arriving, along with all the elf and human guests for this wedding. Then the wedding organization would begin in earnest, culminating in the completion of the bridge and the wedding of Julien's brother and the elf king's sister in the late afternoon and evening.

Vriska's stomach churned as she sat in one of the chairs that surrounded the small table. A *wooden* table and chairs. Not the worn stone of the table and benches of home.

Today, Vriska would attend the wedding at Julien's side. Everyone would find out that she was betrothed to him. As Julien's betrothed, she would join Rharreth in completing the bridge while guests from all three kingdoms watched.

No pressure. She could handle this. After all, she was a warrior of Kostaria. What was a little bit of magic and being the center of attention?

Once the wedding was over, everyone would go their separate ways. Vriska's family would board a train headed for Escarland's capital city of Aldon, along with a number of other troll workers and their families who also planned to move there for more work.

Vriska and Julien, however, would travel to Fort Charibert, an Escarlish fort, along with all of the troll and elf warriors who would attend the wedding. Since warriors from Tarenhiel and Kostaria were already in Escarland, the Escarlish generals had proposed to run a few short war games to test how the three kingdoms could best work together in the event of war.

Something that was even more critical, in the light of Mongavaria's recent poisoning of the smuggled grain.

The war games were something Vriska was looking forward to, here in Escarland. She wasn't sure how the Escarlish could make war into a less dangerous "game" as practice, but perhaps it would be like the fighting bouts in the arena. The kind where the warrior was tested and maybe a little blood was shed, but he yielded rather than died.

But after the war games...she and Julien would travel to Aldon as well, arriving just before the Mongavarian princess. And Vriska would have to pretend she was some kind of diplomat or princess material or whatever.

That was *not* something she looked forward to.

At least her family would be there. She would not be alone, as she had thought when she'd first started writing letters to Julien and considering this arranged marriage.

When would she return to Kostaria? Would she ever return? Even though her family would now reside in Escarland, her shield brothers remained in Kostaria. Her heart would be split across both kingdoms.

Would Julien understand that?

Perhaps he would. His sister—and soon his brother later today—had married an elf, splitting their time between two kingdoms. Would Julien be willing to do the same? Could they figure out how to balance his duty to his king and her duty to hers in a way that satisfied both of them?

The door opened, and Da stepped inside. After a round of good mornings, he kissed Ma's cheek and claimed his own plate of food.

Rikze yawned loudly, rolled from her cot, and stumbled to the table just as Ma placed food in front of her.

Vriska remained quiet as they ate. Throughout, Da told them stories about building the bridge. Only the funny ones.

Vriska could tell, at times, when he was editing out things for Rikze's benefit.

As they finished their breakfast, Ma motioned to Rikze. "Come. Let's wash the dishes."

Rikze grumbled under her breath, but she joined Ma in the kitchen area where a pump gushed water directly into a sink.

Da met Vriska's gaze, then pointed at the door, eyebrows raised in a silent question.

Vriska nodded and followed her da outside. Well, this must be it. The delayed discussion about Prince Julien and the whole betrothal thing.

He sat on the front step, and she sat next to him. Outside, the town didn't have the bustle of the night before, yet plenty of trolls and humans were already up and moving about. There was much to do before the wedding later that day.

While the land around the houses was strangely flat and empty, the homes still had the taste of Kostaria about them. All simple stone, even though they stood by themselves rather than formed out of the mountainsides like the houses at home.

"Now about this Prince Julien..." Da gave her one of those looks, trailing off as he waited for her to tell him whatever she was willing to say. As he'd done when she was little, he didn't press. He didn't ask prying questions. He simply waited.

With a deep breath, Vriska found herself spilling all of it. The treaty and the marriage of alliance. Rharreth coming to her with the offer. Meeting Prince Julien and the months they had spent getting to know each other.

She heaved a sigh and picked up a pebble from the

gravel street before tossing it to land in the dirt once again. "I don't know, Da. I like him, I think. He's kind and far more humble than any troll warrior I've ever met. But I just don't know. I never wanted to be anything but a warrior. I never really thought much about marriage and settling down and all that. My duty is to protect my king. But the war is over. I don't want to spend my life standing outside of doorways bored out of my mind. But I don't know if this is the future I want."

Da didn't reply right away. He picked up a handful of pebbles of his own, rolling them in his palm for several long minutes. "I can't answer that for you."

"I know." She wished he could.

"But I know you." Da smiled at her, his eyes holding an expression that was part proud, part sad. "You are my warrior girl. You don't enjoy cooking or keeping a house. You were never going to marry a common worker."

Vriska winced. "It isn't that I think you or Ma are less because you are common. Rikze will be happy to marry and settle down to a life like yours. But that's not me."

"No, it isn't." Da stared down the street, the rising sun stretching long shadows across the street. "Perhaps you could marry a troll warrior. One from a rich warrior family with their own stronghold. If you can find one who appreciates you for you and doesn't see your strength as a competition with his own. Or…"

"Or I can become a princess." Vriska tossed another pebble into the street.

"Not just a princess. An ambassador for our people." Da glanced at her, his gaze searching her face. "Rharreth is right. There will be many of our people moving to Escarland in the coming years."

"Like you, Ma, and Rikze." Vriska's throat tightened. Even though she'd seen it empty and forlorn, she still had a hard time believing that her family was leaving the home where she had grown up, even if she hadn't lived there since she had begun training to be a warrior.

"Yes, like us. Like many of the workers here." Da shrugged, his gaze swinging to take in the town before he smiled at her. "Whatever you do, your ma and I will be proud of you. We have always been so proud of you."

"I know." Vriska rested her elbows on her knees as she stared at the pink sunrise lingering at the horizon even as the sun made its way higher into the sky.

"I talked to Prince Julien early this morning. He seems like a good man." Da's smile turned wry with a touch of humor. "He asked me for my blessing."

"You what? He did? What did you tell him?" Vriska swiveled to better face her da. Why hadn't he said this earlier?

Of course he hadn't. He'd given Vriska the chance to vent all of her thoughts and feelings before he'd inserted any of his own. If he'd mentioned he'd talked to Prince Julien earlier, she would have held back her opinion until she'd heard his. A trait, it seemed, she had inherited from her father.

Da's smile twinkled in his eyes now. "I told him that since you hadn't punched him when he proposed, then he had my blessing."

Vriska heaved a sigh, her shoulders relaxing. Her da must like Julien. He wouldn't have joked with him or given him his blessing if he hadn't. Even if he had disguised it with the wording that indicated that she could take care of herself.

Why was she relieved? Did she really want her da giving Julien his blessing? As if she was in love with Julien and happy about this marriage and all that romantic stuff.

"Vriska." The smile dropped from Da's face as he, too, turned to better face her. "I have seen your drive and determination to fight for your goals in life. You worked hard to become a warrior, pushing through all the discrimination you faced coming from commoner parents. In the end, you not only became a warrior, but you earned a place in King Rharreth's shield band. I can't tell you what you should do now, but I do know that when you decide what future you want, you will fight for it just as hard as you did when you decided to become a warrior."

Vriska stared at the street, the bustle steadily growing, and let her da's words soak into her.

She hadn't been trying. Not really. Not the way that Julien had been risking his heart for the past three months. It wasn't fair to him the way she'd been letting him do all the work for this relationship.

It was beyond time she decided. She'd thought she'd decided when she'd taken his ring, but she was still holding back. She still wasn't pursuing a future with him the way she would if it was her true goal in life.

She wasn't sure how to go about really trying in this relationship. This wasn't like becoming a warrior. Then, the path had been laid out before her in a list of tasks and challenges to complete.

But this was a challenge of hearts and lives. Far more complicated, and it didn't come with nicely laid out goals to conquer.

She would have to think about it. Really, truly think about it.

"Linsh, Da." Perhaps he hadn't given her an answer, but he had pointed her in the right direction to come to the right conclusion herself.

Da nodded, acknowledging her thanks in his usual way. After a moment, his smile returned. "I hear that you have the honor of finishing the bridge."

"King Rharreth will also be finishing it." Vriska shrugged. "Besides, you and the other workers are the ones who did all the work. I'm just putting in the last few feet."

"Still, I can think of no one I would rather see have that honor than you and our king." Da patted her shoulder, then pushed to his feet. "I hear the kings of Escarland and Tarenhiel should be arriving shortly."

Vriska stood and stretched her tense muscles. Today would be far too busy for thinking.

CHAPTER TWENTY-ONE

Julien stood at the end of the dock on the Escarlish shore as he watched the elven boat glide across the Hydalla River. Over a year ago he'd stood here, waiting for Weylind and Farrendel to cross the river for Essie and Farrendel's Escarlish wedding in the small army outpost.

Today's wedding wouldn't be held inside its wooden walls but instead would take place on the soaring stone bridge that now dominated this section of the Hydalla River. Already, chairs and benches were being set up on both sides of the bridge.

Vriska stood beside Julien, shifting as if she wasn't comfortable being a part of these diplomatic proceedings. Rharreth and Melantha stood next to them and a few steps ahead while Brynjar, Eyvindur, and Zavni stood behind them, guarding their king and queen.

The elven boat docked, and a gangplank grew out of the side. King Weylind appeared at the rail, then strode down the gangplank, flanked by two guards.

Rharreth and Melantha strolled forward and met Weylind at the end of the dock. The two of them nodded to Weylind and Weylind nodded to them in the greeting of kings.

But then Rharreth gave a deeper bow as Melantha curtsied. "Linshi, Weylind, for the aid you sent to help with the poisonings. Your healers saved many lives, and your warriors have been invaluable in locating the poisoned grain before more were sickened. Kostaria is in your debt."

Beside Julien, Vriska stiffened. He, too, felt the weight of Rharreth's words. It was a dangerous thing, for one king to say he was in debt to another. Especially if their two kingdoms had been enemies as long as the elves and trolls had been.

"It was my pleasure to help, and you have my condolences for the losses your kingdom has suffered." Weylind shook his head, his long black hair flowing across his shoulders, dark against the green of his silk shirt and tunic. "There is no debt. This is the strength of our alliance."

After a moment, Rharreth nodded, and the postures of the two kings eased from their official, regal ones to something more relaxed.

Weylind stepped forward and gripped Melantha's shoulders. As Rharreth, Weylind, and Melantha greeted each other and spoke, Julien glanced over his shoulder, catching sight of smoke puffing into the sky.

Julien held out a hand to Vriska. "My family's train is on the way. Would you like to go with me to greet them?"

Vriska glanced toward Weylind and Rharreth, who were headed back in their direction and discussing how to divide up the troll warriors and workers between the two sides of the bridge. Then she straightened her shoulders and took Julien's hand. "Very well."

The two of them strolled from the dock toward the train platform to the side of the outpost. By the time they arrived, the train's brakes were screeching as it ground to a halt before the wooden platform.

Escarlish soldiers from the outpost were already assembling on the platform as well, either saluting or bowing when they caught sight of Julien.

Once the train was fully stopped and the steps lowered, Averett was the first to disembark, already wearing his crown. He strode to Julien and Vriska and clapped a hand to Julien's arm. "Good to see you again. Winstead Palace hasn't been the same without you watching my back."

"Good to be back. Avie, this is Vriska. Vriska, my brother Averett." Julien kept his grip on Vriska's hand, hoping she could sense how much he wanted her to feel at home with his family.

Averett grinned at Vriska and gestured to the sword she wore at her side. "I hear you can give my brother a run for his money when it comes to a fight. I hope you let him win once in a while."

Vriska's mouth tilted with the start of a smile, as if in spite of herself. "Occasionally."

Edmund joined them, his cheeks covered with scruff and his clothes rumpled. Edmund grinned at first Julien, then Vriska. "I see you managed not to get yourselves killed off in a Dulraith since I left."

Vriska grinned and rested a hand on her sword. "We would defeat anyone who was foolish enough to challenge us."

Julien's grin tugged at his mouth. At least Vriska liked

one of his family members, thanks to the month Edmund had spent in Kostaria while he and Jalissa helped track down the poisoned grain.

Julien raised his eyebrows at his brother. "You don't look exactly ready for this wedding."

Edmund shrugged. "An early morning. I didn't have a chance to change or shave before it was time to board the train, and I'm not about to risk shaving on a moving train."

Julien wasn't sure if he dared ask what that early morning involved. If he needed to know, Averett would fill him in once they returned to Aldon.

"I'm fine, Farrendel. I'm not going to fall on my face going down three stairs." Essie's voice came from the train, a hint of a laugh in her words.

Julien glanced up as Essie, hugely pregnant and resting a hand on her belly, navigated the steps one at a time. Farrendel stood behind her, his hands inches away from her as if he wanted to reach for her but didn't dare since she'd said she was fine.

Vriska stiffened, her face going blank.

The tension returned to Julien's shoulders. He had known she and Edmund got along, and he hadn't been worried about Averett.

But Farrendel was Laesornysh. He had been her kingdom's greatest enemy. Even Mongavaria with all the poisonings had killed fewer trolls than Farrendel had, though Mongavaria had targeted women and children in a time of peace while Farrendel had killed warriors when attacked during a time of war.

Essie crossed the platform with surprisingly spry and quick steps, given she was eight months pregnant. She went straight to Vriska, smiled, and pulled her in for a hug, made more awkward due to her belly getting in the way and Vriska's stiffness. "Welcome to Escarland, Vriska. I can't wait to officially welcome you to the family and have you for a sister."

Vriska made a strangled noise in the back of her throat, and her expression twisted with a strange look that Julien couldn't read, though she did pat Essie's shoulder after a moment.

Essie released Vriska and turned to Julien. "We missed you in Aldon. It doesn't seem the same with you gone."

"I was still there," Averett muttered behind them.

Julien grinned and hugged her, though he didn't squeeze as tightly or pull her off her feet as he might have if she hadn't been pregnant. "You are looking well."

"I'm looking very pregnant, you mean." Essie kept grinning as she stepped back and glanced over her shoulder at Farrendel. "Farrendel has been getting very good at lying and saying I look beautiful."

Farrendel gave her that too-blank, dour expression of his. "I do not lie."

"Uh-huh." She eyed him. "And how is all your homework going?"

Farrendel hesitated, glancing away from her and shifting from foot to foot. "I will get it done before we leave for Tarenhiel."

Essie turned back to Julien. "Don't worry. We're staying in Escarland for another two weeks so we'll have a chance to get to know Vriska a bit before we leave. Besides, Farrendel couldn't get more than a few weeks off from classes. The in-person ones are a lot harder to suddenly turn into correspondence courses."

Julien didn't try to interrupt. Nor did he really want the

details. From what he'd gathered now and in the letters he'd gotten from them while he was in Kostaria, they were planning to travel to Tarenhiel for the baby's birth. Partly because Tarenhiel had an abundance of healers who would keep Essie and the baby safe and partly because Farrendel's anxiety would be better when surrounded by his family and having the assurance of lots of elf healers on hand.

"I'm glad you're sticking around for a little while." Julien glanced from Essie to Farrendel. "I'd like a few sparring matches while we're both in Aldon."

"I would like that." Farrendel shifted again, glancing from Julien to Vriska then over to Essie, as if asking what he was supposed to do. At a look in return from Essie, Farrendel eased another step closer and nodded to Vriska. "Elontiri, Vriska."

"Laesornysh." Vriska sucked in a deep breath, her posture and expression still stiff.

Everyone stood there in tense silence for a moment. Julien glanced from Vriska to Farrendel and back.

"Well." Edmund broke the standoff, tugging at his shirt. "I need to get spiffed up before my wedding."

"And I should consult with Rharreth and Weylind about the troll guests." Averett glanced at Julien one last time before he hurried in the direction of the dock and the gathered troll warriors and workers.

As the others scattered, Vriska released a breath and leaned closer to Julien. "He's so young."

"Who? Farrendel?" Julien glanced at his brother-in-law as he and Essie made their way slowly up the hill to the army outpost.

"Yes. He doesn't look old enough to be the great warrior

Laesornysh." Vriska shook her head, that strange expression crossing her face again.

"He started rather young. I gather it was out of desperation." Julien still held Vriska's hand. Where were the two of them expected to go? Should they help with organizing the troll guests? Or should he visit the outpost and see if he could help with preparations there?

Vriska glanced toward Farrendel and Essie again and sighed. "It makes it harder to hate him."

"I think that's the point of this alliance and events that bring our peoples together like this wedding. Or the war games." Julien squeezed her hand, wishing he felt free enough to tilt her face to look at him. "Our kings are doing their best to erase the hatred between our three kingdoms to make us stronger and better than we were before."

She nodded, a furrow creasing her forehead even if she didn't speak.

It was a start, at least. That meeting had gone better than he'd feared, so that was something. He couldn't expect Vriska to see Farrendel as a brother overnight, but perhaps she could get there, eventually.

All his siblings had found spouses who fit right into the family. He didn't want to be the one sibling to fail at that. Nor would he want to bring internal strife. They had been so close. He didn't want to be the one who destroyed that.

JULIEN NAVIGATED the halls of the small military outpost, dodging around the soldiers and visiting nobility that crammed the halls.

At Edmund's door, Julien knocked, then stepped inside without waiting for Edmund's answer.

Inside, Edmund stood in front of the small mirror, his face lathered as he carefully shaved. He wore elven trousers, but he had yet to don a shirt. His gaze met Julien's in the mirror, his mouth quirking with a grin through the lather.

Julien shut the door, then leaned against the wall. "I see you are getting all spruced up for the wedding. Not going for the scruffy look?"

"Jalissa's an elf. She prefers me clean shaven." Edmund's grin left as he scraped the razor across his chin. "I guess I'll never have a beard like yours."

"You're just jealous that you never could've had a beard like mine regardless." Julien grinned and stroked the bristles of his beard, softer than they used to be now that he washed his beard with elven shampoo and conditioner.

After a moment, his smile fled. Did Vriska like his beard? Or would she prefer he, too, were clean shaven, since trolls, like elves, could not grow beards? He wasn't sure how he would feel about that. He rather liked his beard. And he wasn't sure how to go about asking her.

"Very true." Edmund grinned again. "My scruff was always rather pitiful. Guess I've always been an elf at heart."

It was part of what made Edmund such a good spy in Tarenhiel for so many years. He had been able to integrate into their society so thoroughly that he'd never been caught. At least, not in Tarenhiel. And that time he was caught in Kostaria was because he'd done something foolish.

"Ready to marry your elf princess?" Julien didn't really have to ask. Edmund's easy grin was coming even quicker this morning.

"Beyond ready." Edmund scraped the razor over his

cheek one last time before he took the towel and wiped off the remnants of lather. "What about you? How are things with your troll bride-to-be?"

Julien had braced himself for his siblings' questions, but he still wasn't sure how to answer. He pushed away from the wall and sank onto the one chair in the room, buying himself a few more seconds. "As well as can be expected, I suppose."

Edmund turned and crossed his arms. "Now what is that supposed to mean? That doesn't sound like things are going particularly well at all."

"No, it is. It's just..." Julien dragged a hand over his beard again, sagging against the back of the chair behind him. "I like her. But I'm not sure she likes me the same way. Or that she even wants to try."

"Ah." Edmund reached for his elven tunic and pulled it over his head. It settled over his broad shoulders, leaving a large V of his chest still visible. "You can't make someone fall in love with you."

"I know. But I still thought this would be a lot easier." Julien shook his head, not wanting to meet his brother's all-too-searching gaze.

"Love isn't as easy as it appears on the surface. But Jalissa and I had a spark and we were drawn to each other." Edmund's smile took on a wry tilt, hinting at secrets even Julien didn't know and wasn't about to pry to find out. After a moment, his smile disappeared, and his gaze searched Julien's face. "Is that the case for you and Vriska? It looked like there was when I saw you in Kostaria."

Why had he started this conversation? "Yes. Maybe. At least for me."

Edmund nodded, as if he read far more into those words

than Julien had meant to tell him. He pushed up his sleeve and secured his derringer in its holster to his forearm.

Julien needed to change the subject before Edmund probed any further. "Watch your back in Mongavaria."

Since they would be going their separate ways for the week between the wedding and Edmund and Jalissa's departure for Mongavaria, Julien wouldn't see Edmund again before he left.

Edmund grinned, as if he was looking forward to the trip into the bowels of the kingdom who had tried to assassinate the elven royal family six months ago and had poisoned a great many in Kostaria. "I'll watch Jalissa's back and she'll watch mine. And Sarya, Jalissa's rather loyal guard, will keep an eye on both of us. We'll be fine."

"You'd better be." Julien hadn't liked the thought of Edmund and Jalissa traveling to Mongavaria before, but he liked it even less now.

"Mongavaria wouldn't dare harm us, not while their heir is in Escarland." Edmund added a few more of his hidden knives into place.

If this was the precaution that Edmund was taking for a perfectly safe wedding, then surely he would be beyond careful once in Mongavaria.

Julien sighed and shook his head. "Perhaps. But we never would have guessed they would take the opportunity to poison so many trolls. Rharreth is still fending off calls for war because the trolls are so outraged. Did you ever figure out which Escarlish lord is doing the smuggling?"

"I've narrowed it down to two suspects. General Bloam and Averett have been briefed on who they are." Edmund tugged at his sleeves, likely checking that his derringer and knife were fully hidden, before he faced Julien again. "I'm hoping I'll find the final piece of proof I need once I'm in Mongavaria. After all, this noble's ships are stopping somewhere in Mongavaria to pick up grain to smuggle into Kostaria, all while sending his own Escarlish grain with the approved shipments to make himself look aboveboard. I need to not only prove which Escarlish noble is involved but also prove the Mongavarian crown knows about the smuggling and ordered the poisoning."

And that was on top of whatever other information Edmund intended to glean while in Mongavaria. Not to mention, Edmund couldn't be caught doing all this spying. As a diplomat, he was protected…unless he was caught actively spying.

Another knock sounded on the door moments before Averett stepped inside, closing the door behind him.

Averett released a breath and sagged against the door. "It's getting chaotic out there. I'm not sure I'll be able to snatch another quiet moment until this hullabaloo is over."

"Hullabaloo?" Edmund smirked and crossed his arms again.

"Yes. Hullabaloo." Averett grimaced and flopped onto the army cot along one side with a sigh. "I'm pretty sure even my coronation didn't have this much commotion."

Julien resisted a groan. He was likely going to get roped into helping with crowd control, especially since he was the official liaison between Escarland and Kostaria, thanks to his semi-official betrothal to Vriska.

"Apparently this is the international event of the year." Edmund's smirk remained in place for another moment before his gaze swept over both Averett and Julien, something changing in his expression.

It took Julien another moment to sense what had caused

this change. This was likely the only quiet moment they would have as brothers before Edmund's wedding. From this day on, their lives would change again.

Essie's marriage had already taken her to Tarenhiel, at least part of the time. And Edmund's role of spy had also taken him far from Escarland for many years. Yet once he married Jalissa, he would again spend much of his time in Tarenhiel.

Averett sat up, glancing between them. He braced his arms behind him. "You're going to live for hundreds of years like Essie, aren't you?"

"Probably." Edmund nodded, solemn. "She won't be alone."

Averett turned to Julien. "You aren't allowed to get one of these heart bond things too, got it?"

Julien hadn't wanted to think about that too much. How awkward would it be to marry Vriska and age so quickly? Sure, she wouldn't age as slowly as an elf, but she would still outlive him by many hundreds of years. "Vriska is a troll. I've never heard anyone mention that trolls still have heart bonds."

"About that..." Edmund shifted as both Averett and Julien turned to him. "You might want to ask Vriska about it. Trolls are technically mountain elves."

Edmund's voice had that quality to it that said he knew something that he wasn't telling Julien outright.

"Great. I'm going to be the only one of us to live a normal human lifespan, aren't I?" Averett gave an exaggerated sigh and flopped back on the bed again.

"Don't worry." Edmund stepped forward and poked Averett's side. "We'll still be your brothers even when you're old and crotchety and we're young and handsome."

Averett dodged away from Edmund's finger and rolled to his feet. "I'm going to hold you to that."

Julien glanced at his two brothers. This would be the dividing line between them. If Edmund's hinting was correct, then Julien likely would watch Averett grow old and die long before he did.

If he married Vriska. If he could convince her to fall in love with him beyond this tepid respect that they had developed. If they could have a relationship like Averett with Paige, Essie with Farrendel, Edmund with Jalissa.

And right now, Julien wasn't sure that was possible, much less likely.

CHAPTER TWENTY-TWO

Vriska waited at the starting line, her muscles ready but not tensed. A reckless surge bubbled in her chest, eager for the burst of energy, the beating of her heart, the adrenaline of the contest.

In front of her, an obstacle course of ropes, wood planks, and a tall wooden wall stretched before her with muddy pits to soften any falls, should they occur.

Behind her, a mixed team of elves, trolls, and humans waited, their various uniforms and clothing spattered with mud and dirt from previous obstacle courses, wrestling matches, and combat bouts they'd done that morning already.

And beside her, Julien waited at the head of his own team, a broad grin framed by his beard as he shot her a glance. By this, their second day of team exercises, his beard was more scraggly and scruffy than she'd ever seen it. The black paint his team had smeared across their cheeks added to his wild look.

Here in Escarland and at Fort Charibert, Julien had an extra confidence to his step, his shoulders broader, his head higher. He was in his element here in a way he hadn't been in Kostaria.

And both the confidence and the wildness were attractive. Very attractive.

She jumped at the sharp whistle that signaled the start, and she surged off the line a heartbeat behind Julien. With a growl, she pounded forward, catching up with him by the time they reached the zigzag pattern of thin beams stretching over a mud pit.

He started over his beam, and she ran lightly over her own. At the end, she halted and spun to check on her team members, calling back encouragement and orders to hurry them along.

One of the trolls on Julien's team reached over and shoved one of her elves off the beam. With a short cry, the elf plunged into the mud below. He came up sputtering and disgruntled.

Before Vriska had a chance to shout an order, one of the trolls on her team slugged the one on Julien's team, sending the troll into the mud as well.

"Don't slow down to get into a brawl!" Julien motioned the elves on his team past him, and they threw themselves at the dangling ropes over the next mud pit.

"Help him up and get moving!" Vriska stepped aside as the other two elves on her team made it to her side of the beam.

The troll who'd slugged the other in retaliation gripped the muddy elf's hand and hauled him to the beam. When the elf struggled to gain his footing since he was so muddy, the troll all but slung him over his shoulder and carried him the rest of the way across.

The humans on the team were slower to cross than the elves or trolls, but soon all of them were across and swinging on the ropes. The elves managed the ropes easily, and they helped the less agile human soldiers manage the feat. The trolls weren't as aerially gifted as the elves, but they were strong and agile enough to cross the ropes without help.

At the tall wall, the trolls stood at the bottom and hefted each of the elves and humans onto their shoulders, boosting them to the top. At the top, Vriska and the others then reached down and pulled the troll team members up.

Julien's team still beat them, their last team member beating hers by a second. While his team celebrated, Vriska circled her team. "Well done. We'll get them on the next one."

The trolls on her team growled. The humans grinned and pounded fists into palms. The elves were more subdued, but they still nodded with hints of fierce smiles creasing their too-beautiful faces. Well, too beautiful except for the one who was currently covered in quickly drying mud.

At the end of the obstacle course, two more teams—one led by Zavni, the other led by a female elf warrior—gathered at the starting line to take their turn. Zavni was flirting outrageously with the female elf, and she was rolling her eyes and slinging insults back at him.

Julien halted next to Vriska, and she gave him a light punch on the arm. "Well done on the win."

"Linsh." Julien grinned and gestured at their teams. Each of the teams were joking and laughing together as they took a moment to drink water and rest for a moment before they headed to their next event. "The generals' idea to spend two days on team bonding events seems to be paying off."

The elf, troll, and human generals had decided to spend two of the five days on team events like this obstacle course to work out any trouble between the three armies before they launched into staged war simulations. On the first day, tensions had broken out, but they had been quickly quelled. The troublemakers—whether they had been troll, elf, or human—had been sent home. And the threat of being sent home in disgrace was enough to keep everyone else in line.

Besides a few lighthearted incidents like the one that had happened during the obstacle course, the threat seemed to have worked.

"Yes. Though I'm looking forward to starting the actual war games tomorrow." Vriska accepted a filled canteen from the young Escarlish boy who had been tasked with distributing water among the soldiers and warriors.

Tomorrow, the real fun would begin. The warriors and soldiers would be split into two sides, and they would have two and a half days of simulated warfare. The last day, Farrendel Laesornysh would arrive for a final battle, complete with magic and artillery.

Strangely, she was even looking forward to that fight against Laesornysh. It would be something to see him wield his magic without the danger of instant death a moment later. It had been a sight to behold when she'd witnessed his destruction of Gror Grar and again when he'd built the Gulmorth Bridge alongside Rharreth. Julien assured her that his brother-in-law's magic was even more impressive now.

All the effort of these war games was supposed to help the generals and commanders develop strategies for working together, should the three kingdoms be forced to fight a war as an alliance. These five days here at Fort Charibert were only the start, the first of many war games to be held in all three kingdoms in the future.

Vriska swept a glance over her team, Julien's team, then on to the obstacle course where Zavni and the elf warrior led their teams across the beams, Zavni still flirting even as their teams competed. Beyond the obstacle course, other teams roamed about Fort Charibert's training facilities while the Escarlish staff kept things running smoothly. A few elven healers clustered along the side, ensuring that injuries were dealt with promptly.

Vriska resisted the urge to roll her eyes. Of course the elves would get a little squeamish at the thought of someone getting hurt.

Though, it probably wouldn't go over so well if anyone were killed at these war games. This was supposed to be a chance to work together in peace, not start fighting each other again for real.

Beyond the healers, the wooden buildings of Fort Charibert sprawled against the lightly forested practice ranges. Long Escarlish artillery guns lined up under tarpaulins, impressive even at rest.

Vriska caught her breath and stared out over the forested hills and the Escarlish guns casting long shadows. This was her new future. Not one of boredom where she spent her life standing guard outside of doors. But one where she fought in these war games and led the change in her peoples' warriors. She would help her people as they integrated to a new life in Escarland while also never forgetting her roots in Kostaria.

This was a new dream worth fighting for. This was something she could put her focus into achieving the way she had to become a warrior.

And in this future, Julien was there, with his scruffy beard and grin daring her to push herself further. It was both strange and not strange at the same time how she couldn't banish him from these dreams, hard as she tried.

Her world was changing. Kostaria was changing under Rharreth and Melantha. Her family was changing by moving to Escarland. Was it time that she changed too?

JULIEN GRIPPED HIS SWORD, keeping his back to Vriska as he stuck close enough that her shield of magic protected them from the lashing roots of elven magic, a barrage of stone troll magic, and stray bolts of Farrendel's magic.

Ahead, Farrendel stood in the center of a small cluster of elf and troll warriors and human soldiers. Their small army had been backed into a corner formed by large boulders at the edge of one of Fort Charibert's vast training ranges.

Vriska marched another step forward and planted her magical shield in the ground, waiting as Julien and the human soldier assigned to them took another step forward to match her.

Next to them, the other trolls and elves in their teams worked in groups to protect the human soldiers. In the pauses, the humans stepped out from the shields to shoot their muskets or rifles before ducking into cover.

The majority of the elves, trolls, and humans who had gathered for the war games currently stretched in a half-circle facing Farrendel and his small knot of warriors. Long lines of artillery guns boomed, filling the air with smoke and reverberating noise, while repeater guns spat blanks above the heads of the gathered army.

It looked terribly unbalanced, with Farrendel and so few facing such an army arrayed against him.

But this was Farrendel. Even the token army assigned to him was probably superfluous.

Julien frowned as he and Vriska marched another few steps forward before taking up their new position. He couldn't put his finger on it, but something didn't seem right. Farrendel was wielding his magic, yes, but he was sticking to the minimum defense, providing a shield from the empty artillery shells and repeater gun blanks. But he was letting the vast army surround him and press his soldiers into this corner.

Sure, this current display was impressive. But Julien had seen Farrendel wield his magic since he'd gained more control of it. He could do more than he was.

Why was he holding back? Was his old anxiety of hurting others preventing him from using his magic in full force the way Julien knew he could?

Perhaps it was a wise precaution and a genuine fear. After all, not even the best healer could mend someone if Farrendel's magic incinerated them.

But the point of the war games was to test not only their capabilities but also their limits. They needed to know the limits of what Farrendel could handle or how an enemy might try to take him out, if they were to prevent such a thing happening in the event a real war should be declared. It did them no good if they defeated Farrendel because he was holding back too much.

Vriska glanced over her shoulder, her reckless grin changing to a frown. "Is something wrong?"

Julien had to shout to be heard over the boom of artillery, crack of repeater guns, pop of muskets, shouting warriors, and the sizzle of magic roaring in the air. "Something is wrong. Farrendel is holding back."

"This is holding back?" Vriska grunted, her magical shield momentarily wavering under the mere brush of a bolt of Farrendel's power.

"Yes." Julien advanced another few strides with her. They would likely engage Farrendel's beleaguered soldiers in a few more minutes.

Around them, the entire front line of the army advanced. Even the rear of the army was now in view, clustered around the guns, which had been at the front when they'd cornered Farrendel here.

Farrendel swept another glance over the lines of soldiers, his magic still swirling around him and protecting those with him.

Then, he smirked.

"We're dead." Julien sighed and lowered his sword.

Vriska glanced over her shoulder at him again. "What—"

A wall of Farrendel's magic burst from the ground behind the rear ranks of their army. The shouts turned to a few screams at the sight, the disciplined ranks breaking apart. Seconds later, a similar wall burst in front of them, running between them and Farrendel's small army.

The two walls rose, enclosing their larger, seemingly superior army. Then, as if to prove that their defeat was total, a light layer of Farrendel's magic washed over them, coating the guns and the people without burning them.

Julien sucked in a breath as the tingly feel of Farrendel's magic coated his exposed skin and prickled along his scalp.

With a sigh, he sheathed his sword. "Well, that's it. Farrendel totally crushed us."

Vriska straightened, her magical shield utterly annihilated in the face of Farrendel's awe-inspiring magic. She lifted her hand, gaping at the layer of blue, fizzling and sparking magic coating her skin. "This is incredible."

After another heartbeat, Farrendel's magic dropped, bursting into fizzles and sparks. The two walls slammed back into the ground, shaking the earth beneath their feet before everything went quiet.

Vriska shook herself and drew in a breath that had a hint of a shudder to it. "I'm glad Laesornysh is on our side now."

"Me too." Julien stretched and shook out limbs that were sore after the grueling last few days. He was looking forward to sleeping in his own, comfortable bed at Winstead Palace that night. Not that he would admit it to anyone.

The generals and commanders called the warriors and soldiers to order. As they gathered, General Freilan launched into a speech about the success of the war games and how he looked forward to more war games in the future.

But Julien turned in the other direction. Surprisingly, Vriska fell into step with him with less reluctance than she used to show around him. The war games had been good for them. Her grins as they fought side-by-side gave him hope that perhaps he wasn't as mistaken to be attracted to her—to have asked her to marry him—as he'd feared.

Farrendel strolled toward them. No, more like sauntered. Julien wasn't sure if he'd ever seen his brother-in-law strut with that kind of confidence before. It was both good and rather amusing to see.

"Your head is going to get too big for your shoulders at

this rate." Julien crossed his arms and grinned as Farrendel came within talking range.

Farrendel's brow wrinkled. "I guess it will match my ears, then."

In anyone else, Julien might have worried about arrogance. But not Farrendel. "I'm sure Essie will like you no matter how arrogant you get."

Farrendel's smile turned a hint soft at the mention of Essie's name. "She told me to show off."

"Of course she did." Julien shook his head, a fond smile tugging at his beard.

No one cheered Farrendel on quite as much as Essie did. She celebrated every accomplishment, every victory, with an excitement that had given Farrendel the confidence to keep pursuing his goals and pushing forward when he faced difficulties.

Essie had been right, all those months ago. For years, Julien's job had been to look after his siblings. But Essie had Farrendel. Edmund had Jalissa. Averett had Paige and didn't need Julien to stand at his back as he once did. It was time for Julien to let his siblings live their lives while he found his own.

With Vriska. Would Julien have the chance to cheer Vriska on the way Essie cheered Farrendel?

Farrendel gestured in the direction in which the fort lay. "You are welcome to share my train back to Aldon. Unless you need to stay to finish your duties here?"

Julien glanced toward the armies. The commanders were currently breaking the warriors into groups, organizing them for the hike back to the fort. At the fort, they would break camp and start boarding trains to return to Kostaria and Tarenhiel.

"We need to grab our things, then we'll be all set, I think." Julien held out a hand to Vriska. "Do you have any duties you need to see to before we leave?"

She shook her head. "Brynjar, Eyvindur, and Zavni are going to see to those returning to Kostaria."

She flicked a glance at Farrendel, her stance going stiff again. She likely wasn't looking forward to spending a few hours on a train with Farrendel, yet she didn't make an excuse to stay and wait for the next train either.

"Very well." Julien turned back to Farrendel. "Yes, we'll take your train to Aldon. If you don't mind us intruding on your after-battle quiet time."

Farrendel waved the comment away as he started to turn toward the train. "I will be on the roof most of the trip anyway. You will not intrude unless you too wish to use the roof for exercising."

"Not a chance." Julien shook his head, giving an exaggerated shudder. He'd poked his head out the window once to watch as Farrendel flipped about on the roof as if entirely unafraid of falling off the speeding train and getting ground into a pulp by the wheels. No way was Julien trying that.

Vriska huffed and muttered under her breath just loud enough for Julien to hear, "*Elves*."

Perhaps Farrendel, with his elven hearing, caught her mutter as well because his smirk widened as he strode away with that hint of a jaunty saunter still in his steps.

Julien and Vriska followed at a slower pace, swinging toward the sections of tents where they would separate to grab their things before boarding the train. It was becoming increasingly comfortable, striding next to her like this as the fort and outlying troll and elven encampments bustled with activity around them.

Soon, they would be in Aldon. Facing the Escarlish court and the Mongavarian princess.

Would this new ease he felt with Vriska survive that? Or would the intrigue of the Escarlish court—so different from her world in Kostaria—send her away from him once and for all?

CHAPTER TWENTY-THREE

Julien stood next to Vriska in the front entry hall of Winstead Palace. At any moment, the train carrying Averett and the princess of Mongavaria would arrive.

Paige and Mother also stood in the front entry with them, both of them wearing silk dresses and tiaras. In contrast, Vriska wore a nicer version of her leather vest over a gray shirt and brown trousers. Her only jewelry items were the decorations in her hair, complete with his ring winking in the sunlight coming through the high windows.

Even though Farrendel and Essie were still in residence at Buckmore Cottage, and would be for another five days or so, neither of them were present for this official meeting. Essie was far enough along to beg off official functions; it was considered improper for her to attend for anything less than a wedding at this point, and even that had caused gossip that she would dare go out in public in her condition. And Farrendel wasn't about to participate in a social function if he didn't have to, especially not without Essie at his side.

Besides, neither Averett nor Julien was eager to have Farrendel or Essie around the Mongavarian princess if they could manage it without appearing rude to the visiting royalty. The Mongavarian spies had tried to assassinate Farrendel and Essie six months ago. Julien wouldn't put it past this Mongavarian princess to whip out a pistol and try to shoot Farrendel, if she had the opportunity.

Was that the reason the Mongavarians had pushed for this diplomat swap? Their spy-assassins had failed, so now they sent in their princess to finish the job instead?

No, surely not. She would be caught if she tried to kill Farrendel and Essie, and the Mongavarians wouldn't risk their only heir.

Still, Farrendel and Essie wouldn't attend any of the formal dinners or functions with the Mongavarian princess. If they could avoid even seeing her, that would be the best thing.

Vriska shifted, her gaze darting about the hall as if looking for an escape.

Julien laid a hand over hers where it rested on his arm. "Life as royalty is surprisingly boring. You spend a great deal of time behind the scenes waiting around just to make the perfect entrance or the right impression."

A hint of her smile broke through her hard, neutral expression. "Being a warrior involves a great deal of standing around, guarding the king and queen while they are standing around."

"True." Julien tilted his head, hoping that the faint sound he heard was the train pulling into the small station inside the palace walls. He gave her a larger smile, hoping she could read the depth of his sincerity in his eyes. "I'm glad you're here with me. It has been a little awkward, standing by myself at these functions when all of my siblings are paired off."

He kept his voice low so that Paige and Mother wouldn't hear more than the fact that he was whispering to Vriska. He had been serving as Mother's escort, and he wouldn't want her to think that he resented that.

Vriska snorted, waving toward the door with her free hand. "I heard all about how the Mongavarian princess was hoping to get her claws into you while she was here, you being the only unmarried Escarlish prince. You're just glad I'm here to protect you from her."

He grinned, glad that they were at a point where they could banter reasonably well. "That's the plan."

Vriska's grin held the hint of a snarl, her eyes glittering. "I'll punch her if she tries anything."

"Please don't cause an international incident on my account." Julien eyed her, taking in the way she clenched her fist, her other hand tightening around his bicep. She wasn't really planning to punch the Mongavarian princess, was she?

"It wouldn't be only on your account." Vriska's grin dropped, replaced with gritted teeth. "I would be more than happy to give any Mongavarian royalty a taste of my fist for what they did to my ma and sister and all the others they poisoned in my kingdom."

"We don't know that the Mongavarian royalty was involved." Though they strongly suspected. It was unlikely someone else had conducted such a poisoning effort on their own without the Mongavarian king at least giving tacit approval at best, direct orders at worst.

"Of course they were. No one believes otherwise, even if you won't admit it officially." Vriska flexed her fingers, her jaw as hard as the stones of Winstead Palace around them.

Julien swallowed back the rising panic. He wasn't sure he could stop Vriska if she took it in her head to punch the Mongavarian princess. He might agree with her about what the Mongavarian royalty deserved, but they were currently standing on Escarlish soil. It wouldn't be good if the Mongavarian princess was assaulted during an official welcome.

Even beyond the ramifications it would have for their relations with Mongavaria—shaky as those already were—there would be consequences with other nations who would hesitate to send diplomats to Escarland, thereby isolating Escarland and thus the whole alliance. And if Mongavaria took advantage of that isolation to make alliances of their own…

It wouldn't be good. It just wouldn't.

Vriska glanced at him and something between a grimace and a smirk eased some of the hardness from her jaw. "Don't worry. I'm not going to just haul off and punch her. Not unless she does something to deserve it."

That was probably the best he was going to get. He kept his hand over hers on his arm, as if he could keep her in place at his side.

At the entryway, two footmen pulled open the heavy, ornate doors, standing to attention.

Julien quickly schooled his features to the blank, royal mask that he'd been raised to wear. Next to him, Vriska still looked like she wanted to kill something, but that was likely to be expected.

Averett strode up the palace steps with a young woman around Essie's age on his arm. A swarm of guards trailed behind them, wearing Escarlish and Mongavarian colors and eyeing each other warily.

The Mongavarian princess's blonde hair glinted in the afternoon sunlight. Her perfect, porcelain skin matched her delicate features and the grace in her movements. Her demure, lavender dress draped around her lovely, corseted figure while white gloves covered her slim fingers.

She was the image of the perfect princess. Utterly beautiful. Delicate. Poised. Graceful. Everything he had once thought he would like in the woman he married.

Nothing at all like the troll woman standing at Julien's side.

Vriska stiffened still further, her stance going rigid while her eyes were flinty.

Glancing between her and the Mongavarian princess, he eased a little closer to Vriska. Of the two, she was the one he wanted at his side.

Perhaps the Mongavarian princess was nice enough, but he didn't know her.

He knew Vriska. Her love for her family. Her drive to achieve her goals. Her loyalty to her king and kingdom. Her faithfulness to her duty. Her strength when facing difficulties. The way she had trusted him to see her break and cry when she never let anyone else see her that weak and vulnerable.

And, yes, apparently he had a thing for tall, muscular women who could beat the stuffing out of anyone who hurt her family.

Averett halted in front of Mother and Paige, released the

princess's arm, and stepped to Paige's side. "Princess Bella of Mongavaria, may I present to you my wife, Queen Paige of Escarland, and my mother Queen Mother Ariana of Escarland."

Princess Bella swept into a lovely curtsy. "It is my pleasure to meet you, Your Majesties. I bring you greetings on behalf of my father and grandfather and on behalf of the Mongavarian people."

Paige smiled and returned the curtsy with a nod. "Welcome to Escarland, Princess Bella. I hope your stay will be comfortable and beneficial to our kingdoms."

With another smile, Princess Bella moved to Julien and Vriska, Averett at her side. With another of his practiced, king smiles, Averett nodded to each of them. "This is my brother Prince Julien and his betrothed, Lady Vriska, shield sister to King Rharreth of Kostaria."

If he hadn't been watching, Julien wouldn't have seen the brief tightening of the princess's rosebud mouth and the flash in her eyes before she schooled her features behind the pleasant mask.

She had been hoping for a betrothal to him, as they had guessed from the wording of the Mongavarian king's letter. But Averett hadn't promised a betrothal, and she couldn't argue if Julien happened to already be betrothed.

Julien patted Vriska's hand and glanced at her, adding a little edge of charm to his voice and warmth to his gaze. "I met Vriska on my recent trip to Kostaria and fell head over heels for her."

Vriska met his gaze, a hint of a frown teasing the corners of her mouth. Perhaps he had laid it on a tad thick.

Princess Bella smiled, any hints of disappointment

banished from her face. "How fortunate for you. Love can be such a rare thing for those of our rank."

Instead of disappointment, a hint of hurt colored her words. Vulnerability flashed in her blue eyes before she turned away.

"My family has been blessed in that regard." Averett held out his arm, and Paige took it, snuggling closer to Averett than was likely proper, though not excessively so. With a smile, Averett gestured to one of the maids standing at the edge of the room. "The maid will show you to your rooms, and the footmen will bring your luggage."

"Please let the staff know if you need anything to make your stay more comfortable." Paige also remained smiling, the picture of a gracious queen. "Your rooms have already been prepared, if you would like to rest before supper after your long journey."

"Thank you." With another curtsy, Princess Bella followed the maid with her guards trailing behind her. The footmen would already be at work, carrying her luggage from the train, through a side entrance, and up the back stairs to her rooms.

Once the princess was gone, Julien allowed his shoulders to relax as he turned to Averett. "How did the exchange go?"

"It went well enough. Farrendel's magic didn't cause any problems with travel over the border." Averett's jaw tightened.

They had worried that Farrendel's protective magic along the border wouldn't allow the Mongavarian princess and her guards to enter. But the magic seemed to sense that they weren't a direct attack and had allowed them inside Escarland. Perhaps that was an indication that the princess didn't have any nefarious schemes planned while she was here in Escarland.

Though, she didn't seem the nefarious type. She was too delicate. Too much a princess. Surely she was innocent—or mostly so—of any schemes that her father and grandfather might have. She might try to marry into the Escarlish royal family on behalf of her kingdom, but she likely wasn't an assassin.

"Edmund and Jalissa?" Julien's stomach tightened. By this point, Edmund and Jalissa would have been in Mongavaria for most of the day, traveling down the Hydalla River to the coast where a ship would take them to the Mongavarian capital city of Landri.

"Edmund looked eager to leave." Averett sighed and shook his head, as if he thought their brother was a touch crazy. Julien couldn't help but agree. "As worried as I am for them, I'm glad Jalissa is with him. He won't do anything too foolish when she's there."

Perhaps. But Jalissa was more daring than she seemed on the surface. She had to be, to have married Edmund. Perhaps Edmund wouldn't do anything too reckless, but that didn't mean the two of them wouldn't take risks if they thought it would get them the information their kingdoms needed.

"They'll take care of each other." Paige squeezed Averett's arm, sending a glance toward Mother, whose face had gone tense. "Now, let's enjoy the rest of our afternoon before the formal supper this evening. Vriska, I'd love to get to know you better. Let's retire to the garden where we can chat."

Vriska shifted, but she nodded and let go of Julien's arm.

After how tightly she had been gripping him, his arm tingled a bit as blood flowed back into his skin and fingers.

JULIEN SAT between Vriska and Princess Bella at the long oak table in the private, formal dining room.

Vriska stabbed at her steak and devoured large chunks at a time. Still, it wasn't like she chewed with her mouth open or let meat juice dribble down her chin. She just enjoyed her food with gusto.

On his other side, Princess Bella neatly sliced off small bites and chewed gracefully, keeping up a steady conversation with Averett at the head of the table and Paige across from her. Occasionally, she glanced at Julien and included him in the conversation. Nothing overtly flirtatious, but she didn't interact with Vriska at all.

Not that Vriska attempted a conversation with Princess Bella either. It made for a rather frosty supper, sitting between them.

As they finished, Princess Bella hung back. She rested a light hand on Julien's arm, peering up at him with large blue eyes framed with dark lashes. "May I speak with you a moment, Prince Julien?"

He glanced around. The others had moved to the door, but Vriska had paused, crossing her arms as she shot a death glare at Princess Bella. Averett, too, had halted, his gaze a silent question, asking if Julien wanted him to stay.

Julien made a subtle motion with his hand, telling him that it was all right if he left. At least one Escarlish guard would remain just inside the doorway, and the princess's guards would likely linger as well, so there was no danger of them being left alone.

Averett said something in a low tone to Vriska, and they left the room.

Julien turned back to Princess Bella and nodded. "Yes, of course. Was there something you needed, Princess Bella?"

She clasped her hands in front of her, something vulnerable twisting her beautiful face. "I suppose I should congratulate you on your betrothal, but I'm afraid I find myself rather disappointed. I was hoping when I came here that you and I…" She gave a self-deprecating laugh, a hint of pain in her eyes. "Well, obviously those hopes were in vain since you have already fallen in love with someone else."

"Yes, I have." Julien stated it quickly, hoping he sounded sincere. He was falling for Vriska, even if their relationship wasn't what they were pretending.

Perhaps he hadn't managed enough sincerity. Her head came up, her heart-shaped face framed by golden hair arranged in curls. She met his gaze, reached out, and rested a light hand on his arm. This time, she didn't withdraw it. "Are you in love with her? Or is it an arranged marriage? I can recognize the signs, you know. My parents had an arranged marriage. They were cordial with each other, but they never truly loved each other."

Cordial with each other. That described his relationship with Vriska all too well.

He shouldn't confide that to Princess Bella. Not only was she a foreign princess of an enemy kingdom, but it would be disloyal to Vriska.

Julien forced a smile and eased back as subtly as he could until her hand dropped from his arm. "Vriska is my choice."

"I understand." Princess Bella smiled, a liquid sadness

pooling in her blue eyes. She dropped her hand back to her side as she glided toward the door. A few steps past him, she half-turned around, that vulnerability still present in the way she carried herself. "But if you do wish an escape, please consider me an option."

Julien kept his mouth shut and just held her gaze until she turned and left.

He didn't want an escape. And even if he did, he wouldn't choose Princess Bella.

CHAPTER TWENTY-FOUR

Vriska scowled at her reflection in the mirrors. She looked like a seal. A big, fat seal stuffed into a silk casing.

She held her arms out, keeping them away from the pins that the Escarlish seamstress was stabbing into the silk she'd draped around Vriska in the vague shape of an Escarlish style dress.

Instead of accentuating a tiny, petite frame—like that rather breakable-looking, all-too-pretty Princess Bella—Vriska's lack of a waist and sturdy frame just looked huge in this dress.

She wasn't fat. Logically, she knew that. A good warrior always carried a little bit around the middle, needed for stamina and endurance. Not a hanging gut by any means, but not the unhealthily defined muscles that was the stereotype. A skinny little elf warrior could fight well for an hour or two, but she'd take a troll warrior's endurance any day.

Yet this dress wasn't designed for a warrior. It was meant

for a body like that full-figured, but skinny-waisted perfect princess.

Was that what Julien wanted? Vriska wouldn't ever be that shape. And why did she even care what Julien thought? Why did she get this burn inside her chest every time she saw the way that princess looked at him? As if she hadn't already had enough reason to consider breaking that perfectly straight nose in her punchable porcelain face.

The seamstress stood back, one hand on her hip, the other still clutching that pincushion filled with deceptively tiny needles that could pass as torture devices. "What do you think, Your Majesties?"

Julien's sister-in-law Paige and his mother sat on a couch along one wall of the sitting room in the suite Vriska had been given. Apparently, dress fittings were a whole public production here in Escarland. The maid had even brought tea and a tray of sweets for them to munch on while they watched the seamstress stuff Vriska into this dress.

Vriska glanced again at the tall tri-fold mirror that the seamstress's assistant had set up. Just to make sure Vriska had an excellent view of just how large she looked in this Escarlish dress.

She hated this dress. Hated the formal dinners and double-talking undertones running underneath the conversations when anyone besides Julien's family was present. Hated the rigid schedule and duties that had kept them so busy she hadn't even had a chance to see her family, even though she'd been in Aldon for four days. Only the stones of the palace felt familiar, even if they were all covered up with wooden paneling, fine furnishings, and opulent carpeting.

She'd thought she could handle this. But a mere four

days at court had shaken her resolve and confidence more than she cared to admit.

Paige stood, cocking her head as she paced around Vriska for a moment. "It is…" She trailed off, as if unsure what to say.

Julien's mother, too, regarded Vriska with a furrow puckering her forehead. "The work is excellent, as always. And there is nothing wrong with you, Vriska. It is just…"

A knock sounded on the door a moment before Princess Essie, Julien's sister, trundled through, shutting the door behind her.

Vriska grimaced. Even hugely pregnant, Essie managed to look better in the flowing dress than she did.

Essie halted a few steps into the room, her gaze focused on Vriska. "Oh dear."

The seamstress winced, then sighed. "I quite agree. This style is not right."

Paige breathed a sigh, as if she hadn't dared say such a thing out loud. "Exactly. Vriska needs something that captures her stately beauty, and the current Escarlish fashion doesn't do that. Perhaps we could include hints of her Kostarian culture?"

Stately beauty? Vriska had never heard herself described that way. She certainly didn't feel stately or beautiful at the moment.

She started to cross her arms, got stabbed by a host of needles at her underarms, and halted. "I don't see why I need a new dress for this ball. Can't I just wear my Kostarian clothes? I don't care about fitting in or anything like that. I'm a troll. I'll dress like a troll."

"I understand that. And I know you don't care about the gossips. Not that you should. You should ignore them."

Essie walked closer with a slight waddle. "But a dress is a kind of armor. Perhaps not the type of armor you normally wear, but you'll quickly learn a ballroom is a battlefield, and your dress is your shield. When you look your best, you'll feel confident enough to take on the gossips."

"Well, I'll feel more confident in my old clothes." Vriska stuck her arms out again, waving her hands to indicate the dress. "Not this."

"Perhaps you would." Julien's mother held her gaze in that same, soft look that Vriska got so often from her own mother. "Or you would feel even more out of place."

More out of place. Had Julien and his family seen how off Vriska felt, here in Escarland? It was as if the whole world had tilted, and she had yet to regain her footing.

"We all agree that you shouldn't be asked to give up your troll heritage. Of course not." Paige shook her head and joined Essie. "Any ideas? You have a better eye for style than I do."

"Perhaps." Essie reached for the sketchbook the seamstress had set aside and turned to a fresh page. "Maybe something like this?"

She sketched something on the page, out of Vriska's line of sight. The seamstress and Paige leaned closer.

After a moment, the seamstress's eyes widened. "It is daring, Your Highness."

Paige grinned and nodded. "But perfect, I think. Besides, who's going to argue? As Vriska said, she's a troll. She needs to reflect that in her style."

Essie flipped the sketchbook around and held it out to Vriska. "What do you think?"

Vriska took in the rough sketch. She didn't have much imagination to envision what she was seeing on paper as a dress on herself. But it did seem better than the sausage casing she was currently wearing. "Sure. Whatever you think is best."

The seamstress nodded, then started divesting Vriska of the pins and fabric. Once she had refolded the fabric, she bowed and mumbled something about fetching more supplies before she and her assistant hurried off.

After Vriska dressed in her shirt, leather vest, trousers, and boots, Essie waved her toward the chair across the table. "Have a seat while we wait for her to return. Take a moment to enjoy the refreshments. I know you don't get much of a chance to eat when the seamstress gets a hold of you."

Vriska took in the array of tiny, sugary-looking desserts. Far too sweet and delicate compared to what she was used to.

She wanted *home*. Her ma's cooking. Moose steaks. The cold autumn winds blowing with the promise of snow.

Paige stirred honey into a cup of tea. "Why don't you tell us about your family, Vriska? Julien mentioned you have a sister?"

Vriska blinked and stared at her callused palms. Rikze. How was she settling into her family's new home in Aldon? Where was this new home? Was it in a decent neighborhood or in one of those slums Vriska had heard about?

But when she glanced up, she found Essie, Paige, and Julien's mother watching her with compassionate gazes. They had been looking out for her, just as Julien said they would.

Would Vriska eventually learn to see Essie and Paige as sisters? And Julien's mother as an additional mother-figure in her life? It was strange, to think about gaining so much family once she married Julien.

But he had accepted her family so readily. If this was the future that she was going to grasp with both hands, then she should put in the same effort with his family.

They weren't as bad as she'd feared. Not even Laesornysh.

JULIEN STROLLED through the palace gardens, drawing in a deep breath for the first time in the past few days. With Vriska busy with a dress fitting, odd as that seemed, and Averett escorting Princess Bella to a meeting with Parliament, that left Julien with free time on his hands. He didn't even have his guard duties to keep him busy, now that they had been officially handed off to someone else while he had been in Kostaria.

He set off down the short path between the trees that connected the palace gardens with the back garden of Buckmore Cottage. Fresh gravel crunched beneath his feet, showing that this path was more well-maintained now that Buckmore Cottage was Essie and Farrendel's home here in Escarland.

When he didn't find Farrendel in the back garden, he knocked before stepping into the cottage and halting just inside the door. "Farrendel?"

"In here." Farrendel's voice came from the parlor.

Julien strode down the corridor, then leaned on the jamb in the doorway, taking in the sight of Farrendel's version of doing homework.

Farrendel was sprawled on his stomach on the coffee table, books and papers spread on the floor below him. His swords lay in their sheaths under the coffee table. Within easy reach, but not in the way. Essie and Farrendel's fluffy orange cat Mustache curled on Farrendel's back between his shoulder blades. The cat looked supremely smug.

"That doesn't look comfortable." Julien couldn't help his grin. He was never sure where he would find Farrendel—sitting on the table, hanging from a rafter, upside down on the couch—but lying on the coffee table was new.

"It is not." Farrendel eased onto his elbows, freezing when Mustache shifted. "But I cannot move."

Of course not. How dare he move and disturb the cat?

"No, I can see how that would be difficult." Julien crossed the room, avoiding all the books and papers, and sank onto the couch. "That's a lot of homework."

"It is four weeks' worth. I need to turn it in early for the time I will miss." Farrendel heaved a sigh and set his pencil down on the book on the floor below him. "Having a baby in the middle of the semester is not ideal."

If he had been Edmund, Julien might have made some joke about how Farrendel should have thought of that before…but Julien wasn't and therefore didn't.

With a laugh, Julien leaned his elbows on his knees. "Probably not. But it looks like you're managing all right. Will you get it all done before you leave tomorrow?"

"Most of it." Farrendel pushed all the way onto his elbows and shrugged.

The movement shifted his long silver-blond hair. Mustache sprang to his feet and pounced, biting at the strands of Farrendel's hair and getting a mouthful of shirt while he was at it.

Shaking his head, Julien reached over and picked up Stache, detaching the cat's claws from Farrendel's shirt. He settled the cat on his lap, scratching its head.

"Linshi." Farrendel sat up, shifting into a cross-legged position facing Julien. "I do not have to finish all of it. Just the first three weeks. Anything after that, I can submit after we return to Escarland. But I would like to finish as much as possible. When we return, it will be close to final exams, and I do not want to add additional work on top of them."

Not to mention he would be only a few weeks into new fatherhood. Julien had heard those first few weeks with a new baby were rather sleepless. Not that he had any personal experience, of course.

A pang surged through his chest. He likely never would.

He shoved the thought away. It was fine. He was fine. He would simply enjoy being an uncle to Bertie, Finn, and soon this new niece or nephew. Hopefully several more after that. His life would be full, even without children of his own.

"I believe I will still be here in Aldon when you and Essie return." Assuming Vriska didn't make a break for Kostaria before then. "We can resume our morning practices, if you'd like."

Stache jumped down and sauntered across the room, strolling over Farrendel's papers before plunking himself down in the middle of the book still open on the floor.

Farrendel's tired expression creased with a smile. "I would like that."

Julien thought he would. Farrendel would need the stress relief.

And Julien would need the stress relief too, considering how strained his own life had been lately.

Farrendel's silver-blue eyes studied him. "You look like you could use a practice bout now. Is everything all right?"

Julien sighed and sagged against the back of the couch. He wasn't sure how much to tell Farrendel. The past three months had been wearying. In Kostaria, he'd had to be constantly on his guard, and even then he'd been beaten within an inch of his life. Mongavaria had poisoned hundreds, if not thousands, of trolls, and he'd witnessed the horrors of death in a way he'd never seen outside of a battlefield.

And then there had been Vriska. Every time he thought he made progress, something happened that set him back.

"You and Essie made falling in love in an arranged marriage look so easy." Julien grimaced and couldn't look at Farrendel. Why hadn't he just kept his mouth shut?

Farrendel snorted, then barked a short but real laugh. "If it looked easy, it was because Essie made it so. It certainly did not feel easy to me." Farrendel sobered and leaned forward. "You did not see the first three months. I was gone fighting at the border for weeks at a time. Essie did not know elvish or what to do. We were a bit of a mess."

"You seemed close by the time you came to Escarland for that first visit." Julien couldn't help but smile, remembering how Essie had turned all fierce and defensive when they'd given Farrendel a hard time.

"We were getting there, yes. But what you could not see was that while we were here, I finally told Essie about my weakness to stone and what happened the first time I was tortured. She finally admitted to me how much she missed Escarland and her family." Farrendel looked down at his hands where they rested on his knees. "That is where Essie and I were at three months into our relationship. You and Vriska are not Essie and I. I do not think you can compare the paths we take. And if you are not at the same place we were, I do not think that is a reason for undue concern."

Julien drew in a deep breath, then let it out slowly as he

let Farrendel's words settle into his chest. It had only been three months, with three months of stilted letters before that. While he might be the type to fall in love quickly, Vriska wasn't. She needed patience and time to take things slowly.

But the fact that she was here in Escarland—enduring a dress fitting of all things—had to mean something. She was trying, in her time and her way. She needed Julien's patience, not his discouragement that she wasn't falling in love at the same pace he was.

Julien lifted his head and met Farrendel's gaze. "When did you get so wise?"

"I have been married over a year. I should hope I learned a thing or two in that time." Farrendel's tension disappeared as he smiled and relaxed into the lighthearted tone.

"One whole year. More than enough time for you to become an expert in this whole marriage thing." Julien grinned back, thankful to move back to banter rather than serious discussions.

"And by next year, I will be even more of an expert than I am now." Farrendel's smile widened into that mischievous one that had been so elusive before.

"Still, I'm the big brother. I'm supposed to be the one with all the good advice." Julien crossed his arms, trying to look affronted. He didn't think he succeeded.

"My monthly dose of wisdom and life advice during my counseling sessions must be doing some good." Farrendel's grin didn't waver. To him, the counseling sessions were such a normal, healthy part of his life now that he could joke about them.

"That could be it. Or your machasheni is rubbing off on you. She is also very free with dispensing advice." Julien reached down and petted Stache. The cat remained curled where he was, though he broke into a loud, rumbling purr.

"Her advice is never what you expect." After a moment, Farrendel's grin faded, and he stared down at his homework with a glum expression. "I suppose I should get back to work. Unless you wanted that practice fight now?"

Julien couldn't possibly refuse the eagerness in Farrendel's voice. He probably shouldn't encourage Farrendel's procrastination, but he well understood the need to do anything besides academic work.

Besides, he hadn't had a chance for a workout that morning, and he was itching to stretch his muscles.

"Sounds good to me." Julien gave Stache one last scratch, then stood. "I've been getting beat up by too many trolls recently. It's time I was beat up by an elf again."

That just made Farrendel grin as he reached for the swords he'd set under the table.

VRISKA MATCHED her stride to Essie's short, slow steps as they navigated the path through the forest.

Not that Vriska minded the pace as she usually would. Despite the comforting stones of Winstead Palace, it was good to be outdoors, even if the smell of trees and earth was mixed with a hint of coal and the general stink of the sprawling city. The air was strangely warm, the weather still holding on to summer even though it was rapidly changing to fall in Kostaria at this time of year. She relaxed, soaking up the moment of quiet after several days of the restrictions of life in the Escarlish palace.

"You seem relieved that the fitting is over." Essie shot her a grin, a twinkle in her green eyes.

"Yes." Vriska couldn't help that the word came out in a growl. That dress fitting had been sheer torture.

"Don't worry. Now that the seamstress has figured out a general style, future fittings won't be nearly as long or torturous." Essie's smile remained in place, as if utterly oblivious to the fact that her words weren't exactly reassuring. She rested a hand on her belly. "I wish I could stay and see you wear it, but I'm afraid this little one won't wait for anyone, much less for a formal ball. Not that I'd be attending in my current state anyways."

Vriska nodded, but she didn't try to add anything to the conversation. Princess Essie could give Rikze a run for her money when it came to chatter, and it was strangely relaxing just to let Essie chatter on without any demand for input from her.

"I'm looking forward to a little peace and quiet in Tarenhiel." Essie slowed even more as they approached a large tree root that jutted into the path. "Unlike the Escarlish press, which would be hounding the front gates trying to get one of those newfangled photographs of the baby, the elves appreciate the need for privacy. Well, except for Farrendel's family. They are going to hover atrociously, but I suspect I won't mind the help. I know Rheva will probably volunteer to watch the baby while I get a shower and a nap."

As Essie gingerly stepped over the tree root, Vriska reached out a hand and steadied her. Babies sounded like a lot of discomfort and work.

So why did an image of a strong, female troll warrior with a reddish tinge to her hair pop into Vriska's thoughts?

Or a male warrior with a hint of scruff that few other trolls could grow?

Try as she might, she couldn't immediately shake the thought away like she usually did. If she had children, then she wouldn't be the sole warrior in her family. No, she would be the beginning of a warrior family line.

But getting to that future of full-grown sons and daughters…that was the part that gave her pause.

"I'm thinking I might get one of those new cameras for Farrendel for his birthday. Though, his birthday is still months away, and it might be nice to get a family photograph long before then. Photography has come such a long way even in just the past few years." Essie gave a slight shrug. "I have a feeling Farrendel will find cameras fascinating, once he can tear himself away from homework long enough to examine one."

How had they gone from babies to cameras? Vriska hadn't thought she'd missed that much of the conversation.

"Perhaps you and your family can visit one of those photography studios that have set up shop in the main district of Aldon. They are quite the thing right now." Essie glanced at Vriska, but only for a moment before she focused once again on the path ahead of them. "I wish I'd had a chance to meet your family. Perhaps once we return from Tarenhiel?"

That question seemed to need an answer. "Maybe. You will like my little sister Rikze."

It still seemed strange, both to think about introducing her family to even more royalty and to think that she would still be here in Aldon in a month or so when Essie and Farrendel returned after the birth of their child.

Essie's grin brightened her face once again. "Of course I

will. We youngest children need to stick together." After a moment, her grin dimmed back into her more neutral smile. "I hope you have a chance to visit your family soon. Perhaps you and Julien can sneak away after you see our train off tomorrow morning. You are overdue for a tour of Aldon anyway. Not that you seem the sort to enjoy excessive shopping, but Aldon is a sight to behold."

It was sure to be. So many people, crammed into such a small space. The entire population of Kostaria could get lost in the bustle of Aldon.

How would her family survive as such a small group of trolls overwhelmed by so many humans?

Vriska cocked her head as a noise rang from the forest ahead of them. The clash of swords filled the air, but the voices that went with it held more laughter than anger. A practice bout, then, not an attack.

Essie kept walking, likely not yet hearing the noise thanks to her less acute human hearing. "I know the engineers are eager to get to work on the new sewage system now that the troll workers are here. An underground sewage system will be a big improvement, especially in the most crowded parts of Aldon."

"My da is excited to get to work. There is very little left to build in Kostaria, and an abundance of trolls who can do it." Vriska shrugged, listening to the clash of swords as it grew louder the closer they came. "He really enjoyed building the bridge."

"Alliance Bridge, as Parliament has dubbed it." Essie tilted her head, likely hearing the noises now. "I'm glad he has enjoyed his time in Escarland so far. I wish I could guarantee that their integration into Aldon will be as smooth, but

I fear discrimination and prejudices against trolls and elves still exist, much as I wish they didn't."

"As there is still prejudice against elves and humans in my kingdom." Vriska grimaced, remembering the way Julien had looked all battered and bloody after Brathac and his cronies ambushed him.

She and Essie rounded a corner in the path. Before them, the path entered another garden, this one surrounding a brick patio at the rear of the wooden manor house. At first glance, the manor house appeared slightly overgrown with plants. Yet a further inspection revealed that the twigs and leaves were actually growing from the house itself. The work of elven plant magic, no doubt.

Just inside the surrounding forest, Julien, Laesornysh, an elf, and a human Vriska didn't recognize were locked in a practice bout. Laesornysh kicked off a tree, flipped in the air, and came down with his swords aimed at the soldier.

The human soldier took a step back, raising his shield and his sword to protect himself.

Laesornysh lightly leapt from the shield and landed on his feet on the ground, parrying a thrust from the other elf as he did.

Essie's smile took on a fond tilt as she halted to watch the practice fight. "After Farrendel was rescued from Charvod, Julien was the first one to realize that Farrendel needed to resume exercising and practice fighting to come back to himself after the torture. For months, Julien got up early with Farrendel and was out here, rain or shine. Farrendel was happy he had a chance to return the favor when Julien asked for his help to prepare for the fighting bouts he'd face in Kostaria."

Vriska swallowed at the mention of Laesornysh's torture

at the hands of Charvod. Back then, she'd applauded the treatment of Kostaria's enemy. Only Rharreth had pointed out the dishonor in the torture, and he'd been punished for it by his own brother.

Clearing her throat, Vriska tried to keep the guilt out of her voice. "All that work paid off. Julien gave a good account of himself during the fighting bouts."

So much so that he'd earned a beating at the hands of a troll who didn't appreciate being bested by a human. But Vriska wasn't about to tell Essie that.

"Julien is good like that. He will quietly step in and do what needs to be done to take care of his family." Essie glanced from the practice fight to Vriska, her eyes far too knowing. Essie might look and sound cheery and oblivious, but that just masked her true ability to read people.

Vriska shifted, resisting the urge to look away. "Yes, he is."

He'd jumped right in and looked after Vriska's mother and sister when they'd been sick. Even before then, he'd gone out of his way to include Rikze, treating her as a little sister right from the beginning.

He spent so much time and effort on taking care of others. But who took care of him? Who did he trust enough to carry his burdens since he was so busy taking burdens from everyone else's shoulders?

She could help him. She wouldn't be another burden he'd have to carry, but she was strong enough to help him carry the burdens he took on. As he would help carry hers.

Together, they would protect both of their families, their kings, and their kingdoms.

She had feared having to choose between their kings, their peoples, and their duties. But that wasn't the case, was it? Julien's siblings were proof that it was possible to balance duties to two kingdoms. It made for a more complicated life, but it could be done, and done happily.

She wouldn't have to give up the life she loved but instead add Julien to it. As he would add her to his life in a way that she would have to grow used to. It might mean a few torturous dress fittings and an opulence that she didn't like, but perhaps she was strong enough to face the change.

Beside her, Essie grinned and turned toward the manor house. "I see I've done my sisterly duty for the day. I'd invite you inside, but I can tell you'd rather join them for a fight than me for another cup of tea. Go ahead. I'm sure the parlor is strewn with homework and not fit for company right now anyway."

With that, Essie headed for the cottage, her steps sure on the smooth bricks of the patio.

Vriska shook her head. Who knew that she would find herself liking Laesornysh's wife? And after this practice bout, she was probably going to find herself bonding with Laesornysh himself.

It was about time, though. They were Julien's family, and family meant a great deal to him.

She strolled into the forest and rested a hand on her sword. At her approach, the four men halted and turned toward her. She gestured to them. "Mind if I join?"

The soldier and elf guards looked to Laesornysh. Laesornysh glanced at Julien.

Julien grinned. "Of course." He turned to Laesornysh. "Vriska and I against the three of you."

Laesornysh raised his eyebrows. "You will be outnumbered."

"Nah. We can take you." Julien shifted so that he stood with his back to Vriska and faced the others.

Vriska felt her own savage grin tugging at her face as she strode to his side and drew her sword.

Oh, yes. He was the man she wanted at her side and guarding her back, as she would guard his.

CHAPTER TWENTY-FIVE

Vriska strolled through the streets of Aldon in the early morning hour. Only a small cordon of guards surrounded her and Julien, though she was torn about how she felt about their presence. It was strange, needing guards. She could take care of herself. Yet the number of humans milling along the streets even at this hour was boggling. The few guards didn't seem like enough if they were swarmed by angry humans.

But Julien strode down the street with an easy confidence, occasionally waving back at the people who stopped and bowed.

However, they soon veered off the main shopping district into a darker, dirtier side street. As they walked, the small wooden shops transitioned to tall, wooden buildings looming over the street. Lines strung high above the street waved with drying laundry.

Yes, it was a tiny street in Aldon. The buildings were wood or sometimes brick. The road beneath her feet was slimy, and the stench of excrement hung in the air. The faces that peered down from windows were human.

But even with all that, a part of Vriska eased at the sight. This back alley, rather than the grand palace, was where she had come from and in many ways still belonged.

They halted in front of a large brick building that filled a large portion of this block. Faded, painted words declared this the *Aldon Times*.

Vriska glanced at Julien, raising her eyebrows.

He shrugged and gestured at the building. "This used to be a newspaper office. When the *Sentinel* was discovered to be a front for a Mongavarian spy ring, the *Aldon Times* jumped on the chance to buy their building since it is in a nicer section of the city. The city council bought this building for cheap since it is conveniently located for the new sewage system. When my brother and Parliament arranged for troll workers, it made sense to house them here." He shifted, glancing away. "I'm sorry it isn't in a nicer part of the city. This street is still decent. It isn't a dangerous section. But it isn't..."

It wasn't like the clean, pristine streets surrounding the palace.

Vriska waved his concerns away and strode toward the large double doors that led into the former newspaper building. "You saw where I grew up. My parents and many of these families would be uncomfortable in the wealthy sections."

"This is still a far cry from the clean back alleys of Osmana." Julien grimaced down at his boots, scraping them on the stone steps.

"Well, you humans clearly need our help since you can't properly dispose of your own waste. And you definitely need a lesson in cleanliness." Vriska wrinkled her nose. She supposed one got used to smelling filth day in and day out, but it was appalling that the humans had allowed their streets to get this bad. Even the worst street in Osmana smelled as fresh as the icy mountain winds. "While we trolls are no prissy elves, we at least observe basic hygiene in how we maintain our streets."

Julien laughed one of his deep, loud chuckles that rang along the street. She liked that about him, the way he laughed. None of this timid laughter.

Before he had a chance to open the door, one of the doors slammed open, narrowly missing Julien. A tall troll with brawny arms and shoulders marched out. He muttered an apology, then continued on his way.

Julien caught the door, then gestured for her to enter first. A human custom—as she learned—that dictated that a gentleman let a lady go first. She might have argued, but she was too eager to see her family to stand there debating a random human custom.

When she stepped inside, she found the inside of the building utterly transformed. The troll workers must have hauled Kostarian stone with them when they traveled here, likely leftover stone from the Alliance Bridge.

A small atrium filled the center of the space with a two-story opening all the way to the roof, where a portion had been replaced with steel and glass skylights. Around the edge of the two stories, inner stone walls had been built. Doors marked each apartment while a landing with a railing circled the second story.

Trolls—mostly women and children—bustled around the space. Some hung laundry over the railing or on lines strung across the atrium. Younger children played on the ground floor of the atrium, kicking a leather ball back and forth.

This was a small community, built inside of the shell provided by the old newspaper building.

At the far end of the atrium, a set of stairs led down into what had likely been the basement. Male voices rang from down below, though Vriska couldn't make out what they were saying.

"Vriska!" Rikze shouted from somewhere above her.

Vriska craned her neck and found her sister leaning over the railing and waving at her.

"Come on up. You have to see our new place. Da and the others built all this over the past week. We slept on blankets in the basement until it was finished." Rikze motioned, then halted and grinned even broader. "Julien! You have to come too!"

Julien let the door to the building swing closed before he joined Vriska. As they strode toward the stairs, he leaned closer to her, whispering, "I knew your people were impressive, but it is amazing what they've done to the place in a mere week."

Vriska glanced around as well, running her fingers over the handrail as she ascended to the second story. Perhaps it was the contrast between this and the tenement housing outside, but even she was impressed. Her family—and the families of the other troll workers who had made the decision to move here—had taken to this new life with gusto. They weren't holding back, missing the kingdom they'd left behind.

It was time she stopped looking behind and instead focused ahead. She needed to grasp her new future with the same determination and joy that her family showed in reaching for theirs.

At the top, Rikze led the way around the balcony to one of the doors—an actual wooden door the likes of which were rarely seen in Kostaria—set into the stone wall. She knocked, then opened without waiting for an answer.

"Ma! Look! Vriska and Julien came for a visit!" Rikze strode inside with the same confidence that she used to have about their home back in Kostaria.

Vriska and Julien. Rikze said their names in a rush, together. In her sister's mind, they were already a pair.

Vriska strode inside and got the first look at her family's new home.

In many ways, it didn't look much different than their house in Kostaria. The walls were stone, though far straighter and more square than the more rounded shape of homes in Kostaria. This place had the same basic layout with a wall of kitchen cupboards along one side and two doors in the back. Their same, worn stone table and benches filled the center of the room.

Ma sat at the table, cutting off the ends of the green beans. She was still too thin after her poisoning, her hands a little shaky as she wielded the small paring knife.

But her color was better, and she seemed recovered from the strain of the journey from Kostaria to Escarland.

"Vriska." She started to push herself to her feet.

"No, don't get up." Vriska hurried to Ma's side and sat next to her before she could think about standing. "You appear well, Ma."

While the warmth of the weather was surely better than the chill already descending on Kostaria at this time of year, the stink of these back streets couldn't be healthy.

"I am fine. Your da and sister have been taking good care of me." Ma smiled first at her, then over her shoulder. "And I see Prince Julien has been taking good care of you."

"I try." Julien wielded that charming but sincere smile of his as he sat at the table across from them. "But Vriska needs no one to look after her."

No, she didn't. Julien didn't need anyone to look after him either.

But that didn't mean they couldn't *want* someone to look after them all the same. It didn't make them weak. After all, Rharreth hadn't been weakened by marrying Melantha, even if Vriska had thought that would be the case. No, they had become stronger together.

Perhaps that would be the case for her and Julien. Could she be stronger with Julien at her side than she was alone? And would he be stronger with her?

"Is there anything you need?" Julien focused on Ma, taking in the room once again with a swift glance.

"No, we have been well provided for." Ma lopped the end off another bean. "We have plenty of food and a snug shelter."

"We don't have our own washroom, though." Rikze grimaced. "We have to share a communal water closet in the basement. Did you know that they don't have running water in this part of Aldon? We have to haul our water from a community pump down the street. And don't even get me started on the lack of waste removal."

"Rikze, hush." Ma reached out and rested a hand on Rikze's arm. "There isn't anything the prince can do."

"I'm afraid there isn't." Julien shared a grimace with Rikze that somehow still managed to hold the hint of a smile. "That's why we had to call in your da and the other workers. Lack of clean water and adequate waste removal has plagued this city and needs to be fixed."

"Da and the others will get it fixed in no time." Rikze grinned and slid onto the bench on the other side of Ma. "They're in the basement right now, you know. Meeting with the human engineers and plotting out a map for the new system."

"This place is only temporary." Ma waved at the room around them. "This building will eventually become one of the main pumping stations. We are already looking for a building we can rent or preferably purchase to build a more permanent community much like this."

"I will let you know if I hear of anything." Julien nodded, his eyes going a little distant as if he were mentally cataloging the city and where a building might be found.

Ma's mouth pressed into a tight line. "We can make it on our own, Your Highness. We do not need the charity of the Escarlish crown. You have already provided much for us. My husband and the others have been saving the money they earned while building the Alliance Bridge. We will be able to make our own way."

"I understand." Julien reached across the table and rested a hand over Vriska's. "But I am marrying your daughter. It is my duty as the liaison between our peoples to see that you and the others are well settled here in Escarland."

How well he understood the troll mindset, that he appealed to duty rather than anything else.

Instead of yanking her hand away, Vriska gave in to the impulse to twine her fingers with his. His calluses fit against hers in a way that sent a strange, pleasant tingle up her arm.

Her and Julien's gaze locked over the table, something heated passing between them.

The snap of Ma slicing through another bean broke the moment.

Ma had her head down, studiously ignoring them. "In that case, your help is appreciated, Prince Julien."

"It's just Julien." Julien's fingers tightened over Vriska's, as if he was thinking about withdrawing his hand but was reluctant to do so.

Vriska cleared her throat, hoping her voice came out normal. "We came to ask if Rikze wanted to join us on a tour of Aldon. You're welcome to come too, Ma, if you'd like."

"That's sweet of you to offer, but I believe I'll stay here." Ma smiled, her smile widening as Rikze all but bounced on her seat. "But I can see Rikze is eager to go. Rikze, if you could pick up some things for me on your way, I would appreciate it."

Rikze nodded, grinning from ear to ear.

While Ma gave Rikze a verbal list of food items they needed, Julien slipped out. After Vriska also memorized the list to be on the safe side, she and Rikze left, strolling down the stairs once again.

They found Julien in the basement, talking with the human engineers and the troll workers, including Da. After a moment, Da slapped Julien on the shoulder before Da glanced at Vriska, meeting her gaze across the room. He gave her a nod.

Vriska's shoulders relaxed a fraction. She and her da would talk later once both of them had a chance. But for now, that nod was all that was needed between them.

The human engineers bowed, then Julien crossed the room to join Vriska and Rikze at the base of the stairs.

Together, they strode up the stairs and exited the troll

community, where the Escarlish guards fell into a protective formation around them once again.

Within a few minutes, they strolled from the dark, dingy alleyways of the tenement housing to the nice, but still low rent shopping district of Aldon. From there, the streets became increasingly nicer, the people walking on the boardwalks dressed in finer clothing. Many of the people looked askance at them, though they looked away quickly, bobbing a bow, when they noticed Julien walking next to them.

Were they staring because Vriska and Rikze were trolls? Or because they weren't dressed in the rich silk of the fashionable Escarlish elite? Perhaps it was a mix of both.

Would it be any better at the ball? Or would Vriska still stick out, despite the Escarlish made dress? The dress wasn't the current fashion, and the seamstress had seemed to think it a bold choice.

It wasn't like Vriska was ever going to blend in. Not with her height, her muscles, her gray skin, and her very troll appearance.

Right now, Julien didn't seem to care about the attention they were getting. Perhaps he wouldn't care at the ball either.

Rikze paused by every shop window, gaping at the displays and commenting on everything.

Julien shook his head. "I wish you could have gone shopping with my sister Essie. She enjoys this kind of thing and knows all the best shops. The shop owners adore her."

"She was very welcoming." Vriska could picture Julien's sister and Rikze strolling along the street, chatting away and admiring all the fancy things in the shop that just looked like too much opulence to Vriska. With a glance at Julien, Vriska drew in a deep breath and forced herself to ask the question.

It was time she took more of an interest in his family. "She's due soon, isn't she?"

"Yes. I think in a few days, but it could be any day, really." Julien shrugged and grinned. "We're all rather eager for another nephew or our first niece."

"I can't wait until I have nieces and nephews." Rikze shot the two of them a grin before she peered into a nearby shop window.

Julien's grin went stiff, and he stared straight ahead rather than looking at Vriska.

Vriska caught her breath, not sure how to respond. Of course Rikze would assume Julien and Vriska would have children someday. It was what everyone would assume.

And Vriska wasn't sure how she could handle seeing the flash of pain in Julien's eyes that he tried so desperately to hide. He was willing to sacrifice for her, no matter how hard.

What was she willing to sacrifice for him?

The question settled uncomfortably in her chest and gut. Since she had become a warrior, she had willingly put her life on the line for her king, kingdom, and the members of her shield band. Her life had seemed like a small sacrifice in the face of war.

Yet marrying Julien would demand a different kind of sacrifice. A relationship couldn't be built on a foundation where one person always sacrificed and the other only took. Both needed to sacrifice for each other, putting the other first.

Julien had been doing that for the past three months. Was she willing to do the same?

It turned out, neither she nor Julien needed to respond. Rikze kept walking and, after a moment, asked about one of the shops ahead.

As they turned the corner, a large brick building came into view. It took up a full city block with large double doors forming the entrance and a sign declaring it the "Aldon Market" hung above the doors.

"This is my sister's favorite place in Aldon." Julien waved to it.

"I know. Queen Melantha told us about it after she visited here with Princess Essie last spring for the treaty celebrations." Vriska took in the famed Aldon Market. "She was rather effusive about it."

"Really? I can't picture Queen Melantha sounding *effusive* about anything." Julien smiled from Vriska to Rikze. "I'm sure you'll enjoy it."

"And me?" Vriska raised an eyebrow. A lightness filled her chest, making her want to reach for his hand as she hid her smile.

"You'll tolerate it." Julien's smile tipped into that familiar, wry grin. Perhaps he read her mind because he held out his hand. Inviting, but not pressuring.

Vriska didn't let herself hesitate for more than a moment before she clasped his fingers. "Just so we don't get separated in the crush of people."

"Of course." Julien pointed to Rikze, who was already darting ahead of them through the open doors. "Perhaps you should be holding her hand, then."

"Probably. But..." Vriska waited a heartbeat, the unfamiliar flirtatious words sticking in her throat. But they still felt so right that she managed to force them out. "Your hand is better."

Inside, the market bustled with humans, packed into the aisles between the booths so densely that it was hard to move at times. The building rang with noise, the sound of so many chattering people reverberating off the steel girders and glass skylights far above.

Among the humans, a few elves wound their way through the press, standing out in their silken shirts, trousers, and tunics and long, flowing hair. The humans gave them room but didn't stare with hostility the way they glared at Vriska and Rikze.

Would her people someday stroll through the Aldon Market with such lack of fear? The elves and humans had begun to build a beautiful thing between their two peoples. It was time the trolls fully joined this alliance.

Rikze halted next to a booth with fine, embroidered tablecloths. She pointed at a table runner embroidered with mountain lupine and forget-me-nots. "Ma would love something like this."

Vriska didn't dare look at the cost. It was surely too dear for the few coins she carried in her pocket. Nor could Rikze spend any of the coins Ma had pressed into her hand to buy food. "Yes, she would. Perhaps someday we'll get something like it for her." She turned to Julien, quickly cutting him off before he could speak. "These are Kostarian flowers."

"You'll find a few Kostarian designs have made their way to Escarland, even if your people are only just beginning to come here. The war, short as it was, had a big effect on the soldiers who fought in your mountains." Julien dug into his pocket and pulled out a few coins. He faced the woman running the booth. "We'd like this runner, please?"

"Of course, Your Highness." The woman smiled, bowed, and whipped out a sheet of brown paper. With deft, practiced motions, she folded the embroidered table runner into the paper, then tied the packet with a length of twine. With another bow, the woman handed the package to Julien.

Julien passed it to Rikze, who hugged it to her chest, grinning.

Vriska waited until they moved on and were out of earshot before she said in a lowered tone, "You didn't have to do that."

"It isn't charity. It's a gift." Julien lifted a shoulder in a half-shrug. "I wanted to do it."

Still, Vriska wasn't sure how comfortable she was to keep accepting gifts from him. Everything she had in life had been something she earned.

But he was a prince, and those few coins were a small thing to him. And they were betrothed. Gifts were a part of the deal.

"Still…" Vriska wasn't sure why she was still protesting. He'd done something nice, and it had made her sister happy. Ma would like it, once she got over her own discomfort over receiving the gift.

"Besides, it wouldn't do for me to stroll through the market without supporting a few local vendors. Essie is better at that than the rest of us, but it wouldn't be a good look if I appear stingy with my troll bride-to-be." Julien's smile quirked even further, and he swung their clasped hands. "If you see anything you like, please let me know. You will be helping my public image."

This was the prince side of him. In Kostaria, she'd mostly seen the warrior and the gentle, caring man.

But he was also a prince, well-versed in things like his public image, diplomacy, and all things Vriska barely comprehended. How could she possibly stand as a princess at his side if she couldn't even see the simple things like the ramifications of buying or not buying a table runner her sister had shown interest in?

She had known that marrying Julien wouldn't be simple, but it had seemed less complicated back in Kostaria.

As they wandered the market, Julien also purchased each of them one of the quirky, troll-themed ear mugs that Queen Melantha had in her healing clinic. And of course, he purchased boxes of chocolate for Rikze at several of the candy booths until Rikze struggled to hold them all as she raced between the booths.

At a leather works booth, Julien halted, inspecting something. Vriska would have peered over his shoulder to see what he was looking at, but Rikze had darted off to the next booth. Vriska had to let go of Julien's hand to avoid losing sight of her sister in the crowd.

She found Rikze a few booths over, looking at an array of baked goods.

When Julien caught up, he held something in his hands. "I know you aren't much of a jewelry person, but this made me think of you."

A wide leather band rested on his hand. A bracelet, though it was wide enough to almost look like a small bracer. The leather was embossed with a pattern of swords laced through a geometric design.

His gaze lifted from the leather band to her. "Do you like it?"

All she could manage was a mute nod as she held out her wrist. He gently secured the band around her wrist, buckling it so that it was snug but not too tight. His fingertips brushed the tender skin of her wrist, sending those tingles up her arm and down her spine again.

"How is that? Is it too tight?" He was looking at her with those deep brown eyes again, all open and vulnerable.

She had to swallow several times before she could speak,

and even then her voice came out as a croak. "No. It's fine. I mean, it's lovely. Linsh."

What was this extra sizzle between them? Why did Vriska want to lean into him, despite the crowds around them and her sister standing nearby?

"Prince Julien, Lady Vriska. What a pleasure to see you here."

The lovely, melodic voice drove a knife through the heat flaring between them. Vriska jerked back a step, and Julien straightened, his grin instantly replaced with a neutral mask.

Princess Bella glided toward them, dressed in a pastel pink dress edged in delicate ivory lace around the collar and down the bodice. Four Escarlish guards trailed her, along with two of her own Mongavarian guards. The crowd parted in front of her, the Escarlish people staring at the Mongavarian princess in their midst.

Or, perhaps, they were staring at her utter beauty. She wasn't as ethereal as the elves, but she held a waifish beauty that only the humans could achieve.

Next to her, Vriska felt like she was a hulking brute. Too tall. Too muscular. Too lacking in a waist or a proper figure. The leather band Julien had just secured around her wrist was too plain and poor compared to the diamond and ruby bracelet adorning the princess's delicate wrist.

A wrist Vriska could snap in her fist if she squeezed too hard.

Princess Bella halted next to Julien, then rested a delicate, pale hand on Julien's arm. "I decided to tour your lovely capital city and see the pride of Escarland for myself. Such an industrious city you have. It doesn't have the charm of Landri since it lacks an ocean view, but the Fyne River provides a beautiful backdrop nonetheless."

"I have heard that the ocean is a sight to behold, but I've never seen it for myself." Julien glanced over his shoulder at Vriska, as if unsure what to do.

Princess Bella threaded her arm through Julien's and neatly steered him into place next to her as they started down the aisle once again. She did it so skillfully that Julien would've looked rude if he'd resisted. "You'll have to visit Landri someday and see the ocean for yourself. Personally, I love the long, sandy beaches."

Vriska clenched her fists and stalked after them, suddenly relegated to the position of guard in the background once again.

Julien could see the ocean from Kostaria as well. Sure, Kostaria was all cold ocean and rocky shores—none of those warm shores and sandy beaches that Princess Bella was describing—but that just made the ocean all the more deep and mysterious. The elves, too, had stretches of shoreline he could visit. No need for him to go to Mongavaria.

But that wasn't really what the princess was hinting at, was she? She didn't mean just for a visit. She was trying to dig her claws into Julien.

He didn't seem to notice. He nodded along politely, falling into step at Princess Bella's side as if strolling with her was the most natural thing in the world. Neither of them displayed the awkwardness that plagued Julien and Vriska.

Just when Vriska was actually making progress, that golden-haired beauty had to swoop in and tear it all to pieces with her perfectly manicured nails.

The Mongavarian guards shouldered between Vriska and Princess Bella, cutting Vriska off from Julien. The Escarlish guards sent her a glance, as if unsure about their duty, before several stepped between them as well, leaving Vriska to trail behind in the rear with the rest of her and Julien's original guard detail.

Rikze trotted to Vriska's side, sending a scowl at the back of Princess Bella's head. "What's she doing here?"

"Touring Aldon like we were, apparently." Vriska flexed her fingers, trying to relax her aggressive stance.

"Aldon is a big place. Don't you think it's odd that she ended up at the same place we did?" Rikze clutched her stack of parcels, still glaring at Princess Bella.

It was odd, and that same thought had niggled at Vriska.

But she sighed. Perhaps both of them were reading too much into it. "Perhaps. But the Aldon Market has become well known. Maybe they've heard about it in Mongavaria too."

"Maybe." Rikze sighed and stared down at the bundles in her arms. "I think I'm sick of shopping. Can we go home to Ma, now?"

"Yes." Vriska didn't have the stomach for any more either. Especially not with the way Princess Bella was batting her eyes at Julien.

Perhaps it was cowardly to retreat. But Vriska wasn't allowed to punch Princess Bella, and if this was a fight that came down to womanly wiles, then Vriska didn't stand a chance.

Julien and Princess Bella had paused at a booth up ahead.

Vriska nudged one of the Escarlish soldiers. "My sister and I are going to return to the troll community in the old newspaper building. Could you let the prince know?"

The soldier nodded, then shoved his way past the other guards to whisper in Julien's ear.

Julien turned and met Vriska's gaze, a hint of something

pained and frustrated twisting his features. At least he didn't seem to be enjoying himself, stuck to the princess's side.

After a few moments, the soldier hurried back to them. He barked an order, and three more of the soldiers fell in behind him, leaving a few men to continue to guard Julien, before he turned to Vriska. "The prince has ordered us to escort you. He also said to give you this." The soldier held out a handful of coins. "He said to buy your family a feast."

Rikze's eyes widened. "With this, we could buy a feast for everyone!"

They could, though they would likely need to find a grocer in the poorer section of Aldon rather than shopping here in the upscale district.

Vriska accepted the coins. When she glanced back at Julien, the princess already had him by the arm, leading him away.

Well, that was the end of her tour of Aldon. Vriska straightened her shoulders and forced her smile back on her face for Rikze's sake. And, perhaps, for her own. No way was she going to let that princess see she'd won this battle. "Then let's do that then. We'll get the items Ma requested as well as a bunch of other food, then we'll have a feast tonight to celebrate your new home in Escarland."

The grin returned to Rikze's face as she hurried toward the market's exit.

Vriska lengthened her stride to keep up, something hard settling deep inside her chest.

Princess Bella might have won this round, but she was going to find out that Vriska didn't yield that easily.

JULIEN GLANCED over his shoulder one last time as Vriska and Rikze disappeared into the crowd. His heart wanted to be there, with them. But he was a prince, and his duty to his kingdom demanded that he act the proper host to Princess Bella.

Her hand on his arm was small, with slim fingers. As they strolled through the market, she paused to speak with those running the booths and with people in the crowd. Her face lit, her eyes sparkled, as she talked with his people.

In that moment, she reminded him of Essie. Perhaps because they were both princesses who had been raised from birth to interact with people in that gracious manner.

Unlike Vriska, who interacted with others in a stiff, abrupt manner. She was never going to win the hearts of the people with the seemingly effortless manner of Princess Bella.

Yet Julien found himself wishing he still had Vriska at his side. Princess Bella's trilling laugh grated on him in a way neither his sister's loud laughter nor Vriska's chuckles ever did.

That reaction didn't make sense. Princess Bella was everything Julien should have been looking for in his future wife. A marriage that would bring a political alliance. A cultured, lovely woman who would fulfill the role of princess with ease. With her golden-blonde hair, lovely figure, and clear blue eyes, she was the epitome of human beauty.

And yet, she didn't appeal to Julien as she might once have.

After another interminable hour of strolling through the Market, Princess Bella steered him to the exit. There, a carriage pulled by matching white horses waited to return the princess to the palace.

The carriage was small with only a single bench seat. Julien was forced to sit next to her on the bench, close enough that their legs brushed when the carriage jolted over uneven cobblestones.

At this time of day, the crowds on the sidewalks spilled onto the edges of the streets. Carriages, horses, and laden wagons clogged the roads until their pace was a crawl.

Julien gritted his teeth and suppressed his sigh at the slow pace. He couldn't allow his frustration to show, as it might be considered rude to Princess Bella.

Princess Bella swiveled to face him, her blue eyes luminescent with a wet sheen. "Prince Julien, I've been hoping for another moment alone with you."

Julien glanced around the carriage, even knowing that they were, indeed, alone. The carriage windows weren't covered, nor was the window to the driver, but it was still verging on scandalous nonetheless. "We will arrive at Winstead Palace shortly."

"At this pace, we will have plenty of time to talk." Princess Bella clasped her hands in her lap, her fingers trembling against her pale, pink silk. "I was hoping you had given our last discussion some consideration. I know my grandfather intimated that he expected a marriage of alliance between me and you to be the result of this visit. And I understand why that cannot be the case, given your recent betrothal."

Julien resisted the urge to edge away from her. Not that there was anywhere he could go. His back was already pressed to the carriage's side. He didn't try to speak, just held her gaze and waited for her to continue.

Her eyes dipped from his gaze to focus on her hands. "I, too, was hoping for a marriage of alliance with you. Not for any political reasons, but for escape."

The pain in her words and the vulnerability in her posture tugged at him. Julien found himself leaning forward. "Escape?"

"I'm sure you don't have the best opinion of my father and grandfather here in Escarland. They are hard men and care more for their power than they do for their own people, even their own family." When Princess Bella glanced up again, her eyes glittered with even more of a liquid sheen. "I don't agree with my grandfather's methods. He is cruel, and my father is becoming more and more like him. I was hoping that by coming here—by marrying you—I could escape them."

Julien's spine softened as the first tear trickled down her pale cheek. A protective urge welled inside him, and he had to clench his hands against his knees to stop himself from reaching for her.

He was betrothed. For the first time, he had trouble remembering that while in Princess Bella's presence.

But perhaps there was something he could do for her, even if he couldn't marry her. He wasn't sure if Escarland could offer her asylum. It would be a political nightmare, and Mongavaria would accuse them of kidnapping her. Perhaps they might even go to war to get her back. But maybe he and Averett could think of something. "Have they…hurt you?"

It was a very forward, personal question to ask. But they had gone far beyond the bounds of normal propriety in the past few minutes anyway.

"No." She paused, her shoulders hunching beneath the

beautiful dress. "Not yet, anyway. But before I left, there was a moment...I feared..." She shuddered, her thin frame appearing even more delicate. "And I fear returning to them now that I've failed in their mission to secure a betrothal to you."

"I am sorry." He wasn't sure what else to say. He couldn't promise Escarland's help, not without talking to Averett first.

"I know there isn't anything you can do." Princess Bella lifted her gaze again as another tear traced the line of her smooth cheek. She reached out one trembling hand and rested it on his arm. "I'm not asking you to break your betrothal. I hope you're happy with her. But if you find that you aren't, all I ask is that you consider me as an alternative?"

He would be happy with Vriska, and he wasn't going to even entertain the thought of someone else. Besides, even if he was free to choose, he wouldn't choose Princess Bella. Perhaps she was telling the truth and her plea was genuine. But he wouldn't dare tie Escarland to Mongavaria. Not after what her grandfather had done, both in the assassination attempt on the elven royal family and the poisoned grain sent to Kostaria.

She was asking that he didn't hold her family members against her. He could do that. After all, he didn't hold Charvod or Drurvas against Rharreth, and they'd been his family.

Julien glanced out the window, thankful to see the gates of Winstead Palace approaching. The carriage sped up as the traffic cleared around the palace. He faced Princess Bella and gently eased her hand from his arm. "I will see if there is anything I can do to help, but I cannot make any promises."

"Thank you." Princess Bella opened her reticule, pulled out a kerchief, and dabbed at the tears on her cheeks. Drawing in a tremulous breath, she sat forward again, her face returning to that perfect, princess mask that hid her hurt and vulnerability.

As the gates opened and the carriage rolled through, they lapsed into silence. For which Julien was grateful. She'd given him far too much to think about.

All this time, he'd assumed Princess Bella was just as scheming as her father and grandfather. But what if she didn't know about their schemes? Or, at least, didn't agree with the violence and death they had caused?

But if she was attempting to escape, what would that mean for Edmund and Jalissa in Mongavaria? Princess Bella was supposed to be the guarantee of their safety. Yet if she had no intention of returning...

He would have to discuss this with Averett. Though he wasn't sure there was anything even his brother could do, tied as his hands were by politics.

JULIEN WALKED through the dark streets of Aldon, four Escarlish guards watching his back. He'd spent most of the afternoon with Averett, discussing Princess Bella. Neither of them had come up with any solutions. Any help they gave her would cause a sticky situation for Escarland. Nor was Averett convinced that she was telling the truth.

But Averett hadn't seen the look in her eyes. It hadn't seemed like an act.

Still, Julien was all for exercising caution. Just because a compassionate part of him wanted to believe her, that didn't mean he trusted her.

Nor was he about to break off his betrothal to Vriska, no matter what Princess Bella tried to hint.

After his meeting with Averett, he'd learned that Vriska still hadn't returned to Winstead Palace. She'd sent word that she was spending the evening at the troll community and would return late.

As he neared the former *Times* building, the thumping of drums and stomping feet reverberated into the night. Light spilled from the doorway, the doors propped open.

At the doors, he was halted by two male trolls, their arms as big around as his legs. But as the light fell across his face, they grinned and stepped aside. "Vriska's Prince Julien! You're always welcome, of course."

"Linsh." He nodded to them and stepped inside the building.

Someone had set up a stone table in the center of the atrium, and its top was laden with fruits, vegetables, and various dishes that he recognized from his time in Kostaria. The space around the table was packed with people. Not just trolls, but humans wearing plain clothes crowded around the tables, talking and laughing together. Even the balconies around the upper stories were packed with trolls and humans.

The trolls must have invited people from the surrounding tenements. A wise move, to earn the goodwill of their new neighbors.

Yet Julien didn't think it had only been done out of such a cold-hearted reason as buying goodwill. No, these trolls had been gifted a feast, and they wanted to share. They had seen the poverty of this section of the city, and they had shared the little they had. Though how they'd managed to put all this together with the mere handful of coins he'd passed along to Vriska, he didn't know.

As he shoved his way into the press of people, several of the troll women smiled as he passed, thanking him.

He didn't deserve their thanks. All he'd done was share a few paltry coins. A little thing to him. These people were the generous ones. They could have kept the food those coins purchased to themselves, yet they shared freely anyway.

"Julien!" Rikze appeared at his side, wearing a nice, but worn blue dress edged in fur that he guessed was her best one. "Ma loved the table runner. And thank you for the coins. Vriska and I got a whole bunch of food and look at the feast Ma and the others made."

"It looks delicious." Julien had already eaten supper, and he wouldn't want to take from these people when he certainly didn't need it. Besides, he wasn't sure he could shove through the crowd to claim any of the food. He glanced around the crowd, but he couldn't spot Vriska. "Where is your sister? Last we heard at the palace, she was still here."

"She's upstairs with Ma. Come on!" Rikze gripped his arm and tugged him through the crowd.

While she dodged between people with ease, Julien found himself bouncing off trolls and humans as he was yanked between them. He muttered his apologies and hurried after Rikze.

On the second story, Rikze led them to her family's home. The door stood open, and Da and a group of the workers stood outside, talking.

Julien nodded to them, but he continued inside, where he found Vriska, her ma, and several other women gathered around the table. The new table runner graced its surface while one of the troll ear mugs sat in its center with a few dandelions poking from it.

Ma smiled at him, giving him a nod, before she continued her conversation.

Vriska's expression, however, remained a stony, blank mask. She sat stiffly at the end of the bench, not participating in the conversation.

Julien held out a hand to her. "Can we talk?"

Her mouth pressed into a tight line, but she nodded. When she took his hand, her grip was firm and tight, on the verge of painful.

There wasn't anywhere to go that was truly private, unless they braved the press of people to step outside. And he didn't relish the thought of braving the crowd just yet.

Instead, he pulled Vriska into the corner of the tiny kitchen near the door to one of the two bedrooms. "I'm sorry about earlier. I didn't want to abandon you when Princess Bella latched onto me in the market."

"I understand." Vriska's jaw remained stiff, and she wouldn't meet his gaze. "You are Escarland's prince. You didn't have a choice but to be a good host to the visiting princess."

If she understood, then why was she angry?

Julien gathered his courage, hoping she wouldn't punch him, and gently rested his hand against her cheek. Her face was hard beneath his touch, yet her skin was smooth like polished granite. When she didn't sock him in the nose for daring to touch her, he took that as a good sign, even if the muscles in her jaw remained tight and angry beneath his fingers. "The entire time I was with her, I was wishing I was with you instead."

She snorted and half-turned away from him, the movement causing his fingers to drop from her face. "Really? Why? She's the flawless kind of princess you should have at your side."

Julien released a breath, nearly giving a laugh. This wasn't anger. It was jealousy stiffening her spine and flashing in her eyes. Granted, it looked a lot like anger. But then again, most of Vriska's emotions did.

And maybe he was just asking for that broken nose, but he let a hint of a smile cross his face. "Is that jealousy I hear?"

"No." Vriska crossed her arms, turning back toward him to better glare at him.

"Good." Julien stepped as close to her as he could with her crossed arms forming a wall between them. "Because there's nothing to be jealous of. You're the one with my ring woven into your hair. You're the one I want at my side. I find I rather like knowing the woman at my side can punch the living daylights out of anyone who dares attack us."

Vriska lowered her arms to her sides, the heat seeping out of her gaze. "She still was flirting with you. In case you hadn't noticed."

"I noticed. But I didn't flirt in return." Julien scrubbed a hand over his beard. "She claims she wanted to marry me as a way to escape her father and grandfather. She says she doesn't agree with their policies."

"And you believe her?" Vriska gave that soft snort again, shaking her head.

"I don't know. Maybe? She seemed genuinely scared when she talked about her family and what they might do to her when she returns without a betrothal to me." Julien tried once again to shrug away the protective tug at his heart when he thought of Princess Bella's soulful eyes begging for help.

"Don't be foolish." Vriska's stance became hard once again. "That princess has claws, even if she hides them with her fancy dress and pretty face."

Julien nodded, though he wasn't sure what to think. Was Vriska right? Was it an act? Or was this her jealousy talking once again, making her read things into Princess Bella's actions that weren't there? "In that case, I'd better stick even closer to you from now on. You promised to punch her if she tried anything."

Vriska's spine relaxed a fraction, her jaw softening with the hint of a smirk. "Does that mean I get to punch her for flirting with you?"

"Probably be best if you didn't. But that glare you gave me a few minutes ago might work." Julien faked a shudder. "You had me quaking in my boots."

"Clearly." Vriska huffed and jabbed a finger toward the door to the balcony. "Let's see if there's any dessert left. I'm hungry."

With that, she spun and headed for the door without waiting for him.

Julien followed, still mentally kicking himself. She might understand and she might have even forgiven him, but she was still hurting. He never should have let Princess Bella drag him away, politics or no.

He would have to do better, especially at the upcoming ball.

CHAPTER TWENTY-SIX

Vriska gaped at her reflection in the mirror in the suite of rooms she'd been given in Winstead Palace.

Unlike the last time, this Escarlish dress was stunning. Its dark blue bodice laced up the front and fitted in a way that gave her a waist and accentuated the curves that were normally hidden by her stiff leather fighting vest. Like her vest, it had a high neckline but left her shoulders bare. Yet while her fighting vest did so to show off her muscles and give her a good range of motion, her bare shoulders and the line of her collarbone seemed different when framed by this dress.

At the waist, the dark blue silk flared into a layered skirt that draped to her ankles in the back but only went to her knees in the front. A decorative belt hugged her waist with a matching sheath for her sword. The skirt had been expertly tailored so that it fell smoothly beneath the sword rather than bunching. Beneath the skirt, she wore dark brown trousers and knee-high boots that matched the belt and hugged her legs in a way that made her calves look amazing.

The dress felt dangerous. A dress she could fight in, if required, yet remained beautiful all the same. A dress that remained very troll—very *her*—while also lending her an air of elegance that her leather and furs didn't.

Perhaps Julien's sister Essie was right. The right dress was a kind of armor that lent confidence. Not just for the battle of the court but also in the battle of building a relationship.

Was this the right dress? Except for the fabric, it didn't look much like what the Escarlish women would be wearing.

Julien wouldn't care. He would see *her*—had seen her—no matter what she wore.

A knock sounded on Vriska's outer door, a moment before the door opened and Queen Paige's voice filtered inside. "Vriska? May I come in?"

"Sure." Vriska crossed her arms and glared at her reflection in the mirror again.

Two sets of footsteps crossed the sitting room before Queen Paige stepped inside. She came to a halt, her polite smile widening into something genuine. "Wow. You look stunning."

Vriska fisted her hands in the skirt, then forced her fingers to relax as she faced Queen Paige. "Are you sure?"

She was supposed to be confident. The right dress as armor and all that. But it would be nice to have someone else confirm it.

"Yes, of course." Paige gestured at her. "You always have a kind of striking beauty. But that dress just takes that and brings it out in a way that just gives you a presence."

Really? That was what others saw?

"Linsh." Vriska wasn't sure what else to say. She could

handle compliments about her fighting skills. But her looks weren't something she worked hard to achieve. So why did she want the reassurance anyway? And feel better when she got it?

Ugh. Feelings. They were way too confusing.

Paige waved toward the open door to the sitting room. "My maid can help with your hair, if you'd like. Not that you need help. You are beautiful as you are. But I thought you might like your hair done to match the dress."

Vriska sighed and sank into the chair in front of what she'd learned was a dressing table. She'd already had her clothes made over, and that hadn't turned out as bad as she'd feared. Perhaps it wouldn't hurt to let this small part of her be changed as well. "Sure, why not? But I'm not going to wear one of those fancy tiaras or anything like that."

"Until your wedding to Julien, you aren't entitled to a tiara, so no worries there." Paige gestured, and a young woman in a simple black dress and white apron stepped inside.

The maid held a small wooden box, which she kept perfectly level even as she bobbed a curtsy to Vriska. As if Vriska were some kind of lady instead of a common, usually grubby and sweat-stained warrior.

Paige took the box and opened it. "I was thinking we'd use this instead."

Inside rested a slim necklace formed of diamonds and royal blue sapphires that matched the color of Vriska's dress.

Vriska grimaced. "I'm not wearing a necklace." The thought of something looped around her neck, choking her, didn't appeal in the least.

"It'll go in your hair." Paige's gaze dropped from Vriska

to the box clasped in her hands. "You often wear decorations in your hair."

Vriska drew in a deep breath. The pressure of this ball was making her snappy, but she shouldn't take it out on Paige. Julien's sister-in-law was just trying to reach a hand out in friendship. "Fine. Do what you wish with my hair."

The maid approached, pulling a small hairbrush out of the front pocket of her apron. "If you will allow me, my lady. Please sit still, and I will set to work."

Vriska faced forward, only to see herself in the mirror again. Ugh. She was not about to sit there and watch the maid work. Before the maid had a chance to move, Vriska stood, turned the chair around, then sat with her back to the mirror.

The maid pursed her lips, but she didn't comment as she set to work. Vriska could feel the way she was disentangling the bits of bone and leather from Vriska's hair, setting them one by one on the dressing table behind her. Divesting Vriska of the last bits of Kostaria still on her person.

Besides her sword. Vriska rested her hand on the hilt, gripping it to reassure herself that it wouldn't be taken away from her too.

Queen Paige smoothed out her dress, then sat on the end of the bed. Her turquoise silk dress set off her straight blonde hair, which had been braided into a crown, then slicked into some kind of bun at the back. A sparkling tiara perched in her hair while a matching diamond necklace graced her throat. She was every inch the regal queen—everything Vriska wasn't.

The maid removed the last decoration from Vriska's hair—Julien's ring—before she attacked the snarls and knots with the hairbrush. Vriska resisted the urge to wince. She was a warrior, after all. A little hair-tugging was nothing to flinch over.

Paige straightened her shoulders and met Vriska's gaze. "I understand that tonight is intimidating, even if you don't want to admit it. I know what you're going through because I've been there myself. I wasn't raised to be a queen. I wasn't even born into the nobility. My father was the general in charge of protecting the king, a rank he'd earned through merit."

Then Paige came from a line of warriors, not the nobility. For the first time, Vriska felt a true kinship with this queen who might someday be her sister.

"Essie and Jalissa were raised to be princesses. There are things that they do so effortlessly that don't come as naturally to me. Even after all these years, I still feel like I'm learning how to properly fill the role of queen." Paige shared a small smile with Vriska. "While I love Essie and Jalissa dearly, I am thankful to get one sister-in-law who, like me, wasn't raised as a princess."

Vriska found herself smiling in return, even as the maid tugged and twisted at her hair. "Linsh, Your Majesty." She paused, struggling against her instincts. "I worry I will be an embarrassment."

Paige gave a lopsided smile. "I still worry that before every ball and court event. But as my mother-in-law told me, hold your head high and don't let the court see your fear. You outrank nearly everyone there. Or, at least, you will once you marry Julien."

Vriska pressed her mouth into a hard line. She could do that, even if it would be tricky since she couldn't just punch anyone who sneered at her as she would in Kostaria.

Paige stood and halted in front of Vriska. "But don't hold

your head high just for Julien's sake. Do it for your people. Tonight, you are the closest thing your people have to a princess. So be a princess of the trolls."

Now *that* was something Vriska could do. She had been worried about embarrassing Julien and not fitting into Escarlish culture. But Paige was telling her that she shouldn't try. At least, she shouldn't change herself to do it. Instead, she should be herself, stand at Julien's side, and show this Escarlish court just how tough a troll warrior could be.

She lifted her chin and gave Paige a sharp nod.

"And now you look the part of princess of the trolls." Paige grinned and motioned for her to turn around.

Steeling herself, Vriska turned in her chair to face the mirror once again. Despite herself, she caught her breath.

The maid had deftly woven the necklace into a braid around the top of Vriska's head, giving her the appearance of a crown without the presence of a tiara. The maid had added a few small braids to frame Vriska's face, and she'd braided Julien's ring and Vriska's troll decorations into them. The rest of her hair had been left loose to flow over her shoulders and back.

She did, indeed, look like a princess of her people.

"Now to plan your grand entrance." Paige grinned and glanced at the ticking wall clock. "I've instructed a maid and one of the guards to escort Princess Bella to the ballroom shortly after Averett and I arrive. She won't like it since she would've wanted to wait until after you arrived so that she could make the grand entrance. Once she has arrived, Darla will fetch you."

The maid gave another curtsy. She must be Darla.

"By arriving after Princess Bella, your entrance will make

a greater impact." Paige's grin held a gleam. The glint of a commander plotting to win a battle. "By arriving last, you will be shown to be the guest of honor rather than Princess Bella."

Vriska raised her eyebrows and matched Paige's grin. "You are as devious as a warrior."

"I've learned a thing or two while queen." Paige swept one last glance over Vriska, as if to make sure her job was done, before she and her maid left the room.

VRISKA STOOD in front of the double doors to the ballroom, her heart beating harder than it did when she went into battle. In a battle, she knew her place. Knew her duty. Knew the strength of her arms and the skills of her fingers.

But this was a different kind of battle altogether. One she didn't have the skills or experience to fight, even if she was dressed as if she could.

She clenched her fists, lifted her chin, and eyed the doors. No matter. She was a troll warrior. She didn't back down from a fight.

Perhaps sensing that she was ready, the Escarlish guards nodded to the footmen. The footmen swung the doors open, and one of them shouted into the crowded ballroom, "Announcing Lady Vriska, shield sister to King Rharreth of Kostaria."

Vriska let her lips twist at the sound of the title tacked on to her name. She wasn't technically a lady, but it seemed the Escarlish people didn't know how to handle her rank as a warrior and shield sister without adding a noble title to it.

And perhaps that was the point, wasn't it? As Rharreth's

shield sister, she was acting in the role of a lady of noble rank by agreeing to a marriage of alliance. She had to be seen as a lady to be a match for Prince Julien, third in line to the Escarlish throne.

Head held high, Vriska rested a hand on her sword's hilt and marched into the ballroom. Somehow, she had ended up entering on the second story of the ballroom at the top of a sweeping marble staircase. Paige's doing, no doubt, since these were the doors to which the maid had led her.

The orchestra was tucked somewhere beneath the staircase, the music swelling all around Vriska. Still, most of the eyes of those below swung toward her. Her palms were clammy, but she refused to flinch under all those stares.

Across the ballroom, King Averett stood with Paige at his side. Next to them, Julien was a tall, brown-haired figure dressed in muted browns and blues. The cut of the coat accentuated his trim waist and broad shoulders in a way that felt like a punch to Vriska's gut yet somehow was more pleasant than painful.

Princess Bella had her arm looped through his. Not tugging, for that would be too undignified. But she seemed to be trying to convince him to join the swirling dancers in the middle of the ballroom.

As Vriska reached the top of the stairs, Julien's gaze swung toward her. The hard politeness dropped as his eyes widened. Then a slow, broad smile stole across his face. He brushed Princess Bella's hand off his arm without so much as a glance in the princess's direction and strode through the crowd, the people making way for him.

Something in the casual way he ignored Princess Bella brought a savage twist to Vriska's smile. Let that blonde-haired beauty simper all she wanted. Julien was Vriska's.

Vriska strode down the stairs, the silk of her skirt fluttering around her ankles behind her. By the time she reached the bottom of the stairs, Julien was there, waiting for her.

His gaze swept over her, something in his deep brown eyes heated. "Vriska. You look…dangerous in that dress. You always look deadly—like you are about to kill someone—but that dress…" He trailed off, as if searching for the right word. He didn't need to find it. The look in his eyes told her exactly what he thought and felt.

"I should have worn a dress earlier, if that's what it took to render you speechless." Perhaps it was the dress, causing this bold confidence to hum through her veins. Vriska held out her hand before he had a chance to reach for her. "May I have this dance?"

"I'd be honored, my lady." Julien took her hand, then tugged Vriska toward the center of the ballroom.

"You'll be less honored once you realize I don't know any Escarlish dances." Vriska matched his stride. Her skirt fluttered around her knees, the silk rippling in a way that caught the lamplight and shimmered.

As they passed, several of the ladies batted their fans, then leaned their heads together to whisper. Their gazes above the edges of their fans held a venom that made Vriska's back prickle and her fingers itch to draw her sword.

Julien halted them near the edge of the dancers. "I know it doesn't come naturally to you but follow my lead. The steps of this dance are simple."

"I can take orders like any good warrior." Vriska eyed the other dancers. How were they supposed to pick up in the middle of the dance? She clenched her teeth and faced Julien. They might as well get this over with.

"I'm not talking about following orders but following my

lead." Julien rested his hand on Vriska's waist, then tugged her far closer than they usually stood. His voice held a low tone she'd never heard before, yet it somehow sent a tingle down her spine. "I've heard dancing compared to sword fighting. But there's something entirely different about partnering in a *dance* rather than a bout."

His hand was warm against her waist, something she could feel through the thin layers of silk in a way she wouldn't have if she were wearing her leather vest. With gentle pressure, he guided her back and forth through the steps of the dance. She stomped on his foot several times, but he kept his winces to a minimum, though it had to have hurt.

He leaned in even closer, his breath brushing her ear. "Relax. You'll stumble less if you aren't so stiff."

How could she relax with his hand on her waist and his breath tickling her ear? He was so close that she felt the heat from his body and caught a whiff of the same scent she'd smelled on him in the tunnels of Khagniorth when he'd held her after she cried.

Dancing was definitely *not* like sword fighting. It was still visceral. Raw. Heated. But in a completely different way.

Yet as she drew in another deep breath that tasted far too much of the mix of perfumes that clogged the ballroom, she relaxed into Julien's touch. As she relaxed, her steps grew more confident, her body moving with the rhythm of his guidance more than the music.

All too soon, Julien halted. Around them, clapping broke out, startling her. Had she nearly rested her head on his shoulder? In front of the entire ballroom?

Vriska stepped back and forced her expression to go blank again.

Julien bowed over her hand, as if she truly were a lady of his court instead of a troll warrior who had stomped all over his feet. "Thank you for the dance, my lady."

Then, inexplicably, he pressed a soft kiss to her knuckles.

Two months ago, Vriska might have snatched her hand back. Before meeting Julien, she would have punched anyone who dared such a thing. But now she found herself catching her breath. As if she was some weak-kneed lady to swoon over the brush of his lips on her knuckles, even callused and scarred from battles as they were.

She was still processing the feelings churning inside her chest as Julien led her to the edge of the ballroom once again until they joined King Averett and Queen Paige as they, too, returned to the side after the dance.

Julien quirked a smile at her, though it held more regret than warmth. "I fear I can't monopolize you all evening. Even if we are betrothed, it would still be considered scandalous."

A part of her wanted to grip his arm and force him to stay at her side. He couldn't leave her to face the battle of his court without him.

But she was a warrior. She was brave enough to face this alone, if that was what it took.

"I'd be happy to claim your next dance." Averett held out his hand, his lopsided smile showing his resemblance to Julien.

"You'll be less happy once I've stomped on your toes." But Vriska took his hand anyway.

This second dance wasn't at all like the first. She couldn't relax as fully as she had with Julien, and she stomped on Averett's feet several times hard enough to make him wince.

But the third dance was even worse. She ended up with

some random nobleman, and his hand on her waist just made her all prickly and punch-happy. She tripped over her own feet once and bumbled into several of the other dancers. In Julien's arms, she'd felt dangerous and beautiful. But with anyone else, she was just a brute.

As Vriska stumbled through the final steps, the ladies around her didn't bother to hide their tittering. A few whispered, loudly enough for her to hear. Words like *brute. Barbarian. Looks like a trollop in that dress.*

They were just words. Just cruel laughter. They shouldn't hurt. She didn't care what they thought or said. She didn't want or need their approval.

But that didn't stop the hurt from stabbing her anyway. She'd thought she could handle the Escarlish court. But it turned out she was still a common troll from the mountains at heart.

As soon as the Escarlish nobleman released her, Vriska shoved her way through the crowded ballroom. She probably caused more sneers and gossip, but she didn't care. She needed a moment in the fresh, night air to gather the confidence she'd had earlier. Just a moment before she plunged back into the battle.

The glass doors leading outside beckoned her, and she took the shortest path toward them. It didn't matter who she brushed aside or nearly ran over in her haste.

As she reached the doors, she glanced over her shoulder. Her gaze caught on Julien across the ballroom. His back was to her as he danced with Princess Bella. The princess was laughing, her eyes sparkling. To Julien's credit, he was holding Princess Bella as far away as possible, his steps stilted, his back stiff.

"Now there's a match I'd like to see." One of the nearby

Escarlish young ladies whispered none-too-softly from behind her fan to the lady standing next to her. "Prince Julien and Princess Bella make for quite the lovely couple. Too bad he seems smitten with that *troll* he brought back from the north."

"There's no accounting for taste, I suppose." The other lady agreed with a tilt of her head. "I wonder what he sees in the troll?"

"Perhaps he likes..." The woman lowered her voice to the point that Vriska couldn't hear the rest of her comment through the din of voices, dancing feet, and lilting music. But the titters that followed told her everything she needed to know about how crude the rest of the statement had been.

Vriska's knuckles made cracking sounds, her arms shaking with the urge to swing a punch.

The lady fluttered her fan again. "First elves, and now a troll. What is our royal family coming to? Good thing this is the last of them to marry off, or they might start making alliances with the ogres to the south next."

"Oh, can you imagine? I guess a troll isn't the worst creature our prince could have chosen."

Vriska had to leave. Now. If she didn't, she'd punch those ladies for their crude comments. And here in Escarland, that would only make a spectacle of herself and embarrass Julien and his family.

Against this attack, she was utterly helpless. No amount of confidence from a stunning dress could silence the gossips or the heat building in her chest and pouring into her fists.

All she could do was retreat. It would likely cause even more gossip, and everyone would assume she'd left because of Princess Bella. But the princess and her futile attempts to lure Julien away from Vriska had nothing to do with it. No, running was simply better than causing a ball-room brawl.

Vriska shoved open one of the glass doors and escaped into the cool night air. Torches lined the garden pathways while the fountain in the center glowed with the torches set around it.

It would have been peaceful, except for the Escarlish couples wandering the paths or kissing in the sheltered alcoves. Definitely not the privacy Vriska was looking for.

She picked a pathway at random and charged down it. An Escarlish couple had to throw themselves into the bushes to avoid getting trampled. At the edge of the gardens, she barged through a section of the tall hedge, its branches scraping at her arms and tearing at the flimsy silk of her dress.

It didn't matter. She loved this dress and yet hated it. She wasn't sure she could bring herself to wear it again.

On the other side of the hedge, she found herself in the dark, quieter gardens that were reserved for the royal family, though Vriska had seen them several times on the walk to and from Buckmore Cottage before Laesornysh and Princess Essie left for Tarenhiel.

Vriska halted, her hands fisted at her sides. There weren't any convenient rocks to pummel, except for the wall of the palace, and she didn't think pounding her fists into the Escarlish palace would be appreciated.

She wanted to go home. To Kostaria. To the comfortable stone passageways of Khagniorth Stronghold, the familiar streets of Osmana, and her ma's hearty cooking.

Except that her ma wasn't in Osmana. And Rharreth no longer needed her for guard duty, now that he had other shield bands for those duties.

There was nothing left for Vriska in Kostaria. Her future was here in Escarland, with her family and with Julien.

But that would mean putting up with more balls. More events like this where she bumbled around like an oaf and brought down the gossips on her and Julien's heads.

She growled and punched at the hedge, even though it was far too weak and scratchy to make a suitable target for her anger. She attacked it anyway, not caring if her skin tore and bled from the grasping branches.

The hedge a few feet away rustled, then Julien stumbled through. He brushed at his clothes, shedding leaves and sticks, before he faced her. His deep brown eyes swept over her, warm even in the faint light of the stars overhead and the glow of the city gaslights. "Are you all right?"

"No." Vriska growled and punched the hedge one last time. The crunch of leaves and twigs was supremely unsatisfying compared to the heat in her chest.

But without the release, that heat threatened to prick into tears at the corners of her gaze. She swallowed it back. No way was she crying in front of Julien yet again.

She spun away from him. "You should be inside."

"But I'm not. I'm here. With you." Julien's warm hand rested on her shoulder. "Is this about Princess Bella? I told you, she's not the one for me."

"But maybe she should be." Vriska whirled to face him, shoving his hand from her shoulder as she went. "I want to fight at your side. I want to organize the war games and teach our peoples' warriors to work together. I want to be here for my people as they adjust to life in Escarland. But I can't do this." She swept her hand from the palace to herself and the fancy dress she wore. "I can't even manage three dances without embarrassing myself. I'm never going to be the princess you need."

"I don't want that kind of princess." Julien reached for her again, but she stepped away. He let his hands fall back to his side, though he still held her gaze. "I know life at my side is going to have demands. There will be court events that I have to attend. But I can get out of most of them, especially once Edmund and Jalissa return from Mongavaria. He owes me for all the times I covered for him while he was off spying. It's time he took his turn representing the family."

"I'm still me. I'm not going to change." Vriska crossed her arms and glared back.

"I'm not asking you to." Julien gestured, both palms up. "You'll have two princesses and a queen for sisters. They'll help. They'll show you how to be a princess and still be yourself."

Vriska ground her teeth, suppressing a growl. He still wasn't listening. Wasn't hearing what she was trying to tell him.

Yes, she'd met Essie and Jalissa. Neither of them gave her the same prickly feeling that Princess Bella did, yet they were both proper princesses. And Queen Paige was a common girl just like her who had found herself elevated to a position she'd never expected.

But this wasn't about what Vriska was or wasn't willing to learn from her future sisters-in-law. She was trying. She'd put up with that dog-puke-awful dress fitting. She'd even found a style of dress that she liked. She'd shown up at this snow-blighted ball. She'd done everything asked of her.

None of it was enough. She wasn't enough. She couldn't just put on her dress-armor and ignore the gossips the way a good princess was supposed to.

Not when the gossips—cruel though they were—spoke what she feared was the truth. It didn't matter if she wore a pretty dress. She was still a brutal warrior of the mountains. And that wasn't going to change because she didn't *want* to change.

And yet she wanted Julien. And she wanted that feeling she'd gotten when she'd seen herself in the mirror in this dress. And she wanted all these blasted, complicated feelings to just go away for even half a second so she could think without them whispering all these confidence-stealing thoughts into her mind.

"Vriska?" Julien took a tentative step closer.

She released the snarl building in her throat and gestured at herself. "What do you even see in me, anyway? Am I just a duty to you? Because I don't think duty is enough anymore. I don't want to be just the troll you married because you had to." She hated the way her voice caught and quavered before she could continue, staring at her hands because she couldn't look at him. "But I'm a troll. I'm a big ugly bumbling brute and—"

His arm wrapped around her waist and pulled her to him with a suddenness that stole the rest of her words. His hand grasped her chin with a touch that was still gentle yet more insistent, more demanding than anything he'd dared with her before.

She found herself looking into his burning brown eyes almost against her will, his hand against her cheek keeping her from looking away even if she could have pulled back if she'd gathered the will to do so.

"Don't *ever* call yourself that again." Julien's voice dropped into a low rumble, almost like a threat if his eyes hadn't burned with an intensity that speared into her. "You asked what I see in you. I see a deadly woman with hard-earned calluses and scars of war. I cheer your accomplishments as a warrior and a member of the king's shield band. I see the way you love your family fiercely and how much your kingdom is a part of your heart. And, yes, I also see an attractive woman who is beautiful in either bloodstained fighting leathers or a grand ballgown."

His thumb traced her cheek while his eyes swept over her as if he truly was seeing a woman he found beautiful.

She had never been attractive before. She'd always been just a shield sister. Someone to punch on the shoulder and joke with like everyone else in the shield band. And that had been all right. It was still all right when it came to her shield band. She didn't want any of *them* to look at her like this. They were her brothers-in-arms. It would just be awkward.

But it wasn't enough with Julien. With Julien, she wanted *this*. The heat simmering unspoken between them. The way he saw and appreciated all of her. Not just the warrior part. Not just the woman part. With him, she could be whole in a way she couldn't with anyone else.

She should say something in response. She forced her mouth open, her voice squeaking for a moment before she could force out the first thing that came to her. "I'm going to make a lot of mistakes."

It wasn't what she really wanted to say. But her heart wasn't ready to speak more just yet.

"So am I." His gaze remained locked on her. If he was disappointed that she didn't offer any stirring declarations in return, it didn't show in his tender, fervent expression. "As long as we can make those mistakes together."

She leaned into his touch. The gentle tingle through her skin banished the last of her tension. Somehow, in all the change in her kingdom and her life, Julien had become her rock. With him, she forgot about her worries for the future or the cattiness of the Escarlish gossips. She could just *be*.

When Julien tugged her closer still, she didn't resist. They swayed to a slower version of the dance they'd done before. The faint strains of music spilling into the garden provided the background even if they set the rhythm.

Julien's breath and beard tickled her ear a moment before he whispered, tender and low, "You aren't just a duty to me."

Vriska rested her head against the crook of his neck as she had months ago in Khagniorth Stronghold. She probably should whisper something to him in return, but she couldn't bring herself to break the moment with words. As the music of both ballroom and night swirled around them, it seemed only natural to turn her face and press a soft kiss to his neck.

As close as they were, she could feel the change in him. The way his breath caught and his grip on her tightened.

She tilted her face a bit more, then he was kissing her. His beard tickled her skin. Not rough and scratchy as she might have expected, but a pleasant sensation that made a growl build in the back of her throat as she dug her fingers into Julien's hair and drew him closer.

He trailed soft kisses along her cheek and down her neck, his beard tickling her skin the whole way until she couldn't help but gasp.

He froze, then drew back. His eyes searched her face, as if worried he'd crossed a line.

Her brain was still too fuzzy, and all she could think about was how she wanted to get back to kissing. "Your beard..."

Instead of inspiring him to more kisses, the heat in his

eyes snuffed out, and he stepped even farther back, rubbing a hand over his beard. "If it bothers you, I'll—"

This foolish, self-sacrificial man was about to offer to shave off that delightfully ticklish beard. And after he'd just given her a whole speech about he liked her as she was and wasn't going to ask her to change.

Vriska gripped the front of his shirt, cutting him off before he could finish making the offer. "Don't you dare. I like your beard."

Julien grinned, the look almost boyish. "Good. I rather like my beard too."

Since she had just kissed him, it didn't seem so daring to reach out and trail her fingers over his beard. The bristles prickled her fingers, yet had a sleek, almost soft feel to them. "It's softer than I would have expected."

His eyes held a twinkle as he rested his fingers over hers on his beard. "I probably shouldn't admit it, but my beard is my one vanity. You don't get a beard like this without a great deal of care, you know. Combing it, trimming it, and now I've been using elven conditioner on it. I've been rather happy with the results."

"At least the elves are good for something." Vriska tightened her grip on the front of his shirt, rubbing the thumb of her other hand over that fascinating beard. Who knew she would find beards so attractive, considering it was a rare troll who could produce a bristle or two?

With the night-darkened garden surrounding them and the music wafting from the ballroom, this was a time for kissing, not talking.

She was about to tug him in for another kiss when a soft, strained voice came from the darkness behind them.

"Julien, shashon."

Vriska stilled, a flare of a different kind of heat flooding through her. Whoever had just interrupted them could go jump in a glacier-fed lake for all she cared. She just wanted to go back to kissing.

But Julien's gaze snapped away from her to focus on something behind her. He stiffened, the color draining from his face.

Vriska whirled, her hand dropping to the sword buckled at her side in its fancy sheath.

Princess Jalissa and her elven guard stood there, swaying, their faces so ashen and wan that they looked half-dead. Prince Edmund hung between them, his arms slung over their shoulders, his body limp.

CHAPTER TWENTY-SEVEN

All thoughts of kissing Vriska fled as Julien rushed to his brother. Before he could reach them, Jalissa's knees gave out, and the three of them all but collapsed to the ground, Jalissa and her guard Sarya still desperately clinging to Edmund between them.

Julien dropped to his knees in front of them. He pressed his fingers to Edmund's neck, feeling a faint, but steady pulse. "What happened? What are you doing here? *How* did you get here?"

They were supposed to be in Mongavaria, completing their diplomatic mission.

"He has been poisoned." Jalissa kept a grip on Edmund's hand as she met Julien's gaze with deeply shadowed eyes. "I will explain later. Right now, we need a healer."

"Of course. Here, let me carry him to the cottage." Julien gripped Edmund's limp body and hefted him over a shoulder. As he stood, Jalissa staggered to her feet, still clutching Edmund's hand.

Before he could take so much as a step, Jalissa's face

whitened, and she sagged against him as if she were too weary to walk even a step, much less all the way to the cottage.

Sarya moved to help, but she appeared almost as done in as Jalissa.

Julien half-turned, steadying Edmund on his shoulder with one hand. "Vriska?"

He didn't have to explain. She nodded, then swept Jalissa up, carrying her. In Vriska's bulky arms, Jalissa almost appeared a child, tiny and fragile, except for the darkly determined cast to her face as she twisted to grab Edmund's hand with both of hers.

"I will fetch the healer." Sarya bowed, then disappeared into the darkness before Julien even had a chance to nod.

No matter. Sarya had been here with Jalissa when the elven healers who had volunteered to serve in Escarland had arrived. She would know where to find the palace's elven healer in the small gardener's-cottage-turned-healing-clinic on the far side of the gardens.

Julien turned in the other direction and set off down the path that led to Buckmore Cottage. Vriska, with her long strides, kept up easily, sticking close enough to his side that Jalissa could keep her grip on Edmund.

Once they reached Buckmore Cottage, Julien entered and turned down the first floor hallway that led to the section of the manor house that Edmund and Jalissa had claimed as their own, since Farrendel and Essie had settled into the second floor.

He fumbled with the latch to their bedroom door, then nudged it open with his foot. In two strides, he reached the bed and laid Edmund on top of the covers.

Edmund's head lolled, his eyes squeezed shut and his

mouth pressed tight in pain even while unconscious. He wore only a loose shirt, the top few buttons undone. His trousers and boots were travel-stained and dusty.

Vriska set Jalissa down on the bed, and Jalissa scooted until she lay next to Edmund, never releasing her grip on his hand. She rested her other hand on the bare skin of his chest, over his heart. "Wake up, darling. We made it, as you said we would."

The gesture was too intimate and too raw all at the same time, something Julien didn't feel comfortable witnessing. Yet he couldn't look away either, not with his brother so still and pale on the bed. He dragged a chair closer and sank into it.

Edmund groaned and wrapped his free arm around his stomach and curled in on himself, beads of sweat breaking out on his forehead. Jalissa dabbed them away with her sleeve, the fabric stained as if she'd performed such a gesture many times over. Edmund's face tilted to her, and he mumbled something too low and slurred for Julien to make out.

Jalissa must have understood for a hint of a teary smile played around her mouth and in her eyes. She whispered something into his ear, then kissed his forehead.

Edmund's eyes cracked open, and his expression twitched with the hint of a smile. Then he tilted his head, taking in the room, Julien sitting next to the bed, and Vriska standing next to him.

Julien rested a hand on Edmund's shoulder, not sure what else to do. "What happened?"

Edmund drew in a deep breath, as if to rally his strength enough to speak. "The Mongavarian king is dead. Poisoned by his son. Poisoned me too."

There had to be a story behind that, since Edmund would have been paranoid to the extreme. Especially since he had Jalissa with him, who could test for poison.

But now wasn't the time to ask.

"Warn Averett..." Edmund's eyes drifted shut again. "She might be in on it..."

The *she* must be Princess Bella, based on the context. Julien squeezed his eyes shut, trying to get his brain to follow the same train of thought that Edmund would have already figured out, even while poisoned and dying.

If the crown prince had poisoned his father, it likely hadn't been a mere whim. Not with the poisoning of Kostaria shortly before. If so, then why send his daughter off to Escarland, unless she had a part to play in the overall scheme?

And what was that scheme? It seemed that the Mongavarian crown prince had gotten tired of waiting for his turn for the crown and had decided to hurry his father's death along.

Maybe the crown prince of Mongavaria had been behind the poisoned grain as a way to weaken Kostaria and one kingdom in the alliance. If that were the case, then it would stand to reason that Princess Bella was here to weaken Escarland in some way.

Such as a mass poisoning of the Escarlish royalty and nobility at a big event. A ball, for example.

Jalissa's smile faded as Edmund lapsed back into unconsciousness. Still, she met Julien's gaze with a strained but determined look. "We discovered that your Lord Farnley was the smuggler. But it seems he was ignorant of the poison. He has been illegally importing luxury goods from Mongavaria into Escarland ever since Averett introduced the higher tariffs. When merchants in Mongavaria approached him about smuggling grain into Kostaria, he jumped on the chance to double his profits by selling the Escarlish grain from his holdings to Kostaria legally and smuggling Mongavarian grain on the side."

Beside Julien, Vriska's knuckles cracked as she ground one fist against her palm, then the other. Perhaps it would be best if Julien didn't point out Lord Farnley if he happened to still be at the ball.

Julien straightened and pushed to his feet. "We need to talk to Averett. Jalissa?"

"Go. We will be fine until the healer arrives." Jalissa nodded toward the door. "There is nothing either of you can do."

They weren't healers, and Julien didn't even have magic. Jalissa was right. She and Edmund would simply have to hang on until the healer arrived.

With Vriska on his heels, Julien jogged out the door and down the hall. At the outer door, he nearly ran into Sarya and the healer as they hurried inside. The elf healer Nylian gave Julien a nod as he hurried past.

Once outside, Julien broke into a run along the path back to Winstead Palace. In her dress and boots, Vriska kept up easily. She probably could have outpaced him if she wished, but she matched her stride to his.

At the garden, Julien slowed to a walk and held his arm out to Vriska. "We don't want to draw attention to ourselves or cause a panic."

She nodded, rested her hand on his arm as if they had just been out for a moonlit stroll, and fell into step next to him as he wound his way through the garden paths back to the ballroom doors.

When the footman opened one of the double doors for them, Julien had to squint at the flood of light, the music and noise slamming into him after the quiet of the night outside. After a moment to adjust, he found Averett talking in a group of noblemen.

As they threaded their way through the crowd, Julien cast another glance around the room, then leaned closer to Vriska. "Do you see Princess Bella?"

"No." Vriska's head swung from side-to-side as she openly stared around the ballroom, not at all subtle. Still, the looks they received seemed to focus more on her hand on his arm and the close way they were standing than the obvious manner in which Vriska was peering around.

When they were halfway across the ballroom, Averett glanced up and caught Julien's gaze. Julien motioned toward the nearest door as unobtrusively as he could. Averett seemed to understand his meaning, for he gave a slight nod, then turned back to his conversation, appearing to wrap it up as he eased away from the noblemen he'd been talking to.

Julien veered in a new direction, nudging Vriska into place next to him as he strolled instead for the set of doors nearest where they stood. Once they were in the nearly empty corridor, they quickened their place, winding their way around the ballroom until they reached where Averett stood.

Several Escarlish guards had trailed behind Averett, and they now blocked off the hallway on either side, preventing anyone from interrupting their conversation or attempting an assassination.

"What is it?" Averett glanced between them, a furrow creasing his brow.

"We were out in the garden." Kissing, but Julien wasn't about to tell his brother that. Then again, the faint flush that crept up his neck at the memories probably gave that away without him saying anything. "And Edmund and Jalissa arrived. Edmund has been poisoned. The healer is with him now."

"Will he be all right?" Averett took a step in the direction of Buckmore Cottage, as if by reflex, before he halted and met Julien's gaze.

"I don't know." Julien, too, found himself glancing in the general direction of Buckmore Cottage. "We didn't stay to find out. But I think so. By the way Jalissa was gripping his hand, I think they've formed a heart bond."

He'd seen the telltale signs of a heart bond many times over with Essie and Farrendel. It had been obvious enough that even he could recognize it.

Averett blew out a breath, his shoulders sagging for just a moment, before he straightened and his hard, king mask returned. "If Mongavaria dared to attack our diplomats while their princess is here, then she must have a mission of her own. Likely an attack that would break the terms of the diplomat swap and place her at risk regardless, so it wouldn't matter if the Mongavarians broke the terms further by killing our ambassadors."

"Exactly." Julien resisted the urge to wince at how quickly Averett had put it all together with far less information than Julien had been given. That was why Averett was the king and Edmund the spy. They had the brains for it. Julien was the brawn. "Where is Princess Bella?"

"She retired to her rooms, claiming a headache." Averett's frown deepened, and he glanced in the direction of the guest wing. "She also received a message shortly before that."

If Edmund had traveled all the way from Mongavaria, then likely a message from her father confirming that her grandfather was dead and their plan had been set in motion could also arrive.

"We'll check her rooms." Julien glanced at Vriska, receiving a nod. She was there, ready to guard his back no matter what they faced.

"Confirm she's there, then quietly station guards outside. We can't openly arrest her. Not yet, anyway." Averett grimaced. "There's a full squad guarding Bertie and Finn, but I'll send a guard to alert them to the danger. And I'll ask Elluin to quietly check the banquet food for poison once again. He's been checking throughout the night, but if she slipped poison into the punch…"

If that happened, she could have poisoned half the Escarlish court. It would be a bother, but with five elf healers stationed at Winstead Palace and the hospitals of Aldon, they could likely handle the poisonings without any fatalities.

Would she have risked slipping poison into the food? She knew Escarland had elf healers on hand. She had to know the elf warrior loitering near the food had been sent by Weylind to check the food while the Mongavarian delegation was in Escarland. It seemed like a useless plan, to try to poison anyone in Escarland while they were on high alert after what had happened in Kostaria.

But what else could she be planning? The Mongavarians had already tried an assassination plot and failed. Farrendel and Essie weren't even in Escarland right now.

Perhaps her presence was just a diversion while

Mongavaria went through their own internal strife. Maybe the crown prince had wanted her safely out of the kingdom while he staged his coup, preventing any of his father's supporters from getting revenge by killing her.

If so, then why poison Edmund? Why bring Escarland into this at all?

Was it merely an attempt at a marriage alliance? Was her only mission to secure a marriage to Julien now, then later Averett, Paige, Bertie, and Finn could be quietly disposed of, making Julien—and thus her—ruler of Escarland?

Did that mean Princess Bella had been telling the truth? Was her only plan to use marriage to escape her father and grandfather? If so, he couldn't blame her. Her father had just poisoned her grandfather. That wasn't something that happened in a healthy family.

It didn't matter the reasons. Hers or her father's. Right now, Julien just had to find her, prevent her from leaving her room, and then figure out the rest later.

Sharing one last glance with Averett, Julien hurried down the corridor, flanked by Vriska and several of the Escarlish soldiers.

The guest rooms occupied a wing directly off the ball-room. Convenient for the guests, and convenient for Julien now as he all but ran to the set of rooms assigned to the Mongavarian princess.

But instead of the four Escarlish guards he'd expected to see outside her door, the corridor was empty.

Not a good sign.

Julien didn't bother knocking. He turned the latch and shoved the door open. Inside, the gaslights had been turned so low only a dim glow remained to illuminate the four lumps sprawled across the sitting room rugs.

He fumbled to turn up the lights, his heart already heavy in his chest even before the flaring lights revealed four Escarlish soldiers, their uniforms and the rugs below them stained with blood.

One of the guards who'd come with him knelt, pressing his fingers to the neck of the nearest prone soldier. After a moment, he shook his head and moved to the next one.

Two of the soldiers took up stations next to the door while the last soldier eased past them and entered one of the bedrooms that connected to the shared sitting room.

As if she had trained with them for years, Vriska stalked toward the next bedroom in the suite and entered, her stance wary and her knife already in her hand.

Julien strode toward the second to last bedroom and stepped inside, leaving the door open behind him. Inside, the bed remained neat as the maids must have left it that morning, not a bedsheet or piece of paper out of place. He strode around the room anyway, checking under the bed and behind the drapes just to be thorough.

"Julien." Vriska's voice held a strange note to it that he'd never heard. "You'll want to see this."

He strode from the empty bedroom and entered the room she'd been searching, stopping short in the doorway.

The surfaces of the desk, dressing table, night stands, and even the bed held bottles and vials and a strange apparatus that he couldn't name. A pot still sat in a faintly glowing bed of coals, giving off a whiff of cooking beans with an acrid undertone that burned his nostrils.

"Don't touch anything." Julien wasn't sure if they should be even breathing in there. Ricin poison could be inhaled just as easily as ingested.

Vriska rolled her eyes at him as she backed away from

the array on the desk. "Of course not." She glanced around one last time before joining him by the door. "Safe to say, she's been cooking up poison from the moment she arrived. Everything looks empty, so she either took the poison she's made with her or…"

"Or she's already used it." Julien took in the bedroom again. He had no idea how much ricin a setup like this could make in the little over two weeks the princess had been in Escarland. He stepped out of the room, closed the door behind Vriska, then turned to one of the soldiers. "Secure the area. Don't let anyone into this room until the elf warrior Elluin and one of the boys from the Intelligence Office can get a look at it."

Julien might not know what he was looking at, but they would.

The soldier nodded, saluted, then stationed himself in front of the door with his back to it.

"Well, this answers one question." Vriska's mouth twisted, as if she was torn between a grin and a grimace. "That princess isn't a helpless innocent caught up in her father's scheme. She fed you a load of tears and musk ox dung."

And he'd come far too close to falling for it. If not for Vriska's presence in his life, he might have been taken in by Princess Bella's teary blue eyes and innocent demeanor.

Julien scrubbed a hand over his beard. "Where did she even get the castor beans and all this equipment to make the poison? We had her luggage searched. Both by soldiers and by elves specifically searching for ricin or castor beans. Surely this much couldn't have been missed. Unless…"

He met Vriska's gaze, seeing his realization reflected in her expression.

"Unless it was smuggled in, and she retrieved it once she was here." Vriska turned to the door before she'd finished speaking.

Julien was only a step behind her, though he halted by the soldiers guarding the door. He pointed at one of them, a soldier he knew to be particularly reliable. "Wake General Bloam. Tell him that he needs to send an expert in poisons to examine these rooms. He also needs to organize a raid on Lord Farnley's townhouse and warehouses. Tonight, if at all possible. I assume Prince Edmund has the proof the general will need. The general can find the prince in Buckmore Cottage. Vriska and I are on our way to Lord Farnley's."

If they hurried, perhaps they could still catch Princess Bella before Lord Farnley assisted in smuggling her out of the kingdom.

There wasn't time to round up guards for a proper raid. The Mongavarian princess would be long gone by then. Besides, Julien had Vriska at his side. Surely the two of them could overpower the two Mongavarian guards the princess had with her, even if those guards had the skills of trained assassins, given that they had dispatched the four Escarlish guards quickly enough to avoid causing a commotion.

As Julien had known he would, the guard saluted and hurried off without asking any questions.

With Vriska at his side, Julien jogged down the corridors of Winstead Palace and out a side door.

At the castle gate, the squad of soldiers were all alive and alert. Thankfully.

They hadn't seen Princess Bella, so she had likely left via another gate or she and her two guards climbed the wall. From what he'd seen, she'd left her luggage behind and was leaving with next to nothing, so they weren't burdened with anything that would impede their escape.

After commandeering two of the guards, Julien led the way down Aldon's streets. The streetlights cast an orange glow over the streets that still had a subdued bustle despite the late hour. Even here, in the upscale neighborhood, the streets of Aldon were never entirely empty. Nobles returned home from Winstead Palace. Merchants delivered goods so that they would be available before the shops opened the next morning. The city watchmen patrolled with clomping steps, alert for thieves.

While Lord Farnley was wealthy, he lacked the rank to have a townhouse in the most elite street of Aldon. Instead, his townhouse stood along a square off one of the lesser, though still exclusive, streets.

When they arrived, lights blazed from many of the windows of Lord Farnley's home. Julien marched up to the door and pounded on it. If this had been the official, Intelligence Office raid, then he would've had the authority to break down the door and barge inside.

Instead, he waited, hand on his sword, until a sour-faced butler opened the door and looked down at Julien with a dour frown. "How may I help you, sir? The family is not in at the moment."

"Tell Lord Farnley that Prince Julien of Escarland is here to see him." Julien stared the butler down. He didn't throw his title around often, but in this case he didn't mind bringing the weight of the crown to bear. "He *will* see me."

The butler didn't even flinch, though he did bow deferentially as he swung the door wider. "Very good, sir. If you would care to wait in the parlor, I will fetch his lordship."

After Julien instructed one guard to remain at the front

door and the other to go around back to prevent Lord Farnley from making a break for it, Julien and Vriska trooped inside. Once he'd shown them to the parlor, the butler quietly ducked out.

Julien didn't bother to sit. Vriska paced in front of the delicate, rose-patterned settee. Her silk skirt fluttered around her knees as she moved, yet her stalking steps made her look more dangerous than beautiful at that moment.

After only a few minutes, Lord Farnley stepped inside. He still wore the black, tailored suit and neckcloth he'd been wearing at the ball, yet his forehead had a sheen of sweat along his hairline and there was something tight about his stance, even if he tried to hide it. "What can I do for you, Prince Julien? It's rather late for a social call."

"Then it's a good thing there's nothing social about this call." Julien stepped closer, using his extra few inches of height to loom over the lord. "Where is Princess Bella?"

"Princess Bella?" The lord gave an unconvincing wave of his hand, his gaze dropping away from Julien's. "Why would I know where she is? Isn't she still at the ball?"

Julien wished he could grip the front of the man's shirt and shake him. But until the Intelligence Office put together the proof and conducted an official raid, Lord Farnley wasn't under arrest and Julien had to be careful how he approached this. "I know you smuggle goods from Mongavaria. I know you smuggled Mongavarian grain into Kostaria. But what you probably didn't know is that your smuggled grain contained poison. You are responsible for the deaths of hundreds, if not thousands, of trolls."

The lord's face paled, and more sweat beaded his forehead and temples. "I...I don't know what you're talking about."

"Look. I could hand you over to Vriska here. She's rather eager to get her hands on the person responsible for poisoning her family. And trust me, trolls aren't known for their mercy." Julien didn't glance over his shoulder. But he heard Vriska's knuckles crack, and he could only assume she was at her most hard-edged, brutal warrior self just then.

Lord Farnley's knees wobbled a bit before he steadied himself. He swallowed, his eyes so wide that Julien could read the fear there even if the man still wouldn't meet his gaze.

Julien's smile felt sharp as his sword. "Or you can tell me what I want to know. It's your choice."

"I want immunity," Lord Farnley squeaked, tugging at his collar.

"You know I can't promise that." No way was this lord going to get off after what he'd done. His greed had killed thousands, even if he'd been an ignorant participant. Julien waited until, finally, the lord dared lift his eyes long enough to meet Julien's gaze. "But I can promise that you will be judged by Escarlish law, not Kostarian law. But that is all I can give you."

Rharreth probably wouldn't like it, especially since there wouldn't be any way to punish the true murderers—the Mongavarian crown prince and his daughter—without starting a war to do it.

But Lord Farnley was an Escarlish citizen. Averett would be the one to pronounce judgment.

After one moment—and a furtive glance past Julien at Vriska—and Lord Farnley nodded vigorously. "All right. All right. Yes, I've seen Princess Bella. She demanded that I smuggle her out of Escarland. She blackmailed me. Told me that if I didn't do it, she would make sure King Averett and

King Rharreth found out about my smuggling. What else was I supposed to do?" The man's voice rose as he gestured wildly. As if he considered himself a helpless victim in all this.

"And?" Julien crossed his arms and gave the man a hard glare.

"And I sent her off with some of my men to my warehouse in River's Hollow, off Pattenly Street. I've a shipment of elven goods leaving tonight, bound for Mongavaria." Lord Farnley's knees wobbled again as a line of sweat trickled down his temple. He must be scared, if he was blurting out information about yet more illegal smuggling activity. "That's all I know. If you hurry, you might be able to catch them."

Julien nodded, spun on his heels, and marched from the room without any of the normal social niceties. Lord Farnley didn't deserve them.

Outside on the stoop, he halted by the guard he'd left there. "Don't let Lord Farnley leave. General Bloam should arrive shortly with backup."

"Yes, sir." The guard saluted and adjusted his rifle against his shoulder.

Julien and Vriska would have to go alone to the warehouse. There wasn't time to wait, and Julien had to leave the soldiers here to ensure that Lord Farnley didn't take it in his head to try to weasel out of justice.

As Julien set off down the street, Vriska matched her pace to his, her blue eyes hot and furious. "You shouldn't have promised him anything. You should have just made him tell you without making any concessions."

"Perhaps I could have, but that might have taken more time." Julien shrugged and broke into a steady jog. Thanks to all the training with Farrendel and the months of fighting practice bouts in Kostaria, he had enough breath to jog and talk at the same time. "Besides, it wasn't much of a concession. As an Escarlish lord, Averett wasn't likely to turn him over to Rharreth for judgment anyway, no matter what he did or how much he deserved it. But don't worry, Averett isn't going to let Lord Farnley off. He's going to make an example of him so that no one else gets the idea that such smuggling is a wise investment."

Vriska scowled, her fists clenched as she ran. "I still would've liked to see him suffer the Dackath."

The death of the dishonorable. A troll execution.

"I know." Julien glanced at Vriska, taking in her hard jaw, her far harder eyes. "But given the evidence I assume Edmund has, at the very least he will be stripped of his title, his wealth, and all his holdings. He will certainly suffer, even if he isn't executed."

And for a man like Lord Farnley who loved wealth as he did, losing it would be a slow death rather than the quick death of an execution.

No time to think on it at the moment. Right now, Julien needed to focus on the fight ahead. Lord Farnley's smugglers wouldn't be happy to find an Escarlish prince on their doorstep when they were in the middle of leaving with an illegal load of elven goods and a princess on the run. Julien didn't even know how many smugglers he might be facing, on top of Princess Bella's two guards.

But he had Vriska at his back. Surely the two of them could take on any ragtag band of Escarlish thugs.

CHAPTER TWENTY-EIGHT

Julien jogged down the dark Aldon streets, Vriska at his side. His fancy trousers and tailored dinner jacket weren't ideal for going into battle—nor was his lack of any weapon besides the single-shot derringer he'd hidden in an inside pocket of his coat before going to the ball—but it couldn't be helped.

While River's Hollow wasn't the worst section of Aldon—that distinction belonged to Dock Row across the Fyne River—it was still along the waterfront in an area filled with warehouses, dockyards, and manufacturing buildings. As Julien and Vriska entered the district, they passed groups of loitering men, the smell of alcohol heavy on the air. One group took a step, as if to bar their way, but one look at Vriska sent them scurrying off to the shadows once again.

At Pattenly Street, Julien turned toward the river. The huge warehouse took up most of the block, the only one that could fit the description. Silhouettes moved against the dark river, lit only by a single torch tucked just inside the warehouse to keep it from being spotted from farther than a few yards away. The men were loading a small river barge tied alongside the wooden dock.

Was the princess already on the barge, hidden among the crates and barrels? Or was she in the warehouse?

If Julien had Edmund's stealth, then he would have sneaked inside and searched the place before he made any kind of plan.

But he and Vriska weren't that type. They were more the head-on charge kind of people.

He pulled out the derringer, the gun feeling all too tiny in his hand, and glanced at Vriska. "Ready?"

Vriska's grin flashed in the faint light of the distant street lamps. "To break some noses? Always."

With her at his back, Julien marched toward the men loading the barge. "Halt in the name of King Averett. I demand to know where—"

The closest man dropped the crate he was carrying and whipped out a pistol, aimed, and fired.

A gray shield of Vriska's magic blasted out in front of Julien. The bullet ricocheted off the magic as it might have stone, pinging into the warehouse beyond and sending shards of brick falling to the cobblestones.

Julien ducked around Vriska's shield and fired his derringer in return. He didn't hit any of the men, but they at least ducked for cover instead of attacking all at once.

Before any of them could fire again, Julien charged forward and punched the man in the face with the derringer. The man crumpled like a reed, clutching his nose and dropping his pistol. Tossing aside the derringer, Julien swiped the man's pistol from the ground and spun to find the next smuggler charging at him.

There wasn't time to cock back the hammer and rotate in

another shell. As the man lowered as if to tackle him, Julien jumped out of the way, then slammed the pistol into the man's cheekbone. Bone cracked as the man howled in pain, joining the first lolling on the dock.

Vriska charged, wading into the attacking smugglers with both fists flying. With her troll strength, the smugglers toppled like scythed wheat.

She was magnificent. All brawny and brutal in that moment with blood glinting on her knuckles, a snarl twisting her mouth, and death in her eyes.

And yet her silken skirts delicately fluttered about her, the diamonds and sapphires winked in her white hair, and there was no mistaking her for anything but a woman.

His woman. How he'd gotten so lucky, he didn't know.

As she gripped the last smuggler by his collar, lifted him off his feet, and prepared to punch him, Julien caught her arm. "Wait."

She froze, glancing at him but not questioning him. Simply looking to him for the next cue, as one might a fellow soldier one acknowledged as the leader.

Julien faced the man, who was squirming and all but whimpering in Vriska's hold. "Where is the princess?"

The man's gaze flicked upward, toward the second story of the warehouse, before he went back to cringing and blubbering near incoherent begging.

Julien glanced over his shoulder, spotting a light in one of the second story windows. He nodded. "I see. Vriska?"

With a huff, as if the man wasn't even worth punching, Vriska tossed him into the river as if he weighed no more than good river rock used for skipping stones. The man screamed at an impressively high pitch as he flew through the air before he hit the water with a splash a good ten feet away from the dock.

All around them, the downed smugglers lay groaning and fumbling for weapons. They would stagger to their feet, if given a few minutes to recover, but there wasn't time to properly secure them. They couldn't risk Princess Bella getting away. Capturing her was the only way they could force the new Mongavarian king to pay for his crimes without risking a war.

When Vriska turned back to him, Julien just pointed at the light in the window. Vriska nodded, a grim grin darkening her features. Together, they stalked back down the dock toward the warehouse.

VRISKA'S BLOOD pumped in her veins, her heart thrillingly loud in her ears. If her knuckles stung or a cut traced her cheek from a lucky blow, she didn't feel it. Not yet.

Right now, there was only the heat of battle and the urge to feel bone break beneath her fists and sinew part beneath her sword. Before this night was over, she'd fight, and perhaps kill, and her family would have a bit of justice for the poison that had sickened Rikze and nearly killed Ma.

As she stepped into the warehouse, the single torch illuminated only a small circle of space near the door. The rest remained black and deadly.

Vriska drew her sword and stepped into the lead since her night vision was better than Julien's. He took up a position behind her and a little to her left, as if he'd planned all along to follow her once they reached the warehouse and its impenetrable darkness.

She entered the maze of crates, wooden boxes, and stacks of barrels. As her eyes adjusted, she could make out their darker shapes against the gray gloom, providing her with enough cues to navigate.

Only a few steps in, a noise came from behind her, then Julien sucked in a pained breath, muttering on the exhale. She glanced over her shoulder as he fumbled his way forward, his hands blindly patting the space around him. With his human vision, he was even more blind in this darkness than she'd realized.

She caught his left hand with her left hand. It was an awkward clasp, and she had to twist her arm behind her back, but it left both of their right hands free for her to wield her sword and him the pistol he'd picked up from the smugglers.

After a pause, as if he'd needed to regain his sense of space and direction, Julien gave her fingers a squeeze, letting her know that he was ready to continue.

She led the way, pausing at each intersection to peer around the corner for danger before she stepped into them.

Of course, their enemies were all just as human as Julien. Presumably, they would be as blind as he currently was in the darkness.

Perhaps one of the guards was lurking down here, but more likely, they would be somewhere near a source of light. Not right next to it, since they wouldn't want to ruin their own, paltry night vision. But they would need something more to help them see.

At a broader intersection in what she guessed was roughly the center of the warehouse, Vriska slowly peered in each direction. There, toward the back of the warehouse and to their left, a faint gleam indicated a light. It wasn't the torch they'd left behind at the door, as she could still see its hint of a glow when she glanced over her shoulder.

Instead of heading directly toward the light, Vriska continued straight until she reached the far wall of the warehouse. With the wall guarding them from the side, she crept closer until they came around a stack of crates and found a set of iron stairs leading up to the second story. The light was beaming down from above, providing enough glow that Julien's steps steadied, indicating that he could see once again.

They had to go up those stairs, but from this angle, they couldn't see if anyone lurked above just out of sight. Their enemies were too smart to stand so close that they cast a shadow or anything as foolhardy as that.

But she had Julien at her back and her magic at her fingertips. She might not be Laesornysh who could incinerate a storm of bullets as if it were a mere pattering of rain, but she could still deflect a bullet even at close range. Together, she and Julien could handle whoever was waiting at the top of the stairs for them.

Sword in hand, she stalked up the stairs, crouching to stay as low as possible. With the angle, she had to let go of Julien's hand. He didn't need her guidance any longer.

Yet she flexed her fingers at her side, missing the feel of his hand in hers. It wasn't exactly practical to go into battle holding hands, but perhaps afterwards. Maybe then they'd do a little hand holding. Maybe get back to that interrupted kissing.

She gave herself a good mental shake. It was time to focus on the danger above, not the man at her back.

At the top of the stairs, she pressed herself against the wall and peered through the open doorway. All she could see was an empty room. The outer wall was brick while the rest were wood. Not even a box or a crate filled the space.

But she couldn't see the corners on either side of the door. Not without poking her head inside.

Nothing for it but to charge in, swords and fists swinging, and face what came.

She didn't have to glance behind her to know Julien was ready. They'd fought like this often in the fighting bouts and in the Escarlish war games. He would move when she did, just as ready as she was to take what came.

Bracing herself, she blasted a shield of her stone magic in front of her and charged through the doorway.

A gunshot boomed from her right. Her magical shield shattered half a heartbeat before something punched into her shoulder hard enough to send her staggering.

She growled, whirling to face her attackers.

Princess Bella stood there with her two bodyguards on either side. One held a gun still pointed at Vriska, a wisp of smoke hovering in the air before it vanished.

The princess smiled and patted the bodyguard's arm with the same graceful, languid movements she'd used when in the ballroom. "Thank you, Cedric." Princess Bella turned her wide blue eyes on Vriska. "As you can see, troll, this gun is loaded with magically shielded bullets. While we humans are not as gifted with magic as you trolls or the elves, we are capable of much."

Vriska pressed her hand to her shoulder. Warm, sticky blood poured over her fingers while a deep, stabbing pain lanced through her shoulder.

"The magical protections won't stop that elf's magic, sadly, but as you have discovered, it is effective against most other magics." Princess Bella gave a beatific smile that showed her perfectly straight teeth and glowed in her round, pleasantly rosy cheeks. "Now, Prince Julien, please stop loitering in the stairwell, or I will order Cedric to shoot your betrothed again. And this time, he will put the round between her eyes."

Julien's hands appeared as he set his pistol on the floor just inside the room. Then he stepped inside, his hands raised above his head.

Vriska flexed her fingers on her sword, her jaws clenched so tightly her teeth ached. Even if she lunged for Cedric, he was too far away. She wouldn't make it before he got off another shot, and now she had Julien to worry about as well as herself.

But she couldn't just stand here and surrender. Yes, a good warrior needed to know when it was time to yield.

Yet to yield to this simpering, perfect princess was unthinkable.

The second bodyguard grabbed Julien's arms and started to twist them behind his back. Julien struggled, resisting.

Princess Bella whipped something out of her reticule, then held it up so that both Vriska and Julien could see it.

It was a hypodermic needle filled with a cloudy liquid.

Princess Bella's sunny smile remained in place. "This is filled with ricin. A far more potent concentration than what tainted the grain sent to the barbaric trolls. A dose of this will kill far faster. Maybe you will be able to get to an elf healer in time, but perhaps not. I don't think you want to find out."

Vriska flicked a glance between the princess and Julien. Surely Julien had a plan. Of the two of them, he was the more strategic.

But he was focused on her, a pained look in his eyes. He

was as helpless as she was as the bodyguard shackled his arms behind his back.

Princess Bella pointed the hypodermic needle at Julien's neck, the tip less than an inch away from his skin. "My dear Julien, you are going to come with me. It would have been better if you'd married me willingly as planned, but it seems kidnapping you and holding you hostage will have to suffice until we can quietly kill your brother and his heirs."

She said it so lightly, as if she were discussing the perfect tea blend in one of those fancy Escarlish shops. If not for the needle pointed at Julien, Vriska might have risked the gunshot just for the satisfaction of breaking that pretty, button nose.

"At least I will be able to return to Mongavaria with something to show for this endeavor." Princess Bella rested her other hand on Julien's arm, almost possessively. "It seems your brother Edmund was poking around where he ought not, and my father was forced to accelerate our plans. I hate to inform you, Julien darling, but your dear brother passed away in the Mongavarian countryside."

Julien glared down at her, but he didn't correct her.

Vriska didn't either. It was likely wise to let the princess continue to think Edmund was dead.

"I thought I would be lucky if I simply escaped Escarland with my life, but it seems you fell right into my arms after all." Princess Bella's hand halted on Julien's upper arm. "Now, I believe I've talked long enough that the men you attacked below will be sufficiently recovered so we can resume our journey to Mongavaria. Sadly, troll, you aren't needed. Cedric, if you will?"

In the split second as Cedric shifted the gun a hair, Julien's eyes widened, and he rammed his shoulder into the bodyguard holding him. The two of them stumbled into the princess, sending her off balance and knocking the needle from her fingers. It shattered on the ground, its contents spilling into the wood.

Still Cedric remained steady, his gun leveled at Vriska's head.

"Go!" Julien shouted, his gaze meeting hers, before the bodyguard's fist slammed into his temple, snapping his head to the side.

Cedric's finger tightened on the trigger.

Vriska blasted her magic into a shield and threw herself backwards into the wall of brick behind her. Beneath the force of her magic, the bricks exploded, shards of brick and magic swirling around her for a moment. If there was a bullet in there, she didn't feel it.

Then she was falling, the ground far below rushing up to meet her and the shattered remains of bricks falling with her.

She flung out her magic, calling to the stones of the cobbles and the deeper stone of the bedrock. Begging them to enfold her rather than harm her.

Then she slammed into the ground and the cobblestones swallowed her.

CHAPTER TWENTY-NINE

Julien fought the darkness, his face throbbing. His body refused to obey while his brain felt like it was shouting incoherent orders he couldn't understand.

He became aware of hands on him, dragging him. A wad of something was stuffed into his mouth before a gag was tied tightly around the back of his head.

His body thumped hard onto wood, his shoulder bruising from the impact. The pain jarred him all the way to wakefulness, though he lay still to assess the situation.

Was Vriska alive? Had she escaped? That had been a perilously long fall, and she'd already been wounded. Would her magic have been enough?

It had to have been. He refused to think she lay out there somewhere, dead and broken.

The barge rocked beneath him, and the smuggler crew whispered quiet orders as they shoved away from the dock. A gentle thrum vibrated through the wooden deck below him, and if he were to guess, this barge must have been powered by a magical device rather than the more traditional steam driven turbines.

Of course it had a magical power source. The smugglers would need a quiet boat.

If he made enough noise, would someone notice he was aboard and investigate? There was a checkpoint just outside of Aldon where boats coming and going on the river were stopped and inspected.

Yet the smugglers had to have a way around being stopped. Or they simply bribed the officials.

A set of dainty footsteps approached, then halted in front of him. A whiff of Princess Bella's floral perfume wafted around him, carried on the thick, river and algae scented breeze.

"I know you're awake, Prince Julien. There is no more need for such pretenses with us." Her voice came from just above him, and when he cracked his eyes open, he found that she crouched next to him in proper lady-like fashion, balanced on her toes while her skirts pooled gently around her.

She gave him another one of her chillingly innocent smiles. "There, you see? That wasn't so hard. Your life will be much easier from here if you continue to cooperate with me. Your troll girlfriend is dead. By the time your soldiers figure out where you went, we will be long gone. There is no rescue coming. You might as well surrender."

Julien couldn't so much as spit out a retort, not with the gag in his mouth and the wadding drying out his tongue.

Vriska was alive. She was a troll warrior. He refused to believe something as simple as a bullet and a fall to a stone street below would have killed her.

Was this the utter helplessness that Essie and Farrendel

felt when they had been captured by the Escarlish traitors a year ago? As royalty, they'd been trained to watch and wait for the right opportunity to escape in situations like this. And that was exactly what Essie had done.

But she hadn't mentioned how agonizing the wait was. Nor did Julien have Essie's advantages. She was a woman and thus underestimated. She'd still had a weapon, and she'd had Farrendel with his magic to provide a distraction for her.

Julien's captors weren't about to untie him or leave him unguarded. He was weaponless and currently helpless.

But there was no way he was going to let Princess Bella smuggle him all the way into Mongavaria. The consequences would be too dire, not only for Escarland but also for Tarenhiel and Kostaria since they were a part of this alliance.

"Perhaps I'll even allow you to live once you marry me and we inherit Escarland after the sad demise of your family." Princess Bella reached out and ran her fingers through his hair. Unlike when Vriska had buried her fingers in his hair during their kiss, Princess Bella's touch didn't do anything but give him the urge to roll away and punch her.

Perhaps he should have encouraged Vriska to punch this princess at the ball when she'd had the chance.

"It really was good of you to show up before I left." Princess Bella kept stroking his hair. "I was afraid I'd have to return to Mongavaria empty-handed. Though, your brother Averett likely hasn't discovered the little gift we left him in the food stores of Winstead Palace. With elven healers, there likely won't be many deaths. But the few moments of chaos will provide my father the chance to solidify his crown before your cute little alliance thinks to act."

She'd poisoned the food at Winstead Palace. Surely Averett would ask Elluin to check the food, especially given the setup found in Princess Bella's rooms. There was likely very little danger of anyone ingesting the poison, though it would mean tossing the food and replacing it at great expense.

And what did she mean, that her father needed a chance to solidify his crown? What was the true situation in Mongavaria? Was it perhaps not as united and powerful as it appeared?

Edmund would have the answers to those questions, once he woke.

He would wake. Julien wouldn't allow himself to believe otherwise. He'd seen the strength of a heart bond between Essie and Farrendel. Jalissa had kept Edmund alive while they crossed two kingdoms. By now, the healer had likely healed him and he was just fine.

Although, Princess Bella didn't know that. She had been wrong about Edmund. Surely she was wrong about Vriska too.

Vriska would come for him. And when she did, she'd come with the savage vengeance of her people. If not for how much Julien loathed Princess Bella and her guards, he might have almost felt sorry for them.

Almost.

"Milady?" Cedric approached out of the gloom. He still carried the pistol loaded with the magically protected bullets.

Princess Bella patted Julien's head. "Don't go anywhere, darling." She rose gracefully, then she and her guard strolled a few yards away. They spoke in whispers too low for Julien to hear.

Right now, listening in on their conversation was the least of his priorities. Princess Bella would likely tell him her entire plan just to taunt him.

Besides, he had more important things to do. Like set himself up to escape.

It had been years since he'd done this, but years ago he and his siblings had practiced methods to get out of their bonds if captured. While Julien's hands were currently shackled behind his back, the extra length of chain between his hands gave him enough room to pull this off, hopefully. If he was still flexible enough.

With one glance around to make sure no one was watching him, Julien rolled onto his back, his arms beneath him, his shoulders straining.

If he'd been wearing his leathers and armor, he couldn't have done this. His tighter, tailored outfit wasn't great either, but he gritted his teeth and strained the seams.

He scrunched his knees up to his chest and curled into as tight a ball as he could manage. Holding his breath, he wiggled his hands and the shackles underneath him and over his legs, keeping the chain taut the whole time so that it wouldn't rattle.

Finally, the chain came free, and his hands were now in front of him instead of behind his back. Releasing a relieved breath, he uncurled and rolled onto his side. He pressed his arms to his sides and hid his hands against his stomach, using the darkness to disguise the fact that his hands were now in front of him.

He stilled as Cedric glanced back in his direction. Cedric's eyes were sharp, the gun's barrel swinging to point more fully at him again, before Cedric returned to his conversation with the princess.

Julien flexed his fingers and settled as comfortably against the wooden deck below him as he could.

Vriska wasn't dead, and she would come for him. All he had to do was be ready.

VRISKA WOKE to pain and darkness. Her breaths hovered hot and stale around her face while a heavy weight pressed around her.

Every inch of her ached with a deep throbbing as if she'd been thoroughly pummeled. Agony stabbed her shoulder with every breath

But she was alive. That was the main thing.

She wiggled first her fingers, then her toes. It hurt, but she could move them. Not very far before they brushed stone, but there was movement and sensation that sent waves of pain through her.

Princess Bella. The bullet piercing Vriska's shield, then her body. The desperate dive through the brick wall and into darkness.

Julien. That witch still had Julien.

With a growl, Vriska gathered her strength and shoved against the layer of stone on top of her. It groaned, then fell away with a thump and a cloud of gravel and dust.

She turned her groan into a deeper growl as she heaved herself from the pit and rolled onto her hands and knees on the cobblestone street beside the warehouse. In the morning, the Escarlish people were going to be puzzled by the troll-shaped hole she'd left in their street where her magic had used the stones to cushion her fall.

It took another groan-growl to stagger to her feet, and

once upright she had to press a hand to the brick wall next to her as her head swam and the road beneath her tilted as if trying to tip her back into what would have been her grave if she'd had any other power beside stone magic.

Blood soaked the front of the silken bodice and onto the skirt. The skirt itself was in tatters, and even her trousers below were ripped and stained. The boots and fancy leather belt were scuffed instead of shined as before.

Where was her sword? She'd had it in her hand when she'd jumped through the wall.

Vriska rolled to put her back to the wall, then scanned the dark street until she caught a flash of light reflecting off steel.

A few feet away, her sword had fallen tip first, burying itself nearly to the hilt in the stone cobbles. The influence of her magic, no doubt.

She stomped over to it, gripped the hilt, and let some of her magic flow over the sword to pour into the stones below. With a grunt, she withdrew the sword as if it were in its leather sheath instead of stone.

A gargling noise came from the darkness to her right. She glanced up to find a hunched Escarlish man dressed in reeking rags standing there on the street, clutching a bottle half-filled with liquid to his chest. His jaw hung open, emitting a strangled noise, as he stared goggle-eyed at her.

"What? You've never seen someone pull a sword from a stone before?" Vriska swiped the dust and dirt from the blade against her skirt. In Kostaria, it wasn't exactly rare for trolls with stone magic to embed their weapons in stone to store them.

As he continued to stare at her, she marched over and snatched the bottle from his nerveless fingers. She put the bottle to her lips and downed half of what was left in several large swigs. The Escarlish liquor burned down her throat, but the warmth that spread through her helped numb some of the ache.

She shoved the bottle back into the man's hand. "Linsh."

His fingers closed around his bottle, but that was the only movement he made. She wasn't even sure if he blinked.

With the alcohol numbing the ache, Vriska set off around the warehouse, forcing herself into a jog despite the fact that every foot-fall shot pain into her shoulder.

As she neared the corner, she slowed and peered around the building.

The dock and the river flowing past remained dark. And completely empty. No barge. No smugglers. And no Julien.

Blast. She was too late. The smugglers had already shoved off. How long ago was it now?

Vriska glanced upward, but the city lights obscured the stars so much that only a few broke through the haze. Not enough for her to gauge how much time had passed.

Surely it couldn't be long. There should still be time for her to catch them.

They would be heading upriver, following the Fyne as it wound its way north. Would the smugglers take the river all the way until it met the Hydalla, then take that to Mongavaria? Or did they stop somewhere else and offload onto a train that would take them directly east?

It didn't matter. Either way, Julien was likely lost to them if the smugglers got him out of Aldon.

She couldn't let that happen.

Steeling herself against the pain, Vriska broke into a jog, then a faster run. Instead of sticking to the riverbank, she swerved onto the streets that paralleled the river, though she stayed on the straight ones instead of curving into the warrens that followed the contours of the river. Yes, she would miss seeing a few stretches, but she gained ground whenever she could.

Each time the river curved back toward her, she peered both directions, searching for a dark silhouette against the water.

How much farther? Had she caught up, or was the barge —with its propulsion and the river at its back—traveling too fast for her to even have a hope to catch up?

No, she couldn't give up. Julien was hers, and she wasn't about to let that viper keep him.

As she ran alongside another empty stretch of river, she poured a thread of her magic into the cobbles beneath her, then deeper until she reached the bedrock. She sent her power out, searching beneath the river. For what, she wasn't entirely certain.

There. A hint of a vibration traveled through the stone. So faint that it took her a moment to figure out what it was. The propeller of an engine churning the water and the water sending a hint of that churning into the stones below.

Vriska drew on her remaining strength and forced her legs to pump faster into a sprint. She raced past a marshy stretch of docks, then around another large warehouse.

As she rounded the warehouse and came within sight of the river again, she finally spotted a dark shape in the broad expanse of the rippling water.

Vriska skidded to a halt and knelt, pressing her hand to the stone. With a snarl curling her mouth, she shoved a blast of her magic into the earth.

The rumble of her power raced through the bedrock, a deep purr that settled into her bones.

With an eruption of water, a wall of stone shot out of the

river to the front and side of the barge. A few short screams carried over the water as the wave of the dispelled river shoved the barge off course and toward the bank where Vriska knelt.

It wasn't far enough, however. Here, the Fyne River flowed wide, and the barge only shifted a few yards in her direction.

Still pouring her magic into the willing bedrock below, Vriska straightened and strode into the river. A pathway of stone rose to meet her feet so that her boots didn't get more than damp.

As the smugglers on the barge fended off from the wall, Vriska hammered another blast of magic into the bedrock. Another wall of stone exploded from the river below, pinning the barge between them so that it was stuck fast.

Pinned and helpless. All the better to await her vengeance.

Vriska stalked toward the barge on her pathway of stone, her grip steady on her sword. What was the pain of her shoulder or the aches in her bones compared to the fury heating her blood and strengthening her muscles?

"Don't come any closer, troll." The bodyguard Cedric stepped to the side of the barge, leveling that gun at her again with its annoying, magically shielded bullets.

Vriska released a howling, troll war chant and broke into a charge. Let the man shoot her. She would get her hands on his scrawny neck before she died.

Before Cedric had a chance to pull the trigger, Julien leapt from the gloom, wrapped the chain of his shackles around the man's neck, and hauled him backwards, taking him all the way to the deck and out of Vriska's sight.

Julien. He was here, and he was fighting. The sight sent a

surge through Vriska's blood, and she released another heady howl.

Several smugglers grabbed muskets or pistols and aimed at her. She shoved her magic into a stone-like shield in front of her, and the bullets pinged off. Apparently only the Mongavarians had their guns loaded with their fancy bullets. They hadn't deemed it necessary to share with their smuggler allies.

Vriska charged the whole lot of them, battering them with her magical shield before she leapt over the low rail.

More bullets flew around her, buzzing with all the harmless annoyance of a fly.

This time, there were no fists. No mercy. Just her sword and blood.

The smugglers knew it too. They came at her with guns and knives, for all the good it did them.

A few took one look at her and threw themselves over the sides, stroking frantically at the water to get away from her as quickly as they could. One of the smarter ones tried to run across her stone bridge, but he slipped and fell on the damp stone, bashing his head before he rolled into the water.

She whirled, searching for another enemy. Cedric lay on the ground, unmoving.

Julien wrestled with the second Mongavarian guard. He'd wrapped his chain around the man's wrists, keeping the man from stabbing him with a knife. Even as Vriska lunged to help, Julien swung the man around, bashing him face-first into one of the stacks of crates. The man collapsed in a heap, and Julien disentangled the chain.

Together, they turned and faced Princess Bella.

She huddled next to the rail, her back pressed to a stack

of crates. Still standing, but shaking like a leaf as she wrapped both arms around her middle.

As they stalked closer, she turned a tear-streaked face toward them, her blue eyes wide and pleading. "Please don't hurt me. Please, please. Just don't hurt me."

Vriska marched forward and threw a punch right into that upturned, button nose. It made a rather satisfying crunch beneath Vriska's knuckles.

With a high-pitched whine, the princess collapsed to the deck, blood pouring down her chin. The princess clutched at her face with both hands, an item dropping from her fingers where she had been concealing it against the inside of her arm.

Another hypodermic needle, filled with ricin poison.

Vriska pinched the needle between two fingers and picked it up, holding it well away from her body. She glared at the princess. "*Curuska.*"

The princess wouldn't understand the insult. But it made Vriska feel better to say it out loud. And surely the princess understood the tone and the meaning behind it, even if she didn't know the exact word.

"Does that mean what I think it does?" Julien's voice, delightfully alive and strong, rang from behind Vriska.

"Probably. Ma would light into me good if she heard me say it." Vriska shrugged, turned, and set the poison-filled needle on the top of a tall stack of crates where only she or Julien would be able to reach it. "It's rather rude. But she deserves it."

Julien's grin quirked in that wry expression. He stood before her, balanced on two feet with a confident stance that said he was uninjured. Iron shackles still bound his wrists with a short length of chain between them while a cloth gag hung around Julien's neck where he must have tugged it when freeing himself.

His grin disappeared into something darker and grimmer as he glared past her at Princess Bella. "I don't hold to crude language normally, but if ever there's a person best described by it, she would be it."

"I'm surprised you recognized it. Your brother-in-law Laesornysh doesn't seem the swearing type." Vriska cleaned her sword on the tatters of her skirt, then sheathed it. Not that her skirt was all that clean, grimed with dirt and soaked with her own blood as it was.

"No, I definitely didn't hear it from him." There was that wry grin again as Julien strode closer. "I think my brother Edmund might have said it a time or two. He has quite the vocabulary in elvish."

Now that didn't surprise her.

She reached out and gripped the chain between Julien's hand. With a swell of her magic, she crushed the metal chain, snapping the links. He'd need someone else to remove the shackles, but at least he'd have more freedom of movement.

His brow furrowed as his gaze swept over her. "You're still bleeding."

The bullet in her shoulder. Vriska pressed a hand over the wound, feeling the fresh warmth of blood between her fingers. She'd forgotten about it during the rush of battle. Now it throbbed with pain, her head suddenly swirling.

"I think…I might sit down." Vriska sank onto the nearest crate. A wave of throbbing pulsed through her muscles and lanced deeper into her shoulder.

Julien picked up a pistol from where it had fallen on the deck, then he sat next to her on the crate. He kept the pistol loosely trained on Princess Bella where she curled on the deck, mewling. "General Bloam search the city once he tracks us to the warehouse, and he'll find us sooner or later. Once he gets here, we can get you a healer."

"I'll be fine until then." Blackness joined the dizziness swirling through her vision. Vriska closed her eyes, slumped, and rested her head on Julien's shoulder. "Don't let her get away."

"I won't." His voice held a deeper, soothing rumble when she was this close to him.

"And she's my prisoner. I punched her. I get to keep her."

"Of course."

"And don't let that elf healer fix up her nose too soon. That would defeat the point of punching her."

"I'm sure the healer will be too busy with you to worry about her for quite some time."

"Good." Vriska heaved a sigh and let herself sag more heavily against him. He was so thoughtful. So nice to indulge her bloodthirsty tendencies. And, even better, she got to keep him.

He put an arm around her shoulders, the chain cold against the bare skin of her arm. Not that she minded. Right then, she was weary from battle. She was loved by a kind-hearted warrior. And she'd gotten to punch her enemy in the face. Life didn't get much better than that.

CHAPTER THIRTY

Julien paced back and forth outside Vriska's door. As he wasn't her husband yet, he had been relegated to waiting outside while the healer tended her.

She would be fine. She was strong. And the elf healer Nylian was one of the most skilled healers of Tarenhiel.

But that didn't stop him from worrying. She had been loopy with blood loss before General Bloam had found them and they'd been transported back to Winstead Palace.

The throbbing in his head and cheek wasn't helping much. He'd taken quite the clobbering to the head, though he wasn't going to speak up until after Vriska was healed.

The door opened, and Nylian strode into the corridor, his long hair perfectly in place despite the fact that it was the middle of the night. He stared down his nose at Julien. "The troll is healed and resting."

How did the healer manage to pull off that snooty tone, even here at Winstead Palace? Nylian had gotten better around humans during the war, but it seemed trolls still brought out his uppity side.

"Can I see her?" Julien flexed his fingers at his sides, almost ready to shove the healer aside and enter.

"If you must." Nylian started to stride past Julien, then halted. He swept his gaze over him, locking on Julien's face. "I suppose you have not been healed."

"Vriska was the priority." Julien's face throbbed, but it was likely just a bad bruise. He could live with it easily enough.

Nylian sighed, then lifted fingers surrounded by green, healing magic. "Hold still."

Julien froze and refused to flinch when the elf healer's cold fingers brushed against his aching face. While the elf's bedside manner was lacking, he was an excellent healer. In a heartbeat, the soothing magic washed over Julien's face and eased the throbbing. His head felt clearer too, less muddled and fuzzy.

"You will not collapse now." Nylian withdrew his hand, then strode down the corridor before Julien had a chance to thank him.

Shaking his head, Julien pushed open Vriska's door and stepped inside. As he entered the sitting room, Paige's maid was crossing the room, carrying a small wooden jewelry box. As she caught sight of Julien, she dropped into a curtsy before hurrying out the door.

Julien strode to the inner door. It was open, but he halted in the doorway and knocked on the open door.

Vriska lay on the bed, her white hair taken out of the style it had been in earlier and now spread across her pillow. The blanket was pulled to her chin, though a hint of her bandaged shoulder peeked out. She turned her head toward him, her eyelids drooping.

Paige sat in a chair next to the bed. She half-turned at his knock, then waved him inside.

Julien crossed the room and knelt next to the bed. "How are you feeling?"

"I'm fine." Vriska flapped her hand, her face scrunching in a look that was more annoyed than anything else. "I don't need all this fuss and bother."

"I know. But it's all right to rest." Julien gently brushed a strand of her hair from her face before he leaned down and pressed a kiss to her forehead.

"That isn't a proper kiss." Vriska's words slurred sleepily. "We won. I want a real kiss."

"Later. I promise." Julien straightened. He couldn't help but trail his fingers through her hair one last time. The strands slid over his finger with a silken softness that he hadn't expected.

When he turned, Paige's mouth quirked. "I'll look after her."

"Thanks." Julien managed a weary smile before he forced his dragging feet out the door and into the hallway.

There he found Averett leaning casually against the wall. He still wore his black trousers and dinner jacket from the ball, though his remained unrumpled, unlike Julien's stained and torn clothing.

With him, Vriska's family waited. Her da paced. Her ma rested an arm around Rikze's shoulders. Rikze's eyes had a wet sheen, as if she were on the verge of tears.

Julien left the door open wide behind him. "She's fine, and she's awake—mostly—if you want to see her."

Rikze tore away from her ma and rushed inside. Her ma

followed at a slower pace, and she paused long enough to give Julien a weary smile as she passed. Her da rested a hand on his shoulder, giving a firm squeeze, before he, too, entered the room.

How many times had Vriska's family been called to her side after she'd been wounded? And in those battles, there wouldn't have been an elf healer on hand to patch her up afterwards.

As Julien closed the door behind Vriska's family, Averett pushed off the wall. "I'm glad both you and Vriska are well."

"Yes. She tracked me down and took out the smugglers before they even got me out of the city." Julien rubbed at his wrists. One of General Bloam's men had fished the keys out of the pocket of one of the princess's guards and unlocked the shackles, but the memory of iron around his wrists still remained. "Our family should avoid balls for the foreseeable future. Bad things always seem to happen at balls lately."

Essie and Farrendel had been kidnapped after a ball. The Mongavarian spies had broken into the records room during a ball. And now Princess Bella had poisoned food and used the cover of the ball to escape.

"You have a point." Averett sighed, his mouth quirking as if torn between a scowl and a hint of a grin. "I'll be sure to mention that to the nobility when I decide to cancel all formal occasions."

"What about the poison here?"

"None of the food at the ball was poisoned." Averett grimaced and rubbed at the back of his neck. "But poison was discovered in our grain stores and dried fruits and vegetables. Elluin is sorting through what is tainted and what isn't as we speak. Beyond the hassle of wasting so much food and the expense of replacing it, no one was hurt and no real damage was done. It seems to be a poorly executed act of desperation since Mongavaria has failed to strike Escarland in any other meaningful way."

"And Edmund?" That weight dropped into Julien's stomach again.

"He's fine. He was awake and talking strategy as of a few minutes ago." Averett's quirked mouth took on more of a grin for a moment before the grin faded back into a grim expression. "He reports that things aren't as united in Mongavaria as they seem. There's a faction among the nobility who hasn't been happy with the power the king has acquired, and they were especially furious over the crown prince poisoning his father. He tried to pass it off as Edmund's doing, but no one was fooled."

"And Edmund got all that while poisoned and fleeing across the kingdom?" Julien could only shake his head. That was Edmund. Barely surviving being poisoned, and he was already thinking through the tactics of it all. Of course he would take the time to gather information while he and Jalissa were fleeing back to Escarland.

Averett shrugged, as if he, too, wasn't all that surprised. "We've already started the process of reaching out to the leaders of this faction. Edmund and General Bloam think they will be very interested in knowing that we have the Mongavarian princess in custody. If we're clever about this, we'll be able to use her and this faction to force Mongavaria to back off, at least for a while. The new king is going to be too busy with internal affairs to strike out at the alliance for many years to come."

"Good." It wasn't a permanent solution. But it would buy time. And that was what the alliance needed right now.

Averett clapped him on the shoulder. "Now you need to rest as well. You've been up all night."

"So have you." Julien raised his eyebrows.

"But I didn't spend part of it getting beat up and kidnapped." Averett's quirked, grim smile returned. "I just pretended everything was fine while I closed out the ball and had the food stores searched. Nothing too strenuous."

But taxing all the same. If he had a choice, Julien would choose the getting beat up and kidnapped option over handling the politics. "And that's why you're the king, and I'm the warrior."

Averett nodded toward Vriska's door. "And why I'm glad you're going to have a woman like her guarding your back. She's been good for you. You've been too content to simply stand in my shadow. With her, you're going to make your own place."

"I didn't think there was such a thing as being too content." Julien thought he understood what Averett meant, but he wasn't going to admit that out loud. He'd rather give his brother a hard time.

"Perhaps not. And, selfishly, I would have been happy to have you always there, guarding my back and quietly stepping in wherever you were needed." Averett shrugged, staring down the hallway. "And perhaps you and Vriska will still quietly step in wherever you are needed. But you both will have a role in molding how the alliance between Kostaria and Escarland shapes our peoples, the way Essie and Farrendel have shaped our relationship with Tarenhiel."

It wasn't the future he'd expected for himself, but he was eager to embrace whatever came. Organizing war games. Visiting troll settlements in Escarland. Helping Escarlish immigrants adjust to life in Kostaria.

With one last nod, Averett strode down the hallway. Near the corner, one of his aides rushed up, bowed, and appeared to be giving a report.

Yes, ruling was a job that Julien was happy to leave to his brother.

As Julien strode down the corridor in the opposite direction, he found his feet turning not toward his suite of rooms, but toward the doors to the family gardens that would lead him to the path to Buckmore Cottage.

Tired as he was, he let his feet carry him into the gardens. A gray hint of dawn hung over the hedges and shrouded the trees of the parkland. The coolness of early morning washed over him, the peace of the quiet gardens and woodlands sweeping away the last of his tension.

When he reached Buckmore Cottage, he entered and strolled down the hallway toward Jalissa and Edmund's rooms. If they were asleep, then he'd leave rather than disturb them.

But he needed to reassure himself that Edmund was all right.

The door to Edmund and Jalissa's room stood open, and low voices came from within. When Julien peeked inside, he found Edmund awake and alert, talking softly with their mother.

Mother perched in the chair next to the bed, quietly stitching a piece of embroidery as she talked.

"May I come in?" Julien stepped into the doorway but didn't fully enter the room.

Mother glanced over her shoulder, then stood. "Please, take my seat. I could use a moment anyway." As she walked from the room, she halted at Julien's side and rested a hand on his arm. "I'm glad you and Vriska are all right."

"Vriska took the brunt of it." Julien shrugged. "I just played the part of helpless prince until it was the right time to fight back."

"Not a role you play often." Edmund sprawled on the bed as if completely at ease, though he kept his voice low.

Jalissa curled against Edmund's side, her head on his shoulder. Her hand lay on Edmund's chest, as if even in sleep she was determined to make sure he stayed alive. Edmund rested his hand over hers while his other arm wrapped around her shoulders, holding her close. He might appear relaxed, but the hints of fear still lingered in the way the two of them held each other tightly.

Mother gave Julien a quick hug before she left the room.

Julien strode across the space and settled into the chair she'd vacated. "You're looking better."

"I'm feeling better. Elven healing magic really is remarkable." Edmund tilted his head so that he peered down at Jalissa's sleeping face. "She is remarkable. I wouldn't have survived, if not for our heart bond."

Jalissa gave a small sigh in her sleep, shifting, but she didn't wake. Lines of weariness still etched across her face, testament to the toll that keeping Edmund alive had taken on her.

"I'm glad you have her. And that you've formed a heart bond." Julien settled more heavily against the back of the chair.

Edmund's arm tightened around Jalissa's shoulders. All traces of his usual, lighthearted mask disappeared, leaving a more weary, more somber look that Julien had rarely seen on Edmund. "It's different than I thought it would be. I wanted a heart bond and yet…it's painful, knowing that I'm taking so much from her. She's giving me her years willingly, and yet I don't like knowing the extent of the sacrifice she's making for me."

Julien remained silent, not sure what to say. Edmund didn't seem to want him to say anything.

"Then fleeing across Mongavaria, I saw the way keeping me alive was killing her." Edmund turned green-blue eyes toward Julien, a tortured pain lurking there. "There was a moment when she dozed that I thought about letting go, crawling away before she had a chance to wake, and dying before I hurt her any more. I didn't do it, but I thought about it. It's not a part of the heart bond that Essie and Farrendel talk about."

"No." Julien wasn't sure what else to say after Edmund's admission. "But the two of them both know that the years he'll live with Essie will be far longer than however long he would have lived without her. But Jalissa..."

"Jalissa would have lived a long, full life if she'd married an elf instead of me." Edmund sighed and stared at the ceiling. "I knew it, but I wouldn't let myself dwell on it. Until the past few days forced me to face it."

If Edmund's hint back at his wedding was to be believed, it was something Julien would have to face as well. Assuming the trolls had some version of a heart bond.

Could he handle knowing that, to live a longer life at Vriska's side, she would give up her own years and strength for him? Or would the guilt of taking so much from her eat away at him as it was eating at Edmund now?

"Forming the heart bond was her choice as it was yours. From what I've gathered, you both need to love for it to work." Julien leaned forward, rubbing a thumb over his palm. "You aren't stealing from her but accepting what she is giving willingly. Feeling guilty would be disrespecting her choice."

Julien would have to remind himself of that, if he found himself struggling with such guilt. Not just over the heart bond, but whenever the thought of Vriska going into battle at his side and putting herself in danger itched at his protective instincts.

"I know." A hint of Edmund's smile returned, though the pain still lingered in his eyes. "When it's your turn to get married, I don't recommend heading off to an enemy kingdom as part of your honeymoon. Just stick to a nice, calm honeymoon on the beach or wherever your troll wife prefers."

"I think she prefers battles." Julien couldn't help what was probably a sappy smile that crossed his face. Vriska had looked downright gleeful when she'd punched Princess Bella.

"Ah, well in that case, I know who to volunteer for the next mission to Mongavaria." Edmund's grin flashed in full force now.

"Thanks, but no thanks." He'd had enough of Mongavaria lately.

"We should have known the princess was going to make trouble." Edmund shook his head against the pillow, a wry smile tugging at his mouth. "Her full name is Princess Bella Gertrude Donna Yenene of the Royal House of Ghentren."

Julien ran the name over in his mind, but he was missing something. "So?"

"Bella. Donna. Belladonna is a poison. I don't think that was a coincidence."

"Her father named her after a poison?" Now Julien was shaking his head. That was dedication. And it meant that the former crown prince—now Mongavaria's king—had a thing for poisons even when his daughter was born twenty years ago.

"Let's just say I think we're going to need to negotiate for an elf to be permanently stationed here at Winstead Palace to check for poisons. At least, plant-based poisons like ricin or belladonna." Edmund grimaced and sighed. "And the Intelligence Office will need to step up our monitoring for Mongavarian interference. But if we play this right, we'll be able to stop any active attacks, at least for a while."

Soon it would be over. Thanks to Vriska's capture of Princess Bella and the information Edmund had brought back from Mongavaria, they would force Mongavaria to back off. Their three kingdoms would have peace.

CHAPTER THIRTY-ONE

Vriska pressed her back to the far-too-flimsy living wood wall of the elven treetop room as the others crowded around Laesornysh, Princess Essie, and their week-old babe.

The babe was cute enough, as babies went. Tiny pointed ears, a shock of red hair, and easy-going enough that he had yet to snivel even though he was being passed around like a steaming hot potato.

And with Julien's mother, Rharreth, Melantha, King Weylind, Queen Rheva, King Averett, Queen Paige, Edmund, Jalissa, and Julien all packed into the room—not to mention the proud parents—that was a lot of arms and passing around.

Vriska crossed her arms and studied Laesornysh. No, Prince Farrendel. With that beaming smile and the strut that all new proud fathers had, she couldn't think of him as the cold warrior Laesornysh. He was too...young. Too happy. Too like the little brother that Julien saw when he looked at him.

And because Julien saw him as a little brother, she would see him that way too. It might take some time, but she would get there.

She'd never had a little brother before. Once she married Julien, she would get two of them. An elf and a human. Strange, that. And two more little sisters. Also an elf and a human.

Would she manage to be a good big sister to them? For many years, she'd been so busy being a warrior and a good sister to her shield band that she'd failed to be a good big sister to Rikze.

Julien would help her. By his example, she would learn how to be more self-sacrificial. She would become a better sister, a better friend, a better person, with him at her side. Not because he demanded or forced. But because he inspired.

And she would make sure he didn't give of himself until he was empty. And when he was near empty, she would be a source of strength for him. Perhaps she could inspire him to step out of the shadows to become a better person as well.

Julien's mother, the person currently holding the baby, glanced around the room. After a moment, she weaved her way through the crowd and halted in front of Vriska, giving her a smile. "Do you want to hold him?"

Vriska stiffened. What could she say, especially as she felt all the eyes in the room turn to her? No? She would only draw more attention to herself if she did that.

She forced herself to nod, and she held out her arms. She felt so large and awkward as Julien's mother passed the small baby to her, the babe's head looking tiny against Vriska's bicep.

As the baby—what was his name?—settled into Vriska's

arms, she waited to feel something. Anything. Shouldn't she get some kind of warm and fuzzy feeling now that she was holding a baby? All she felt was a panicked clawing in the back of her throat that made her want to pass the baby on to someone else as quickly as possible.

When she glanced up, she found Prince Farrendel's gaze locked on her. If anything, his eyes were wider and more frantic than she felt. Given what he'd gone through at the hands of her people, she couldn't blame him if he felt uncomfortable seeing his newborn in the hands of a troll.

Julien appeared at Vriska's side. "Mind if I take a turn?"

Vriska breathed a sigh of relief and gently handed the baby over. As soon as the baby was safely in Julien's arms, she sagged against the wall, the tension leaving her.

Julien smiled down at the baby, who blinked up at him. Julien cradled the babe in one arm, then reached out to touch one of the baby's hands. The baby curled his tiny fingers around Julien's much larger finger, and Julien's smile widened. "Hi, Fieran."

Vriska caught her breath. The feelings she hadn't felt while holding Fieran herself now stabbed into her chest at the sight of Julien holding the babe. He just seemed so right with a baby in his arms.

Could she really ask him to give that up? He would be an excellent father. More, he was made to be a father down to his very heart the way she was made to be a warrior.

Julien's grin took on a hint of a smirk. "I'm going to be your favorite uncle, aren't I?"

Across the room, Averett and Edmund both gave huffs and eyerolls. Weylind crossed his arms and just looked grumpier. Rharreth's mouth twisted as he tried to hide his smile beneath a fake grimace.

"My turn." Melantha eased forward and claimed Fieran from Julien. The hard edges of her face softened as she made soft, indecipherable noises to the baby.

"Are you all right?" Julien asked in a lowered tone, his fingers brushing Vriska's.

She clasped his hand, tucking their hands next to her where the others likely wouldn't be able to see. "I'm fine. Your family is a hoot when they are all gathered together."

Over the next few minutes, Fieran was passed from Melantha to Rharreth. From there, Weylind claimed the baby.

Almost as soon as Weylind picked him up, Fieran started wiggling and fussing. Seconds later, he gave the first, whimpering cry.

Edmund grinned, leaning against the wall with an arm around Jalissa's waist. "I guess we know who isn't Fieran's favorite uncle."

"He is simply tired." Weylind's tone managed to be both stiff and affronted as he quickly handed Fieran to Essie.

"Or hungry." Essie tucked the squirming baby against her shoulder. Fieran quieted, though it was likely only a temporary reprieve before the squalling began in earnest.

"That's our cue to leave." Averett strolled into the center of the room, then halted next to Farrendel. "You don't have to come if you don't want to. You'll just be there for backup if negotiations go sideways."

Farrendel glanced around the room, his forehead scrunching. His arm around Essie's shoulders tightened, but he sighed. "If I did not go, I would worry."

"You will not be needed. We trolls can handle it." Rharreth waved his hand, a savage grin on his face.

Vriska couldn't help her own grin. Since she'd captured

Princess Bella, Rharreth had argued that the princess was Kostaria's prisoner, even if she'd been held in Escarland's Old Tower dungeon. Besides, it was Kostaria that Mongavaria had attacked with their whole poisoning scheme. Kostaria should be the one to confront them.

Farrendel eyed Rharreth, his face almost too carefully blank. "A bunch of trolls are in charge of peaceful negotiations. Forgive me if I expect things to go awry."

Rharreth barked a laugh. "You have a point."

Vriska squeezed Julien's fingers, fighting her own grin. Who knew Laesornysh had a sense of humor?

"Regardless, we want to keep you in reserve unless the situation becomes dire." Averett's grin disappeared as he grimaced and shared a glance with Weylind. "We've already shown Mongavaria too much of what you can do. The fact that they are trying to develop shielded bullets is proof of that. It's time we concentrated on giving Mongavaria a united front and showing the other strengths of our alliance."

"Like the fact that Kostaria was hurt by the poisoning, but we aren't weak." Rharreth's deep blue eyes held a dark look that it often had before battle.

Weylind sighed, deep lines grooving his face around his mouth. "Why do I doubt that these negotiations are going to remain bloodless?"

"No idea." Rharreth patted his sword's hilt.

After a moment, as if by an unspoken agreement, Rharreth, Weylind, Averett, and Farrendel all turned to their wives, whispering quiet farewells.

Vriska glanced at Julien. He didn't have to say a goodbye because she, too, was a warrior. She'd be going into this battle—or not battle, as the case may be—at his side.

He squeezed her fingers and gave her a nod. A silent reassurance that he was glad she would be there to watch his back. Or, perhaps, he intended to watch hers since the trolls would be taking the lead.

Farrendel pressed a kiss to Essie's temple before he brushed gentle fingers over Fieran's hair and kissed the baby's forehead.

Essie touched Farrendel's cheek. "I have access to your magic. I will protect both myself and Fieran while you're gone."

"I know." Farrendel's forehead remained scrunched, his light silver-blue eyes pained.

Rharreth stepped closer, sharing a glance with Melantha, before facing Essie. "I trust you will be able to protect Melantha as well?"

Essie's eyebrows furrowed as she glanced between Melantha and Rharreth. "You won't be going along this time?"

Melantha shook her head. "Not this time. Not when..." She paused, a hint of a smile brightening her face. "I must protect the heir to Kostaria."

Essie squealed and hugged Melantha with one arm, still cradling Fieran with the other. "I'm so happy for you."

Jalissa gracefully sank onto a seat on the plush cushions of the seating area. "Congratulations, isciena. In that case, while they take care of the little matter of Mongavaria, we shall discuss how to properly welcome our new nephew and our soon-to-be niece or nephew to the family."

As the other women flocked around Essie and Melantha, Vriska felt a strange lump rise in the back of her throat. A part of her was torn that she didn't fit in with the other women here, who were no less strong because they looked forward to a discussion about babies. Yes, they stayed behind. Yes, they weren't warriors. But they held the solemn duty to protect their loved ones and children, and they had the strength to do so if called upon.

And yet another part of her—the larger part—was beyond grateful that she could get out of there as quickly as possible to head off into battle instead of joining that discussion.

Even as she left with the warriors, Julien's mother hugged her. Essie sent her a grin. Paige asked her in a whisper to protect Averett and the others. Jalissa and Melantha gave her knowing, solemn nods.

Vriska was one of them, even if she was a warrior. Even if she preferred bashing heads to holding babies, she was still a woman. They respected her for the kind of woman that she was, and she respected them for being the women that they were. That was what made them all sisters.

As she stepped from the elven treetop room, she gripped Julien's hand with one hand, her sword's hilt with the other.

It was time to make Mongavaria pay for what they did to Kostaria and to her family.

JULIEN STOOD next to Vriska on the tall bluff overlooking the bay at the mouth of the Hydalla River. From here, they could only catch a few glimpses of the far-off ocean since clusters of islands filled the bay. Not to mention that the bay itself was hundreds of miles deep as it widened until river and ocean mixed with no firm line between them.

On the shore and the islands, the trees were vibrant with hues of orange, red, and gold as every tree put on a show of autumn splendor. In Kostaria, they had already gotten their first snow for the year, the fall colors long gone according to the warriors who had come with Rharreth and Melantha.

In the bay below, a line of Mongavarian warships steamed around the nearest island. Most were wooden ships, their masts still holding sails even as the added steam engine powered them through the water. But three of the ships had been plated with iron over their wooden hulls.

Ironclads, Mongavaria was calling them. Escarland didn't have any, yet. Nor did Tarenhiel. But if these tensions kept up, they'd have to consider it, despite the expense.

Still, the Mongavarian ships stuck to their side of the river. A faint blue glow cut down the center of the river, through the islands, and into the distance, marking the magical wall that Farrendel, Rharreth, and Weylind had embedded into the bedrock months before, just waiting to shoot into the sky if the Mongavarian warships attempted to cross to the Tarenhieli side of the river.

"Iron boats." Vriska gave a savage grin. "The extra weight should make them easier to sink, don't you think?"

"Maybe." Julien eyed the ironclads. The Mongavarian king was likely on one of them. If he'd deigned to come. "Our cannons won't do more than dent them."

"I doubt there's enough iron there to stand up to a good squeeze in ice." Vriska's fingers flexed on her sword's hilt.

"Farrendel was right. You trolls are going to start a war, aren't you?" Julien rested his hand on his own sword.

Behind them, the assembled armies of elves and humans waited. It wasn't their full armies, nor were they armed with the latest Escarlish weaponry. But it was still an impressive sight. Especially with Farrendel and Weylind standing on a boulder, both dressed in their full elven fighting leathers and the crackle of magic clinging to them, even if Farrendel didn't unleash the power he held within himself. Next to the two elves, Averett appeared short and unwarriorlike, though Julien would never tell him that. His crown and his regal bearing made up for it, though.

But between them and where Julien and Vriska stood, the lines of troll warriors gripped their weapons and glared down at the ships far below. In their midst, Princess Bella stood with hunched shoulders, staring at her captors warily through eyes still surrounded by bruising beside her now slightly crooked nose. Her one remaining guard stood several yards away, also well-guarded by a squad of trolls.

Weylind turned to Farrendel and said something. Farrendel nodded, though his jaw hardened and his silver-blue eyes deadened to his Laesornysh look.

After a moment, Weylind and Averett hopped down from the boulder and strode through the ranks of trolls, a small contingent of elf and human guards trailing behind them.

Ah, that would explain Farrendel's look. He wasn't happy at being told to stay behind with the army while Weylind and Averett went with Rharreth and Julien to confront the Mongavarians.

But none of them wanted to let Farrendel anywhere near the Mongavarian king. Besides, Farrendel would provide better protection up here, overlooking the whole bay, in the event that something went wrong. He didn't have to be close for his magic to be effective, and he would spot any double-crosses or stuff like that better from there.

Weylind and Averett halted next to Rharreth. Rharreth glanced between all of them. "Let's get this done."

The other members of Vriska and Rharreth's shield band

closed around them. Zavni drew his ax, grinning. Eyvindur let tendrils of ice curl from his fingers while Brynjar crossed his arms and gave a hard nod.

Julien straightened his shoulders. He didn't have magic or superior fighting abilities. But he was honored to stand with this shield band.

The female elf warrior Zavni had been flirting with at the war games trailed behind Weylind, guarding her king. Zavni leaned closer to her and whispered something into her ear.

She slugged his shoulder and stared down her nose at Zavni. But the faint twitch to her lips hinted that she was more amused than angry.

Perhaps theirs would be the next wedding in the shield band, after Julien's and Vriska's.

Vriska and Zavni knelt, and their cold, gray magic seeped into the stones of the cliff beneath them. With a groaning of stone, steps formed into the cliff's face, leading down to the water far below.

Rharreth strode down the stairs with his shield band at his heels. Julien fell into place between Vriska and Zavni, matching his stride to theirs as naturally as if he'd fought with this shield band all his life. He tried not to look down. The steps weren't all that wide, and his footing felt strangely wobbly when he thought about how he'd die if he tripped and fell.

In front of him, Averett also appeared a little white while Weylind was trailing one hand along the stone next to him. It might have looked like it was for reassurance, but Julien was close enough to see the way tiny roots sprang out of the earth and twined over Weylind's fingers. Apparently walking across the treetop pathways was fine by Weylind, but these stone steps down the cliffs weren't.

As they reached the bottom of the cliff, the Mongavarian ships halted. Shouting voices carried on the wind, and the hatches on the nearest ship squeaked open. The long guns were run out, black and gaping like the maws of a many-jawed beast.

"I see a more impressive show of power is needed." Rharreth stood at the edge of the water, then glanced over his shoulder. The rest of the small army of trolls had also reached the thin strip of rocky beach between the cliff and the river's edge. He motioned to them. "Let's freeze them out."

Julien braced himself a moment before an icy blast seared through him. In a blink, a blizzard whipped down the bay, turning fall into winter. Frost rimed the colorful leaves. A layer of ice crackled along every mast, rigging, and sail.

Then Rharreth flung a wave of his magic into the growing storm. The bay froze over, each wave freezing where it stood. A layer of ice coated the ships and completely sealed off the guns and their ports. A good cannon blast probably could shatter the ice but firing such a cold gun could damage it, if not cause it to catastrophically explode.

Rharreth marched onto the ice. Averett strode after him without hesitation, but Weylind paused and took a deep breath before he stepped onto the ice.

It must be strange, trusting the trolls so completely. Weylind would be cut off from anything green and growing. And yet he walked out onto the ice beside the troll king.

Julien strode next to Vriska, careful not to slip on the ice beneath his boots.

Even he could feel the shiver as he stepped over the

glowing, blue line beneath the ice where Farrendel's magic marked the border.

As they strode across the border, the activity on the Mongavarian ships increased. This was, in a sense, a mini-invasion of Mongavaria, since the ships were technically in Mongavarian waters. Well, ice.

Rharreth strode straight to the ironclad that flew the Mongavarian king's banner. Steps formed in the ice so that he, Weylind, and Averett could ascend the ship as easily as they did the marble staircase in Winstead Palace.

Julien and Vriska followed quickly behind, as did a contingent of guards. The rest of the trolls remained in ranks next to the ship, making sure men from the other ships didn't decide to assist their king.

The Mongavarian king had the same blue eyes as his daughter, though his blond hair was darker, almost verging on brown. Threads of gray showed at his temples. He wasn't short by any means, yet both Weylind and Rharreth towered over him. He held his head high, staring down his nose at them as best he could. "You have kidnapped my daughter and trespassed on Mongavaria's sovereign waters. What is the meaning of this display of unwarranted aggression?"

"Unwarranted?" Rharreth snorted and glared back with deep blue eyes that were even icier than the frost crusting the ship. "And what was the meaning of your unwarranted aggression when you poisoned the grain that was being transported to my kingdom?"

"I am not responsible for the actions of a few lowlife smugglers. Smugglers that came from Escarland. Perhaps you should ask your supposed ally why they would wish to poison your people?" King Jimson of Mongavaria smirked and motioned to Averett, as if even now he thought to foster distrust between Kostaria and Escarland.

"I did ask them. And they have punished the smuggler responsible." Rharreth pulled a piece of paper from his pocket. "But perhaps, Your Majesty, you would do better to destroy incriminating papers rather than leave evidence lying around where anyone could find it. Here is a copy of the orders to poison the grain being smuggled to Kostaria."

Another Mongavarian man joined his king. This man was dressed in similarly expensive silk, and his brown hair was neatly combed and trimmed. He held out his hand to Rharreth. "Your Majesty, I am Lord Crest, member of King Jimson's Consular Prime. May I see your evidence?"

Julien worked to keep his face neutral as Rharreth handed over the piece of paper. Lord Crest was one of the lords they'd secretly contacted to set up this meeting. But it was best if King Jimson didn't realize that some of his lords had gone behind his back in these negotiations.

King Jimson's face mottled, and he clenched his fists at his sides. "It's a forgery, obviously. A sheer fabrication."

"Maybe so. But I'm sure the Consular Prime will be interested to examine it to verify its authenticity." Lord Crest folded the paper and tucked it into his pocket.

Julien hoped Lord Crest was smart enough to avoid eating or drinking anything given to him by King Jimson for the next while. He was likely to find himself on the king's hit list after this.

King Jimson's eyes all but bulged from his reddening face. "King Rharreth, you might as well march back where you came from. I refuse to negotiate with those who would fabricate such lies and invade my kingdom."

"You don't have a choice." Rharreth took another step

closer, menacing by his sheer size and presence even if his hands weren't even fisted. "I have your ship. I have your daughter. You will sit down and listen to my terms."

King Jimson's jaw worked, and his eyes strayed to the clifftop as Rharreth motioned in that direction.

Farrendel stood at the edge of the cliff now, surrounded by the elf and human armies. A few trolls had remained behind as well, and they had the princess and her guard stationed where they would be in full view. From here, Julien couldn't see the princess's expression, but he had a feeling her beautiful face was twisted in a similar look of rage to the one that her father currently wore.

Lord Crest stepped up, nodding to Rharreth. "I believe we should hear them out, sire. Restoring peaceful relations with our neighbors is in the best interest of Mongavaria."

King Jimson's jaw worked, but he glanced from Lord Crest to some of the other men gathered behind him. Other lords of this Consular Prime, most likely. The king's eyes flashed even brighter. "Fine."

Julien would have to congratulate Edmund on a job well done. So far, Edmund's information about the tension between the king and his Consular Prime was proving correct. As long as their alliance could leverage the Consular Prime, they could keep the Mongavarian king in check.

As had happened several times in the past year, a table was brought out. The kings sat at the table with their chosen diplomats and hammered out a treaty. And, once again, Julien stood along the wall—or in this case, a ship's rail—and simply guarded his king while Averett took care of the important stuff.

That was all right. Standing in the background on guard was where he belonged. Even better, this time he had Vriska standing with him. He almost wished something would happen, just so he'd have the pleasure of fighting at her side again.

But nothing happened. King Jimson's hands were too well tied between pressure from his Consular Prime and Kostaria holding his daughter hostage.

Unlike the previous treaties, this one wasn't even much of a treaty. It simply pledged nonaggression. Escarland and the other nations of the alliance didn't even promise to lift the restrictions they'd placed on trade with Mongavaria. All that signed piece of paper did was give the Consular Prime the leverage it needed to keep their king in check. And it prevented Mongavaria from trying to make allies among the other human nations by claiming that the nations of the alliance were the aggressors.

It was enough. For now.

CHAPTER THIRTY-TWO

Julien stood next to Averett as they watched the Mongavarian king's ship beat a hasty retreat around the nearest island. Farrendel stood on Averett's other side with Weylind and Rharreth next to him.

Averett sighed and shook his head. "I'm not going to make a fancy speech about how we achieved peace for our time." His mouth quirked, a glimpse of humor laced with a grim twist. "Peace for *my* time, perhaps. But not for the rest of you. The benefit to living a normal human lifespan."

Julien wanted to reach for Vriska's hand again, but she had retreated to stand with her shield brothers. Would he live a longer life? Or a normal human lifespan? That was one discussion he and Vriska had yet to have.

"War with Mongavaria is coming. I might not live to see it, but the rest of you likely will." Any hint of Averett's smile faded as he glanced between them. "I fear I've just placed the burden of that war on my children and grandchildren."

Rharreth crossed his arms. "My people want blood and vengeance for what was done to us. They will not like being told that they must wait. But our alliance isn't ready for that war. Not yet. We need time to train together and learn to trust each other. My people will understand the need to wait for the right time. When the war comes, we will be ready."

Farrendel stared after the Mongavarian ships, now just a smudge and a plume of smoke on the far horizon. His silver-blue eyes held pain, and he was probably already imagining having to fight yet another war after enjoying such a brief taste of peace.

Weylind rested a hand on Farrendel's shoulder. "Do not let the worry plague you, shashon. If war comes, it will likely not be soon. We can hope that the situation in Mongavaria will change before it ever comes to war. Perhaps they will become so consumed with internal strife that they will never turn their attention outward. As for me, I intend to enjoy this time of peace with my family for however long it lasts."

Averett raised his eyebrows at Weylind. "You've come a long way. That was the most optimistic thing I've ever heard you say."

"It seems I have spent too much time with your sister now that she is also my isciena." The lines around Weylind's mouth deepened with a smile this time instead of a frown.

Averett barked a laugh. "Be thankful she isn't here. She would likely have all of us squashed into a group hug by now."

Weylind gave a hint of a shudder, and Farrendel took a step back as if to bolt before Averett suggested doing just that anyway.

Rharreth grinned and slapped Farrendel on the back hard enough to make him stagger a step. "Let's go home. Our wives and my new nephew are waiting for us."

That banished the pained expression from Farrendel's face, replacing it with that soft, mushy look that took over whenever Essie's name was mentioned. Or Fieran's. Or home.

Julien turned to look for Vriska. It was time he found his own home.

VRISKA LEANED against the boulder at her back as the salt-laced breeze wafted up from the bay far below. Her hand was warm where it was clasped in Julien's, and she hoped he couldn't tell if her palm was going a little clammy.

With his free hand, Julien gestured to the bay before them. "I've seen the ocean now."

"Sort of. This is just a bay. The real ocean is much bigger." She tried to keep her tone as light as his.

Why was she so nervous? She already wore his ring woven into her hair. His intentions were already plenty clear.

But this moment still felt important. He might have embraced this relationship, but it was time she made it clear how she felt.

And feelings weren't exactly her strength.

Julien continued to stare at the bay rather than look at her. "This is our future. The others will prepare Escarland, Tarenhiel, and Kostaria for a possible, future war with Mongavaria. But we will be the ones actually training our armies. Together, we will protect all three kingdoms, now and in the future."

"I know." Vriska let the duty settle onto her shoulders, the rightness filling her. Instead of just guarding her king, she would guard her entire kingdom. And not just her kingdom, but all the kingdoms of the alliance. She would always be a protector, even if that duty had grown. "It'll be a good future, I think."

"Yes." Julien paused, flicking a glance at her before focusing straight ahead once again. "I haven't asked yet, but do trolls have a version of the heart bond? How long or short is this future going to be?"

Vriska snorted a laugh and squeezed his fingers. She probably should have thought to bring this up long before now. "We trolls call it *elraithan*. A blood bond. Why do you think we slice our palms and mingle our blood in our wedding ceremonies? It's a rare couple who doesn't form a blood bond. It allows couples to share their strength. I suspect that because I'm sharing my strength with you, it will function like a heart bond and lengthen your life. The elves just got all squirmy about blood and violence, so they switched to paint and runes and hoping that a heart bond forms."

"I see." Julien finally looked at her, a smile half-hidden beneath his beard. "Then I guess I've been worrying for no reason."

"No reason whatsoever." Vriska shared his grin.

After a moment, his grin faded, and his deep brown eyes searched her face. "If those in a blood bond share strength, then won't it be detrimental to you that you're marrying me? I'll just be a drain on you."

The person she'd been a year ago had seen things that way. But she'd come a long way since then. Both in how she viewed Melantha and now Julien.

"There is more to life than physical strength." Vriska shrugged but couldn't hold his gaze. Instead, she focused on the waves rolling onto the stony beach far below. "Vorlec, Rharreth's father, married a commoner. Yet in time, he came to despise her when she couldn't give him the strength he desired. And he despised Rharreth for taking after her in temperament. Instead of appreciating the strengths they did have, Vorlec drained his wife physically and emotionally. He abused her, abused Rharreth, and ingrained such abuse into the culture of Kostaria itself. And I came far too close to buying into that mentality."

Vriska shuddered, remembering the way she'd treated Melantha. The way she'd viewed humans a mere six months ago.

Julien squeezed her fingers again, not turning away from her even when she admitted her failings. "And now?"

"Now I've seen the way Melantha makes Rharreth stronger. And her strength of healing magic saved many during the poisoning." Vriska forced herself to look Julien in the eyes. She was no coward, and she wasn't about to become one when it came to baring her heart. "You and I will be the same. You've shown me the strength of your heart and your humility. You've pushed me to become a better person, and I want to do the same for you. And together, we will pass that strength to our kingdoms and to our children."

That had him stiffening, his expression going too blank. "Children?"

"I don't like babies; that hasn't changed. But you like them. And I realized that I wouldn't be doing the parenting thing alone. We'd both be parents. That's the point, isn't it? That we balance out each other's strengths and weaknesses." Vriska squirmed under his searching gaze. She wasn't sure how to go about explaining this. "And I kind of like the thought of a bunch of warrior sons and daughters who will continue to protect our kingdoms long after we're gone. I might not enjoy the baby stage, but I'm willing to face it to reach that dream. After all, I endured a lot to follow my dream to become a warrior. This isn't any different."

"Vriska…" Julien rested his hand along her cheek, his eyes going soft. "You know I'd never pressure you into anything. If this isn't what you want—"

"And there you go again. Always putting yourself second and others first." Vriska gripped the front of his shirt, startling his words to a halt. "You'll willingly empty yourself if that's what it takes to be second. And I love that about you. But I also realized that what you need in your life more than anything is one person who puts *you* first. Your family can't do that. They have other obligations that must come first. But I can. That's what people in a relationship do. They put the other person first and themselves second until, in the end, it doesn't matter who is first and who is second because the two of you are simply one. Together."

"Together." Julien spoke the word as a promise. A glittering depth to his eyes betrayed just how hard her words had hit him.

Yes, it was beyond time someone put him first. He had been putting others first for so long that he didn't even know how to take it when someone offered to do the same for him.

"We're a different sort of couple. We would have been fine if we'd never met." Vriska shrugged and glanced away, unable to hold his gaze just then. "I would have been content with never getting married and guarding Rharreth as part of his shield band. And it would have been a good life. You probably would have married an Escarlish woman, and you likely would have fallen in love with her. You, too, would have had a good life."

"Should I be worried about where this is going?" His voice held a strained puzzlement. After she'd just confessed she would be all right with having children, and she'd all but said she loved him, this probably sounded odd.

"What I'm trying to say is that we would have had good lives regardless." This wasn't coming out at all how she'd meant it to sound. She forced her gaze back to his. "But I've decided to choose you. Life with you is worth it. Maybe not better, exactly, than what I would have had. Certainly not worse. Different struggles. Different joys. But I'm deciding that these are the struggles and joys that I want to have in my life because you are worth it. Because I love you."

There. She'd said it. Finally.

"You love me?" The tense look vanished from his eyes, replaced with the broad smile that lit his eyes and tugged at his beard in that way she found adorable. Not that she would've used that word before.

"I'm sure you were starting to get worried about that." She tightened her grip on his shirt and tugged him closer. "Yes, I love you. Took me a while to realize it, but I'm a troll. We're rather hardheaded when it comes to some things."

"So I've learned." Julien leaned forward, only inches separating them. "I love you too. Stubborn troll warrior that you are."

While she would have liked nothing better than to get on to the kissing part—there had to be some benefit to all this mushy, uncomfortable heart-sharing after all—Vriska forced herself to release his shirt and put some space between them as she dug into the pocket at her waist.

Before Julien could give her more than a puzzled look, she held out a ring that she'd fashioned out of the stone of Kostaria's mountains. "I made this for you. We trolls don't have any traditions when it comes to getting betrothed. The elves have this whole fancy, gift exchange ceremony, so we trolls went the other way and just punch each other on the arm and say, *Hey, want to marry me?* and that's that. But a ring is a human tradition, so I thought maybe I'd try that instead."

"The tradition is for the man to give a ring to his future bride." Julien was still grinning as he trailed his fingers in her hair, tracing the ring she'd woven there. "And I've already done that."

"Yes, but that was out of duty. I didn't know I loved you then." Vriska gave him a light punch on the arm, then held out the ring again. "So what do you say? Do you want to marry me? Not just out of duty, though duty will always be a big part of our lives. But because we love each other and we've both realized that now?"

Julien gave another one of his deep, rich laughs and took the ring from her. "Of course I'll marry you." He slid it onto his finger, then flexed his hand. "That's surprisingly comfortable. It doesn't feel like stone at all."

"That's because I used my magic to make it so." She'd spent far longer than she'd care to admit fiddling with it to get it just right. While she wasn't about to wear a ring, she knew he would. And she wanted the ring to be as comfortable as possible.

He reached out and touched her face again, and this time she didn't pull away when he leaned closer.

"We're going to make quite the team, aren't we?" Julien whispered before he kissed her.

She drew him closer, pressing him back against the boulder as the kiss deepened.

"Julien," a voice came from somewhere behind them, only vaguely breaking through her hazy thoughts, "Averett says to tell you that the train—oh."

Julien pulled back, then glanced at someone past her shoulder.

Vriska blinked and turned, debating whether or not she should punch whoever had interrupted what was turning out to be a rather nice kiss.

Farrendel Laesornysh stood there, the tips of his ears red, as he looked at the sky, the ground, the bay below. Anywhere but at them. He cleared his throat, rocking back on his heels awkwardly. "Now I know why Averett volunteered me to fetch you."

"Tell Avie we'll be there in a minute." Julien spared just a brief glance for his brother-in-law before he focused on Vriska again. "You know what's the best part of having little brothers? Teasing them relentlessly."

Without waiting for an answer, Julien kissed her again.

Laesornysh muttered as he spun on his heels and darted back the way he'd come.

Vriska couldn't help but smile, just for a moment. Then all she could think about—all she could feel—was Julien's kiss and how much she wanted to spend her life with this human prince with the heart of a troll warrior at her side.

EPILOGUE

EIGHT MONTHS LATER...

Julien stood on the Tarenhieli side of the Peace Bridge, the stone bridge that spanned the Gulmorth Gorge. At the far side, the Kostarian train waited to take him, Vriska, and their guests to Osmana for his and Vriska's wedding.

Next to him, Farrendel had gone dead white as he stared across the bridge toward Kostaria. He gripped Fieran to his chest, though the baby was peering about and squirming to be set down.

"You don't have to do this." Julien had known that holding his wedding in Kostaria might mean that Farrendel and Essie wouldn't be able to come. He and Vriska had discussed it, and even though both of their families were in Escarland, it hadn't felt right to have the wedding there. This wedding was about Kostaria and its place in the alliance. That kingdom should be the one to host it.

Still, Julien didn't like to see the panic in Farrendel's eyes.

He never wanted to be the reason his brother-in-law was hurt. "I understand if you and Essie can't come. I know you'll be at the reception in Escarland. It's all right."

Essie rested a hand on Farrendel's arm, though she didn't say anything. Likely communicating through their heart bond what she couldn't put into words out loud.

Farrendel pressed his face against Fieran's hair, drawing in a deep, shaking breath. When he looked up again, his face was hard. "I need to do this. If I do not, then I will raise Fieran to fear Charvod's Kostaria instead of embracing Rharreth and Melantha's Kostaria. Fieran will grow up in a world where Tarenhiel and Kostaria are not only at peace but are trusted and respected allies. Some of his cousins will be half troll. If I do not face this now, then he will be the one who will pay the price."

Julien raised his eyebrows. That was wise, but it seemed rather more self-reflective than he would've thought Farrendel capable of, given his current panic.

A hint—just a glimmer, really—of a smile cracked the hard look on Farrendel's face. "I discussed this at length with my counselor before this trip. And I already have a counseling session scheduled for after our return to talk through the fallout. I will be fine."

But Julien wasn't. He couldn't be all right with knowing that Farrendel had to go to such lengths to prepare for his wedding. He never should have asked this of him.

Was it too late to call it off? Just grab Vriska and get hitched right there? Or back in Escarland?

"Both of us need this." Essie tucked close to Farrendel, her gaze lingering on Fieran for a moment before she met Julien's gaze. "I haven't been back to Kostaria, except to briefly cross the border for the Dulraith, since we rescued

Farrendel. You and Vriska love Kostaria so much. I want to see it the way you do instead of dwelling on the memories I have."

"It is beautiful right now." Julien glanced across the way again, though Kostaria's beauty was mostly hidden by the stone town that surrounded the train station. Thanks to the bridge, this was the main hub of trade between Kostaria and Escarland, with the trade flowing through Tarenhiel to get there.

He and Vriska had picked a wedding date during the height of Kostaria's summer for just that reason. At this time of year, the flowers would be blooming in the high mountain meadows, showcasing Kostaria to its best advantage to all the foreign guests who would visit for this wedding. This was a chance to properly introduce the Escarlish court to Kostaria.

Vriska joined them and glanced between Farrendel and Essie. "You will be safe in Kostaria. My shield band—and the other shield bands loyal to Rharreth—will see to it."

"Linshi." Farrendel faced the bridge again, his shoulders straightening. "Besides, Rharreth and Melantha asked for my help with the poisoned grain. I cannot refuse."

With that, Farrendel strode onto the bridge, each step too firm and deliberate. He reached out and gripped Essie's hand, still cradling Fieran in his other arm.

Julien watched them go, then clasped Vriska's hand. "I know many in your kingdom will never see him as anything but Laesornysh. But I wish they could see his courage in this moment."

If he were in Farrendel's shoes, Julien wasn't sure he would've been able to step foot in a kingdom where he had once been tortured, especially not with his wife at his side and baby son in his arms. Yet that was what Farrendel was doing, dredging up every last shred of courage he possessed to face the past so that he could raise his son as best he could.

"We'll keep him safe." Vriska squeezed Julien's hand, letting him know that she didn't just mean her shield band this time. But she and Julien, together, would see to it that his family remained safe during their visit to Kostaria.

"I can't believe I get to stay at Khagniorth Stronghold." Rikze's voice broke through the tension of a moment before. She wrapped an arm around Vriska's waist.

Julien half-turned as Vriska's parents joined them. "You are welcome to stay in Khagniorth as well, I'm sure."

Vriska's ma just shook her head. While she still tired easily, she had regained much of her strength in the nearly ten months that had passed since she'd been poisoned. "We look forward to the chance to catch up with the friends we left behind in Osmana."

"You've already done enough in taking care of our travel for this visit." Vriska's da shifted the bag he held over his shoulder.

Julien resisted the urge to roll his eyes. As if he was going to let her parents pay for the cheap seats on the passenger train for their daughter's wedding. He was a prince. The least he could do was invite them to travel in the royal car.

But that was the pride and stubbornness of the trolls.

"Thank you, Ma, Da, for letting me help. Even in this small way." Vriska smiled at each of them before she shared a look with Julien.

It was frustrating that her parents wouldn't take help, but they were making their own way and thriving in Escarland, along with the rest of the community at Little Kostaria. Julien couldn't help but admire them for it.

As punishment for his smuggling, Lord Farnley's warehouse by the Fyne River had been confiscated and given to the trolls, and they'd accepted only after Vriska had convinced them that it was the least Lord Farnley could do as part of his dishonor. Her da and the others had quickly transformed the building into a large community of homes that now boasted a far larger population than the original group of troll immigrants.

The rest of the money from Lord Farnley's estates had gone to help those most hurt in Kostaria. A small measure of comfort, after all the death that had been caused by his smuggling and the machinations of the Mongavarian crown.

A crown that was still locked in a power struggle with the nobles of the Consular Prime. Last Julien had heard, Lord Crest had strong-armed King Jimson into marrying his daughter to Lord Crest's son. Julien had a feeling that match was likely a supremely unhappy one.

As Vriska's parents set off across the bridge, Edmund and Jalissa paused next to Julien and Vriska. Edmund smirked at him. "And you said my wedding was too much hoopla. Yet here you are, making all of us travel hundreds of miles to attend yours."

"Admit it. You're just glad for another excuse to wander into Kostaria without Rharreth kicking you out." Julien grinned right back at Edmund.

"Didn't you hear? Jalissa and I are now heroes in Kostaria. I doubt Rharreth will be kicking me out anytime soon."

Jalissa patted Edmund's arm with a smile that said she knew him all too well. "Then behave yourself at this wedding, darling. I doubt Rharreth will be so lenient if you are caught snooping."

"When am I ever caught?" Edmund kissed Jalissa's knuckles, then together they swept across the bridge.

"Don't worry." Averett nudged Julien with a shoulder. "He's under orders to keep this trip strictly a relaxing holiday in the mountains."

"For some reason, I think he believes snooping *is* a relaxing holiday. I don't think he will be able to resist." Julien sighed and crossed his arms.

Vriska spread her hands wide. "He's on his own. I can't keep an eye on all your brothers."

"He won't get himself into too much trouble. And Jalissa will bail him out if he does." Averett grinned and gave Julien one last nudge. "Now let's get you safely married off."

THE TRAIN HALTED at the old platform outside the ruins of Gror Grar instead of the newer one beside Osmana. In the past few months, the old platform had been used once again, this time as the tainted grain from all over Kostaria had been transported to Gror Grar.

Julien stared at the massive dome of rock and ice that encased the pile of sacks, barrels, and various leather bags that contained the rotting, contaminated grain. It filled what was left of the courtyard of Gror Grar. Only a small section of wall bordered one side of the plateau while a deep fissure still scarred the courtyard at their feet.

Next to him, Farrendel stood tall, though his hands shook at his sides despite his efforts to hide it. Essie, too, was pale as she gazed at what was left of Gror Grar, though Fieran squirmed in her grip as if the baby just wanted to get down and explore with all the fearlessness of an eight-month-old who doesn't yet know the world is dangerous.

Rharreth, who had met them at the station, gestured to the dome and the pile of grain. "Thank you for coming and being willing to do this. I could think of no better way to get rid of this grain."

Farrendel nodded, though he still stared at the courtyard around him with a pale, shaky look as if he were about to bolt.

Julien wasn't sure what to do. He had a feeling that if he rested a hand on Farrendel's shoulder or so much as moved the wrong way, Farrendel would snap like a twig bent too far.

Rharreth, too, took in the courtyard once again, his gaze lingering first on the place where Farrendel had killed Charvod, then on the small section of wall where Farrendel had pinned him but hadn't killed him when he'd destroyed the rest of Gror Grar. "Once before, you cleansed Kostaria by the destruction of Gror Grar. Now, Kostaria will be in your debt when you use the destructive power of your magic to cleanse my kingdom of this poison."

Essie leaned closer to Farrendel so that she could touch his arm without unwrapping her arm from around Fieran. She waited, face turned up to Farrendel, until he glanced down at her. "You've learned a lot in your classes about how to use your magic for ways other than destruction. But you can't forget that destruction isn't always bad. Sometimes war is necessary to protect your kingdom. Sometimes destruction is needed to wipe a horror from the earth or the taint of poison from the ground. If Fieran inherits your magic, he needs to be taught this too, not just to work the power in non-destructive ways."

Julien looked away, the moment uncomfortably personal to witness. Instead, he glanced at Vriska next to him. She glared at the pile of grain, as if she wished she had magic destructive enough to utterly incinerate it off the face of the earth.

There had been little satisfactory justice for the trolls over what had been done to them. Perhaps witnessing the destruction of the poisoned grain would at least give Vriska some closure, if nothing else.

With a deep breath, Farrendel strode forward, the trembling gone from his hands and a harder light burning in his eyes. He knelt a few yards from the dome and rested his hand on the stone of the courtyard. The faint blue light lingering in the cobbles flared brighter, attuned to Farrendel even after all this time.

Rharreth knelt and rested his hand on the stone. His icy white magic swirled around his hand before spreading into the stone, racing forward until it flared brighter in the protective dome. "Whenever you're ready."

The crackle of Farrendel's magic filled the air before a blue light burst inside the dome. Bolts of power curled around the dome, and Rharreth flinched, his jaw working as he fought to keep his protective shield in place around the onslaught of Farrendel's magic.

Julien couldn't tear his gaze away from the sight. No matter how many times he saw Farrendel wield his magic, the awe that rooted him to the spot never diminished. Farrendel's magic was just so…raw. So powerful.

And strangely, it made him all the more grateful for

Vriska's magic. She wasn't insanely powerful like Rharreth or Farrendel. She had a nice, steady kind of magic.

Farrendel's magic built until the pressure of it squeezed Julien's chest. Yet the bolts remained contained within the dome, the power unleashed to utterly consume everything inside.

The tainted grain disappeared in a blink, incinerated into ash and the very ash melted away into smoke consumed by the magic.

Farrendel held his magic for a moment more before he slammed it into the ground and the surrounding dome of Rharreth's magic.

Rharreth grunted, but his magic flared against Farrendel's. He collapsed the dome of stone and ice, melding it back into the ground while still containing any remnants of taint that might linger.

With one last flare and a boom that reverberated deep inside Julien's chest, both Farrendel's and Rharreth's powers clashed, then disappeared.

Julien blinked away the flares in his vision as the searing brightness of all the magic faded.

Vriska released a long, slow breath. "It's gone."

Julien took her hand and squeezed, understanding the pain and relief in her voice. The grain was gone. That particular attack on Kostaria was fully over. Only now could the two of them relax and enjoy their wedding day.

VRISKA TRIED to hide her grin at Julien's confusion as Zavni, Eyvindur, and Brynjar all but abducted him from the train the moment it pulled into the station at Osmana after the short trip from the ruins of Gror Grar. They even went as far as blindfolding him before hustling him through the passages of Khagniorth.

Vriska didn't bother to follow. Her shield brothers would take the long route through Khagniorth, playing up the ruse for as long as possible.

In the courtyard of Khagniorth Stronghold, Melantha greeted her family, showing off her and Rharreth's two-week-old son. The gray-skinned, black-haired little bundle was cute, though Vriska had no desire to stick around for all the cooing and fawning.

Instead Vriska waited to the side with the members of the other shield bands who served as Rharreth and Melantha's guard detail. Even if this was her wedding day and she wasn't on duty, it didn't feel right to leave Rharreth and Melantha without any of his shield band to guard them.

Finally, Melantha's sister Jalissa offered to watch Rhohen for a few minutes, though it seemed like babysitting was going to be a group effort as the rest of them all crowded around their new nephew, wanting a turn.

Melantha joined Vriska, a third of the guards trailing behind her. At the moment, she looked especially warrior-like in gray trousers, tall boots, and a leather vest over a black shirt. Her quarterstaff was slung in a carrier across her back. "We'd better hurry before Rhohen realizes we've left him."

Rharreth glanced over his shoulder, a hint of a smile softening the hard line of his jaw. "He doesn't seem to mind being passed around among your family."

"As long as he doesn't get passed to Weylind. For some reason, babies always cry with him." Melantha smiled and shook her head, though she glanced over her shoulder again as they strode toward the entrance to Khagniorth Stronghold, as if she was apprehensive about letting Rhohen out of her sight even for a moment.

At the doors, Vriska half-turned as well, waiting for Rharreth and Melantha to enter first. The newborn Rhohen had somehow made his way into Farrendel's arms while Essie held Fieran. They seemed to be introducing the cousins to each other, though Fieran was doing more squirming and peering around the courtyard than looking at the baby.

Two thirds of the guards remained around Julien's family, the elven royal family, and Rhohen. What with their own human and elf guards also keeping a wary eye out and the powerful magic Farrendel could wield, they would be fine.

Vriska entered Khagniorth Stronghold behind Rharreth and Melantha, the doors swinging shut behind her a moment later as the last of the guards entered. The cool stone of the entry hall wrapped around her, a comforting and familiar weight.

She and Julien would likely spend much of their time in Escarland—since both of their families resided there—but Khagniorth Stronghold would always be home, even if Escarland also became home. Kostaria held a special place in her heart, and she was thankful that Julien also wanted to spend long visits here. If they did have children, she wanted them to grow up knowing this side of their heritage as well as their Escarlish one.

When she, Rharreth, and Melantha reached the training arena, they took a side entrance rather than the main one. Even through the thick stone, the shouting and laughter of the trolls waiting to enter for the upcoming fighting bouts were still audible, echoing down the corridors and through the doors.

Inside, the arena was empty. The others hadn't arrived yet with Julien.

Melantha drew her quarterstaff. "It's much more fun being on this side of things. Though, you didn't go through such trouble when you made me an honorary member of the shield band."

Rharreth wrapped an arm around her waist and tugged her closer. "That's because making you a member was a romantic gesture on my part. And it didn't seem right to needle you since you'd had the honor delayed far longer than it should have been."

"And this is my shield brothers' way of giving Julien a hard time." Vriska sighed and drew her sword. "You know brothers."

"Yes." Melantha's smile transformed the angular edges of her face, giving her a beauty that was harder, sharper, than that of her sister Jalissa.

The sounds of laughter echoed from outside a moment before the door to the side entrance was flung open. Zavni led the way, grinning, while Eyvindur and Brynjar each gripped one of Julien's arms, steering him inside with unnecessary jostling.

Julien wasn't resisting as they shoved him across the training arena, then forced him to a halt with a grip on his shoulders.

A hint of a grin played around Julien's mouth, half-hidden by the beard. "Let me guess. We've arrived. Finally."

"Yep." Zavni tugged off the blindfold, then stepped back, drawing his ax.

Julien blinked, his forehead scrunching. "You took that long just to get to the training arena?"

Eyvindur and Brynjar retreated, filling in the last spots in their circle. The rest of them drew their swords and pointed them at Julien.

Vriska worked to keep her expression hard when all she wanted to do was smirk. Julien was being a good sport about this. Another reason she loved him.

Julien raised his hands, but that half-grin returned. "This is some kind of test before I marry Vriska, isn't it? Let me guess, I need to defeat her brothers in combat before I can claim her hand or something like that?"

Vriska snorted. If that were the case, she could fight for her own hand. She wouldn't need her shield brothers to do it for her.

But that wouldn't be necessary. Julien had won her hand long ago. Not with combat—though his skill in the fighting bouts hadn't hurt—but with his gentle patience and humble perseverance.

"Prince Julien of Escarland, we name you an honorary member of the shield band." Rharreth's deep voice boomed in the cavernous space around the arena. He flipped his sword around, holding it lightly by the blade as he extended the hilt to Julien. "We pledge to you our steel, our loyalty, and our honor. For the shield band!"

"For the shield band!" The others extended the hilts of their weapons to him as well, even Zavni who had to grip the head of his ax to extend the shaft. Only Melantha didn't bother to flip her quarterstaff around since both ends were the same.

Vriska held out her sword with its hilt to Julien.

Julien glanced at each of them, giving them a nod. Brynjar, Eyvindur, Zavni. Vriska's loyal brothers. Rharreth, her brother and king. Melantha, the sister she'd never wanted but had learned to respect.

Then Julien's gaze met hers, and something hot flushed through her veins as he gave her one of his gentle smiles.

She attempted a smile back, conveying her own eagerness for a wedding she hadn't thought she'd want.

Julien drew his sword and extended it hilt first to Rharreth. "I pledge to you my steel, my loyalty, and my honor. For the shield band."

"For the shield band!" Vriska echoed again, this time at a shout. Her words were drowned out in the roar of the others' yells.

The sound nearly tugged another smile out of her. They didn't have to be this accepting of Julien. Especially not after the way Vriska had stood in the way of Melantha becoming a part of the band.

But here they were, welcoming Julien with as much enthusiasm as if he were a troll.

Did it really matter that he wasn't? Troll, elf, human. The differences were only superficial, in the end. At their heart, they were all simply people. With a heart, a soul, a mind. Those were the important things, not the surface appearance.

There would always be those in Kostaria who would look down on Julien because they saw humans as weaker. There would always be those in Escarland who would scorn Vriska because they saw trolls as brutal barbarians. Julien and Vriska couldn't change that since they couldn't change anyone's heart. But they could focus on their own hearts.

Vriska's heart had been changed in the past year from the

prejudiced person she'd been. Thankfully, there was forgiveness for this, too.

Rharreth flipped his sword back around so that he gripped the hilt once again, but he didn't sheath it. Instead, he turned to face Vriska and rested the flat of the blade on her shoulder.

Vriska stilled as the others quieted. This wasn't a part of the ceremony to make a spouse a member of the shield band. No, this was a part of…but surely not.

Rharreth held her gaze. "You have proven yourself a worthy warrior of Kostaria. I name you Vriska, first of the warrior family Ardon, and I give to you and your heirs the stronghold of the town of Akarak to rule in honor and justice from this day forward."

Vriska stared, trying to swallow past the rising lump in her throat. She'd never thought to hear her family name elevated to that of a warrior family. Nor had she dared to dream of a stronghold of her own. A stronghold that was conveniently located along the main rail line so travel back and forth from Escarland wouldn't be an issue.

Well, now she would have to have children. She couldn't very well establish a warrior family line if she didn't.

Her shield band was cheering again, but she barely heard the roaring past the crackle in her own ears as she sought and found Julien's gaze where he still stood in the center of the circle. Julien gave her a nod, his gaze warm, silently celebrating this honor with her while humbly disappearing into the background.

But she didn't want him in the background. This honor belonged to him too.

She stepped forward so that she stood at his side,

gripped his hand, then faced Rharreth. "We are honored, my king."

Julien's thumb brushed across the back of her hand, sending a tingle up her arm. This warrior line wouldn't just be hers but his as well. And their heirs would be all the better for being human as well as troll.

Zavni sheathed his ax, then slapped Julien on the back hard enough to make him stagger. "Welcome to the shield band. Didn't think Vriska would have it in her to actually go through with it."

And…there it was. The annoying, joking brothers.

But this time, Vriska had ammunition of her own.

Vriska punched Zavni's arm hard enough that Zavni winced. "And when will we get to welcome your elf warrior to the band?"

"Ah, yes, about that…" Zavni shifted, then cleared his throat. "Think the two of you will be back from your wedding trip in a month or so? Tiriana has a few duties to wrap up in Tarenhiel, then she will move here to Kostaria."

"We'll be there." Julien held Vriska's gaze, that hint of his adorable smile framed by his neatly trimmed beard.

"Yes. I suppose we can cut short our tour of northern Kostaria. Just for you." Vriska slugged Zavni's shoulder again just for good measure.

She and Julien had been planning to be back in a month or so anyway. Any longer than that, and they'd risk finding themselves snow-bound in some remote outpost all winter. Not that Vriska minded the thought of being stuck alone with Julien all winter. But their families might worry, and they had winter war games hosted by Kostaria that she was not about to miss.

"She will be welcome." Melantha smiled first at Zavni,

then up at Rharreth. "We could use a few more elves around here."

"Yes, especially warriors with her skill." Rharreth clasped Zavni's forearm. "She will bring honor to Kostaria and to her own people."

"Enough about you, Zavni. You'll have your day in a month." Vriska glanced at Julien, standing at the edge of the group where he'd naturally started to drift. Putting others first, himself second as he always did. "Today belongs to me and Julien. And I don't want my wedding delayed because of your chitchat."

"Right." Zavni draped an arm around Vriska's shoulders, then motioned to Julien. "Let the fighting bouts begin!"

JULIEN SAT in his usual seat beside Vriska in the fighting arena, but this time he had Farrendel, then Essie on the other side of him. In front of him, Weylind, Rharreth, and Averett filled another bench and behind him, Edmund and Jalissa were at his back. Even Ryfon and Brina had been allowed to come this time, and they sat on the other side of Jalissa. Brina's eyes were huge as she took in the furor of a troll fighting bout for the first time.

Next to Julien, Farrendel's knees bounced, his muscles wound tight. Essie gripped one of his hands in both of hers, as if trying to hold him together. Even with moss earplugs in place, Farrendel flinched whenever the gathered trolls roared or stomped or cheered.

If only Farrendel had the freedom to hide in his room rather than attend. But it wouldn't have been a good look if the elves' foremost warrior scorned the fighting bouts.

It didn't help that they'd decided to leave Fieran behind with Melantha, Paige, and Rheva. They were well guarded, but it couldn't have been easy on Farrendel, having his son out of his sight while they were in Kostaria.

As the latest bout ended, a troll across the way stood up and challenged Vriska. She grinned as she stood, her sleeveless leather vest showing off her toned arm muscles.

"Go trounce him good." Julien kissed her knuckles before letting go of her hand.

"Of course. It wouldn't do to be defeated on my wedding day. But I wouldn't mind a bruise or two, just so I can get married in proper style." Vriska grinned back, then strode down the steps.

She drew her sword and faced off against the male troll warrior, her about-to-punch-someone expression hardening her features.

Julien leaned back on his hands. That was his woman down there about to beat the stuffing out of her opponent. And he had the pleasure of sitting here watching and admiring her every muscled curve and beautiful attack. What a way to celebrate their wedding day.

Edmund jabbed him in the ribs from behind. Julien didn't even bother to turn around, knowing Edmund was likely smirking at him. Well, Edmund would just have to put up with Julien going all mushy-eyed over his soon-to-be wife. He'd put up with enough of that from all of his siblings. They would just have to deal with it now that it was his turn.

The troll warrior charged, and Vriska parried easily. She sidestepped and darted a strike at his side that forced him to stumble back. Before he could regain his balance, she struck again, pressing her advantage. Within a few more seconds, his sword hit the sand while Vriska's sword rested against his throat, forcing him to yield.

She returned to her seat amid cheers, and Julien shared a grin with her. "Well done."

Before she could respond, another troll stood, though this time he glared across the way first at Farrendel, then at Rharreth. "King Rharreth, are your guests up for a challenge? Or are the elves too scared to face a troll warrior in the arena?"

Julien gritted his teeth, suppressing a groan. Not this. Again. It seemed every time a Drurvas or a Brathac was defeated, another one reared his nasty head.

Rharreth glanced over his shoulder at Farrendel, speaking in a low tone. "You don't have to accept."

"But it would be better if I fought." Farrendel sighed, his shoulders hunched slightly beneath the swords he wore strapped across his back.

Rharreth hesitated, then nodded. "You won't gain everyone's respect, but there are a few who will grudgingly give it. But they have seen you fight without your magic before in the Dulraith. It isn't necessary now, if you don't wish to."

Farrendel sighed and toyed with the buckles for his swords. "I expected I would have to fight. It is all right."

Rharreth nodded, then faced the challenging troll. "You may challenge my elven guests, but that challenge begins and ends in the arena. You will fight with honor, and you will win or yield with honor. Understood?"

Julien kept his face as blank as he could. He could hear the undercurrent in Rharreth's words, reminding the trolls about Brathac and his disgrace in not leaving his defeat in the arena as an honorable troll should.

Would this troll accept defeat at the hands of Laesornysh? Or would he resent it? Julien's muscles tightened, and a part of him wanted to hold Farrendel back and urge him not to fight.

The troll's jaw worked, but he nodded. "Yes, my king. I understand." He turned to fully face Farrendel. "Laesornysh, I challenge you."

Farrendel unbuckled his sword sheaths and handed them to Essie. After only a heartbeat's pause, he dragged his shirt over his head and let it drop to the bench where he'd been sitting. Drawing his swords, he stalked down the stairs, the lights of the arena highlighting the scars across his back and shoulders.

The troll warrior hopped down into the arena and drew his sword, grinning like he thought he intimidated Farrendel. He charged with a roar.

Farrendel dodged the swing, then used the wall of the arena to launch himself into the air. He landed on the troll's back hard enough to knock him face first onto the sand. A kick sent the troll's sword spinning out of his hand while both of Farrendel's swords rested against the troll's throat.

Rharreth shook his head. "Perhaps I should have warned Farrendel about humiliating my warriors rather than worry about them trying to hurt him."

From that point on, troll warrior after troll warrior challenged Farrendel until he rarely had a chance to leave the ring, as if the troll warriors were determined to keep fighting until one of them managed to defeat Laesornysh one-on-one.

At some point, Farrendel's tension eased, and a hint of a smile touched his face. He was beginning to have fun, the exercise of the bouts working away his tension.

Good. At least all these bouts were helping, rather than harming.

Farrendel had a few chances to catch his breath when

Vriska quickly stood and challenged one of those that Farrendel had defeated. Weylind also took a challenge, which he defeated, though not as quickly as Farrendel did his.

Even Ryfon got into the moment and challenged a young troll warrior who had been sitting with his parents a few benches away. The troll warrior soundly defeated Ryfon, giving him a black eye in the process. Ryfon seemed a bit embarrassed, until the troll laughed, held out his hand, and helped Ryfon to his feet as if the two of them had been good friends for years.

After Farrendel defeated yet another troll warrior, Julien quickly stood before anyone else could. "I challenge Laesornysh."

Farrendel nodded, breathing hard and sweating. The raw edges to his stance were back. Time to put an end to all the challenging.

Julien tossed his shirt onto the bench, giving Essie a nod. She could probably tell even more than he could that Farrendel was ready to be done and pulled out of there.

Drawing his sword, Julien entered the arena and faced Farrendel. He had an advantage that the other trolls didn't. He'd practiced with Farrendel for months. He knew Farrendel's tricks and fighting style better than most, even if he was still soundly defeated in the end.

Julien eased into his fighting stance. "Go easy on me. It's my wedding day, after all. Maybe you could even let me win for once. As a wedding gift."

Farrendel just raised an eyebrow at him, waiting for him to make the first move.

Oh, no. Julien wasn't going to fall for that. This time, he was going to make Farrendel attack him.

Farrendel's mouth quirked, as if he knew exactly what Julien was doing. But he launched himself at Julien anyway, his swords swinging in blurs.

Julien jumped back to avoid the swings, then parried Farrendel's next few blows as best he could. Something stung his upper arm as he didn't move quite fast enough.

When Farrendel struck again, Julien forced himself to flinch. As he'd known it would, his flinch made Farrendel hesitate.

Dropping his sword, Julien tackled Farrendel around the waist. The move was so unexpected that he managed to take Farrendel all the way to the ground, pinning his wrists so that Farrendel couldn't swing with his swords.

Only when Farrendel's eyes widened, his body stiffening, did Julien realize his mistake. He'd just pinned Farrendel flat on his back. In Kostaria. While he was in a room completely made of stone.

Julien eased his hold, keeping his hands there for show but loose enough that Farrendel could break free if he chose. "Do you yield?"

The sound of his voice snapped Farrendel's gaze to him, something in Farrendel seeming to sink in on himself. He nodded, his throat working, before he said, "Yield."

The victory didn't feel the way Julien thought it would. He released Farrendel and stood, holding out a hand to his brother-in-law. All around them, the trolls cheered. Apparently Julien counted as enough of one of their own that they, at least, were thrilled with his defeat of Laesornysh.

Farrendel switched both swords to one hand, then took Julien's hand and let him pull him to his feet.

Julien didn't fully let go, draping an arm around Farrendel's shoulders. "Let's get you out of here."

Pausing only long enough to retrieve his own sword, Julien steered Farrendel out of the arena and back to their seats.

Farrendel sank onto the bench next to Essie, wrapping his arms around her and burying his face in her hair for a long moment as she simply held him.

Julien wanted to punch himself. What had he been thinking, pinning Farrendel like that? Especially here, of all places? Thanks to Melantha's magic, Farrendel had doing so well inside the stone of Khagniorth Stronghold that Julien had briefly forgotten how hard this was for him.

As Zavni loudly challenged another troll warrior, taking the attention away from them, Rharreth half-turned to face them. "The rest of the shield band and I will stay to the end, but you should leave to prepare for the wedding."

Vriska nodded as she handed Julien his shirt. "We'll escort them out."

Taking his shirt, Julien held her gaze for a moment. He couldn't express how much of a relief it was to have her here at his side, also shouldering the duty of protecting his family.

Leading the way, Vriska urged Averett, Weylind, Ryfon, Brina, Edmund, and Jalissa toward the side entrance. After waiting for Essie and Farrendel to go first, Julien took up the rear. A few more troll, human, and elf guards fell into step around them.

As soon as they were in the quiet of the corridor, Julien hurried to catch up with Farrendel. "I'm sorry. I didn't mean to...but I shouldn't have pinned you like that."

Farrendel drew in a shaky breath, but some of the panic was already fading from his eyes, leaving behind a cold, weary dullness. "I am fine. It was not you, but the memories."

"Don't beat yourself up about it, Julien." Essie gripped Farrendel's hand. "We know what you were trying to do. Thanks for ending the challenges."

Somehow, Essie's reassurances didn't make him feel any better. He only felt worse when Weylind glanced over his shoulder, his brow deeply furrowed as he took in Farrendel's slumped shoulders and dragging steps.

After another few minutes, Farrendel drew his shoulders straighter, a strained but genuine smile curving his mouth. He swerved to bump his shoulder against Julien. "You beat me."

"You let me win. You could have thrown me off there at the end." Julien forced a lighthearted tone into his voice, casting off the darkness of a moment ago.

Farrendel gave a one-shouldered shrug. "Perhaps. But as you said, it is your wedding day. Enjoy your victory. It will not happen again."

Probably not. Farrendel wouldn't hold a grudge. He'd already forgiven Julien, even if Julien still beat himself up for it. But Farrendel likely would hold back a little less than he usually did the next time he and Julien sparred. Just because.

Vriska brought them through Khagniorth to the passage that held the king and queen's suite of rooms. All the guests would be housed in nearby rooms, and a whole host of guards were currently stationed at the entrance to that particular tunnel to prevent any attacks.

When Vriska knocked, Melantha opened the door to her room. She held Fieran on one hip. With a huge grin, Fieran just about launched himself from Melantha's arms, screeching, "Dadadadada!"

The last of the weary look dropped from Farrendel's face as he hurried forward and took his son from Melantha. Fieran draped himself backwards over Farrendel's arms, squirming, then laughing when Farrendel obliged by dangling him upside down by his feet.

Essie sighed, though her smile had returned. "It's always Dada. Sometimes hissing noises when I ask him what the cat says. I think he's only said Mama once or twice."

Julien nodded, not sure what to say. At least Farrendel was back to smiling and laughing.

Melantha gestured down the corridor. "I will show everyone to their rooms. Essie, Farrendel, you will have the balcony. We thought you might prefer to sleep outdoors rather than surrounded by stone, and when Rharreth returns, you can fortify it with your magic."

Julien eased away from the crowd of his family. He found Vriska waiting for him in the corridor, and he wrapped his arms around her.

She embraced him and rested her head against the crook of his neck for a moment. "Your brother-in-law is all right. You need to let him be strong when he can. They'll turn to you if you're needed."

"I know." Julien let himself lean into her for a moment, soaking up her strength as he tried to release the guilt. It had been an accident. It was time to let his siblings go so they could live their lives while he lived his. They would look to him when he was needed. After another few seconds, he pressed a kiss to Vriska's temple. "The next time I see you will be at our wedding."

"Finally." Vriska released him and stepped back. "Fighting bouts are fun and all, but I'm ready to get to the marrying part."

So was he. Their nine-months-long engagement had been good. They had needed the time to enjoy falling deeper in love. But now he was ready to finally be married to his troll warrior.

VRISKA BRUSHED at the deep blue silk skirt of the dress she wore. It was designed much the same way as that gown that had been ruined the night the Mongavarian princess tried to make off with Julien. Except this time, Vriska wore a leather vest over the shirt-like bodice. With the skirt rising to her knees in front with her trousers and boots beneath, she knew from experience that she could fight rather effectively in this dress if needed.

Besides, it was her wedding. If ever there was a day to wear a dress, this was it.

Still, she had her sword buckled at her waist and a knife lay on the table, waiting to be stuffed into her belt before the ceremony. Instead of a bracer, she wore the leather bracelet with sword designs that Julien had bought for her on their first trip to Aldon.

"I know you don't like tiaras, but…" Paige's voice came from behind her. "You are allowed to wear one today, if you wish."

Vriska turned to face her future sisters-in-law Essie and Paige, soon-to-be mother-in-law, her own ma, and Rikze.

Paige held out a box, then opened it, revealing a slim silver band set with tiny diamonds and sapphires. A single, larger dark blue sapphire was set into the center, forming a slightly larger peak to give the band the hint of a crown-like appearance. "This is the tiara that matches the necklace you wore in your hair for your first ball in Escarland."

That would explain why it had a familiar look to it.

Rikze leaned closer, her eyes widening. "That's so cool. You really are going to be a princess."

She was. Even though she'd been betrothed to Julien for nine months now, that part didn't seem real. He didn't act much like a stuffy prince. Most of the time, the two of them were out in the dirt and grime with the warriors from the various kingdoms, training the armies to fight together. When they weren't doing that, they visited the troll communities forming in Escarland, worked with the generals of all the kingdoms to plan the next war game, or helped the Kostarian towns hardest hit by Mongavaria's poison.

A part of her wanted to refuse. She wasn't really the tiara-wearing type.

But she could see the way her sister was just about drooling over the tiara. A tiara that Rikze would never be able to wear in public since she wasn't a princess.

And Vriska had seen the way both common and warrior trolls alike had begun looking to her thanks to the title she'd soon add to her name. It wasn't a job she'd thought she'd want, but she'd seen over the past months how her people needed a princess to work among them.

Even many women in Escarland—the ones who didn't fit the mold of petite and tiny—had embraced her as *their* princess. The catty noblewomen still remained, but with time Vriska had met many of the ladies of the court who were nice and gracious rather than petty.

More than that, her future sisters-in-law had rallied around her and helped her navigate the court. It had been a pleasure to watch the three of them—regal Paige, poised

Jalissa, and apparently innocent Essie—go to battle and utterly savage the gossips in defense of Vriska, yet retaining smiles and class even as they fought the war of words and intrigue. Vriska couldn't ask for better sisters to guard her back.

Word of how Vriska had broken and permanently altered the shape of Princess Bella's nose had also caused the gossips to back off. Sure, they still whispered behind Vriska's back. But they were a lot more careful in how they did it, as if fearing their perfect noses would be next.

Vriska would wear a tiara today. Not to prove the gossips wrong but to be a princess for her people. Both the trolls of Kostaria and the humans of Escarland. "Sure. But only if Rikze gets to try it on first."

"Really?" Rikze's eyes somehow managed to widen even further, though she sat on her hands as if to resist reaching for the tiara.

Ma glanced between Vriska and Paige, as if worried the Escarlish queen would be offended.

"That's a great idea. Of course she can try it." Paige held out the box.

Essie jumped to her feet and hurried forward. "Here, let me help. Getting a tiara in place is tricky the first time."

Paige handed the first box to Julien's mother, then pulled out a second one. This time, she revealed the necklace Vriska had worn in her hair all those months ago. "Rikze, I know you can't wear a tiara at the wedding, but this necklace matches the tiara your sister will be wearing. Would you like to have it braided into your hair? It will look a bit like a tiara when we're done."

Rikze froze, gaping at first the tiara, then the necklace. She turned to Ma. "May I?"

"If their Majesties are sure about this. We couldn't impose." Ma sank deeper into her chair, shifting uncomfortably.

"It is no trouble at all." Julien's mother held the box with one hand as she gestured down to the bag she'd stashed by her feet. "I have a necklace to braid into your hair as well, if you'd like."

"Oh, I couldn't." Ma glanced at Vriska, almost desperately.

Vriska rested a hand on her ma's shoulder. "It's just for today, Ma. You can accept, you know. But know that I'll be proud to have you at my side at the wedding whether you're wearing fancy jewels or your grubby work clothes. You're my ma."

Ma drew in a deep breath and gave Vriska a shaky smile. "All right. Just for today."

Julien's mother, Paige, and Essie set to work, and soon they had the necklaces braided into Rikze's and Ma's hair while a braid had been wrapped around Vriska's head before the tiara had been sewn to it with white thread that matched her hair.

Vriska glanced at herself in the mirror one last time. She looked like a princess. A rather deadly, tall, and muscled princess with scarred knuckles and a few bruises from the fighting bouts earlier. But a princess just the same. And she was all right with that.

In the end, she was simply herself. Woman. Warrior. Soon, a wife.

A knock sounded on the door, and Jalissa stepped inside. Her perfect princess smile widened as her gaze landed on Vriska. "You look amazing, isciena."

Vriska grinned back. Yes, she was gorgeous, even if she

did say so herself. "Is everyone ready?"

"Just waiting on you." Jalissa's smile held a hint of a smirk. "Rather impatiently in Julien's case."

Essie strode to the door, her green skirts swishing about her in a gentle rustle. "Then let's go. I can't wait to see the look on Julien's face. He's going to be poleaxed."

Vriska grinned as she reached for the knife she would give Julien in the ceremony. "I own a poleax."

"Of course you do." Essie laughed as she glanced over her shoulder. "I think Julien might have a replica of an ancient Escarlish one hanging on his wall."

Yes, he did. He'd given Vriska a tour of his weapons collection months ago. She wasn't about to admit how weak-kneed and swoony she'd gotten at the sight of his array of historical Escarlish weapons.

She was probably going to go all weak-kneed and swoony again, seeing him waiting there in the center of the assembled guests. Waiting for *her*, looking at her like she was a precious, beautiful sword forged by the greatest smith who had ever lived.

And she'd look at him the same way. Julien, with his rugged beard, muscular form, and that charming yet self-deprecating smile that did funny things in the pit of her stomach.

Checking the knife at her hip one last time to hide the heat stirring in her chest, Vriska strode toward the door. It was beyond time to marry her human warrior-prince.

JULIEN FACED Vriska as they stood in the courtyard of Khagniorth Stronghold. Her family sat in the first row, surrounded by Vriska's shield brothers. Her ma and sister wore glittering Escarlish jewels in their hair and beaming smiles on their faces. Her da had dressed in a clean but serviceable shirt and trousers, his eyes holding an extra sheen. Ranks upon ranks of trolls filled the benches behind them.

His family, the elven royal family, and rows of Escarlish nobility packed the benches behind him. He didn't have to look to know his family was grinning just as much as hers was.

Rharreth performed the ceremony for the trolls while the same Escarlish officiant who had conducted Edmund and Jalissa's ceremony was just as unflappable when melding the Escarlish ceremony to a troll one as he had been with the elven one.

The Escarlish vows came first. Then Rharreth gestured to Julien.

Julien drew the traditional Escarlish dagger he'd noticed Vriska eyeing the last time she'd seen his historical weapons collection, then sliced a line across his right palm. He held the dagger out to Vriska. "With blood and blade, I pledge to you my life and my honor until death overtakes us."

Vriska took the dagger, then drew the knife she had belted at her side. Without a flicker to betray the sting, she sliced her left palm, the blood welling, before she held her knife out to him. "With blood and blade, I pledge to you my life and my honor until death overtakes us."

Julien accepted her knife. Then he clasped her bloody hand with his and stood still as Rharreth bound their hands together.

"Blood and blood, bone and bone, I declare you one and

bound together from this moment until death takes you." Rharreth's voice carried over the crowd.

As Julien turned, he caught sight of Essie and Farrendel in the front row. Fieran draped over Farrendel's knees, observing the proceedings while upside down. Meeting Julien's gaze, Essie grinned, while Farrendel gave him a nod.

This alliance had started with them, but Julien and Vriska made it complete. Escarland, Tarenhiel, and Kostaria were bound together in a way they had never been before. The world was changing, but their kingdoms would face that change with strength thanks to the alliance.

Julien drew Vriska closer with their bound hands. He wasn't sure what the future held for them. Whether they had children or not, whether they would go to war with Mongavaria in some distant future or not, they would be strong enough to face the future because they would be together.

DON'T MISS THE ADVENTURE!

ELF PRINCE

Farrendel would do anything to keep from killing again...even marry a human princess.

Farrendel Laesornysh, the younger elf prince of Tarenhiel, has become the elves' foremost warrior, thanks to his deadly magic. He is no stranger to death. But when the humans propose a marriage alliance during a diplomatic meeting, he is desperate enough to avoid more killing to agree. Even if an elf should never trust a human bargain.

The human princess is probably a spy. Or an assassin sent to kill him on his wedding night. Yet if he can make this marriage work, as his grandmother seems to think, it might be the first breath of hope Farrendel has had in over a decade.

Experience the first adventure from Farrendel's point of view and fall in love with these characters all over again!

Elf Prince gives Farrendel's perspective on the events of Fierce Heart (book 1).

FREE BOOK!

Thanks so much for reading *Shield Band*! I hope you enjoyed Julien and Vriska's romance in this finale to the Elven Alliance series! While I'm sad this is the final book, I hope this whole series has brightened your life and brought a smile. If you loved the book, please consider leaving a review. Reviews help your fellow readers find books that they will love.

If you want to learn about all my upcoming releases, get great book recommendations, and see a behind-the-scenes glimpse into the writing process, sign up for my newsletter and check out my website at www.taragrayce.com.

Did you know that if you sign up for my newsletter, you'll receive lots of free goodies? There are several free Elven Alliance short stories available, along with a standalone fantasy Regency retelling of Beauty and the Beast titled *Torn Curtains*.

You will also receive the free novella *Steal a Swordmaiden's Heart*, which is set in the same world as *Stolen Midsummer Bride* and *Bluebeard and the Outlaw*! This novella is a prequel to *Stolen Midsummer Bride*, and tells the story of how King Theseus of the Court of Knowledge won the hand of Hippolyta, Queen of the Swordmaidens.

Sign up for my newsletter now

ALSO BY TARA GRAYCE

ELVEN ALLIANCE SERIES

Fierce Heart

War Bound

Death Wind

Troll Queen

Pretense

Shield Band

Elf Prince

COURT OF MIDSUMMER MAYHEM

Stolen Midsummer Bride (Prequel)

A VILLAIN'S EVER AFTER

Bluebeard and the Outlaw

PRINCESS BY NIGHT

Lost in Averell

LIST OF CHARACTERS

Book 1 - Fierce Heart:

- Ashenifela – Essie's horse
- Averett – king of Escarland (humans)
- Brina – daughter of Weylind and Rheva. Princess of the elves. Younger sister to Ryfon
- Daesyn – human man from elf legends who formed a heart bond with the elven princess Inara
- Edmund – prince of Escarland. Brother to Averett, Julien, and Essie
- Ellarin – late king of Tarenhiel. Late husband of Leyleira. Father of Lorsan.
- Elspeth – princess of Escarland. Nickname: Essie. Younger sister of Averett, Julien, and Edmund
- Farrendel – prince of Tarenhiel. Younger brother to Weylind, Melantha, and Jalissa
- Illyna – a friend of Farrendel that he made during the war.
- Inara – elf princess from legends who formed a heart bond with the human Daesyn
- Jalissa – princess of Tarenhiel. Sister to Weylind, Melantha, and Farrendel
- Julien – prince of Escarland. Brother to Averett, Edmund, and Essie
- Leyleira – former queen of Tarenhiel.

Grandmother to Weylind, Melantha, Jalissa, and Farrendel. Great-grandmother of Ryfon and Brina

- Lorsan – late king of Tarenhiel. Father to Weylind, Melantha, Jalissa, and Farrendel. Son of Leyleira.
- Master Wendee – chief diplomat for Escarland (humans)
- Melantha – princess of Tarenhiel. Sister to Weylind, Melantha, and Farrendel
- Paige – queen of Escarland. Wife of Averett. Good friends with Essie.
- Rheva – queen of Tarenhiel and Weylind's wife
- Ryfon – son of Weylind and Rheva. Crown prince of Tarenhiel. Brother to Brina
- Vianola – late queen of Tarenhiel. Mother to Weylind, Melantha, and Jalissa.
- Weylind – king of Tarenhiel (elves)

Book 1.5 – Elf Prince

- Fingol – friend of Farrendel's from the war. Skilled with carving wood
- Iyrinder – bodyguard for Weylind.
- Sindrel – chief diplomat for the elves

Book 2 – War Bound

- Albert – Nickname: Bertie. Essie's oldest nephew. Son of Averett and Paige.
- Charles Hadley – owns the largest weapons manufacturing factory in Escarland. Father to Mark Hadley

- General Freilan – Escarland's top general/head of the armies
- Lance Marion – human inventor friend of Essie's and Farrendel's
- Lord Bletchly – one of the lords in Parliament
- Lord Crelford – one of the lords in Parliament
- Lord Fiskre – an elderly lord in Parliament
- Lord Kranshaw – one of the lords in Parliament who actively hates elves
- Mark Hadley – Son of Charles Hadley.
- Phineas – Nickname: Finn. Essie's youngest nephew. Son of Averett and Paige
- Thanfardil – elf in charge of the train system

Book 3 – Death Wind

- Charvod – king of the trolls. Older brother to Rharreth.
- Hatharal – Melantha's former betrothed
- Maxwell – head army surgeon for Escarland
- Nylian – head elf healer
- Rharreth – prince of the trolls. Younger brother of Charvod.
- Vorlec – late troll king whom Farrendel killed fifteen years before Fierce Heart

Book 4 – Troll Queen

- Brynjar - a male troll warrior who is a member of Rharreth's shield band
- Darvek - a male troll warrior who is a member of Rharreth's shield band.

- Doctors Harwell – husband and wife team of doctors specializing in trauma counseling
- Drurvas Regdrir – Rharreth's cousin and member of Rharreth's shield band
- Eugene Merrick – human captain assigned to guard Farrendel. Brother to Miss Merrick
- Eyvindur Gruilveth - a male troll warrior who is a member of Rharreth's shield band
- Ezrec – Zavni's father
- Inersha – troll woman who helps Rharreth and Melantha. Wife of Mymrar
- Leonard Harrington – magical engineering professor at Hanford University
- Lerrasah – Zavni's mother
- Miss Merrick – Essie and Farrendel's cook and housekeeper. Younger sister of Captain Merrick
- Mymrar – troll man who helps Rharreth and Melantha. Husband of Inersha
- Nirveeth - a male troll warrior who is a member of Rharreth's shield band.
- Taranath – Rheva's father and former head elf healer
- Vriska – a female troll warrior who is a member of Rharreth's shield band
- Zavni Rindrin – a male troll warrior who is a member of Rharreth's shield band

Book 5 – Pretense

- General Bloam – Edmund's boss in the Escarlish Intelligence Office

- Merellien Halmar – elf lord Jalissa thinks about marrying
- Sarya – Jalissa's loyal bodyguard
- Trent Bourdon – reporter at the *Aldon Times*. Acquaintance/friend of Edmund's

Book 6 - Shield Band

- Rikze - Vriska's little sister
- Princess Bella - princess of Mongavaria
- King Jimson - Crown prince/king of Mongavaria. Bella's father.
- Brathac - troll who hates Julien (and all humans)
- Elluin - elf warrior stationed in Escarland
- Tiriana - elf warrior who falls in love with Zavni

LIST OF ELVISH

- Amir – prince
- Amirah – princess
- Dacha – father (informal)
- Daresheni – Most honored king (or more literally, great king)
- Elishina – heart bond
- Ellonahshinel – heart of the forest
- Elontiri – welcome, greetings, hello
- Eshinelt - green paint used in elven wedding ceremonies
- Isciena – sister
- Laesornysh – death on the wind
- Linshi – thank you
- Macha – mother (informal)
- Machasheni – grandmother
- Sason – son
- Sasonsheni - grandson
- Sena – daughter
- Senasheni – granddaughter
- Shashon – brother
- Shynafir – fierce heart

ACKNOWLEDGEMENTS

Thank you to everyone who came alongside me and encouraged me while I wrote this book!

To my dad for your insightful comments on the early copy and to my mom for asking how the book was coming. To my brothers Ethan, Josh, and Andy for being the reason the brothers in my books are always so amazing and fan favorites. To my sister-in-law Alyssa for suggesting that this book needed to happen. To my sister-in-law Abby and future sister-in-law Meghan for rounding out the best sister-squad a girl could ask for. To my friends Paula, Bri, and Jill for being there during a tough winter and year. To my writer friends, especially Molly, Morgan, Addy, Savannah, and Sierra for all your help and encouragement, both in writing and with my recent health issues. To Deborah for your hard work in copyediting the book and providing lots of fangirling comments to keep me smiling during edits! And a special thanks to Tom, Mindy, Tessa, Quinn, and Molly for turning proofreading into a family affair.

Finally, a very, very special thanks to you, my loyal readers! You displayed incredible patience with this book after I pushed the release date back two months due to health issues. All your emails asking after my health and giving me encouragement were so uplifting! I can't begin to express how much I appreciated your support! I'm so thankful for all of you who reached out to share your own stories of struggling with food intolerances and allergies. It is so nice to know I'm not alone in this!

Thanks also for picking up this series and turning it into what it is today. This went from my fun, random elf story that I wrote on a whim to a bestselling series that made it possible for me to quit my dayjob and write full time. I'm so thankful to all of you who have followed along with these characters for six books (seven, counting *Elf Prince*). While we're all sad to be leaving these characters to their happy endings, I hope you all join me for the next adventure!

Made in United States
Orlando, FL
21 June 2022

19019946R00271